CRACKS

CRACKS

Sheila Kohler

Z

ZOLAND BOOKS

Cambridge, Massachusetts

First edition published in 1999 by
Zoland Books, Inc.
384 Huron Avenue
Cambridge, Massachusetts 02138

Parts of this novel were previously published in a
different version in *The Paris Review, Bomb,* and *The KGB Bar Reader.*

FIRST EDITION

Book design by Boskydell Studio
Printed in the United States of America

05 04 03 02 01 00 99   8 7 6 5 4 3 2 1

This book is printed on acid-free paper, and its binding materials
have been chosen for strength and durability.

Library of Congress Cataloging-in-Publication Data
Kohler, Sheila
Cracks : a novel / Sheila Kohler. — 1st ed.
p.   cm.
ISBN 1-58195-008-x (acid-free paper)
I. Title.
PR9369.3.K65C7   1999
823 — dc21   99-27263
CIP

This book is for my beloved husband Bill,
without whose fortitude, intelligence and hard work
none of this would have been possible.

I have been helped enormously over the years in the revising of my work by a number of people whom I have never thanked properly:

Jeanette Perrette, who sat and listened at length after lunch while I haltingly translated my words into French.

Karen Satran, who provided friendship, food, advice — and even a husband.

Stephen McCauley, who would lean forward along the table and say, "Well I liked the passage about. . . ." and for his letters and consistent kindness.

Amy Hempel, who kept me writing with her support and generosity and wisdom.

Therese Svoboda, Victoria Redel, Diane Williams, Lily Tuck, Suzanne McNear, Rebecca Kavaler, Blair Birmelin, Patty Dann, Diane DeSanders, Sondra Olsen, Gay Walley.

Others whose support has been crucial: William Abrahams, Dawn Raffel, Elizabeth Gaffney, Mark Mirsky, and Patrick McGrath.

My agent Robin Straus.

And my darling girls: Sasha, Cybele, and Brett, who are my best readers.

Bring me my Bow of burning gold:
Bring me my Arrows of desire:
Bring me my Spear: O Clouds unfold!
Bring me my Chariot of fire.

— William Blake, *Milton*

The Thirteen Girls
on the Swimming Team

FUZZIE BURLS

FIAMMA CORONNA

JULIE DENCH

MEG DONOVAN

SHEILA KOHLER

ANN LINDT, VICE CAPTAIN

DI RADFIELD, CAPTAIN

PAMELA RICHTER

MARY SKEEN

SANDRA SWANN

BOBBY JEAN TREVELYAN

BOBBY JOE TREVELYAN

LIZZIE TURNER

The Staff

MISS SUNNY NIEVEN, M.A. OXFORD,
HEADMISTRESS

MISS G, SWIMMING
MISS LACEY, ENGLISH
MRS. WILLIS, SCIENCE
MRS. KEILLY, GEOGRAPHY
JOHN MAZABOKO, NIGHT WATCHMAN
MRS. LOONEY, MATRON

PART ONE

REUNION

➤>◄◄

There was Di Radfield, our captain,
So rich and bold and fair.
She wore her blouse wide open
And a pin in her hay-colored hair.

Ann Lindt was the one with the brain.
She was sallow-skinned and lean.
Of Fiamma's friends she was the main,
The vice captain of our swimming team.

Fuzzie differed from the norm
With her curly hair and strange mind.
She sang madrigals at night in the dorm.
She was odd, perhaps, but kind.

Meg Donovan had a pretty face.
An R.C., like all five Donovan girls,
She was full of sultry grace
With her heavy, red lips and her soft, dark curls.

Sheila Kohler, too, was there.
She wrote it down for us.
She watched with her blue-gray stare.
She was interested in lust.

But the one Miss G loved best
Was the one who came from afar.
It was the thirteenth girl who was put to the test:
Fiamma, the princess, our languid swimming star.

The graves of Sir George Harrow and
his faithful bullterrier, Jock

THE WHITE SKY meets the flatness of the plain, pressing down heavily all around. In front of the school nothing moves except the shimmer of heat. It is all distance: flat land, sky, and the slight trace of the river that runs slow and dun beside the graves toward the low, blue hills.

Looking out, so many years later, from the red-roofed buildings of our Dutch-gabled school across terraced lawns and veld toward the river and the wattle trees, we can no longer see the graves, but we can still hear the hum of the mosquitoes that swarm along the banks of the stagnant water. We can still smell the thick smoke of Miss G's cigarette. In our minds' eyes we see Fiamma lying on the gray marble grave beneath the frangipani trees. Her slender hands are crossed on her chest, and the white irises that grow wild along the banks of the river cover her body like candles. A faint breeze stirs the hem of her earth-colored tunic. She seems asleep.

We stand on the veranda, clutching the parapet as if it is the railing of a tossing ship, and gaze at the faint trace of the river, beside which lie the graves of Sir George Harrow and his faith-ful bullterrier, Jock.

Our school, which was renowned for neither academic excel-lence nor illustrious alumnae, had once belonged to Sir George, a high commissioner and hero of the Boer War. He distin-guished himself at Ladysmith and Kimberley. Even his bull-terrier, Jock, was famous for bravery and fidelity. According to legend, he ran a great distance and traversed many dangers in the war-torn veld to summon help for his wounded master. The little lozenge of his grave lies beside Sir George's.

The area around the graves was always out-of-bounds, but we ran there to escape the other girls and pick the purple and white irises, which grew wild by the river. There was a picnic hut with a red, beaten-clay floor and two latrines, which gave off an unholy odor. Vagrants sometimes sheltered there, and we would find their striped blankets and tin mugs under the benches. We would lie in the shade of the frangipanis on Sir George's cool, gray marble grave and cover our bodies with the wild irises and fold our hands on our chests and play dead. We managed to move the heavy marble slab aside enough to gaze down through the crack at the illustrious bones that lay there, white as shells.

The girl in the black shantung

WE WERE SEVENTEEN or eighteen years old, the last time we saw one another. Our world has changed completely: the dormitory called Kitchener is now called Mandela. We have become awkward with one another. We offer up our cheeks to be kissed and then step back, fast. After the first words we stand stiffly in silence with lowered gaze and averted eyes and folded hands. Our breathing alters. Each of us fears the other will notice the changes in us after all these years.

We are careful what we say. Our voices sound odd. The words sound cracked. We have difficulty hearing. We whisper as though someone might overhear. There are silences, clearings of the throat. There is shrill laughter, there are shrill exclamations of delight, professions of surprise. "Not a line, not a wrinkle, my dear, well, only smile marks around the eyes." We do not say that some of the former beauties look old and plain, that some of the once-plain now look youthful and handsome. Nor do we mention that Fiamma is not among us. The subject remains unmentionable among all the bearers of the secret.

Most of the thirteen members of the swimming team are here: Meg Donovan, Ann Lindt, Sheila Kohler. Only Julie Dench and Sandra Swann said they were unable to attend. Even Fuzzie Burls has somehow managed to put in an appearance. She has painted her short, square nails black for the occasion. We have all made some effort at camouflage: we have dressed up, we have masked our faces with heavy makeup, we have donned jewelry. Fingers twist pearls into knots, clutch gold chains, turn watch-bracelets around wrists. Eyes are bloodshot and puffy from the long voyage out.

An impeccably dressed woman in black with a diamond pin in her lapel arrives late, striding firmly across the veranda, her face in the shadows. We do not recognize her at first. Her whole body looks bloated, as if she had soaked up water from all that swimming; even her pebble blue eyes seem watery in her wide face. She is wearing black kid gloves and a double-breasted shantung suit, which makes her sweat.

We are all sweating. We mop the beads from our foreheads. There are rings beneath the arms of our silk blouses, crepe de chine dresses, cotton shirts. One of us pours water from the ice-water jug with the lemon slices.

It has rained the night before, and the brown lawns glisten. A dove coos in a blue gum tree. The late afternoon is still hot, but there is a shift in the weather. Rain threatens again. An eddy of warm air rises with a murmur through the palms, bringing with it the bitter smell of wet zinnias and a distant wail, as of a dreamer's voice, clear and shrill. We fall silent, expectant.

How happy we are to be here. We are all going to have such a *wonderful* time. It is so *nice* that so many have turned up. It is so amazing that some of us have come from so far — Sheila Kohler, all the way from America. How *lucky* for us that the letter from Miss Nieven, our headmistress, was so persuasive. Poor old Miss Nieven: she must be on her last legs by now. Couldn't let the Old Bag die without seeing her one more time. Ann Lindt points out that Miss Nieven had good reason to be persuasive: her tenuous place here, her cottage in the grounds are probably at stake. She and her old school need the money some of us have.

One of us tells the old joke about the parrot and the mustard sandwiches in the brown paper bag, but no one laughs. We leave our sentences unfinished. We ask, "Do you remember how we used to . . ." and then gaze into the distance.

We listen to the grandfather clock in the hall chime the hour. We look at the brass bowl of proteas that collect dust and the narrow staircase that leads from the hall beyond the veranda into the shadows.

In our minds' eyes we see Miss G, our swimming teacher, slender and strong, standing by the staircase in her belted khaki overalls and her shiny brown boots. The balusters cast shadows on her, and her clothes seem striped black-and-white. She has mud on her cheek and boots. She moves her munificent mouth to blow her yellow whistle. She calls us to attention: *Line up, girls, line up.*

After such a long absence the spaces between things have altered, some moving closer together and others farther away. The branches of the jacaranda trees stretch higher toward the sky; the palm fronds are thicker and darker; the once-clipped hibiscus bushes have grown into monstrous, dripping trees. The concrete slabs sag sadly beside the pool. Blood red poppies grow even more wildly among the blue hydrangeas near the round, thatched-roofed changing huts. Low blocks of flats have obliterated much of the veld. The dust roads now are tarred. The free-ranging, flat acres of farmland have been cut up and spotted with small houses. The veld has been fenced, and the long grass, uprooted and planted over.

The rooms do not seem as big as when we first entered here. We are to sleep in the dormitory now called Mandela. We raise our eyebrows and goggle at one another. We remember the hard, narrow beds, the lack of privacy, and the tall Zulu night watchman, John Mazaboko, with his torch that punched holes in the hydrangeas outside the window.

The art room has been torn down and replaced. A water fountain has been installed in the shade by the steps, and a new bench, under the loquat tree. The paneled rooms are still shuttered against the bright light and the heat. The faded reprints of Degas's ballet dancers still line the dusty gray corridors. From the hall rises the polished banister from which Bobby Joe, one of the Trevelyan twins, who was to become an Anglican nun, fell while playing horsie when she was five years old. In the library looms Sir George's portrait. He wears a monocle and looks old and dried out. Beside him hangs the dark painting of his dog, broad-backed, stiff-legged, and panting.

The small black holes where several of us poked the light, oak paneling with iron tongs remain in the common room. "Vandals," Miss Nieven called the perpetrators, whistling every time she pronounced an s: they pillaged, raped, and burned.

We walk down the wisteria-covered pergola that borders the edge of the perfects' lawn, past what was Miss Nieven's study. Fuzzie walks a little behind the rest of us with her odd, catlike walk, stepping lightly and looking down at the stones. She had wanted to be an opera singer like Mimi Coertse. She jangles her bracelets nervously on her freckled arms and flashes her black nails.

Ann, who was always blind and deaf to ordinary things but understood all the extraordinary ones, including our dreams, and who never cared for flowers, whispers to us, reminding us how we stamped our feet at Miss Nieven's Pekingese, Puck, and gave him an occasional kick to make him snarl, as he sat guarding Miss Nieven's door.

Fuzzie stares at us with apprehension from her close-set eyes and says that she has forgotten so many things. Her silver bracelets jangle as she flutters her fingers to convey them.

Two small black boys ride a skateboard up and down the path that goes to the pool. "You wouldn't have seen that before," the woman in the black shantung suit says, smiling at them. As she does so, we see her large, white teeth and shiny gums, and we recall the young girl we have carried in our minds through the years. We can bring her forth, tall and athletic, with her thin, hay-colored hair: Di Radfield, our captain.

We are the best of friends

MISS NIEVEN EMERGES from her room to lurch toward us like a ship on a rough sea. Her face is a web of wrinkles, her thin hair, punished with pins into a tiny bun. She leans on her cane. Called Sunny despite her olive complexion and her melancholy mien, she has more fine hairs than ever growing from the wart on her chin. She presses our hands and offers us her pale cheek.

Unlike us, she does not shy away from speaking of Fiamma. "A perfectly oval face," she says, recalling Fiamma's beauty.

We do not know what to say. Only Meg, dark-haired and Asian-eyed and herself a beauty, nods an assent, as the shadow from her leghorn hat shifts on her cheek. She is still straight and slender and pale. She did not go on to university but married young. Now she moves her hands smoothly in the air. She still has the mask of her soft, dark hair, her heavy lips, and the odd, empty expression in her dark eyes, which give no inkling of her thoughts.

In the shadows of the wisteria-covered veranda, Miss Nieven says, "There she was, lingering languidly outside Miss G's door." Her wrinkled face goes distant and tight. Our presence has stirred her memory. She surveys us blindly and says, "You were such a close-knit team, were you not? Devoted to one another. I was certain the thirteen of you would remain the best of friends."

Sheila, who always tried hard and has surely read the phrase in a book, says, "As close as a hand in a glove." We raise our eyebrows slightly, and we are all tempted to contradict her. In an instant she has touched on the reason we have been avoiding one another for so long.

One of us offers Miss Nieven a chair, and she settles down into the shadow in her mauve dress and amber beads, her back still stiff and straight. She has an M.A. from Oxford and had taught at a girls' school in India. She sat all day in her shaded study, guarded by her gray Pekingese, and made up programs for our activities: classes, prep, music lessons, ballet, riding, sport, and baths. When she made a mistake, she erased her small, penciled letters with her pink, oblong rubber. She wrote her sermons for chapel on Sunday: God of the Rushing Wind, of the Tumbling Waters, of the Mighty Mountains. Her favorite hymn was "Mine eyes have seen the glory of the coming of the Lord/ He is trampling out the vintage where the grapes of wrath are stored."

Miss Nieven rests her hands on her cane, tilts her head back blindly, looking as though she were talking to God, and says in her liquid, wobbly voice, "You were mostly in the water, rain or shine. We never had such a team. We were so proud of you — much prouder, I am afraid, than of our matriculation results that year." She laughs and waves a hand as thin as rice paper in the air.

Miss Nieven believed ambition was not seemly for Christian girls, for the meek should inherit the earth. She pauses, and we are afraid she has lost the direction of her discourse. Meg, who got a third-class matriculation, slips a cushion behind her back. Bobby Joe brings her a footstool. Miss Nieven lifts her arthritic legs one by one with difficulty, fusses with her skirt, and leans her cane against the chair. She opens her arms and exclaims, "The judges were always presenting those trophies to you. There you were, Di, your arms filled with trophies." Miss Nieven's voice has a raspy sound.

"We even beat Kingsmead," Di says, her pebble blue eyes

turning bright as she remembers our many triumphs. She coughs her smoker's cough and turns her head to the light. Her swollen face has a look of ill health. Her long, blond hair is cropped short and dyed copper. She still presents herself as if she had certain rights. She has to be taken into account in her black shantung suit with the padded shoulders and the large, unicorn-shaped diamond pin on the lapel. She has rubbed some dark rouge on her cheeks, and it makes her look much older — hard in a deathly and impressive way. Her once-slender body has run to fat, though she still has her broad swimmer's shoulders.

Miss Nieven says, "I used to like to watch you. If I saw one, I always knew where to find the others. It was almost a sunny dance, perfectly choreographed, a lovely garland of girls! You reminded me of that Matisse painting, you know the one I mean, with the blue background and all the pink figures holding hands, rising lightly into the air. There you were, swallow-diving from the high board in your black racing costumes, doing double back flips, one after another. Up, up you went into the air, light as light can be. I can almost hear the splash. You were so full of energy, enthusiasm, and life!"

No one cries out, "A dance? You call all those furtive, passionate writhings a dance?"

No one speaks of Fiamma's swallow-diving, opening her arms wide on the sky and earth, while Miss G gazes raptly up at her.

Di, who has dared to smoke, now stubs out her half-finished Craven "A" with its crimson smudge, pressing down hard, crushing it out with a spark of her old, uncontrolled temper. It lies smoldering in the dark earth around the potted palm next to the bench, while she crosses her arms, scowling.

Miss Nieven says, "And loyal, so loyal to one another! Always owning up, taking the blame. Diligent, too, and not only at swimming. I remember you, Ann, getting up before daybreak to help Fiamma with her Afrikaans, whispering to her in the window seat."

Ann Lindt, our vice captain, still sallow and thin, stands alone near the parapet, removes her thick glasses, and wipes her small, protuberant, pink-rimmed eyes. She laughs nasally and moves closer into the circle of women around Miss Nieven. Ann says in her pinched, secretive voice, "Fiamma was the best friend I ever had." Di looks at her askance and wipes the trace of crimson from her teeth with her tongue. There is a moment of silence.

Miss Nieven gazes blindly across the damp lawn and says, "Sometimes I think she is still out there and will come gliding across the lawn in her turned-down panama hat."

Sheila's cheeks flush as she says, "If she had to go off, it should rather have been to someplace grand. I can see her married to a handsome Milanese with lots of children, wearing a cloche hat, living in a grand house by a lake like the one she used to tell us about."

Miss Nieven turns toward the sound of Sheila's voice. "You were always making things up. I remember one of your Latin translations, which started out *In sylva,* which you translated "in heaven," and you went on to write of spirits wandering around the Elysian Fields."

No one says anything, but we all look at Sheila and remember how she used to make up long stories in the dark of the dormitory. We would fall asleep to the sound of her voice telling tales of Zulus with skin as pale as lilies or Chinese girls with blue eyes and fair hair. All her stories came to the same dramatic finale: violent death, whole families wiped out by Zulu impis or left to be eaten alive by red ants in a dry donga.

Why did Miss Nieven bring us back?

"YOU FIND THE SCHOOL much changed?" Miss Nieven asks. We evade her eyes and deflect her question. Ann opens up her small handbag and hunts inside, dipping her head and exposing the gray roots of her hair.

Ann had come to our school on a scholarship and had never swum in anything but the brown water of a ditch. She has married a rich black politician and lives in Harare, where she teaches political science at the university. She is one of the richest of us now and wears large corals around her thick neck and a square blue-white on her finger but still looks poor in her crumpled tartan with the big pin and her short-sleeved white shirt. No one asks her if it was Miss Nieven's letter, on the school's pale blue stationery with the dark blue crest at the head, which obliged her to come back to the school she disliked. No one mentions the contents of the letter that has brought us all back.

Miss Nieven says, "Tomorrow you must walk back to the river and visit the graves. Nothing has changed there — so far — but they may have to be dug up completely, as I told you in my letter." She leans her head back against the chair in a thin beam of light, as if overcome by the weight of it all. She stares blindly across the terraced lawns at what is left of the wild veld. She has suffered recently from fainting fits and for weeks has hardly ventured out of her room.

She sips water, pants, hauls herself up, and leans on Meg's arm. She makes an effort to straighten her back. She says that for this school to continue, it needs our help. Of course, it has been in difficulties before: there was all that trouble over Fiamma, she reminds us, blinking her small eyes blankly.

For a moment we think she has lost the thread of her thought. But she puts one hand to her flat, spinster breast, clutches at her amber beads, and says she thinks of our school as one of those monasteries that kept learning alive in the Dark Ages. There are few such places left, where the flames of Christian values, of love and learning, are kept alive. Half the student body comes here from farms with nothing: no money for books or even uniforms. They are beating at the gates.

However generous we may have been in the past, the school now needs our help more than ever. Without it a precious part of our past will be sacrificed. "The next thing you know they'll let a developer bulldoze those graves and turn up those bones." We look at one another, our faces pale.

It is, after all, a splendid summer evening, and the light is dazzling. There is no longer any hint of a storm. The sun, a lambent gold, is sinking beneath the horizon. Beneath it our old school grounds are disappearing into the twilight. The wind has dropped again. The air is sweet with honeysuckle, jasmine, and orange peel. The lawns are incandescent with heat and sheen. The red-hot pokers blaze. The dahlias smolder darkly. We stand and stare in silence. Only Ann is unimpressed. She turns sidewise to the lawns, cranes forward, and shortsightedly studies our faces, carefully. She is muttering some obscure line of poetry: *"Les deserts tartares s'eclairent."*

Miss Nieven moves toward Di and takes Di's gloved hands in hers, saying, "I am so glad you found the strength in your heart to come back." Then she turns, grasps her shiny black cane with the head in a shape of a bird, and totters through the door into the shadows. We hear the tap of her cane, as we stand, gazing into the distance across the veld toward the river.

PART TWO

DISTANCE

✦➤◄✦

How we first heard about Fiamma

WE WERE THIRTEEN and fourteen years old. Meg, who
had been held back because she took a little longer to
learn, and Pamela Richter, the thin girl who always got less than
10 percent in maths, might have been fifteen. Sheila and the
Trevelyan twins were probably still twelve.

Most of us had been confirmed in our white Sunday dresses
and panama hats, because Miss Nieven had said this was not a
fashion show. We had made our first and last confessions.
Sheila had confessed to reading banned books but said she was
not sorry, because they told you the truth about life, and burst
into tears. Ann had told her to stop showing off. Most of us had
had our periods for the first time by then and spent much of
our time peering anxiously at the backs of our tunics, afraid we
might find a dark stain spreading shamefully there.

From the dusty teacher's platform, Miss Lacey, our English
teacher, was saying something about the arrival of a new girl,
Fiamma Coronna. We were probably in the second year of the
senior school. We were all in the classroom, sitting two-by-two
at our wide wooden desks with the tops that lifted to store our
books and our comics, and holes cut out to hold the inkwells.

Ann, who came first at maths, Latin, English, French, history, and backstroke — everything except science, music, recitation, ballet, and gym — was sitting in the front row beside another brainy girl who never made the swimming team. Ann was the only one who read the *Manchester Guardian*, which was sent to us from England on special, thin airmail paper and got pinned to the bulletin board, where it was flapping about in the cold morning air that came in through the open windows. She was wearing the thick glasses she had to wear because she was always reading. She read books by Winston Churchill, who was attacked in an armored train in the Boer War. She sat in the window seat in the early morning before we got up, reading his *Great Contemporaries* and looking up all the words she did not know, like *internecine* and *belligerent*. It was Ann who had asked Miss Nieven why the natives did not have the vote. Miss Nieven had said that democracy took a long time to develop.

Di, who could turn fifty cartwheels on the lawn and do pirouettes all around the assembly hall platform and was first at ballet and gym, was rocking on her chair in the back of the classroom, stretching her long legs. Beside her was Meg, who was reading comic books beneath her desk. Mary Skeen was best at science; she sprawled beside Pamela, who was not good at anything then but later took a First at sex. Fuzzie was first at music and recitation. She sat, peering out the window, next to Sheila in the gold glare of the winter sun. Fuzzie had a lovely voice for both singing and speaking. Miss Lacey often made her recite "Ozymandias" by Shelley at the end of class in order to curb any excessive ambition, not considered seemly for Christian girls. "Look on my Works, ye Mighty, and despair," Fuzzie would say, stretching out her fat, freckled arms and lifting her hands toward us, imploringly. Ann, who knew much poetry by heart, was tone-deaf. The Trevelyan twins, who were orphans, sat side-by-side in the middle of the classroom and were, like her, on scholarship. Miss Nieven said money had no importance and should not be mentioned in polite company. *On ne parle pas de l'argent,* she said then, in the days when the school had money.

Miss Lacey was saying, "May I have your attention, *please,* girls. I am trying to tell you that a new girl is coming all the way from Italy to our school, after the holidays. I want you to welcome her on her arrival. Girls, are you listening to me?"

It is almost certain we were not listening when Miss Lacey told us about the exceptional circumstances — something about a business trip — under which Fiamma was to arrive. We rarely listened. We had difficulty just keeping still. We bit our nails, the skin around our nails, the ends of our pens, the ends of pencils; we sucked our plaits and sometimes even smooth stones; we craned our necks to check for period stains; we scratched, picked, and peeled, at our scabs, our teeth, and our noses. Bobby Joe was presently busy surreptitiously wiping what she had discovered in her snub nose onto the bottom of her desk.

The gold glare of the winter light was coming in slantwise through the north-facing windows. We were sitting in our long-sleeved winter shirts and brown cardigans and striped ties, our breath misty in the early morning air, and muttering about it being worse than *Jane Eyre* in our unheated classroom. The highveld winter mornings were bitter cold, but by midday we would tie our cardigans around our waists, roll up our long sleeves, and lounge on the dry grass in the strong sun. Heating was not considered necessary where the winters were short and the summers long.

"Now I want you to be particularly nice to this new girl, who is coming from such a distance, from another country, another . . . background." Miss Lacey's voice rose in a vain attempt to persuade.

She knew that we were not nice to new girls, wherever they came from. We teased, tormented, and tortured them. We made them eat bitter aloe or swallow something nasty like cod-liver oil, or we gave them the black spot, which was supposed to frighten them, but, because most of them had never read *Treasure Island* and therefore did not know that if someone gave you the black spot it meant you were about to die, they only looked at us blankly.

Sheila told Bobby Joe, when she was a new girl, to put her towhead in the toilet and flush. She refused. "You have to," Sheila said, looking surprised, but Bobby Joe just walked away. Lizzie Turner broke Pamela's doll furniture for no reason at all when she was ten years old.

We were nasty to all new girls, especially foreigners. We were proud of our new country's independence, even if our mothers still called England home; after all, they had never been there. There was a new girl from England, pasty and plump, whom we called a killer. We made a circle around her and chanted, "You killed Joan of Arc." There was an American, Ramona Landsberger, whom we all called Ramooona Hamburger, imitating the way she answered all questions with a drawl, while she spat on her big, red mosquito bites. She did not stay long. The mosquitoes were too much for her. Africa was too much for her; we were too much for her.

We thought of all foreigners as "drips," whose soft feet made them unable to walk barefooted, as we could, across the hot, hard ground. We were sure they would get lost in the veld or fall into a deep donga or eat poisonous berries and die.

Miss Lacey was even older than Miss Nieven. She had blue-white hair and violet-blue eyes and wrinkled skin. She had told us that in her youth, at Oxford, Yeats had fallen in love with her violet-blue eyes. She was always quoting him, particularly his poem "When you are old and gray and full of sleep."

She was not quoting him this morning but informing us in hushed tones that Fiamma was actually a real princess. She told us that Fiamma was from an old, aristocratic Italian family, from the lake district not far from Milan. Her father owned great tracts of land, a large villa on the edge of a beautiful blue lake, famous paintings, rare jewels, a huge fortune. He was himself a prince, she went on, in her breathless way.

No one knew exactly why Fiamma's father had chosen this particular school, so far away from home, but Miss Lacey presumed he had his reasons; perhaps he had come across it in his travels, while searching for something else he wanted.

We shifted about and pulled at our socks and flared our eyebrows and sucked in our cheeks and goggled in mock amazement and awe. Di shrugged her broad shoulders and lifted the top of her desk as though she were looking for a book and mumbled, "So what" to Meg, who grinned. Ann, who never missed anything, turned around and gave Di her twisted smile. Pamela snickered.

We did not like aristocrats.

Naturally, being Italian, Fiamma was Roman Catholic, Miss Lacey went on, but she would attend religious services with the rest of us. She begged us to be gentle with her and to be mindful of her background. She said Fiamma had what she called a breathing disorder. Miss Lacey knew so much about Yeats, but little about young girls.

On the subject of R.C.'s

WE STOOD on the dry lawn during break, the sun warming our shoulders. We sipped hot tea from tin mugs and ate what we called squashed flies and stubbed the square toes of our lace-up shoes in the red sand. Bobby Joe picked her nose and maintained that the Pope kept all his old jewels locked up in vaults in the Vatican, while everyone else starved. Di told us her mother said Catholic nuns buried their babies in the backs of convent gardens. Sheila said her aunt told her those nuns were walled up in cellars when they sinned.

Meg, who was an R.C. herself, looked as if she were going to cry. She said she had never heard of such things, and she was sure no Catholics would do them, and anyway, what did being walled up alive mean?

"If you have done something really bad like having sex, they build a wall around you and leave you in there all alone in the dark to die, slowly, standing up. You can't even sit down to die," Sheila said, enjoying the drama of it all.

"They do that?" Meg's heavy lips trembled.

Fuzzie said, "Don't worry, they won't do that to you, Meg, even if you are an R.C., because you're beautiful and good as gold."

"She's not that good," Ann whispered to Sheila.

On Meg's bedside table she kept the photo of her mother and father with their five girls. The girls were all in faded dresses, and they seemed almost identical, sitting or kneeling on the ground, with their flat, pansy faces uplifted, showing off their slanting eyes and their heavy lips and their dark curls. All the girls were smiling, except for the youngest, who would die young of scarlet fever and was very nearsighted and did not seem to be aware that the photo was being taken, because her eyes were closed.

From the side of her thin mouth Ann whispered to Sheila that Meg's Catholic parents were not as perfect as Meg thought they were. Meg had confessed to her in a moment of confidence — Ann was good at getting our confidences with her probing questions, and Meg was no match for her — that her father beat his five girls once a week. He beat them with a sjambok out on the veranda, leaning over the back of a chair. They were beaten both for the sins they confessed and for the ones they did not.

Bobby Jean, who had been in a convent school, said Catholics were always trying to convert you in order to keep your soul from rotting in hell for eternity.

Lizzie said her mother said Protestants were rational and educated and kept their places of worship tastefully bare, whereas R.C.'s were superstitious and ignorant; they resorted to beads and candles and ghastly pictures of Christ, bleeding, with thorns around his head and nails in his hands.

We had all learned about Bloody Mary in history and how she killed so many Protestants because they wouldn't convert. We had all read a poem by the greatest poet in the English language, a poet who was even greater than Yeats, according to Miss Lacey, in which he asks God to avenge the saints slaughtered by the R.C.'s.

Perhaps Fiamma had seen some slaughtered, and that was why they had sent her away from her lovely villa, which was near a blue lake and mountains, Di suggested.

"We better watch out, the Catholic princess might want to slaughter some of us," Bobby Joe said.

It was then that Ann had one of her blinding revelations. She whispered to Sheila, "Miss G is going to like this new girl, you wait and see." She saw it in a flash.

What are cracks?

We held our breath, we shut our eyes,
We felt our heads spin.
Our souls escaped into the skies,
We heard a frightful din.

In the dark we saw diamonds;
Miss G sallied down the aisle.
She touched us with her hands
And bore us aloft, awhile.

MISS G WAS our crack. When you had a crack you saw things more clearly: the thick dark of the shadows and the transparence of the oak leaves in the light and the soft glow of the pink magnolia petals against their waxy leaves. You wanted to lie down alone in the dark in the music room and listen to Rachmaninoff and to the summer rains rushing hard down the gutters. You left notes for your crack in her mug next to her toothbrush on the shelf in the bathroom. If you accidentally brushed up against your crack and felt her boosie, you nearly fainted.

We all knew how to make ourselves faint. The teachers did not know we made ourselves do it, though they suspected we did. They even had a doctor brought in to examine us, but he said there was nothing wrong with us. He said he had never seen such a healthy group of growing girls. We did look healthy.

Our skins were gold with all the sunshine, and our hair and teeth looked very white in contrast. Weekdays in the summer term we wore short-sleeved white blouses with round collars and brown tunics with their big *R*'s embroidered on our chests and our long brown socks. Our tunics were worn four inches from the ground, measured kneeling, so you could see our knobby knees. In winter we wore long-sleeved blouses and ties.

We took turns fainting in chapel. Before communion, while we were on our knees and had not had any breakfast, we breathed hard a few times and then held our breath and closed our eyes. We sweated and started to see diamonds in the dark. We felt ourselves rush out of ourselves, out and out. Then we came back to the squelch of Miss G's crepe-soled boots as she strode along the blue-carpeted aisle to rescue us. She made us put our heads down between our knees, and then she lifted us up and squeezed our arms.

We leaned against her as we went down the aisle and felt her breath on our cheeks and the soft swell of her boosie. Our hearts fluttered, and we saw the light streaming in aslant through the narrow, stained-glass windows: red and blue and yellow like a rainbow.

Miss G led us out into the cool of the garden. We sat on the whitewashed wall under the loquat tree in our white Sunday dresses and undid the mother-of-pearl buttons at our necks. Miss G sat on the wall beside us and smoked a cigarette, holding it under her hand, so Miss Nieven would not notice if she came upon her suddenly. When Miss G told us to, we took off our panama hats and set them down on the wall. Then we leaned our heads against her shoulder. We got to sit there under the cool, dark leaves of the loquat tree and feel the breeze lift the hems of our tunics very gently and watch Miss G blow smoke rings, until she asked if we felt all right now. Her voice was deep and a little hoarse, like a man's.

Why Miss G called us to her room

> She called us to her room at night,
> She made us drunk on wine.
> We searched the truth with all our might;
> For her we write these lines.

IN OUR FLANNEL pajamas and plaid dressing gowns and flat leather slippers we huddled in Miss G's doorway and halfway down the long corridor, trembling and whispering. Why had Miss G summoned the twelve of us? She had never done so before this evening.

We were all whispering, looking at the faded reprints of Degas's ballet paintings, and waiting until she finished her conversation. We could hear her speaking and laughing on the telephone. To overhear her conversation better, Sheila, who was nosy, tried to get near the door. We gathered she was talking to the witty Mrs. Willis, the science teacher, who was her intimate friend at that time. Later Mrs. Willis became her enemy. Her best friends often became her enemies, because they betrayed her and took advantage of her great generosity, she said.

She was generous in many ways. Bobby Joe told us how Miss G sat by her bed in the sanatorium — a small, white building, set among blood red hibiscus bushes, where we were sent when we were ill — when she had the chicken pox. Bobby Joe forgot her itching while Miss G told her about a man she had fallen in love with when she was nursing in Wales during the war. She massaged his privates for him. Bobby Joe rubbed her small, strong hands together to show us what Miss G showed her.

Was it possible that Miss G had chosen us for her team? we wondered. We knew she banished girls whenever they disappointed her. Nor did they even know how they had disappointed her, or if they were to leave for good or simply to step aside for a while. Had she banished all the girls who had been there before us?

Fuzzie said that when she had gone to the san at the beginning of the term for her physical examination, the nurse had weighed her and measured her fluttering chest and slipped her cold, dry fingers under Fuzzie's warm, sticky armpits and held the ends of the tape measure together, asking her to inhale and measuring her again. "Miss G will want you," the nurse had told her, because she could expand nicely. Now she hummed a hopeful tune, wearing her vest under her plaid pajamas, and twisted her tight red curls around her finger. Her father was a musician and spoke of the four B's: Beethoven, Bach, Brahms, and Burls.

Expanding nicely was not the only reason Miss G chose girls for her team, Ann muttered mysteriously from over her shoulder, while standing on tiptoe to examine the Degas prints with a critical eye.

Meg said she thought Miss G chose the best-looking girls in the school for her swimming team. Sandra du Toit, who was already on the team, was certainly good-looking. And we, too, were good-looking, weren't we, Meg suggested, surveying our group with a benevolent eye.

We were good-looking. How could we not have been, growing up half-wild in fresh air, sunshine, and heat? Meg, of course, was particularly good-looking with her heavy, red lips, her slightly slanting, dark eyes, her slim waist, and her full bust. At fifteen, she looked lovely, even in her faded, shapeless pajamas.

Di flipped her fine, blond hair back from her face and stood on her long, slender legs, complaining to Meg about the wait. Ever since her father committed suicide in the bath, Di's thin lips dipped at the corners. She maintained Miss G chose girls who were rich and could contribute to the team fund. Some of us were rich: she had inherited her father's money. Fuzzie's father, who had inherited her mother's money when she died in a fire, had lots of money; Sheila's father, a timber baron, died of a heart attack and left all his money to her mother, who took to the bottle.

Ann, who was very poor, said Miss G probably chose anyone who could be useful to her. She helped Miss G with her correspondence and with the swimming-team quarterly, which told the school about its triumphs.

No one could think why Miss G had summoned the Trevelyan twins, who were not rich or pretty or useful, with their white hair sticking up on their heads like straw and their snub noses. They stood arm-in-arm, twisting about and putting their hands between their legs and wanting to go to the toilet. They were still horse-mad at twelve and tied their belts around Mary's waist and made her run around the garden, playing horsie and pretending to whip her. Perhaps Miss G chose them because they were orphans and had no one to turn to, Fuzzie whispered to Lizzie, the tall, elegant girl who spoke with an English accent.

Finally, Miss G covered the receiver with one hand and told us we might enter her room and find a perch. We filed in solemnly.

Miss G had acquired a room as large and as pleasant as Miss Nieven's. The bay windows were open to the evening light, which fell onto the silver jug of wet roses.

We could see through the big bay windows across the terraced lawns as far as the river on one side, and on the other up the green-gray hill as far as the pool. Unlike Miss Nieven, who kept her room shuttered and dim, Miss G always let in the sunlight. She believed it necessary to combat her skin malady, something mysterious with a Greek name, contracted as a child, that made her scratch from time to time.

Miss G sat in her wicker chair before her desk in her khaki jumpsuit and scratched at the bristles on the back of her neck in the evening light of her big, open room. She was slim and athletic. She seemed tall, although she was not as tall as Di. She had fine, tapered fingers and what she called good bone structure: high cheekbones and an aquiline nose. Her eyes were wide-spaced and large and as dark as night. They were mysteriously shaded by thick lashes and had a beautiful expression when she was carried away, which she often was. Her forehead was broad and generous, and her hair as glossy as a gypsy's. Her mouth had no droop but was firm and straight. Two deep lines ran from her nose to the corners of her lips. She was wearing what she always wore when she was not wearing her black bathing suit: her starched khaki jumpsuit, with a hand-embroidered belt, and her famous highly lacquered boots with crepe soles. Her clothing was always spotlessly clean and well-pressed and starched, and it made a whispering sound like the sea as she moved.

Sitting on the carpet with clammy, clenched hands and dry mouths, or perching on her bed like birds, we waited expectantly, gazing up at her, our name tags pricking our necks. There was no scratching or picking there; only stillness and docility. Miss G had bribed Mrs. Looney, our matron, with boxes of chocolates and nylon stockings to allow us to stay up at night in her room. She glowed, we thought, as though a halo surrounded her head. She spoke fast and impatiently, as though there were little time left.

"Shut the windows, Radfield," she ordered. She always called us by our surnames, as though we were boys.

We watched avidly as she took out two straw-covered demijohns of wine from her cupboard. She mixed the red and the white, pouring from both containers at once into a big white pitcher, with a glug-glug, something we had never seen anyone do before. She gave us glassful after glassful and told us to drink up. *In vino veritas,* she said. She liked to quote in Latin or from Shakespeare. She told us she was an autodidact, which meant that she had learned everything by herself.

She told us that whatever happened in her room was to remain a secret. We were not to tell anyone. We were not to fidget, not to ask questions, not to speak at all unless spoken to, and not to get up to go to the bathroom.

"I need your whole attention, if we are going to accomplish the great things I have in mind for you," she said, lighting a cigarette. When we had all solemnly promised to obey — we would have promised her anything — she informed us in a matter-of-fact tone that she simply needed some new blood. She was choosing twelve new girls for the team: us.

The whole room, with its bright yellows and blues and its large photos of Miss G's Welsh terrier, who died of some horrible disease, spun around. It was only afterward that we thought of the twelve girls whose places we had taken, especially Sandra, our head girl, a beauty, tall and brainy, slender and athletic, with red-gold hair, who had been Miss G's favorite, and who was suddenly banished.

She informed us that it was of no importance who was on her team, because she could teach anyone to swim. "I could teach a sheep to swim," she said scornfully, and we lowered our eyes and laughed sheepishly. We were certain she could do what she said.

She scratched her cheek, and we did the same. As she spoke, we moved our lips with her words. When she tapped her ash into the ashtray, we tapped our fingers. She held her handsome head high like a fist and pressed her broad shoulders back, soldier-like. We sat up and pressed back our shoulders.

Her hair was cropped so short you could see the bristles at the back of her neck, and she had burned her skin dark that summer, the result, she had explained to us, of the reflected light from the snow on a recent skiing trip to her native Wales.

She said that we were not to be deluded that she had chosen us for our innate ability to swim, or for any other particular abilities we had; on the contrary, she maintained, she had chosen us randomly. Anyone else would have done just as well. She said she chose her swimmers by chance, that is, as a manifestation of God's will.

She told us, "What is important in learning to swim well, as it is in anything, is desire," and her black eyes flickered mysteriously. She told us we could do anything if we desired it enough. We liked the way she said *desire,* and we looked at one another and raised our eyebrows and smiled.

She said we could and should break all the absurd rules that governed our young lives; we were to flout convention. "You can do anything you want. The world is yours for the taking. Nothing is impossible for you, my girls. Live your lives to the full. Do you want to be absolutely free? Do you want to escape your suffering bodies? All you need is to desire it."

She told us to use our imaginations, to concentrate, to think of nothing else, if we wanted to win; that everything was part of the race. She advised us to keep our bodies fit at all times, to eat fruits and vegetables and whole-grain bread and keep ourselves light for the rest of our lives. She told us to swim in the morning, at night, constantly. "Discipline," she said, "not talent, is what counts." Potential was simply the willingness to learn what she had to teach. "Don't let men wreck your bodies or bend your minds; be just like them." Her grandmother gained just fourteen pounds when she was carrying her mother, who weighed seven at birth; her grandmother was riding a horse at eighty. "You can be strong and beautiful until the day you die. Aim high." She lifted her big, strong hands and shook them at the high molding, as we all looked up.

She told us to think of the water as our own true home, to learn to do without breath, without air; to be light. We sucked in our stomachs and straightened our backs. She told us not to make any unnecessary movements in the water, not to roll about or twist our shoulders or lift our heads too high, but to suck a little air fast from the sides of our mouths. She said not to make any splash, to slice silently through the water, to cut through it, to kill. "Swim out of rage," she ordered, "and for God."

She wanted us to know she was not a failed intellectual but an educated woman, perhaps more educated than our head-mistress with her degree from Oxford. She encouraged all of us to read and promised to lend us books from her library, not the books on our school syllabus, not *The Story of an African Farm*, not *The Tempest* or *Jane Eyre*, but books covered with brown paper, written by writers of whom we had never heard: Law-rence, both D.H. and T.L. She told Ann to read her namesake, Ayn Rand.

We stared up at her, trying to follow what she was saying. We often had great difficulty following her, because she spoke so fast and with so many long words and unusual expressions. "If you can't bedazzle them with brilliance, baffle them with bull-shit," she said. Miss Lacey told us she was vulgar, having spent some time in America and picked up certain expressions there, but we knew Miss Lacey was jealous because she was old and washed out. We thought Miss G expressed herself brilliantly. If we could only understand her, we could learn the secret of life.

She went on in her mellifluous Welsh voice. She told us both that we were a worthless bunch who would never amount to anything and that we could be the best swimmers anywhere, with our names inscribed in history. She repeated our names. Radfield, Radfield, Miss G said, shaking her head. She used allit-eration. She called Di, "Reckless Radfield," and Fuzzie, "Burls the Bear," because she was plump and awkward. Ann was "Logical Lindt" and Meg was "Darling Donovan," because she was beautiful and good and was always helping the little girls who came crying to her about their troubles. Mary Skeen was "Sweet Skeen," because she was placid and good-natured, and Lizzie was "Lucky Lizzie," because she got to spend the holidays in England with her father.

Miss G spoke of the importance of honor. She told us about Brutus: that the good of the team should triumph over the good of the individual. She told us that the means justified the end, which was to win and win again.

She spoke of truth and freedom from repression. She said the essential was to look into your heart honestly and to know the truth about yourself and, thus, about life. "If you find the truth within you, it will save you. If you ignore it, it will destroy you," she said. No one else would tell us the truth; we were brainwashed by a bunch of bland spinsters who knew nothing — or would tell us nothing — about life, who gave us a sugarcoated version of the truth. She imitated Miss Nieven sipping a cup of tea, lifting her pinkie in the air and talking about God the Rushing Wind, making us laugh with a delicious sense of complicity.

She said she would tell us about our headmistress, who, if she was not going mad, was at least more and more disorganized. She closed herself up in her room and did not respond to anyone for days. She was getting worse and worse. "All Sunny Nieven thinks of is taking your money. If I were your parents I would complain. She cannot even answer a letter anymore. And that's the truth."

"To thine own self be true, and it must follow, as the night the day, thou canst not then be false to any man," she recited. Now that we were on her team, we had to learn the art of telling the whole truth.

She would even tell us about herself, as an example. She told us her father was a dirt-poor Welsh miner, and a drunk, who made her kneel as a punishment, even when she had the curse, until she fainted; that he beat her mother, who made millinery, sitting up late at night sewing plastic cherries onto felt to supplement their small income; that she, Miss G, stole money from her grandmother's money box, which she kept under her bed, to buy her boat ticket to Africa.

"No inhibitions here! I will have no inhibitions here!" she said sternly. "Repression of libidinal urges only leads to aggression. Give me your secrets, girls, give me the dark depths of your hearts, and I will give you the light. Search your hearts, for the universe lies therein," and we searched and searched. "It is always more grubby than you think," she added, and we nodded our heads, knowing she was right. She said there were certain subjects we should get out of the way, so that we could go about our business. She knew what we were thinking.

"I know what you are thinking about, Darling Donovan, behind that angelic air," she said to Meg, making her squirm about and blush. "You are a quiet one, a regular little saint. But don't think I have not been watching you. You're interested in what everyone else your age is interested in, and it is not swimming."

She looked around the room for another victim. "And if our little saint is interested in it, just think how interested Reckless Radfield must be! Ah, Radfield, you are entirely honorable and good, but you are the most dangerous of all. Isn't she now? She is a sensualist. Are you not? I can see it from the way you throw yourself into the water, from the way you run across the veld, from the way you look at Meg." Di dared to look back at Miss G without blinking.

"And as for Logical Lindt, don't think you fool me either, my dear. You are far too clever for your own good," she intoned, shaking her head. "Your nose may be in a book for the moment, but you're just like the rest."

She proceeded to tell us in detail about the miracle of a man's erection. "Observe them as they swell in their bathing suits when they come near you." We giggled and smirked and imagined men's mysterious parts swelling like sunflowers in the warm light of our bodies. We were transformed into snake charmers, magicians. As the light faded and night fell, she advised us to adopt the habit of clenching our pelvic muscles after we urinated to tighten them, so that they could give pleasure. "Our muscles are like our minds: we must exercise them again and again," she said, as we clenched and unclenched them. *Mens sana in corpore sano*, she quoted. She told us that we must always tell her when we had our periods.

By the time Fiamma arrived, all of us had had our periods for the first time. The hot weather out here makes us develop early, Miss G told us, but Fiamma, being an aristocrat with blue blood, would do so more slowly.

The game of truth

THE MOON CAST its pale light in the long, narrow room as we sat on the floor in a circle whispering. Ann sat on the sidelines and called out "Stop," and Meg's hand was found at the bottom of the pile, so she had to answer the question.

It was Sheila who devised the game. Always one who tried hard, she suggested we practice telling the truth in the dormitory at night, as Miss G had suggested.

We all put our hands one on top of the other to make a pile and then pulled them out one by one, starting from the bottom, playing truth. Someone sat on the sidelines and called out "Stop," and whoever had her hand at the bottom of the pile had to answer a question truthfully. The only one who escaped, because we never asked her to play, was Fiamma — that is, until the day she disappeared.

Ann asked Meg what was the worst thing she had ever done.

Meg had been taught by her Catholic mother and father to keep her mouth shut, to chest her cards, so she said she could think of nothing.

Ann said, "Oh, come on. Out with it."

Meg confessed to putting a hairpin up her winkie, and then covered her face with her hands in embarrassment.

"You did that!" Di gasped, pulling her lips down at the corners, as though she were about to be sick.

Meg now sat on the sidelines and got to ask Di the same question. That is how we found out that Di had actually allowed a boy to put his finger up hers.

"So you're not a virgin?" Ann asked her, impressed.

"Not strictly speaking, I suppose," Di said with a superior air, flashing her strong, white teeth and her rosy gums at us in the moonlight.

After that we followed her around like dogs for days.

When Fiamma first arrived

WE HAD STAKED out our territory, fought over the best beds in Kitchener, and were bouncing on them, when Bobby Joe spotted a car approaching in a cloud of red dust in the distance.

It was the beginning of the spring term and a long period of drought. The October rains had not come to signal the end of a dry winter. Instead the wind blew across the veld, carrying a fine red-clay dust into the classrooms and dormitories. It settled in a thin film over the basins and dresser tops and windowsills.

Dust was flying from the wheels of the dark green Porsche, which came to an abrupt halt under the oak trees. A man got out, trailed by a blond girl, her head drooping like a snowdrop in the early spring. We had never seen such a handsome and elegant man. He looked shiny, striding up the polished red steps between the sandstone lions, two at a time, followed by a servant carrying leather suitcases of different sizes.

Leaning far out the window, Bobby Joe told us the man looked like a fairy with golden eyes.

Miss Nieven, too, was there on the steps in the full glare of afternoon light. She had not greeted any of our parents on our arrival but remained within the thick walls of her cool study, making up programs, or writing in pencil about God for her Sunday sermon, erasing with her big pink rubber when she made a mistake. She had left the task of greeting newcomers to Matron, the least important member of the staff, who had stood with her cardboard-backed list and licked her fat finger to turn the pages, looking for our names through thick glasses and ticking them off one by one.

But for this latecomer Miss Nieven was standing on the front steps in the sun, waving her white lace handkerchief about in the air like someone in a book, the lavender wafting up to us as we hung out the windows. She was wearing her best mauve dress, the one she kept for chapel on Sundays, and she had even pinned a posy of wilting violets to her flat spinster bosom. Her thin voice rose in greeting: "Welcome, welcome," she shrilled, shaking the father's hand, as though she would never let it go.

He was nattily turned out, in tweeds, in exactly the light-colored shirt and pastel tie and shiny shoes that fashion, as we imagined it, prescribed. His dark, glossy hair was perfectly trimmed, and his pale face freshly shaved. Fuzzie maintained his lips had been lightly touched with rouge.

"Definitely a poofter," Bobby Joe concluded, leaning dangerously far out.

We watched him leave, loping down the steps two at a time. The blond girl followed and clung to him. He had to pry her loose, and long after he had gone, we saw her standing there, looking down the dusty driveway, lingering in the shade of the oak trees while the sun set in a rush of red. She was still out there when dark fell swiftly, and we could hear a dog howl with a wild, wolf-like sound. Then she turned her face toward the school and dragged herself slowly up the drive.

Miss Nieven, who had politely refrained from interfering in this parting, was there again with a big smile to usher Fiamma into our dormitory. Tugging at the hair that grew from the wart on her chin, she told us to be sure to make the new girl feel at home, and then stood there as though she wanted to say more. We felt she would have liked to stay all evening to make sure we were kind.

Fiamma came into Kitchener followed by the servant carrying all her suitcases. The moment she entered the room, our eyes turned to her, as though there were something magical about her appearance. She stood there, blinking her dark eyelashes, the tears still on her cheeks, her long neck delicate but not frail, and her oval face tipped to one side. She looked as though she had just risen, naked out of the sea, and stepped into a shell, like the lady we had seen in the painting in art class. We tried to pay no attention to her, but we were all staring.

What drew our attention? Her eyes were unusually big, huge,

still disks, a strange shade of light blue and as clear as running water. Her expression, too, was not one we had ever seen. She did not seem to see us, or rather she seemed to see through us, as though she were looking into the distance or listening to some faint sound. She did not look either sad or happy, but removed, as though she had looked us all over, and found us wanting. It was the uncaring look of the outsider.

Her pale eyes and her pale plait, which lay on her shoulder, matched her milk white skin, which was that of a redhead. But her hair was not red, it was blond. Her nose was unusually straight and seemed pencil-thin at the tip.

The oval of her face struck us particularly. There was something soft and sweet about the curve of her cheek. We recalled it from the copies of Italian Renaissance paintings we had seen in art class. It was the smooth oval of the Florentine Madonnas, the face of the very young mother with her child. It made us feel lonely.

Fiamma turned to the servant who had brought in the leather suitcases, hatboxes, and vanity cases, all initialed, with combination locks and first-class tickets flying. "Thank you so much for your kindness," she said to him, and then, speaking to us in the same clipped English tone, she added, "Fiamma Coronna. Good evening," though no one had asked her her name.

"Good evening, Your Royal Highness," Bobby Joe quipped from the end of the dormitory. Pamela stood up and curtsied, and we all giggled.

A tear ran down Fiamma's pale cheek. It was the only time we ever saw her weep. She did not even weep on the Sunday afternoon she disappeared, after we had played the game of truth.

Ann said, "This one is not going to be with us for long."

Why did our parents send us to this school?

We came here on slow trains from afar,
Traveling through veld day and night.
We followed the evening star.
To arrive at this lonely place in the moonlight.

THE ONLY KIND OF SNOW we had at Christmastime was made from cotton wool, and the holly was made of plastic. It was so hot we sweated when we ate the roast turkey and potatoes and gem squash, and when they flamed the Christmas pudding, the light outside was so bright you could hardly see the flame. The poem we read did not make much sense to us because April was not the cruelest month and bred nothing out of the dead land.

In those days our school was entirely surrounded by farmland. For miles around there was nothing but a few mangy cows, wattle trees, and pale mud huts, their skeletal frames visible in the blinding light. The dirt roads lay dry and white as shells in the sun. Sandy paths led across the veld to the river and the graves. An iron gate closed on the long driveway, lined with ancient oaks, that led up to the school.

No one was here except the girls and the teachers, who were elderly spinsters from England no longer able to find gainful employ in their home country, because of age or eccentricity or the commission of some minor misdemeanor. They clasped their hands to their hearts and looked across the veld to the distant horizon and longed for the lilac in May. The big girls lolled in the leather chairs in the common room and listened to Elvis singing "Hound Dog," and talked about boys. They slept over sums in the classrooms or whispered in the library, while they pretended to look up Latin verbs.

We were sent here as boarders at five or six, because there were no proper schools where we lived. We left our parents on distant farms or in small towns and traveled alone or in little groups for days on trains through wild country. We arrived exhausted and confused, stumbling through the long, narrow passageways, lit only by Matron's torch, and finding our beds among strange sleeping girls. The sheets smelled damp and funny. We lay awake, listening to the clashing of the palm fronds in the dry wind.

We cried for our mothers until Matron came to us in her dressing gown with her gray plait over her shoulder, trying to bring comfort. But she did not smell of flowers like our mothers. She did not feel like them. Her bosoms dangled slackly down to her thick waist under her rough dressing gown with the twisted red-and-white twill. Her hair was not silky like our mothers' — if we dared to touch her limp braid at all. She clucked her tongue at us. She told us our noise would only wake the others. When we got to the hiccupy stage, she took our temperatures with the thermometer she took from a small glass of Dettol with a snap of her wrist. Her name was Mrs. Looney, and we thought she was, too.

Night after night we wept for our mothers. If we went on wailing for too long and woke the other girls, Mrs. Looney took us to the spare bed in her small, stuffy room. We lay awake in the dark, sniffing and hiccuping and listening to her stertorous breathing. We stared up at the sky and tried to find the stars that looked down on our homes, remembering where we ate cold sausages with our sisters, sitting up in the bay window after church on Sunday, looking over the lawns, watching the big white tickbirds picking at the dirt.

We saw our mothers standing in the open window. They came to us in the half dark, their soft breaths on our cheeks, as they sang us familiar songs: "Underneath the budding chestnut trees." They were slipping their rings onto our fingers and toes;

they were rocking us on their knees and reciting rhymes: "She shall have music wherever she goes."

Mornings we saw their faces as we tried to untangle the knots in our hair, or as we lay in the big bath with the claws for feet. We heard their voices coming from down the corridor; they would bring us the cakes of soap we had forgotten in the dormitory. They sat on the branches beside us in the loquat trees and tickled our necks with leaves. We thought we heard them calling our names, and we ran down into the bamboo at the end of the garden, catching glimpses of them parting the bamboo and stepping toward us in green silk dresses, but it was only the cry of a sparrow hawk or the wind in the leaves.

We made up imaginary friends. Sheila's was called Margaret. Margaret came with her to the toilet to talk to her when she had to make number two or ran beside her when she had to run around the hockey field, her breath rasping in her chest.

We felt ourselves spin out into the darkness, round and round, like a leaf on water.

On Miss G's team

WE WERE ALL WINNERS and losers at different times, and our status on the team waxed and waned. We were willing to do anything to improve our precarious positions. We were constantly terrified Miss G might dismiss us, cast us out into the darkness of purgatory, lump us with the girls who were not on the team and who hardly seemed to exist at all.

Once on the team, we rarely mixed with the other girls in our class or any of the other classes. They had become boring. They seemed to have been washed away, to have left the school and vanished. Even Sandra du Toit, our head girl that year, who was beautiful and brainy and good at games, but no longer on the swimming team, no longer mattered. The swimmers were the only ones who did, because they were the only ones who mattered to Miss G.

Besides, Miss G had always tried as much as possible to group her team members in one dormitory on the pretext that we would disturb the other girls by rising early for swim practice. She knew well that it was in the whispered conversations in the night that affinities were formed, that it was while sitting in the window seat, staring up at the garlands of stars hanging low and bright in the African sky, that confidences were exchanged.

We stood on the high board for Miss G, trembling with suspense, looking down at the light fragmented in the water, opening our arms on the air, plunging through it, splitting the surface of the water with hardly a splash, toes pointed to the sky.

We rose early to swim before assembly; we swam two hours after rest in the afternoon and again at dusk. We always had cramps in our toes. Our hair was always wet. Our hands were always damp and cold and our fingers crinkled. Our eyes were always bleary with chlorine, as we gazed dazedly down at our damp books. Our pillows were soaked when we lay our heads down to sleep.

Meg and Miss G

> Behind her dark head was the sun,
> As she leaned across and touched Meg's knee.
> She was marked forever as the one,
> Forever branded by Miss G.

THE SUN LAY in a diamond shape on the soft carpeted floor, filling the big tearoom. A glass vase stood in the window with mimosa branches spreading fan-like against the sky. Women leaned close, the flowers in their hats trembling. They whispered and sipped tea, their little fingers lifted in cream leather gloves. Waitresses wore black dresses and frilled white caps, which floated like boats on the backs of their heads. They pushed tea carts on wheels, piled high with wondrous cakes: éclairs and little tarts with whipped cream and big, ripe strawberries, the kind Meg adored and almost never got to eat, she told us later. Miss G bought her several of them — one with cream and strawberries — and several cups of tea poured from a shiny silver teapot with straight sides and a little matching pitcher of milk. She noticed how Miss G slipped several packets of sugar into her many pockets and patted them with satisfaction.

On Fridays we were allowed to go into town for doctors' or dentists' appointments. This Friday, Miss G had accompanied Meg when she had to go to the doctor for her severe period pains. After the visit to the doctor, she had taken Meg out for tea in a big department store in the center of town, a place where Meg had never been before.

Miss G leaned forward and asked Meg, who was stuffing cakes into her mouth, about her family. She was glad Miss G was asking her this and not, as she often did, something more difficult that she might not understand. "How on earth does your poor father cope with so many girls?" she wanted to know.

Meg took another quick bite of cake and a sip of tea before answering. She felt warm in the sunshine, and started to explain how she tried to help her father by doing as many of the household chores as she could, rising early to clean the floors. Then she remembered how Miss G had said that we should tell all the truth and bring the dark parts of our lives into the light, and though she was not quite sure what a dark part was or whether she had any to be brought into the light, she found herself revealing what she had never told anyone before.

She told her how her father beat her and her sisters, making them lean over a chair once a week out on the veranda so that he could beat them with a sjambok, one after the other; the worst part was watching. She could not stop herself from watching. She drew aside the muslin curtain at the window and watched her father beat her sisters, starting with the youngest girl, the delicate one, watching and listening to their desperate cries for mercy. She knew that her father knew she was watching, that he wanted her to watch — indeed, needed her to watch, and that he would beat her harder than all the rest because she had been doing so, beat her until she lay unconscious on the floor.

When she stopped speaking, she waited, a little breathless and flushed, for Miss G to murmur words of sympathy or approbation for bringing forth into the light such a dark part of her life. She thought Miss G would pat her on the back and tell her how reckless and brave she had been, or perhaps even order a few more cakes as a reward, but Miss G did nothing of the sort. She leaned forward slightly and briefly placed her hand, lightly but unmistakably, on Meg's knee.

"There wasn't anything sexy about it," Meg told us, but it seemed to her that something enormous had happened. She had the strange but certain impression that Miss G was branding her as one of her own. Everything spun around her: the waitresses in black dresses, their little, frilled white caps, the shining silver teapot, the strawberries on the cream cakes, the yellow of the mimosa branches in the vase by the window, even the light in a diamond pattern on the carpet. Meg wanted to hold on to the moment like a precious gift, a jewel, something to be kept wrapped up forever in pink tissue paper.

How Fiamma made the swimming team

> For Fiamma she could skim across the water,
> As fast as can be,
> For she was a prince's daughter,
> And Miss G loved her most passionately.

M ISS G TOLD US she was not entirely satisfied with her new team. She might choose some new members, or get rid of some of those she had already chosen. She was going to make the girls on the team race with the rest of the class. We could choose the stroke we liked and had to swim two lengths of the long pool. She told us to wait on the dry grass by the pool in our thin, black racing costumes, the spring sun burning our tender skin purple.

She liked to keep us waiting, for it enabled her to see who had real character and would stay the course. She said it was character, not talent, perseverance, not promise, that counted.

Fuzzie swatted at mosquitoes, which seemed drawn to her plump, bare legs and arms. Di tossed her long, thin hair impatiently. Lizzie practiced her crawl in the air, stretching her long, white arms. We rose up on our toes or crouched down on our heels with our elbows on our thighs and hands between our legs. We milled around, licking from the palms of our hands the powdered sugar we had obtained from Di.

Miss G called out the names of the whole class alphabetically and had us line up: "Allenby, Arkright, Bell, Burls, Fiamma Coronna . . . ," she called. Our legs felt watery, like the reflections of legs in water. We squirmed. We pulled the straps of our green plastic caps away from our chins. Color washed from the sky. Finally, she raised her black gun in the white air.

The water glittered; the sun blazed. We saw birds shoot up in the air and heard the crack of the gun. We flung ourselves across the water, crowding together. We splashed and kicked and crashed into one another, struggling breathlessly in a series of races, one after the other. When she saw that she was not winning, Sheila threw up her arms and sank down into the water, pretending to faint, so she would have to be dragged out.

The winners of each heat then swam a final one. Fiamma left all the rest of us behind after a few strokes. Miss G had her swim alone, timing her with her stopwatch, while we had to stand and look on. The spring sun was burning our cheeks, and the sweat was dripping into our dazzled eyes. We put up our hands to shade them, watching Fiamma flying back and forth across the surface, silvered by sun and spray.

Miss G stood in the shadows of the changing huts, her arms crossed, her wide lips trembling, and her yellow whistle dangling unused on her chest. The light in her dark face was strange and cast a glow. There was an expression of joy and pain at the same time.

She strode to the edge of the pool and leaned over to give Fiamma her broad hand and pull her out with one swift, strong movement, the water rushing from Fiamma's white skin like silver ribbons. She stood in the sun on the sides of her narrow feet on the hot concrete around the pool, gazing at us directly, as though it had been the easiest thing in the world.

"Hurry up and get her a towel," Miss G shouted imperiously. She draped it carefully around Fiamma like a royal cape and flung her arm around Fiamma's shoulders. She led her away, talking earnestly, bending her dark head toward Fiamma's blond one. They went together toward the changing huts, their shadows mingling in the dry grass.

What Fiamma liked about swimming

SITTING ON THE WOODEN bench in the changing room, where Miss G had left her after the tryouts, her thin, wet racing costume clinging to her narrow body and her pale plait lying on her shoulder, Fiamma lifted her inhaler and pumped to get her breath. She told us she did not want to be part of our team. "I don't want to swim for Miss G," she said.

"You don't?" Meg gasped in disbelief, watching her pump.

Fiamma suffered from a condition that made her use the inhaler. From time to time she placed it in her mouth and pumped on the soft brown bag. The other teachers said she had asthma and allowed her to climb out of the pool and lie down in the shade with her towel over her back or to sit on the bench and run her fingers through her blond, wavy hair, reading a book in gym in her bloomers, which showed off her slender legs, while we sweated and groaned on the hard floor, vaulting over the pommel horse or doing endless jumping jacks, sit-ups, and press-ups, which were supposed to combat any excessive interest in sex. We believed Fiamma was pretending most of the time, using her supposed illness to avoid whatever she wished to avoid.

"I like swimming fast. It feels like flying," she told us. She swam until she felt one with the water. She liked its mysterious sound in her ears — a sound like music, she said. She liked the way her mind floated free. She was never tired out swimming, except when she had her asthma attacks. On the contrary, swimming invigorated her. She was addicted to it, she said, it was like a need for air. If she could not swim she became restless, bored, edgy. Swimming was not a sport for her; it was where you could be who you really were. Besides, it was the only place where you could be on your own in this school. Fiamma said she found the lack of privacy unbearable.

We were not supposed to go off on our own. It was considered dangerous. We were not even allowed to lock our doors. The toilets and the small white cubicles where we washed for exactly ten minutes — baths were no longer allowed because of the drought — remained unlocked. We even took brief showers together in the bathroom under the stairs — Meg, Ann, and Di, all together, scorching themselves under the old shower that was impossible to regulate. Wherever we went, we heard the teachers' low voices and the high-pitched ones of girls. We were together day and night, eating, washing, learning our lessons, reading, sleeping, whispering in the dark, even going to the lavatory in the stalls where we could see feet and heads and talk to one another, while we strained and pushed. It would be unbearable here without the swimming, Fiamma said.

She told us she had no memory of learning to swim. Her father, who had been a championship swimmer himself, even swimming the channel, had thrown her into the water before she could walk. She kept a photo of him in his full-length swimsuit in a beaten-silver frame by her bed. His head was flung back, his dark, wet hair swept from his forehead. There was a towel slung around his neck. He appeared to be laughing.

She had no desire to compete in races, Fiamma said. In all her life she had never had to compete. She had grown up alone in her father's house with only an old servant for company. She had seen her mother and her half sister infrequently on visits to Milan, and neither of them could compete with her. Her father hated the one and refused to recognize the other, rarely mentioning her name.

Furthermore, she told us, she liked to swim because she had been found near the water, or so she was told by the old servant. He was a teller of tales. He was cleaning the changing huts near the lake, he said, when he heard cries. He was afraid some peasant had tried to drown a kitten, as they often did, weighing them with heavy stones and throwing them into the lake, where they would sink down into the dark of the soft silt of the lake bed. Instead, he found a newborn baby in a basket. "Like the story of Moses in the bulrushes. Only there was no massacre of babies, just a note from my mother in my shawl, which read, 'Returning that which belongs to you,'" she told us in her deadpan voice.

How Fiamma came to join the team anyway

THE LONG DESKS stretched all the way across the laboratory. There was a faint smell of smoke and methylated spirits in the dusty air. Ann was standing very straight and small in front of the class and succinctly and clearly explaining some experiment that no one else had understood when the laboratory door swung open abruptly, and Miss G put her dark head inside. She needed to see Fiamma urgently, Miss G said to Mrs. Willis, the science teacher.

Miss G had been Mrs. Willis's particular friend, but now she hated Miss G passionately. Mrs. Willis, the science teacher, had told us that the story about Miss G's parents was utter nonsense, that it was like something out of Dickens, and that Miss G's parents were very much middle-class and doted on Miss G and had sacrificed to send her to the best schools in Wales, where she continuously broke all the rules and was sent home.

Mrs. Willis maintained Miss G had been shut up in a mental asylum for a while, that she had been institutionalized, held in a straitjacket. Her parents died alone and unloved but respectably in an old-age home, according to Mrs. Willis.

Miss G had told us that Mrs. Willis was a lesbian. She had seen Mrs. Willis in the driveway making out with Miss Lacey, the English teacher whom Yeats had once loved.

Everyone said Mrs. Willis was very brilliant. She was sent down from Oxford because of some mysterious scandal, but she still received parcels of books with strange titles from England. Ann maintained Mrs. Willis read Marx and was probably a Communist, and Fuzzie that she was a spy, but Fuzzie always exaggerated. Di believed that Miss G was right, and that Mrs. Willis was a lesbian.

Whatever Mrs. Willis's sexual preference, she was always leaving us to cope on our own with our Bunsen burners, endangering our lives, while she disappeared into the science closet to have a quick drag on a cigarette. We were always blowing up our experiments, singeing our eyelashes, our eyebrows, while Mrs. Willis dragged on her cigarette. She wore a white coat without bothering to do up the bottom buttons, so that you could see her slim knees in her pale gray stockings. She was pacing before the blackboard, a piece of chalk in her hand, listening to Ann explain the experiment, while no one else except Mary listened, at the moment when Miss G put her head in the door to ask for Fiamma.

Mrs. Willis hissed at Miss G in her raspy, smoker's voice, "I am in the middle of a science lesson, if you don't mind," and gave her a furious look with her small, gray eyes. Miss G glanced over the rows of long desks that stretched from one side of the room to the other. Fiamma sat by the wall with her head down on the desk, apparently asleep.

Miss G said, "I don't think Fiamma will miss much of your science lesson. This won't take more than a minute. It's urgent." She told Fiamma to come with her. Fiamma lifted her head and looked up blankly, glancing from Mrs. Willis to Miss G, and blinked her big eyes. Then she shrugged her shoulders with her usual indifference and rose, yawning as she made for the door, almost knocking over a Bunsen burner as she went.

Fiamma was always careless in class. She wandered in late and forgot to bring the right books or dropped them on the floor while someone was reading aloud. She was always losing her pen and borrowing one from Sheila, who had several in preparation for her future career. Fiamma rarely bothered to answer questions, or when she did, answered the previous one. She always got up the moment we were dismissed, sauntering out without her books. She regularly fell asleep over her homework in the evening, her head in her arms. Yet the teachers would watch her, smiling fondly and indulgently, without ever scolding her.

Still, she could answer questions no one else could about history, and she surprised us with her knowledge of the ways of the world. She possessed odd information: she knew about Garibaldi and the Carbonari and Mazzini and about some old Italian king who had said, *"Avanti Savoia!"* She played the Moonlight Sonata so that we were moved to tears, but she did not care for it. When she recited Keats's "The Eve of Saint Agnes" at the drama competition, she forgot her lines halfway through, but the judge commended her on the sweetness and musicality of her voice.

Under the loquat tree at break we formed a circle around her and questioned her. She told us how Miss G had persuaded her to join our swimming team.

In her splendid, sunny room with the big photos of her dead Welsh terrier on the walls, Miss G told Fiamma to sit down in the comfortable armchair and offered her a glass of wine, which she declined. She asked Fiamma if she were happy at our school. Fiamma said she had not expected to be happy here, and hoped not to have to stay for more than a few months. Miss G knew it must be very lonely for Fiamma so far away from her home. She knew how Fiamma must feel, for she, too, was a foreigner, after all, and she, herself, was often lonely out here.

Fiamma said nothing. What was there to say, after all? Then Miss G asked if there was not something — any little thing — she could do to make Fiamma's stay more comfortable, to make her feel more at home. Fiamma said she thought for a while and then confessed that there was one thing she particularly missed.

And what was that? Miss G wanted to know, leaning forward eagerly, her elbows on her knees. Fiamma said it was her breakfasts: the crispy sweet rolls and coffee with steamed milk, brought to her in bed on a tray by the old servant. He always tapped the spoon against the cup to wake her, before he entered. Then he would throw up the shutters to let the sun stream in pools into the room.

"If you promise to swim for me, I will see what I can do," Miss G said, raising her eyebrows and wagging a finger at her, smiling, as Fiamma left the room.

In the long, narrow dining room with its odor of oranges and burned porridge, we cast hostile glances at Fiamma as the servant brought her special breakfast on a tray: sugarcoated white rolls and coffee with steamed milk, served on blue-and-white willow-pattern china. We whispered about Your Royal H —— as we shoveled the dark, lumpy porridge called maltabella into our mouths, washing it down with weak, milky tea from tin mugs that scalded our lips. Even Darling Donovan, who had such a sweet tooth, managed to complain that it was just too unfair.

Now our team had thirteen girls, not twelve. Inevitably, when we lined up double-file to walk to the bus, one of us would be left out. Inevitably, as best friends were formed, one of us would have to be rejected.

Was Ann Fiamma's best friend?

A NN DID NOT WANT to be Fiamma's friend, but she had little choice. No one else wanted to be her friend. No one invited her out on Sundays, when we were allowed to go home. No one invited her for half term. No one ever invited her, because of her small, protuberant eyes, her shiny forehead, and her stilted conversation: she could not chatter inconsequentially, as the rest of us did, but could only hold forth about the French Revolution and the Rights of Man.

"Your head's always in the clouds," Miss G told Ann, as they walked under the heavy leaves of the oak trees along the driveway to the bus. "You ought to think about more practical things, Lindt. For example, your skin. You ought to take care of it. Looks are more important than thoughts, you know. Why don't you ask Sister to give you some medicated soap for your blackheads, my dear," she suggested, looking at Ann's blighted nose and cheeks. "And, I feel obliged to tell you, your nails are not very clean, either, dear. Your fingers are always stained with ink, and you have a big blue bump on your writing finger from pressing too hard."

Miss G told her to pair off in the future with Fiamma. "Walk with her from now on, Lindt; it will do you good. Study her. Learn to put your shoulders back, as she does. Carry your head high. Imitate the way she carries herself. It will improve your prospects."

But Ann could not carry her head high, as Fiamma did, and though she brushed her hair as much as she could and rubbed her skin with Trushay, her hair remained dull and her big forehead shiny and bulbous as ever. She could not write a line that looked the way Fiamma's did, flowing in royal blue ink with rhythmic Italian curves.

Miss G wanted to make sure that Fiamma was never the thirteenth girl, the one rejected. She was determined to spare her any unhappiness. But she was punishing both of them, unwittingly, in throwing them together. She probably thought Ann and Fiamma would talk about books, never bothering to notice that they did not like the same ones.

Fiamma was always reading. Like all of us she read Keats and Wordsworth and Browning, but she also read Italian and French novels of which we had never heard. These, even Ann did not know.

Sitting in the long, narrow dining room in the glare of early morning light, after breakfast, digesting lumpy porridge, we listened hopefully as the prefect read out the names of girls who had received letters or parcels. We hoped for our names to be called, so we could walk up to the head table to pick up our items. Fiamma's name was called every day. So every day she sauntered through the crowded dining room to pick up the fat letters or parcels of dried fruit and cake and nuts from Italy; the chocolates called kisses in large boxes with many layers; the brown-paper parcels covered with stamps, which she opened after breakfast on the lawn, carelessly letting the paper fall to the ground; the piles of gold-embossed, leather-bound books in Italian or French in beautiful, rich colors with silk ribbons in them to mark her progress. She smelled their pages as though they were flowers.

What were the books about? we wanted to know. Fiamma told us Maupassant's story of the fat prostitute who is made to sleep with a Prussian, even though he is the enemy; Manzoni's story of the nun who is closed in the convent against her will; Dante's story of the visit to the underworld led by a slip of a girl. She shut the book with her finger between the pages and quoted the first verses of Dante's *Inferno* by heart in Italian in her singsong voice, when all most of us could quote were the lines we had been forced to learn as a punishment from "The Ancient Mariner": "Water, water, everywhere, nor any drop to drink."

Ann, whose mother and father were too busy on the farm to write and too poor to send parcels, borrowed her books from the library. She preferred history and philosophy and psychology, not poetry and novels, but she was obliged to ride on the bus beside Fiamma when we went to the swimming meets or on our rare visits to town. She was obliged to walk with her when we walked back to the bus, double-file. They walked side-by-side in uneasy silence. The role of the reject was left to Fuzzie, who was confused anyway.

Fiamma's visit to Ann's home

MISS G CALLED ANN to her room and suggested she invite Fiamma home for the short spring holidays. Apparently, Fiamma's father had come down with a bout of malaria during his visit to a game reserve and was in the hospital somewhere, delirious with fever. What could Ann say? she asked us. She knew it would be disastrous, but it was much worse than she had envisaged. To start with, there was the long, slow train ride together all the way to Salisbury, with Fiamma just sitting there, staring sulkily out the window at the veld and complaining about the heat, or reading obscure Italian novels, or writing endless letters to her father, lifting her slim, silver fountain pen to her lips and writing smoothly in royal blue ink.

At the small, hot station with the sun-blanched walls, Ann's mother and stepbrothers emerged from the shadows of the russet tin roof. Ann saw them through Fiamma's eyes: two louts with long khaki socks and short khaki shorts and thick, red necks and white eyelashes and small eyes. Ann suddenly found herself hating them passionately as they stepped forward onto the platform, blinking their sheeps' eyes stupidly in the sunshine.

From the moment Fiamma stepped delicately off the train into the sunlight, with the brim of her panama hat turned down to shade her white skin, and the lovely oval of her face tilted slightly to the side, and her long, blond plait on her shoulder, Ann could see that her stepbrothers had fallen in love with her. They were in love as they both reached for Fiamma's big leather suitcase at once. They were in love as they banged their thick heads together, laughing like idiots. They were in love as they squeezed their long legs and thick knees up to their chins, one on each side of her, in the back of the old, narrow Morris, which bumped over the dust strips all the way to the tobacco farm, where Ann's father kept losing his tobacco crops to the locusts and the heat and drought.

Worse still, Ann saw her mother, as well, through Fiamma's eyes. She had a maths degree from Oxford but had given it all up for love. She had married Ann's father, an impoverished farmer with sandy hair and freckles and these two big, ungainly boys from a previous marriage. Ann saw her mother standing there in the unforgiving sunlight, looking harassed and shabby, her shirt coming out of her drab, gray skirt, her unsupported breasts drooping, and her mousy hair caught back and hanging mournfully on her neck. Ann was ashamed of her shame.

For her amusement Fiamma was taken riding with Ann's mother, leaving Ann behind, for there were only two riding horses. When the horse stepped on a twig and startled a bird into rising suddenly in the air with a great flapping of wings and galloped off, she hung courageously on to its back and was praised for her excellent horsemanship. Ann's mother never praised Ann for anything, despite her consistently high marks. She took Ann's extraordinary brain for granted and always felt obliged to give the tastiest morsels of meat to the two big boys who were not hers.

She suggested the girls help her bake a cake. Fiamma lolled about the big farm kitchen, with its beams and thatched roof, striking interesting poses, one hand on her hip. She looked out the window at the chickens, clucking in the dusty sunlight, or she perched on the side of a table, swinging her slender legs slowly back and forth. When Ann's mother asked her to break an egg into the mixing bowl, she took the egg and held it delicately between her finger and thumb and lifted it up to the sunlight and considered it for a while, as though it might be something precious. Then she broke it on the stone floor, not in the blue-and-white-striped mixing bowl, and stood there, looking slightly surprised, while Ann was made to clean it up.

Fiamma strode off for a walk one morning, taking only the two big ridgeback dogs, a book of Italian poetry, and a bottle of water up the koppie. In those days leopards often came down from the hills to steal a sheep. When she did not come back by dusk, the whole family was in a state of anxiety. The two brothers rushed around, pulling at their hair and searching everywhere, as did Ann's father, when he came back up to the house from the land in the evening.

It was he who found Fiamma lying idly under a baobab tree, resting her head on its roots reading her book of Italian poetry. "You shouldn't have worried. The dogs would have looked after me," she said, when Ann asked her what on earth had made her stay out for so long.

Worst of all were the dinners, Ann told us later. Fiamma sat between Ann's brothers, wearing her lovely blond hair loose on her shoulders. It glowed in the kerosene lamplight, and her skin shimmered like milk, and her clear, blue eyes gleamed. Each time she lowered her lashes, the whole table seemed to tremble.

In the evenings she dressed herself up in the red silk kimono her father had brought her back from a business trip to Japan, all hand-embroidered with dragons and flowers. She wore little pointed silk slippers. Every time she reached across the table, as she did repeatedly, the sleeve of her kimono would fall away, revealing the way up her white arm to her budding bare bosom. The stepbrothers, and Ann's father as well, angled their necks to look.

On her last night, he opened a bottle of white wine, for the first time Ann could remember, and told Fiamma stories about his experiences in the war that he had never told Ann. He looked more handsome than ever to Ann with his sandy hair and freckles and his big, boyish grin. Looking at Fiamma closely, he said, "Those were the happiest days of my life," as Ann's mother pursed her lips into a thin line.

Swimming at midnight with Miss G

> Oh, Miss G, we will love you forever,
> For you we will swim night and day.
> Oh, Miss G, we will desert you never,
> For you we will fight in every way.

IN OUR DREAMS we heard Miss G calling us softly. She stood in the moonlight in the door of the dormitory. She made us get out of our beds in the white light of the moon. We rose, dazed, but in her surprising presence immediately awake and ready to follow. She said "Going swimming. Too hot to lie in bed."

The summer term had hardly begun, and already our hair stuck to our sweating foreheads, our pajamas to our backs. We stumbled about half asleep, looking for our swimming suits in the dark. Miss G told us not to be so absurd. We would not need swimming suits; we would swim in our birthday suits.

"Don't wake Mrs. Looney," Miss G said as we tiptoed down the neon-lit corridor past her door, leaning forward in an attempt to make ourselves small.

In the night-scented garden we huddled close. We whispered and giggled in the hot half darkness, following Miss G. She glanced behind with her dark, restless eyes. "Where's the new girl?" she asked, while Fiamma lingered languidly, staring up at the vast jewel tree of stars. Finally she spoke up. "Present," she said. She adopted the clipped accents of the English, though she had never been to England. She said "drawing room" for "lounge" and "sand shoes" for what we called "takkies." She did not end her sentences with "hey," as we did, and she never used the word "man" as a form of address.

"One finger on my back, Fiamma," Miss G commanded, as we climbed up the hill, going toward the pool in the pale light of the moon. Fiamma looked at Miss G for a moment, not understanding perhaps that Miss G would always have one of her girls pretend to push her up the hill with one finger to her back.

"Just one finger, to get me up the hill, dear," Miss G reiterated, and smiled her munificent smile. Fiamma obeyed, walking behind and pushing Miss G up the hill with her second finger on her back.

"Take off your things, girls; go on," Miss G said, as we gaped at the edge of the water, hesitating.

She unzipped her jumpsuit with one quick gesture, standing firm and lithe, her toes curling over the edge of the concrete. She was smooth and straight as a statue. Her bronzed skin was strange in the moonlight, the deeper dark of the shadow between her legs as quiet and mysterious as a shell.

"You're going to catch a fly," she told Fuzzie, who stood with her big mouth wide open.

"Do you think you're going to be run over by a bus and found without your knickers?" she asked Pamela, who was later to be so good at sex but now clutched her pajama bottoms, protectively.

Miss G lifted her arms, rose on her toes, and dived into the water. She splashed us and told us to get in. "What are you waiting for, kingdom come?" she asked. Then she turned and struck out strongly across the water, reaching valiantly with long arms, kicking up a silver spray in the moonlight.

Fiamma was the first to step out of her pajamas, unashamed. Naked in the moonlight, her white body shone softly. She was slimmer than most of us and lighter-boned. She carried her head high, tilted slightly to one side as though it might roll off. Because we were reading *The Tempest* that year, Miss Lacey called her Ariel.

We watched her open her arms to the stars and the night, and enter the water, her glittering body all gathered together like a white, lacquered bud.

For a moment we stood in silence and watched her swim. She was more at ease in water than on land. She was not good at any of the land sports we played: hockey and netball and rounders, but we had often found her in the pool at dawn, as though she had been there all night, beating back and forth, sending up a rainbow spray into the air, while the sun striped the sky pink and orange and red.

Di muttered, "She swims bloody fast," and threw off her dressing gown and pajamas. We all followed, throwing off our slippers into the wilting hydrangea bushes. We could see Pamela's ribs. Even Fuzzie threw off her vest and stood clutching her plump little boosies, trembling with embarrassment.

We plunged in a pack behind Fiamma, diving into a dream. Di swam breaststroke, her long, strong arms and legs stretched, lithe and fast; Meg swam sidestroke swiftly beside Di, her beautiful head, long neck, and big breasts dipping and rising over the water. Mary plowed through the pool, splashing, doing fast butterfly, and Ann, quick and neat and efficient, swam backstroke, with little splash, while Fuzzie, keeping her face in the water, not taking a breath for long stretches, her body wriggling like a worm, somehow kept up with the rest of us, swimming a crazy crawl. Sheila, too, who always tried hard, swam as fast as she could to keep up. Fiamma, who swam crawl so much faster than anyone else, swam out ahead of us, alone.

In the dim light and the warm water, we slipped back to a timeless time: we were small again, swimming through water to catch Miss G's phosphorescent, shining body. Soon we were swimming around her, under her, Fuzzie at her feet, Di at her head, Meg at her waist. Like minnows around the mother fish, we circled her, we brushed against her smooth body; we touched an arm, a leg, a toe; we felt her all over us in the water. She was swimming fast, turning her head back and forth, breathing in and out, beating the water evenly, surging beside us, and then she was lying still on her back, arms outstretched, staring up at the swirl of stars in the deep blue sky. We too lay on our backs and stared up at the stars. We thought we could hear the music of the spheres; the stars were singing to us; our mothers were chanting to us, we could hear the beating of Miss G's heart. Our heads spun. We floated on beside Miss G in the moonlight and the mysterious quiet of the night, the lights of the school glimmering faintly in the distance, only the crickets chirping.

We saw our mothers waving to us from afar; we saw them coming toward us in the starlight, their silver skirts blown against their bodies; we heard them calling our names with surprised delight. We watched them bending over and reaching out their arms and catching us up and swinging us through the air. We were flying. We were light as light can be. We left our bodies behind and flew, free through the air. We could smell the chlorine and the jasmine and the mysterious verbena scent of Miss G's skin. We felt the water ripple against our naked bodies like air, and we watched our mother's heads come down over us in the half dark to kiss our foreheads, our cheeks, our noses, our chins, and our lips, and their voices whispered, *Good night, good night.* The slapping and the splashing of the water kissed our faces, and the beating of our hearts said, *Good night, good night.*

Miss G was calling us softly. She made us get out of the water and stand by the edge of the pool in the pale white light. Water dripped from our hair. The moonshine was as warm as sun on our faces and on our new breasts. We stared at Miss G's strong, brown legs, the shadow of the shaved hair at the tops. She told us we were her girls. Otherwise she felt far away, removed. She paused. A blankness had come over her face. She said, "I feel at such a distance from the rest of the world."

What Miss G said about Fiamma

"COME UP HERE and sit by me," Miss G said, when Fiamma attempted to slip in late unnoticed and sit at the back of Miss G's room. Her face had a bright, soft look, and when she said Fiamma's name, her voice lingered. Fiamma moved slowly forward. "Burls, make room for her," Miss G told Fuzzie, who had to get up and move elsewhere.

We all sat quietly, waiting for Fiamma to take the only comfortable chair and settle herself down. Meg sat very upright on the floor, her shoulders pressed back and her head held high. Di lounged on Miss G's bed. Sheila sat on a hard stone step and squinted miserably. Mary sprawled on a stool with her legs open.

"Sit where I can see you. Perhaps you can save us, Fiamma," Miss G said.

"I am just a swimmer," Fiamma said.

"No, no false modesty here," Miss G said. She said Fiamma had great style; she had speed and endurance; only she could stay the course (Miss G was fond of nautical metaphors); only Fiamma had attained a consistent level of excellence. *She* was dedicated to the sport of swimming, despite her breathing problems, her homesickness, her father's illness. "You do not catch Fiamma lolling about in bed in the morning. She is up there, rising with the sun, in the water at first light, doing her fifty lengths," Miss G said, looking critically at Meg, who was sitting in her faded pink pajamas, stretching her neck, head to one side, pursing her lips, trying to look like Brigitte Bardot.

Meg slept heavily and late at school, with her dark hair hiding her flushed face, her body sprawled beneath her thin sheet, because she had to rise early at home in Barberton in the Eastern Transvaal. She was obliged to help with the family chores in the humid heat on holidays. She had to make the morning tea for her mother and father, help dress her little sisters, hang all the washing to dry, heap the furniture into the middle of the lounge and polish the floors.

"Unlike Burls, who never gets her racing turns right, Fiamma can turn in a flash. Why can she turn so fast, while Burls takes her sweet time and creates such a lot of unncessary splash? Watch how Fiamma does it," Miss G advised Fuzzie, who sat pressing her fat knees to the floor. "Of course, if you were to lose a few pounds, now, that would also help, you would not have so much mass to move." Fuzzie blinked her close-set, green eyes.

Only Fiamma could make a straight enough dive, Miss G pointed out to Mary, who was clumsy but quick, who had trouble keeping her long body in a straight line and her feet together when she entered the water.

"As for Lindt, she's not willing to take a risk: too cautious, too crafty, too busy weighing the odds."

Miss G said only Fiamma could open her arms wide enough to the sky when she swallow-dived. Only Fiamma was willing to give her all, to throw herself into the air with reckless abandon. What was the matter with the Trevelyan twins? she wanted to know. Why did they not have the necessary spring, the surge, the courage? What was wrong with Lizzie? What made her so precious? Why was she trying to be so perfect? What was wrong with all the rest of us? Why were we so ordinary, so dull, so reluctant to take a chance, to do something reckless and wild? Why did we leave Fiamma to blaze our trail?

Following Fiamma

> Miss G followed Fiamma,
> Watched her with dark eyes
> Hurrying down the corridor,
> Brightening when Fiamma she spied.

THE GRASS WAS DRY and dusty now. The seringa tree drooped over the wooden love seat in the corner. The pale wisteria petals fell to the ground. We watched Miss G walk behind Fiamma as she sauntered down the stone steps and along the edge of the prefects' square lawn. When Fiamma paused to look at a dry leaf stirring, a dove's wings beating, a swirl of dust, Miss G paused, too, and stared at a boot or flecked an imaginary spot of lint from her jumpsuit. When Fiamma turned around, feeling Miss G behind her, Miss G hurried by.

It was clear to us, she was no longer satisfied to see Fiamma in her room in the evenings or in the afternoons at the pool, gazing at Fiamma as she did a back flip from the high board, her luminous eyes straining in the sun. It was not enough for her to turn her head back and forth, as though she were watching a tennis match, as Fiamma skimmed up and down the water, the spray splashing Miss G's face, or to run up and down the edge of the pool through swimming heats, shouting her name like a rallying cry. It was not enough for her to feed Fiamma glucose with a spoon out of the blue-and-white tin between races or massage her feet, so that she did not get cramps, or rub her back with a towel. It was not even enough to call her by her Christian name.

If Fiamma were unable to sleep in the hot, dry nights, if she had one of her frequent attacks, her shallow cough keeping us awake, her breath coming in short, sharp pants, it was not into Mrs. Looney's room that she went for comfort. Night after night Miss G would come to see if Fiamma were well. She would tell Fiamma to follow her to her room. She would allow her to sit in her white smocked nightdress in her wide wicker chair and sip hot cocoa or wine. She slipped Fiamma past Mrs. Looney's room quietly and brought her back into the dormitory and sat on her bed and waited while she knelt and said her prayers in Italian and asked God to make her father well. Miss G tucked the sheet around her gently and arranged her mosquito netting over her bed carefully, so that she would not be bitten.

She made Fiamma promise that if anything were wrong she would come to her, but she never did. We would hear her ragged breathing and the pumping of the inhaler in the night. We could hear her tossing and turning. Miss G came so often that Fuzzie giggled, and Pamela jumped out of her bed and twitched her thin hips suggestively in the shadows, and all the rest whispered.

And now she had taken to following Fiamma about in the day as well. Ann watched her follow Fiamma along the pergola and said, "She's cracking up." We all watched her striding out, slightly flat-footed in her boots, blinking her dark eyes in the glare of light, hunting for Fiamma in the vast garden.

It was easy to lose a girl out there, and Fiamma always managed to disappear. We did not know where she went, or how she did it. Despite the rules, she was always going off on her own. We considered that she made no effort to fit in, to join our group. Before we could snub her, she snubbed us. Even worse, she seemed simply to ignore us. She was thinking of other things. She did not even notice our slights or understand our sarcasm. She smiled at us as she slipped by, dreaming, perhaps, of the cannas flaming orange and red at the edge of the terraced lawns of her villa by the lake.

It was not that she was unkind to us. She never raised her voice, or said anything hurtful. On the contrary, she was given to sudden and unexpected acts of kindness. When Bobby Joe had the chicken pox, Fiamma rose early and picked flowers and thrust them, still wet with dew, through the window at the san. She gave up the role of sleeping beauty to Meg in the school pageant even though the whole class had voted to give it to Fiamma. "You will do it much better than I will," she told Meg, who afterward bore a grudge against her.

Fiamma spoke of honor and loyalty and fidelity, but we con-

sidered she was playacting, and thought her kindness was con-
descension and her talk of higher things showing off and silli-
ness. "Her Royal Highness is holding forth again," Di would say.

We thought her clothes pretentious and strange. In the eve-
ings when we were allowed to change out of our uniforms, she
wore dresses with labels from the big London shops: Liberty's
or Harrods, dresses that looked babyish and odd with flowers
embroidered in the smocking on her budding bosoms. She
wore shoes with bars across the insteps and buttoned with a
buttonhook. She threaded silk ribbons through her thick plait.
She liked to dress up and act, and she loved the films they
showed us once a month in the assembly room through a flickering projector, which was always breaking down.

Fuzzie sometimes said, "Perhaps she is not used to girls, to
young people; she is accustomed to being shut up in an old
house with her peculiar father and some old servant. Perhaps
she would like to be our friend." But no one paid attention to
Fuzzie.

We watched Miss G stride through the garden anxiously,
hunting for Fiamma in all the cool, shady places where she
sometimes hid from us: behind the hydrangeas, or in the dark,
heavy branches of the loquat tree, which hung down so low
they touched the smooth, dark earth.

We followed Miss G as she followed Fiamma. She went so far
as to walk across the veld to the river and the graves in search of
her. We were not allowed to swim the river because of the bilharzia, which infected many of the waters of that region, and
the area around the graves was out-of-bounds, but as the heat
increased in the summer months and the drought continued,
and as the pool was not always available to the girls on the
swimming team, we took to tucking up our tunics in our pants
and running across the veld to linger in the shade of the wattles

and the willows along the riverbanks. We would wade in the river, the brown, half-stagnant water rising up to our thighs.

None of the elderly spinster teachers remonstrated. None of them came to look for us. None of them cared. They did not care about much, during those dog days. They dragged themselves into the classrooms in a state of disarray in the mornings, sitting on dusty platforms, their legs carelessly apart, with the girls giggling and peeping up their skirts. Even Miss Lacey sat mopping her pale brow, stunned by the heat, the dry air, the continuous drought, letting us read popular novels in class. A general lethargy had crept over the staff.

Ann said there was more wine drinking than there should have been in the staff room at night. She had heard raucous laughter. She had seen bottles. She had glimpsed Mrs. Keilly, the geography teacher, staggering down the corridor as though she had no idea where she was. Miss Nieven herself seemed permanently unavailable, shut up in the fastness of her cool study. It was said that she was ill, though no one was able to confirm this report. We were left to our own devices much of the afternoon.

When Miss G caught sight of us following her, she asked what we were doing, but before we could answer, she said, "Has anyone seen Fiamma?" putting her hand up to shield her eyes from the blinding glare. "Have you not seen her anywhere?"

"No," Meg said, she had not. Could we not help in some way, perhaps, Meg asked, but we lowered our gaze, looked away so as not to see the expression of despair in Miss G's eyes. We were ashamed of her shame.

The air near the river was heavy and redolent with the odors from the latrines and the thick smell of stagnant water. The water was evaporating fast, leaving the banks slimy and slippery, the drying mud gray and cracked. The sun burned down through the slate gray haze. Several girls from the matriculation class, who should have been studying, sat by the water, half naked, their bare feet dangling, their fair arms and legs and un-protected faces burning, their skin peeling in wide strips from their shoulders, exposing livid patches of purple. Sheila walked in the riverbed with her tunic tucked up in her pants, the mud seeping up her calves, pretending to be a pirate.

"Over there," Bobby Joe said suddenly, "there she is!" and pointed to where Fiamma lay in the river. She was lying naked in the dark water, her light hair loose, letting the sluggish cur-rent catch her up and carry her slowly along for a way, reaching out lazily to grasp at overhanging willow branches.

We heard Miss G cry half in warning, half in salute. "Oh! Fiamma!"

How Miss G made Fiamma talk of her home

IT WAS LATE, and we were weary and hot, worn out with swimming, wine, Miss G's words, and the increasing heat. We had been sitting cramped and uncomfortable on the floor in her room for hours, or, if we were lucky, perched on her bed.

Only Fiamma sat in the comfortable chair, staring absently before her. She had come in after everyone else and nodded off in her chair by the window. Only she was allowed to come in late; to swing slowly out of the swimming pool in the middle of swimming practice and stand, dreaming, in the sun, staring into the middle distance while the water ran off her white body in silver strands; to lie by the side of the pool during practice in the shade of the mimosa tree with her towel over her shoulders.

"How much land did you say your father owns?" Miss G asked her once again, leaning toward her in her wicker chair. Miss G was fascinated by the aristocracy. We often saw her reading women's magazines with pictures of the Royal Family on the cover, holding the magazine under the desk when she had to supervise our homework. She claimed to have been presented to Prince Philip at court when she had won her medal. She told us that he was from a much better family than that of the Queen, whose ancestors could hardly speak English, coming as they did from a minor German family and having to change their name so that it sounded English.

It was Miss G who told us about Fiamma's pedigree, the history of her family, her place in society. She loved more than anything to make Fiamma describe her house by the lake.

We sat before her and rolled our eyes and flared our eyebrows at one another, blew out our cheeks, sighed, and shifted about, but Fiamma went on and on in her singsong voice. Perhaps she was carried away by her own words, her memories of home, of happier days with her father, who was increasingly ill with bouts of high fever and delirium. While she spoke, Miss G moved her lips as though she were the one speaking.

Fiamma said her house was surrounded by beautiful, regular gardens with gravel paths and ancient trees and a stone wall. It was old and very large. One day it would all be hers, although she knew her mother would try to lay claim to it for her half sister's sake.

There was a profusion of cut flowers in every room — roses and sweet peas and lilacs, lilies and peonies and baby's breath. In the entrance hall there was a forest of flowers. It was like a hothouse, and there was the sweet smell of the many flowers mingled with some other smell, like that of incense. It made Fiamma think of funerals and weddings at the same time.

There were many old, dark paintings in niches, lit up with little lamps hung over the gold-embossed frames. Many were old still lifes where the half-peeled fruit or bleeding hare was barely visible. In one of the paintings two French sisters stare out of the canvas with a pleased expression, as though they are proud of what they are doing. Their hair is coiffed high on their heads, and their stiff breasts are completely bare. One of the women holds the nipple of the other delicately between her curved white finger and thumb.

Her father also owned a famous collection of diamonds, Fiamma said. There was a famous yellow one and a famous blue one, which was supposed to bring bad luck. This was why they had come to our country: her father was buying diamonds for his collection. He had visited Kimberley before going on to the game reserve where he had fallen ill.

When she stopped speaking, Miss G made her go on. "How many servants did you say there were, tending the garden?" she asked while we covered our yawns with our hands and shifted our weight uncomfortably on Miss G's carpet or on the hard floor. Fiamma had never counted all the servants. She said she and her father ate dinner on the stone terrace, often alone. In the candlelight, her father looked so handsome in his cream linen trousers, his damp, dark hair brushed back smoothly. He asked her about her life and listened to her with great interest, as though she were a grown-up. He had read everything, she maintained, all the books we read at school. They talked about Rider Haggard and Kipling and Dickens. He knew all about Miss Havisham walking around and around the decaying bridal feast and about Uriah Heep's damp hands. He, too, loved to watch her swim. When she was a small girl, he had taken her to see walled medieval towns, poppies growing through the stone, the sun setting over the sea at Naples. There she had broken a glass and cut her feet.

Fortunately, Miss G was not as interested in Fiamma's father as she was in her house, her paintings, and her habits, and we were allowed to go to bed.

We left Fiamma behind in Miss G's room, imagining her standing and staring out the window while Miss G paced up and down restlessly, in her khaki overalls, or worse.

Miss G made us suffer

"IS FIAMMA HERE?" Miss G said, as we shuffled into her hot room in our pajamas and slippers, half asleep. It was late, but Miss G could not sleep, and so she had called us into her room to enlighten us. The windows were closed on the hot night, but we could hear the dry wind beating in the palms.

"Where is Fiamma? Why has she not come? I told you to bring all the girls on the team, Radfield," Miss G said, looking anxiously around her room for Fiamma.

Di did not answer. Fiamma had mumbled something rude to her in Italian and refused to rise. "You'll get me into trouble," she had said, but Fiamma went back to sleep.

"She must be unwell, poor girl. Is she unwell? Now she swam well today," Miss G said, looking at Fuzzie. "Why can't you swim as well as she does, Burls?"

She told us to find a perch, picked up her glass of mixed red and white wine, and wiped her wide lips. We could see she was working herself up. She was trying to distract herself from her agony. For a moment we thought she might find someone else to distract her, but her gaze fell again on Fuzzie.

Her father, everyone knew, had contributed hundreds of pounds to the swimming team fund so that Miss G would put her on the team. Everyone knew, too, that she had been expelled from her former school, though no one knew why.

"Burls-the-Bear, excuse my French, but you swam like shit

again today," Miss G said, and we could not help laughing. We loved it when she swore and said, "Excuse my French." Fuzzie blushed as bright pink as her pajamas; and her double chins pressed down upon her chest. She sat cross-legged, her fat knees pressing against the floor.

"What's the matter with you, Burls? Thinking about the boys again?"

Fuzzie did not reply but only blushed redder, so that her freckles disappeared, and her head sank further onto her chest. Everyone was staring at her, laughing, except for Meg, who looked as though she were about to weep. Fuzzie was watching her hand trace the sinister, blue flower pattern of Miss G's carpet.

"What, no reply from Burls? Perhaps it's about the girls that she's thinking?"

We laughed even louder at that, and Pamela made little kissing noises, and we put our arms around ourselves and rubbed our backs.

"No, I'm not thinking about either one," Fuzzie said, blinking her close-set eyes. We were all watching with secret delight, glad someone else was the target of Miss G's ire, as Fuzzie sank miserably into the blue flower pattern, her face flushed with shame.

"Why are you left wallowing around in the water when Fiamma passes you by? She must be exhausted after the way she swam today. Did she remain in the dormitory, or has she gone off somewhere on her own again? She's not ill, is she?" Miss G's voice rose to a panic pitch. She got up and walked back and forth across her room, her boots creaking. She scratched at the bristles at the back of her neck.

No one said anything.

"Don't any of you know? Don't you care? Lindt, what about you? You're supposed to be her friend, aren't you?"

"Yes, I am," Ann said, looking as though she were thinking about mathematics. "But I make it a rule not to talk about anyone behind her back."

"Very wise, Lindt, very wise," Miss G said, sitting down again and turning back to Fuzzie. She scratched her leg, saying, "Burls-the-Bear, now why isn't it Fuzzie-the-Fish? It could be Fuzzie-the-Fish, couldn't it? Actually, you do look a bit green, postively green around the gills tonight. Been eating chocolates on the sly, hey? You ought to watch your weight, don't you think?"

Fuzzie blinked, lowered her head, and said, "Yes, Miss G." No one laughed now.

She went on scratching. "I am only saying this for your own good, you know. No one else will tell you girls the truth. Your parents are too far away, and only I care about you. Obviously no one else does. I could tell you lies as everyone else does. I could tell Burls that she swam well, but what good would that do her? You have got to look into your heart and find the truth, and the truth is you are putting on weight. You look bloated, puffy. Can't you see it when you look in the miror? Are you blind, after all? If you cannot see it, there must be something wrong with you. You will never be able to swim well, if you put on any more weight. Did you ever see a fat swimmer? Besides, doesn't all that fat disgust you? Look at your arms, even they are getting fat. Now no more chocolates, hey? Promise me, will you?"

"Yes, I promise," Fuzzie muttered to the carpet.

"You'd better, if you want the boys to love you, and if you want to swim as well as Fiamma. Don't you want the boys to love you? Why do you eat so much? You ought to think about that; there must be a reason. You've got to find it out. Can't you tell me?"

"I don't know why, Miss G," Fuzzie said with a great sob. The tears were pouring down her fat cheeks, and Meg was weeping, too, in sympathy.

Miss G lit a cigarette and exhaled fast, scratching at her leg.

"What's the matter with you, Burls? Get up and go and find your friend," she concluded. "Go and see if she's all right, Burls, do you hear?" Fuzzie staggered out of the room, saying she had pins and needles in her peg legs.

The team's losses

MISS G WAS increasingly distracted as the long summer term wore on. She did not listen when we talked but gazed across the gray grass and the flowers strangled in the soil. She did not respond to us. She no longer talked about the truth or the wonderful things we could accomplish.

When she did speak, she fell silent suddenly and gazed toward the pool in the fading evening light. She had lost the direction of her thought. We waited for her to continue, but she scratched the back of her head and said, "What's the point? Go on, go and swim, girls, go along."

As we swam slowly up and down the pool, or even lay on our backs and stared at the red sky, she stood beside the pool in her swimming costume, her whistle hanging silently between her dry, chapped lips. She did not run up and down beside the pool as she used to do when we swam in the evening; she did not call our names. Sometimes she even forgot our names, calling Lindt, Radfield, and Kohler, Donovan. She never again called us to swim with her at midnight, despite the increasing December heat.

We all stared up at her in the long shadows of the evening light. We hardly recognized her. She had lost weight; deep, dark circles formed under her eyes; her breath smelled sour. She looked older, though we noticed she made an attempt to cover it up. She had taken to wearing makeup. She applied mascara to her eyelashes but would forget it was there and rub her eyes, causing it to run down her cheeks. She even colored her wide lips with a ghastly, dark rouge that gave her a hard air. She had dry patches on her skin and sores around her mouth. She scratched constantly. Her old skin ailment was acting up in the dry heat. We were afraid she would fall ill, or, worse, leave us. Sometimes she even even spoke of giving up teaching. "For the amount of money they pay us to do this, it isn't worth it," she said; no one appreciated her efforts. No one was grateful. No one cared. What was the point?

We no longer won any prizes. Di no longer flashed her shiny, pink gums and her strong, white teeth in the sun, her arms full of trophies. Instead, her arms hung limply by her sides, her empty hands clutching at the air. Our team came last or next to last. Kingsmead beat us. St. Andrews beat us. Even the convent schools beat us. We slunk back to the bus in the shadows, ashamed. We sat silently and gazed out the windows. We sang no triumphant songs. We scowled at Fiamma, who sat in silence beside Ann on the bus or walked past us with her head tilted and her distant air.

Staring up at Miss G as she stood vacantly by the side of the pool in the evening light, we could not believe that she had fallen for a girl who made no attempt to be charming, who had no desire to charm her, or anyone, who slipped by us like the moon through cloud. To us Fiamma seemed entirely unfeeling. We found her cold, through and through. She never seemed angry or sad or even amused. When we told one another jokes and laughed raucously, rolling about, holding our stomachs on the floor, she only fidgeted and left the room.

None of us could understand how Miss G could get excited

about a girl like her. Italians were supposed to be so passionate and temperamental. They were supposed to fall into rages, to express themselves in song. "Besides," Mary whispered, "Italians aren't blond."

When we complimented her, she shrugged her shoulders, indifferent, as though all she wanted was to pass unnoticed. She never took pains to impress, and yet we found her domineering and mysteriously willful. Ann helped her with her Afrikaans homework; Mary, with her science; Meg baked an extra batch of scones for her at domestic science, because she was not eating much; Sheila lent her silver pens, and she lost them in the grass. Her carelessness created havoc in our hearts.

When we spoke of love or attraction, she said nothing. She was always scrupulously polite, but she was always trying to escape us, slipping by coolly and boldly, as though she wished to make herself invisible.

We could not believe that Miss G, who had told us once she felt at a distance, felt far, far out at sea and alone, could be brought back in and made a fool of by this pale, careless girl.

What to do about Fiamma?

> Meg wanted to be Brigitte Bardot,
> Sheila, to be Scarlett.
> All Ann wanted was to read Diderot,
> But we all wanted to be Miss G's pet.

THE DOVES COOED in the eucalyptus trees. The wind stirred the dust across the dry veld, which had been set ablaze by one carelessly discarded cigarette stub, causing untold damage, reducing a thousand acres to a black stubble. The thatched roofs of the round changing huts had caught fire, saved only when the night watchman, John Mazaboko, had come running with his hose.

The earth had cracked, and the roots of the flowers were strangled in the soil. Only the red-hot pokers and the aloes with their prickly pears still stood stiffly upright. The fan-shaped sprinklers no longer waved back and forth in the evenings on the lawns, cooling the air. When we went for walks in the afternoons, the dust was on our shoes and in our mouths. We were not allowed to bathe at all now except in the basins that ran along the center of the dormitories like a string of coffins. We all splashed 4711 behind our ears and poured it between our new bosoms. Di had put it in the wrong place and screamed when it stung.

We were supposed to lie on our beds for two hours after lunch because of the polio scare. There had been an outbreak of it. The only newspaper available to us was the *Manchester Guardian,* which gave us no local news anyway, but the teachers told us terrible stories of children paralyzed from the waist down, their limbs withered, pushed around in wheelchairs for the rest of their lives.

Because of fear of contagion we were not allowed to go to the few public places usually allowed us: the outing to the Pablo Casals concert, the tour of the art museum. Even our Friday visits to town for doctors' and dentists' appointments were canceled. We no longer went to lie under the sunlamp, burning off our pimples. We no longer left the grounds at all. The iron gate was kept closed except for the one Sunday a month when the girls who had families in the area went home, and the rest of us tried despererately to ingratiate ourselves with someone who would take us along. Some of the parents, like Sandra's, had sent for their children. Those who remained were to wear little cotton bags with camphor around their necks. The teachers, too, lay on their beds for two hours after lunch.

We stood before the mirrors behind the basins in the long, narrow dormitory with its iron cots and whispered about Fiamma and Miss G. Meg pursed her heavy lips like Brigitte Bardot and lisped, "If Fiamma were kinder to Miss G, she would be kinder to us. Why doesn't she care for her?"

Bobby Joe glanced along the dormitory to Fiamma's bed at the end by the wall, where she lay, apparently sleeping, on her side, one arm above her head, and said, "She doesn't care for anyone." She seemed capable of sleeping for long hours, hardly moving on her bed.

Ann, on the bed next to Fiamma, said in her low, nasal voice, "It won't last; nothing lasts long with Miss G," and glowered in the background, looking glum, propped up on pillows, reading about revolutions. She read about the American Revolution, the Russian Revolution, the French Revolution. She read about the eighteen-century French philosophers in her history book: Rousseau and Diderot and Montesquieu, and about the Rights of Man.

Di said, "Perhaps, but in the meantime, I am getting impatient."

Di was half naked before the mirrors, using her school tie as a veil, dancing the Dance of the Seven Veils, pretending to be Salome, getting Herod to give her John the Baptist's head. Mary was dissecting a tadpole she had fished out of the pond to study for science.

Sheila lay on the bed beside Pamela, their feet in the air, comparing their beauty. Sheila was finding her own superior. She said there was nothing we could do about the situation anyway and added that she was trying to decide whether to be bold and rapacious like Scarlett O'Hara or good and meek like Melanie, but was leaning toward Scarlett. Di said she much preferred to be Becky Sharp than Amelia.

Fuzzie, who was singing *"La donna è mobile,"* trying to be Mimi Coertse, said she wanted to be Jane Eyre as a fierce wild child shut up in the red room, not as a meek and mild grown-up who wore gray and fell in love with Mr. Rochester.

Ann blew her thin nose and scolded us. She told us we were all vain, strutting about before the mirrors, and should stop thinking about ourselves and think instead of our fellow man, not trifle our lives away. Instead of hovering before the mirror, contemplating our images, we should be thinking about helping others. What about the poor, the hungry, the homeless, the natives?

When she rose and came over to us, approaching the mirror, she turned away from her reflection, her high, shiny forehead bulging like an egg, her little pig eyes glowing, and went on scolding us. We should all be thinking about the injustice of the natives' position in our country. Wasn't it time someone did something about that?

Mary said she had helped with the African Feeding Scheme in her holidays. She had fed starving little black children peanut-butter sandwiches.

But we went on dreaming of Miss G or Heathcliff, putting our hands between our legs. When Miss Lacey had asked how many girls would like to marry him, all the hands shot up.

Our favorite film stars were Ava Gardner and Gregory Peck. She was so beautiful and familiar, shining with her own light, and he, though dark and handsome and smooth, was all mysteriously wrapped up in a suit. Which one to choose? We wanted them both. Only Miss G was both familiar and mysterious, beautiful and dark at the same time; only she was capable of arousing all our desires.

But why did she desire Fiamma?

Pamela said she thought Fiamma was keeping some deep, dark secret from us. "Perhaps she had a lover in Italy?" she suggested and turned her foot to a more advantageous position in the light. "Can't you see mine is much prettier than yours?" she told Sheila.

"Perhaps she had lots!" Fuzzie exclaimed loudly, but Fiamma did not stir.

"Do you think she is really asleep?" Lizzie asked Ann, who went back to her bed and peered down at Fiamma, who, as though she felt our gaze on her, or had been listening all along, stirred, rose languidly from her bed, went over to the basins, and began scrubbing her cheeks with soap and a toothbrush. She always did that to preserve her creamy complexion.

We pretended to read but spied on her. Di went back to being Salome and Fuzzie, to singing *"La donna è mobile."* Mary said she was going to flush the tadpole down the toilet.

We were always spying on her. Sheila, who enjoyed it, looked on, as Fiamma scrubbed absentmindedly. She whispered, "Her Royal must be preparing for Miss G."

"Now Her Royal must be thirsty," Meg observed, when Fiamma added an Alka-Seltzer capsule to a glass of water to make it fizz, because she never drank flat water. Meg was never given even the pocket money to buy her sanitary towels and was obliged to borrow them from Di.

Di whispered that Fiamma washed her hair with fresh lemon to heighten its blond lights, and took baths in milk to make her skin white. Fuzzie said it was champagne.

The twins rose from their beds. One put her panama hat on her head and walked over to the door. She pretended to come in the door, imitating the way Fiamma curtsied when she shook hands with adults, making a brief bob. They bobbed at one another, giggling. One said, "Your Royal Highness, how delightful, how lovely of you to come to tea."

There was a shuffling at the door, and everyone ran back to her bed. We watched the door open. Miss G came in, wearing her usual khaki jumpsuit and boots.

"What's all this? You are supposed to be resting. What's going on?" she asked, as though there had been an outbreak of fire.

No one answered. "Fiamma, are you feeling all right, dear? No bad news about your father, was there?" she asked anxiously, striding over to her. Fiamma shrugged sulkily and said she was fine and went on scrubbing her cheeks.

"Better come with me, darling," she said in a hoarse voice.

"I'm fine, at the moment," Fiamma said fiercely, glaring at Miss G and at us as well. We were having a fit of suppressed giggles and making little kissing faces behind our books.

Miss G said, "Just come with me."

Fiamma sighed, rinsing off her brush and taking her sweet time. She made Miss G wait. She put on her socks and shoes. Then she gathered up her book. Miss G followed each movement with her ardent gaze.

So did we. She crossed the dormitory in silence like a queen, accepting Miss G's silent tribute, her head tilted very slightly to one side. There was something awesome about her. She was irresistible; she always got her way. We thought she had put a spell on Miss G.

We tiptoed in our socks down the corridor to Miss G's half-open door. We hovered there, listening and trying to see what was happening inside, pushing one another out of the way. We caught a glimpse of Fiamma, as she sat in state in Miss G's wide wicker chair. Her head was poised delicately on her long neck, her languid locks on her collarbone. She stared ahead, reading the bound book that lay in her lap and sulkily sipping from a big cup of cocoa, as Miss G sat at her feet. What was she sulking about? we wanted to know.

Miss G got as close as she could, smiling up at her. She had her big hands around her knees. She was glowing, burning; she was on fire.

We watched, our hearts pounding, waiting for something to happen. But it did not: nothing happened! Fiamma went on reading. She rose and stood silently by the window, gazing at the sky, with her head tilted a little, pulling idly at a loose lock of hair. We had no idea what she was thinking about. All we knew was that Miss G adored her.

What did Miss G see in Fiamma?

WE LAY whispering in the hot, dark dormitory on our hard, narrow beds, troubled by mosquitoes and dreams. Fiamma was with Miss G, once again. As usual, Ann perched with her torch in the window seat, reading her book. She said it was Fiamma's illness and loneliness, her distance from the rest of us, that drew Miss G irresistibly to her. "She identifies with Fiamma's incapacity to fit in," Ann said, twisting her mouth sightly to one side.

It was true that Fiamma took part less and less in our competitions and fierce jealousies. She seemed more interested in inanimate things, trees, rocks, even ants, than in us. We saw her sit for hours, watching the red ants crawl under a log. Was she dreaming of her past, or some unknown future? Did she perhaps see, in her mind's eye, some old Milanese church, where, pushing aside the heavy leather curtain and breathing in the odors of incense rising from the censers, watching the gold light coming in from a high window aslant, she slipped quietly into a pew beside some dark, unshaven man? Did she enjoy her solitude, gathering herself together and escaping from the din and strife around her? Or was she lonely? Did she find peace? Or did she long to join in our games?

She answered our questions about her life briefly but never asked about ours. She seemed to hear and see us all, but distantly, as through a pane of pebbled glass. We never felt she preferred one or the other of us, not even Ann, who was supposed to be her best friend.

Fuzzie said she did not know about Fiamma anymore. Everything was all confused in Fuzzie's mind, since they took her mother away, last year. She wasn't sure what she had made up, and what had really happened. When she came back from a singing lesson one day during the holidays, the house was empty. Her mother was no longer in her room, brushing her long, dark hair, nor was she out in the hothouse, growing her orchids, rather than the dahlias she preferred. They had taken her away to the asylum, and she had died in a fire, which spread because the young psychiatrist had forgotten to do the fire drill properly.

Fuzzie said she kept imagining her mother in her white dress, flitting up and down the corridor, rattling the doorknobs, screaming for help. Fuzzie's father always made a point of telling everyone that, although his wife was Jewish, he himself was Christian.

Ann said, "Fiamma has secrets like everyone else." Some of them Ann had learned. She knew most of our secrets. When Fiamma was visiting Ann's farm for the holidays, Fiamma had told her the story of how her mother had left her father after their wedding night. He had married beneath himself, for love. She may have been the housekeeper or a nurse, a pretty, strong-willed woman with fair, curly hair and a ruddy complexion. She already had a child in tow. His family was against the match, but he married her anyway. After their wedding night —

Fiamma never knew exactly what happened but suspected her mother had actually beaten him after he finished forcing himself on her — her mother went off to Milan. Apparently she was pregnant with Fiamma already, and nine months later came back to the villa to leave the baby by the lake.

The mother and half sister lived in Milan with another man, perhaps several men in succession. Fiamma visited them a couple of times in a small, dark flat near the Duomo, and some man was always lurking around behind the thick, green curtains that divided the rooms. All the furniture was highly polished, and there were artificial flowers in vases on the marble mantelpieces. Fiamma's father did not like her to go there. He was frightened of her mother. "He says she's unscrupulous and ambitious, that she's a whore," she told Ann.

Fiamma's mother adored Fiamma's half sister, who lay in a dark room with the curtains drawn. Fiamma had only seen her once. She wore her hair short with a curl matted down with grease on her forehead and spoke in an affected drawl. She smelled of onions, which her mother gave her for her health, and as a result everyone called her Cipolla, meaning "onion." She was supposed to be suffering from some illness. "She likes to pull the wings off flies," Fiamma told Ann.

Di said in her opinion Miss G was enamored of Fiamma because she was a rich princess. Di said Miss G was fascinated by status. But Di did not even believe that Fiamma was an aristocrat. She had never mentioned her title, after all.

Lizzie said it was Fiamma's elegance: the way she walked and the way she moved her hands so smoothly in the air.

Meg, who read romances, said it was a sort of rapture — that was the word that would describe it in a romance. Miss G was enraptured by the way Fiamma flung open a door or a window, stepped out into the light, and seemed immediately to own the place; her high-handedness and haughty stare. It was because she liked to be herself — careless, dauntless, elegant.

Everyone agreed Fiamma was beautiful, but there were other beautiful girls on our team, after all. There was Meg herself and Di, of course. Fiamma was an exceptional swimmer, but we had other good swimmers as well. Di could beat her at breaststroke, and Ann at backstroke, but no one could surpass her at crawl, and crawl, of course, is the fastest one of all.

Despite Miss G's opinion Bobby Joe was much braver than Fiamma. When Bobby Joe was allowed to exercise the horses that were kept for the paying pupils, she trick-rode. She could stand up on the horse and hang down below its belly. She could do a double back flip from the high board and Fiamma only a single, but none of us was more graceful than Fiamma.

Fiamma told Ann that she found Miss G overbearing, missing the point, which was not lost on the rest of us. "Do you know what she did?" Fiamma said. "She left a pair of swimming goggles on my dresser with a little note, wishing me a happy birthday. I don't know how she knew it was my birthday."

Di said, "Whatever the reason, Miss G's passion is not reciprocated. She does not impress Fiamma at all." At the same time, we knew perfectly well, Miss G was falling more and more desperately in love with her.

What Di Radfield did not tell the detective

D I DID NOT TELL the detective what had happened in the changing hut. She did not want to, when he questioned her after Fiamma disappeared. He was a young man, who must have just finished his training — it was probably his first case.

He seemed ill at ease in her presence, as if he were the one who had committed the crime. He sat there chewing gum, sweating heavily, talking about the drought, and smelling of B.O. Di tried to draw back from him, but she was trapped in the corner of the library. There was no air in there, because the windows and the shutters were closed on the heat.

She found something very grating about the stupid jokes he kept making. He even snickered a couple of times. He was an Afrikaner idjut, she told us afterwards.

At first he just sat there with a fat file filled with papers, then he asked her all the wrong questions. He asked her if she had a boyfriend, making her furious. She wanted to slam her fist down on the table, but she just asked him if he had ever heard of the expression "It's none of your business." He opened his file and read his notes and questioned her about her father's drinking and his suicide, and her sister finding him in the bath, his wrists slit, the blood turning the water pink. Miss Nieven must have given him all sorts of information, because he asked why, when Miss Nieven had said she could go home at that time, Di had preferred to go back to swimming practice.

Di could still see her father in the narrow hallway of their house with the "Cries of London" paintings on the walls. He was balding and his pate was shiny, and he had an orange in his hands. He was explaining, "If you cut it in half you have two parts; if you cut it again, you have four." That's all she remembered of his words.

Di did not say anything about what happened at the pool that morning early, either. She had just arrived to practice her racing starts and found Miss G striding up and down the edge of the pool in her black bathing costume. She could see the shimmer of sweat on her strong arms and the dark shadow of the shaved hair between her strong, brown legs. Miss G was watching Fiamma dive and swim fast, up and down the pool, doing crawl for one length, making a racing turn, and then doing backstroke for the next. She was showing off, doing back or swallow dives from the high board, fearlessly. There were only a few other girls swimming at that early hour.

The pool lay in the soft shadows of the mimosas and the wilting blue hydrangeas. The cool, clear water shone a yellow-green, and dew glittered like splintered glass on the gray grass.

Di tried to keep up with Fiamma, but she could not. She climbed out of the water and practiced her racing starts, smacking her stomach flat on the surface of the water each time. Then Fiamma got out of the pool and did a perfect swallow dive from the high board, opening her arms on the rising sun and orange sky. It was too much.

Di went into one of the small thatched-roofed changing huts. She had just removed her black racing costume and tossed it in a crumpled heap onto the polished floor, and was standing naked in a corner under the bare rafters, when she heard the hinges of the wooden door squeak and felt a rush of cooler air. She remained silent, hidden in the shadows, as Fiamma entered.

Di was not sure why she hid there, what she was planning to do, if anything. She watched Miss G follow Fiamma into the changing room with the light behind her. Di could not see Fiamma's face because she had turned her back. Slowly Fiamma slipped her arms out of her straps and folded down the top of her swimming suit. She spread her arms out on either side and shook her smooth shoulders in a sort of dance. Little drops of water fell onto the concrete floor from the tips of her fluttering fingers. She stepped out of her swimsuit. Di saw her naked back, bare white shoulders, and damp skin, clothed only in the cool morning air.

All the while, Di heard the bells chiming loudly, calling us to assembly, and then, as though awakened by the bells, the crowing of the cocks.

There was not a word spoken. Miss G was watching Fiamma, and her face was wet, her mouth slightly open. Then she moved toward Fiamma, slowly, and put her arms gently around her. She lowered her dark head to Fiamma's boosie and sucked, making noises like a baby. Di wanted to weep because Miss G had never even touched her boosies.

Then Fiamma pushed Miss G away from her, roughly. "Please," Miss G implored. Fiamma said, "Can't you just leave me *alone,*" and walked past Miss G and out of the changing room, leaving the door ajar. Di saw the grass shining white in the early morning light, and the soft flowers on the mimosa trees, like snow on the thin branches. She put on her tunic quickly and picked up her panama hat and ran down the bank toward the school.

How we upset Fiamma

A NN WAS PERCHED on the window seat, reading about Winston Churchill and the armored train and the Boer War in the light of her yellow torch. Sheila was telling a story about violent death. All her plots ended violently. The Trevelyans were lying side-by-side in bed, whispering about our team's recent failures. "Even Helpmekaar High beat us," Bobby Joe said with disgust.

Ann looked up from her book and whispered, "Miss G's lost interest in our winning. She doesn't desire us to win anymore."

Di said, "She's all washed up."

Bobby Joe said, "She's gone completely barmy."

Fuzzie said, "She keeps picking on me. She keeps telling me I'm too fat. Does she think I want to be fat?"

Ann said, "She tells me I have a blight of blackheads on my nose, and my nails are dirty, and I should try and walk like Fiamma."

Meg whispered to Fiamma, who was lying on her back in the moonlight and staring up at the ceiling, "I wish Miss G liked me as much as she does you. What did you do to make her like you so much?" Fiamma rolled over without answering.

Pamela made little kissing noises in the dark, and got up and twitched her thin hips. We all laughed.

Bobby Joe said, "If I hear about Fiamma's villa one more time, I'll strangle her."

Fiamma rolled back and said, "What do you want me to do? She makes me describe it."

Bobby Jean said, "You could at least keep it short and sweet."

Meg said, "If you were sweeter to Miss G, do you see, she would be sweeter to us. She's unhappy, because you are not nice to her, because you either ignore her or are rude to her. That's why she picks on us."

Bobby Joe made kissing noises in the dark and rose from her bed and pulled Bobby Jean out. They danced the tango up and down the dormitory, leaning forward and back while Fuzzie sang: Ta-da-da-dada, ta-da-dada. We all laughed loudly. Mary told us to shut up, we would wake Mrs. Looney.

Fiamma sat up in the moonlight in her smocked nightdress. She looked around at us and said in her bored English voice, "I am not sure you know what you are suggesting."

Di said, "You shouldn't be so bloody superior all the time. You think you're better than everyone else, don't you — even better than Miss G. What right do you have to be so bloody stuck-up?"

Fiamma flopped down again on the bed and turned her narrow buttocks into the air and her face into the pillow.

Meg said, "You could be nicer to her for our sakes, don't you see, just to make our lives easier, even if you don't want to."

Mary said, "The means justifies the end, like she says."

Ann dusted the back of Fiamma's head with the beam of her yellow torch and said, "Lots of people in history have sacrificed themselves for others. God even asked Abraham to kill his own son, and he was going to do it. Judith sacrificed herself, and so did Cleopatra with the asp at her bosom, and so did Lucretia. We should all sacrifice ourselves for the common good, to relieve the suffering of others. I would be happy to sacrifice myself for others, if someone wanted me to do it."

PART THREE
THE DINNER

→>→→

What we talk about

A STARCHED WHITE tablecloth, willow-pattern plates, cut glass, and shimmering cutlery array the trestle table that has been set up in the shade for our feast. White printed menus are propped up in silver holders. Frosted silver pitchers of iced water lie at either end. There are camphor candles in glass bowls all along the table to keep off the mosquitoes.

Meg, the only one wearing a low-cut dress, waves her hand smoothly in the air and lisps, "It looks like a wedding."

Fuzzie has never married, though she has been in love so many times: "Every four weeks, when the moon is full." Her freckled skin is still smooth, and she is no longer ungainly, but she still has the apprehension in her close-set green eyes that makes us, too, apprehensive, as it always did.

"Let's hope the food's improved. Do you remember that ghastly, lumpy porridge they made us eat every morning?" Meg says, pulling a sour face. Di reminds us what wonderful scones Meg made in domestic science. Ann, with that twist to her thin lips that makes her seem detached from what she says, reminds us that Meg, despite her romantic air, was a practical girl, a realist, who said she would marry a rich man. Meg looks from Di to Ann and laughs. "And I did." She still has her leafy scent.

Fuzzie says, "I'm starving." As she leans across the table to reach for the menu, she looks almost willowy. Fuzzie, so fat as a young girl, has become thin. Her hem hangs sadly to one side, and she has tied around her neck a cheap pink scarf, which clashes with her hair, cropped short now but still very red and curly.

Ann whispers to Sheila that she wonders if Fuzzie gave her fortune away to charity in a manic fit. "Do you suppose she still wears her vest as she did as a child, even in the worst heat?" Ann asks.

"Probably," says Sheila, who believes what has happened before will happen again.

"Sit by me, Meg," says Di, now heavy, sitting down at the head of the table. "You sit over there, Fuzzie."

Fuzzie has spent years sitting on the veranda staring at the morning glory creeping up the walls of the mental hospital. Now she sits in the middle of the long trestle table between the snub-nosed Trevelyans. Her years in the asylum, in spite of her repeated shock treatments, seem to have preserved her youthfulness. She looks like a fawn, gentle and timorous, as she bends over the bright anemones in the center of the table and sniffs, saying with surprise, "But they have no smell!"

Sheila sits at the other end of the long table beside Mary and Pamela, the girl who always got less than 10 percent in maths. Pamela is still as thin as ever but now has varicose veins in her legs from all the standing she has had to do while binding books. Sheila frowns. Perhaps she is thinking of her work. She wanted to be a writer like Alan Paton, and write a sentence like his about all the roads leading to Johannesburg, but she has only written thrillers, all of them about murdered girls.

Mary, who has become a doctor, looks jowly, but we recognize elements of the uncomplicated girl in her smile, bowl-cut hair, and shapeless dress.

We sit down, one after the other. Everyone sits apart. We gaze blankly at one another. Ann still has her perpetual cold. She looks slightly feverish, and her high forehead and protuberant eyes shine.

We are all bored. We have nothing to say to one another, after all this time. And if anyone wanted to speak, where on earth would she begin? What do we all expect?

Di jerks her head back and says to Meg, "Tell me what has happened to you."

Meg sits very stiffly, in silence, her shoulders pressed back, her head held high. She looks as though she has practiced this position before a mirror and found it advantageous. She shakes her head and says, "Nothing much, really. It's extraordinary. So many years, without anything special happening."

Ann, who sits opposite Meg, blows her nose and says in her nasal voice, "Oh, come on, Meg, something must have."

Meg says, "Well, I did marry a lovely, rich pediatrician. I actually fell in love with him when I saw him with children. It was the way he put his hand on their heads, ever so gently."

Di looks at Meg and says sadly, "Ah, Meg in love."

Meg goes on, with her slight lisp, "But we have not had children, ourselves. We tried everything, even hormones from menopausal Italian nuns. But we do have one another. We are very happy. We travel. We have a lovely house; I grow roses, you know. You see, nothing out of the ordinary."

Di says, "Really so happy? It seems to me I am left with only objects. Two of my husbands have gone, my children are scattered, and my dog has died." She looks around the veranda, as though the missing might be here in the shadows.

The veranda has grown shabby; the damp has peeled the

paint; there is dust in the corners — even the proteas in the brass bowl look dusty; spiderwebs hang from the beams. We sip drinks in the late afternoon shadows. There is the smell of damp earth. Lizzie rises suddenly, scraping back the long bench on the polished floor and making off with an air of secrecy. She is still slim and elegant, and her gray hair hangs straight to her shoulders. We watch her walking out into the garden, alone.

We break the silence again by speaking about the condition of the country. Ann, who was always interested in it and always went into things in depth, has written several books on the troubles of our country, which were translated widely, even into Japanese. She removes something from a tooth with her nail and says the place is less changed than it should be.

"To tell you the truth, I am sick and tired of talking about this country, sick of it!" Di says.

The silence drops again. We watch the breeze lifting the branches and the lawns running down and down, falling away, strange and gray in the twilight like the mountains of the moon. We listen to the chiming of the clock. Something silver glimmers in the distance and is gone.

Meg reminds us how Di wanted to be a dancer like Margot Fonteyn and kept hoping she would stop growing, but she didn't. She looks as tall and as broad-shouldered as a man.

Di drinks hard liquor fast, swinging her crossed leg. She has married three times: number one, one of her teachers at the Royal Ballet, left her for a black professor of mathematics; number two, a very rich American, died and left her a fortune. Now she has her vast house, acres and acres of empty corridors, the English furniture and the silver. "My second husband was a prudent man. He never ate meat, rode a stationary bicycle every day, and took handfuls of vitamins." She found him on the floor in the bathroom one summer morning in their house by the sea. She remembers the dead weight of his head when she tried to lift it onto her lap.

"How awful for you," Meg says, putting her hand on Di's arm. "Let's not talk about the past; it's too depressing." Meg lifts her lovely hands in the air with the fingers spread, as though she wishes to keep the past at bay.

Ann rattles ice in her glass and says, "Why do you think Sunny brought us here?"

Di says, "Not to talk about our lives, I hope! Perhaps I came here to see Meg."

Meg says, "I came here to see all of you and to have a good time. Let's do it."

Ann, whose husband is as handsome as he is unfaithful, says, "Oh, for God's sake, Meg! You were always having such a fucking good time, weren't you? It was always such a fucking lovely day."

Mary says sternly to Ann, "It's a question of attitude. Some of us see the glass as half full, others, as half empty."

Ann lifts her gin and tonic and lime and squints at it through her thick glasses in the muted light. "It has been said, of course, that there is no such concept as a thing itself."

Meg, as though suddenly inspired by a deep thought, says, "What do things matter when compared with love?"

Fuzzie leans forward to lift her glass, and for a moment, we see the fat little girl with her shiny tunic stretching across her stomach. She says, "Too much pineapple juice."

No one speaks, but we all remember, surely. We see Di moving through the half dark of the dormitory in her disguise as a man, her painted mustache running into her mouth, a glass of spiked pineapple juice in her hand.

Di rises. Despite her weight and her elegant suit, she swings a long leg easily over the bench. She says she has to "cross the bridge," using the school euphemism, though there is no longer any bridge to cross. We listen to her firm, rapid steps. Meg rises and goes after her, moving smoothly and swiftly, as she always did, in the water and on land, flitting slim and specter-like through the shadows. When they have left the veranda, Ann, too, rises in her crumpled tartan and short-sleeved shirt and walks down the table to Sheila. "Di's husband had just taken out an insurance policy in her name for a million rands, the day before he died. *Et comme c'est étrange et quelle coïncidence,* hey?"

Sheila, who once signed her letters "From an undiscovered genius," has perhaps just had an idea for another book she always wanted to write, for she says, to no one in particular, "I have my work. I do have my work, you know."

The candles are lit

UNDER THE STAR-WILD sky we sit on the long veranda, listening to the myriad sounds of the dusk: rustlings and creakings, chirping of the crickets, a door slamming. Our voices seem to come and then flow away like an echo. There are nighthawks. There is the smell of damp earth and cut grass. There is a slight mist rising low and thin, like gauze in the blue air.

Fuzzie says, "The mosquitoes are attacking my calves and eating me alive."

"Light the camphor candles, please; they'll ward off the mosquitoes," Di orders the ancient servant.

He lights them all along the table, bending over in his wrinkled white uniform, his hands shaking, fumbling with the big box of kitchen matches. He shades the flare of the match from the breeze with one pink-palmed, black hand. The candle flames twist and righten in the air. We lean across the table toward the flames, drawn toward them, as if they could protect us from the dangers of the encroaching dark, and our white faces are brought closer, so that for the first time we form a group again, like people on a dark night on a dark beach, taking their holiday.

Then, half bent, he brings the heavy silver platters, laying them out on the side table. There is a fat brown turkey, its shins frilled and crisp, a great ham, its skin scored and dotted with dark cloves, a whole leg of lamb, cooked English style, dark outside and in. Between the meat and poultry are dishes of roast potatoes, gem squash, butter melting in the scooped-out halves, green beans almondine, mint jelly, and gravy boats, a thin film of fat floating on their surface. There are dishes of custard and pears cooked in red wine and a white, iced granadilla cake on a frilled doily.

We serve ourselves abundantly, refilling our wineglasses, and rising for seconds. Our faces flicker and change in the strange light, as we heap the food high on our plates. There is grease around our mouths, down to our chins; our lips are stained with red wine, our lipstick, smudged, our camouflage, undone. We are transformed, unmasked by the fatigue, the food, the candlelight. The breeze picks up, and the candles send shifting shadows across the table. The stars flame brightly above us. The moon rises.

Someone says, "Remember St. Agnes's Eve?"

Each one remembers the night differently, but vaguely, because we were so drunk. Everyone agrees that no one wanted to hurt Fiamma. We just wanted to have fun with her. We wanted Miss G to have fun with her, too.

We remember with a sense of exhilaration, as though we were once again celebrating an ancient ritual. We laugh, and we feel better. We remember the long, narrow dormitory. We see the Trevelyans embracing, their thin shoulder blades milk white in the moonlight, like wings. We hear Meg and Di make the moans we associated with love.

Fuzzie sits before the low bowl of anemones, which seem to

glimmer mysteriously with the light of their deep reds and purples. They flutter in the breeze, opening and shutting their petals like their sea cousins, drifting back and forth in dark waters, as she sings the pure, clear notes of an ancient madrigal.

How horrible is it?

THE CANDLES burn low. Di has removed her black shantung jacket. Grease marks her blue scarf. She is the only one left eating.

Ann says the worst part of her husband's job is the awful, dull dinners for visiting dignitaries they have to attend. So much wasted food, when so many are starving. She says her politician-husband wants her to buy expensive frocks from the Faubourg St. Honoré to wear at these dinners. But what use would such frocks be on her frumpy figure? Besides, whatever she does, her husband leaves her on the weekends for the village where he was born. He dons the loincloth of his childhood, sits in the dust, and smokes dagga. She would love to go with him, but he does not want her there. "You do not belong," he says.

"The villa is empty as a tomb," Ann says, shuddering.

While the moon slips through clouds, Di finally pushes her dish away and speaks slowly, as though she is regaining her memory. She tells us that the irony is that she threw herself into dance after she left school, although she was too tall. She wanted nothing to do with men, but her first husband told her he found her irresistibly attractive. Perhaps it was her fortune he actually found irresistible, she says, laughing. "One was supposed to marry, wasn't one? Besides, I was pregnant," she says, drinking another glass of red wine, surrounded by the remnants of the huge meal she has consumed.

Fuzzie, resorting to the language of our youth, says, "Do you know, when I got excited, I actually believed I could make myself preggie. All I had to do was cross my legs and shake the bed."

Mary watches Fuzzie sip more wine and says, "You should probably not drink so much, with all the medicine you have to take."

Fuzzie stiffens, and her close-set eyes flash. She says, "I don't feel I need my medicine anymore. I haven't felt so good for years," but she looks at us as though she sees some horror about to surface.

Di says, "At first I thought he might have suffered a slight stroke," referring now to her third and present husband, the German industrialist. "He walks in his sleep. I have to keep my door locked at night, because he once sat on my face and almost suffocated me. He forces me to make love to him in odd ways — he is still a large, strong man. I can hear him shuffling in the acres of corridors, bearing down on me. Can you imagine? He wants me to call him my stallion," Di says, lighting her cigarette. He summons her urgently and has her attend to his needs. He wants her to press her naked back against his fat stomach, while he shouts words at her that she does not understand, words that sound harsh and cruel. She has never managed the language, such a difficult one, she complains, even worse than Afrikaans, which she hated, too. She has to let him clamber up on her back and take her coarse, dyed hair in his hands and yank her head back, while she calls him the German word for stallion, a word she always forgets. Then he pushes and prods into her orifices with his thick, gnarled fingers.

"It is horrible, horrible," Di says, bursting shamelessly into tears, to our utter surprise, and putting her head down in her arms on the trestle table with the bread crumbs, the gravy-stained tablecloth, the empty coffee cups, and the cigarette butts.

"Don't worry," Meg says and puts her hand on Di's arm, but

Meg is weeping, too. She weeps not only for Di, or for her un-born children, but also for Fiamma, who is not here. Di lifts her head, the paint running across her bloated cheeks, as it did years ago. She says, "You understand, because you are good. You would understand, too, Ann, because you understand every-thing. I don't. I only know that everything is gone. It came to an end a long time ago."

Sheila, who lived in France for a while, says, *"Tout passe, tout casse, tout lasse."*

"And what about desire?" Fuzzie says, throwing back her head and laughing, as we all hear the echo of Miss G's exhortation.

We remember the moonlit night when Miss G strode sud-denly into the dormitory. We can still hear her voice calling Fi-amma, and our drunken giggles. We all laugh in the moonlight, our faces glowing. We are suddenly unaccountably lighthearted. A mood of revelry has taken hold of us, as though all this talk has washed us as clean and pure as the light of the moon.

Fuzzie is queen of the May

P AMELA SAYS it is a pity there is no piano out here; Fuzzie could play us a tune. But Di says, "It's late. Let's go to bed," and rises from the bench.

Fuzzie, also rising, recites in her lovely voice:

> You must wake and call me early,
> Call me early, mother dear;
> For I'm to be Queen of the May.

The rest of us rise together and leave the table, going through the hall, hurrying past what had been Miss G's door, like the tide rising, flowing up the dusty stairs, going fast, in silence, along the corridor leading to the dormitory now called Mandela, back to where we slept so many years ago. In the muted light of the corridor our middle-aged faces look gray and worn — even Meg's, her dark curls falling lankly into her slanting, Asian eyes.

She says she remembers how her father used to say they should have named a wing of the school Donovan because of all the tuition he had to pay for his five girls. Meg no longer hears from him. He left her mother for a younger woman soon after her little sister died. "It was too much for him," she says sadly. No one speaks.

We hesitate on the threshold of the dormitory once called Kitchener. No one wants to go in first. Someone turns the brass handle of the door gingerly. Slowly we release the tongue of the lock and open the door onto half darkness. We enter and look into the deeper darkness at the row of neat, narrow beds that await us and the basins that run down the center of the room.

The moon has sunk; all the lights are out. It has begun to rain again, a hard drumming on the roof. A great, dark downpour has begun. In it we all see Fiamma, floating toward us, half naked, the crown of daisies aslant on her forehead, gliding across the parquet, her head slightly to one side, her cheek almost caressing her shoulder, playing "St. Agnes's Eve."

PART FOUR

DISGUISE

→>‹←

Why Miss Nieven called us into her room

ON THE NIGHT Fiamma disappeared, Miss Nieven called the twelve of us into her study. We were only summoned there if we had done something seriously wrong, or if there was very bad news.

Before we went in, we were told to shower and change our stained clothes. We were allowed to stay in the shower for as long as we liked, feeling the water on our bodies. We washed our hair for the first time in weeks, because of the drought. We scrubbed. We stared up at the ceiling and thought about Fiamma. We thought of the mosquitoes and the flies — so many of them; we could still hear the hum.

In the study there were no mosquitoes. The windows were kept closed, and the heavy red velvet curtains were drawn in the evening light. We could hear the grandfather clock in the hall chime the hour, and the wind beat in the palm fronds.

A green-shaded lamp cast a pool of light on the baize of Miss Nieven's large mahogany desk. Leather-bound books lined the walls, and a fern grew in a wooden pot. Her personal servant, an ancient black man in a rumpled white jacket, brought a bulb-shaped bottle of water and a glass on a silver tray and placed it beside her, slowly and solemnly, as we, too, filed in solemnly.

We sat cross-legged on the red carpet and spoke in hushed voices. We darted quick glances at one another. We looked changed: cleaner, lighter, paler, ashen beneath the eyes.

We floated in the dim light of the room. It was as though we were dreaming, or had left our bodies behind with Fiamma under the frangipanis. We kept seeing the filtered light, the still water, and her clear eyes staring up at us. We huddled close in our thin dresses. We sweated in the thick heat, filled with the coldhearted thrill of tragedy.

Miss Nieven spoke about Fiamma, pulling as usual on the hair that grew from the wart on her chin. We found it hard to pay attention. We shifted about while she stretched out her sentences. She thought she was reassuring us, but she was not.

She told us that she wanted to hear exactly what had happened on the walk. She hoped, she said, that Fiamma would be found before nightfall, that everything was being done to find her, but that, if she were not, and if we did not clear up the mystery, she would be obliged to call in the police.

Search parties had already been sent out. They had dogs with them. They might have to drag the river, but she was still hoping nothing worse than a sprained ankle had befallen Fiamma. There was always the possibility that she might have got lost out there, and that someone would have found her and would call the school at any moment. Her voice trembled as she added that Fiamma was not a very strong girl, with her breathing disorder, nor was she familiar with our veld. She may have underestimated the dangers of the terrain, the wide open spaces, the heat, the monotony of the landscape. She may not have been aware of how easy it was to lose oneself out there.

Fiamma had been protected from danger. She was used to straight paths and gardens with clipped hedges and ancient, shady trees. She might even have fallen asleep in the sun; it might be a case of simple sunstroke. There was no reason to panic, or to think she could have drowned in that little stream, superb swimmer that she was. There was no reason to jump to the worst conclusions.

Nothing like this had happened before at this school. Still, all necessary precautions had to be taken, and it would be very helpful if we would tell her what we knew. We were, after all, not only the last ones to have seen her but also her teammates, were we not? We were likely to know if Fiamma had said anything unusual, if something had upset her, or if she had taken it into her head to go off to telephone her sick father. She was headstrong.

We shifted about and looked at one another and stared blankly. Ann took off her thick glasses to wipe her small, red eyes, and her face looked naked. She was sweating. Two tears ran down her sallow cheeks. Fuzzie whispered to Sheila something about her mother just wanting to grow dahlias and not orchids, but Sheila told her to shut up. Di looked almost green around the lips. She was holding on to Meg's arm so tightly that Meg winced. The Trevelyans said they had to cross the bridge and walked out, holding their stomachs. They looked deathly pale from all the fermented pineapple juice they had drunk the night before.

Miss Nieven said, "Everything will remain between us, *intra muros*. We are all on the same side, after all," whistling again when she pronounced the *s*'s and exposing her row of yellow teeth.

She told us not to try to protect anyone. We knew to whom she was referring: one who had pulled at one cigarette after the other, grinding them out beneath the heel of her boot, whose eyes were as dark as midnight and showed a gleam of terror, a wild hare's look.

Miss Nieven told Di that as captain of the swimming team, she should speak up first. What did she remember about the walk to the river? What had happened in the dormitory, last night?

There was a long silence. The stilled sounds of evening were all that came to us, the sounds of the rain-stunned garden. Di stared ahead. Her deep blue eyes looked black, and her light skin seemed to have lost all its glow. Miss Nieven looked her in the eye and said in a sweet voice, "Well, Diane, what do you have to say?"

Di rose to her feet, and we all turned to look at her. She seemed to have grown ungainly in her height and the heavy muscles of her brown legs. She caught her spill of thin hair and pulled it from her face. She said what we already knew. She said the girls on the swimming team had organized a midnight feast, that we had spent most of the night eating a lot of oily sardines and peaches in sweet syrup, and drinking condensed milk and fermented pineapple juice. Fiamma had had a good time along with the rest of us. No one had slept well after it, because we all felt sick. She said it had started to rain very hard, this afternoon on the walk, and we had taken shelter in the picnic hut. Then the sun had come out again, and there were lots of mossies, and it got very hot. We had last seen Fiamma lying in the shadow of the frangipani trees. She'd seemed quiet and calm. When Miss G had asked if anyone had seen her, we had hunted for her everywhere. Then Miss G had told us to line up, and we had come back to school. Di sat down again, and Ann, who had lost her handkerchief that afternoon, borrowed Di's and blew her nose loudly. Fuzzie let out a little noise that might have been either a giggle or a sob.

We trooped out of the study and stumbled down the wisteria-covered pergola. The school was very quiet, more so than usual for a Sunday evening. The place seemed empty, as if the girls were absent and the constant hum of their voices, silenced. The seringa tree drooped lifelessly over the wooden bench; ivory clouds were pinned to a still blue sky. We listened to the hollow sound of our shoes on stone.

A group of girls was huddling together in the shadows and light of the long pergola. They were whispering. One of them bent down to pull up a brown sock and lifted her head to stare at us, as the others did when we filed past. They went on staring at us sullenly, as we walked down the steps that led into the long, covered corridor. Slowly we descended them, linked like a chain, one after the other.

Whose idea was the feast?

THE IDEA for a midnight feast came to Di after she had seen Miss G and Fiamma together in the changing hut. She immediately told the twins, and they eagerly agreed, because they were always starving, because they did not receive any parcels with extra sweets and biscuits, as everyone else did. Orphans, they sat in agony after each breakfast, hearing the long list of names called out; their names were never called. They did not even receive books about horses. They were always trying to borrow *Thunderhead* or *My Friend Flicka* from Mary, who had the whole series and would part with them only grudgingly, because she was also horse-mad. Sometimes the twins slipped out of their beds at night and went and lay down in the stables on the straw to be near the horses. The smell of manure and sweat, the swish of the tails, the stamping of hooves on the stone floor, a sudden sweet whinnying, comforted them. They were the ones who spiked the pineapple juice by leaving it to ferment for ages under the oak tree by the hockey field.

Di suggested the dancing and the dressing up, because she wanted to dance with Meg in the disguise of a man.

And, certainly, it was Sheila who thought of acting out the roles of all the characters in Keats's poem, which was her favorite. She thought it was brilliant. She said, "Some of us can be Madeline and some, Porphyro. We can dress up and have a beadsman and a beldame. Someone can hobble around."

Mary said, "I'll be Porphyro with his steed," and began rushing around the room, waving an imaginary whip in the air.

Meg murmured, "I will be Madeline and pray for a dream lover in the moonlight," getting down on her knees, spreading her dark curls on her shoulders, and putting her hands together in mock prayer.

Pamela said, "Fiamma can be Madeline, and Miss G can be her Porphyro," and we all clutched at one another feverishly and giggled.

Then Ann recited the part of the poem we liked best:

> Her rich attire creeps rustling to her knees:
> Half-hidden, like a mermaid in sea-weed,
> Pensive awhile she dreams awake, and sees,
> In fancy, fair St. Agnes in her bed,
> But dares not look behind, or all the charm is fled.

St. Agnes's Eve

> Fuzzie sang songs of long ago.
> Ann recited to the moon.
> Never before had Fiamma feasted so,
> While we, in lovers' arms, swooned.

> We drank, we ate, we discarded our clothes
> The moon shone on our flesh.
> We lay together, we dreamed of love,
> We lost ourselves, enmeshed.

WE HAD NEVER seen Fiamma have as much fun as she did the night before she disappeared. It was the same for most of us. We liked the food, the dressing up and pretending, the drink, the excitement, and the dreams of love in the moonlight. The languid moonlight advanced, as we lay side-by-side in the dormitory, trying to stay awake until midnight.

We waited up impatiently with the windows and curtains open. We sweated in the heat. Some of us hid in the bathrooms, reading our books to pass the time and swatting at the mosquitoes, jumping up to kill them with our slippers, the blood marking the walls. We listened to the grandfather clock in the hall chime midnight. Then we rose and slipped down to fetch the flowers from the bathroom under the stairs.

Miss G had suggested we ask Fiamma to help decorate the dormitory with the flowers: "You know, Fiamma is wonderful with flowers." When we told her what we were planning, Miss G's eyes had turned brilliant, and she had said longingly. "Italians are very artistic. They have the imagination, the flair. They are full of surprises." Then she had brought forth the business about no repression of libidinal urges and how repression led to aggression and told us to let our imaginations soar, our emotions rule our hearts.

And to our surprise Fiamma had acquiesced, rising obligingly from her bed and mixing goldenrod with lavender in big jars by the windows. We discovered her gift with her hands that night. When she had finished with the flowers, she piled up fruit and tins of sardines in the basins along the center of the dorm. Finally, she helped us with our disguises.

Naturally, Ann was designated as our reader. She perched in the windowsill with her torch, intoning the lilting verses of "The Eve of St. Agnes" in her monotonous, nasal voice and blowing her nose from time to time. While she read, we acted out the poem: we ate and drank and discarded our clothes as Madeline does, before we climbed into our beds to wait for our imaginary lovers. We hid behind doors or under our beds in the role of the real lover, Porphyro.

Di, in her panama hat, tilted at a rakish angle, and galoshes, danced up and down the dormitory with Meg, holding her around the waist and turning her around and around. Fuzzie sang madrigals with flowers in her red curls. The Trevelyans shimmied around the dormitory completely naked, hugging one another like lovers, their thin shoulder blades like white wings in the moonlight.

By the end of the feast we were all wandering about half naked, our makeup smudged, crushed flowers in our loose hair. We were drunk on the juice and wine. We sweated and giggled and sighed, playing the lovers in one another's beds. Then the batteries on Ann's torch failed, and she had to stop reading the poem.

What many of us were to remember best was the white, full disk of the moon. There was thunder and lightning, but no rain. Fuzzie, who was always particularly sensitive to smells, was to remember those of the flowers, mingled with those of hot, sweating bodies, which increased as the night went on.

Why the game of St. Agnes's Eve?

> Our robes drifted to our knees.
> Half-hidden like mermaids in seaweed,
> We dreamed awake and saw
> In fancy, Miss G, fairest of all.

"THE EVE OF ST. AGNES" was our favorite poem, although, or perhaps because, Miss Lacey had said we would do much better to read Milton's "Samson Agonistes." Of course, our feast did not take place on St. Agnes's Eve. We did not know when that holiday was. Ann maintained it was probably in December or, anyway, sometime in midwinter, because the poem speaks of such bitter cold. Now it was midsummer for us, and thus the appropriate time.

We wanted, insofar as possible, to make the feast resemble the one in the poem. We wanted to have the same sort of food — the candied apple, the quince, the plum, but in the end all we could procure was the usual midnight feast food: tins of condensed milk and sardines and peaches in sweet syrup. Of course, we had no beadsman, no beldame; we had no Porphyros for our Madelines, but we made believe.

When the detective asked us about the feast, we told him about the food and the alcohol, but no one mentioned Di jumping out of the cupboard in her galoshes and painted mustache and panama hat and not much else, in her role of Porphyro, and climbing into bed with Meg, where they made the sorts of noises they associated with love. No one spoke of passing the pineapple juice to Fiamma, or of her drifting drunkenly around the dormitory, stumbling blindly into the basins in the center of the room.

No one mentioned Miss G.

Who was invited to the feast and why?

ONLY THE GIRLS on the swimming team were invited, naturally. We were all there: Fuzzie, her sheet slipping down her plump, shiny hips, and her daisy chain tilting into her eyes as she sang madrigals; Pamela, half asleep in pajamas tied with a belt around her thin waist, eating peaches, the syrup dripping down her arm; Ann, sitting up in the window seat with her yellow torch and her thick glasses, her collarbones protruding from the sheet tied around her neck, blowing her nose; Di, in pajamas and galoshes, sporting a painted mustache; Meg with a scarf tied tightly across the lilt of her full breasts, lisping softly in Di's ear; the Trevelyans in nothing at all; Lizzie, elegant in white pajamas; Mary in her riding boots and plumed hat, pretending to be Porphyro arriving at the castle on his wild steed "with heart on fire"; and Sheila, spending her time eating tinned sardines and dreaming of love and death.

What Fiamma did at the feast

> Around a neck a knot she ties,
> She drapes a sheet around.
> While her loss draws nigh
> With daisy chains we are bound.

NONE OF US KNEW exactly what cards Fiamma was playing at the midnight feast. We do know that we asked her to join in with us, and to our surprise she did so with enthusiasm. Perhaps she had simply been waiting to be asked, or perhaps the dressing up made her think of her father, who was still languishing in some small hospital somewhere, suffering from increasingly high fever, Miss G said.

Fiamma told us that her father had once taken her to Venice during the carnival season. Everyone dressed up in costumes with masks, so that no one could tell who they were. They had kept their costumes a secret even from one another. Fiamma had made her own costume. She had dressed up as a mermaid with a wonderful tail and mask, and in the crowd of people and the confusion, her father had asked her to dance, not knowing who she was.

Fiamma threw herself into our preparations. She used our sheets, blankets, and scarves to make us look like knights and ladies from long ago. She draped our sheets around us, tied scarves around our heads, and threaded a flower through a plait, standing back to survey her handiwork critically. Instead of jewelry she used the flowers we had stolen from the cutting garden and hidden in the bathroom under the stairs. She made flower chains for our ankles and wrists and foreheads, splitting the stems with a knife and linking them together.

She made up our faces so that we hardly recognized one another. She outlined our eyes with dark pencil and flecked our cheeks with gold paint, so that those of us who were playing Madeline looked like angels. The Porphyros — usually the taller girls: Di, Mary, Pamela, and Lizzie — wore pajama trousers and loose shirts and raked panama hats and, sometimes, galoshes or boots. Fiamma painted their upper lips with black pencil to make them look like men. Like a magician she transformed us. We felt like the inhabitants of some strange, distant land, and in our anonymity and the half dark of our dormitory, we could do anything, say anything, be anything we wanted. We were wild and free. Afterward, because of the heat and sweat, much of the makeup ran, streaking our faces like those of savages.

Fiamma, too, was transformed. We would always remember her, pretending to be the beadsman, telling her rosary on her knees and shivering with cold in the hot dormitory. She looked suddenly old, her smooth brow wrinkled, as though her whole life had passed her by, and she had become the ancient beldame, hobbling blindly down the moonlit dormitory, leaning on a stick for a cane and warning an imaginary Porphyro of the dangers in the house.

> Saying, "Mercy, Porphyro! hie thee from this place:
> They are all here to-night, the whole blood-thirsty race!"

Other staff members who knew about the feast

W E FOUND OUT afterward that Miss Lacey was awakened by the noise. She told Sheila, her favorite, that she had heard a noise coming from Kitchener, but she remembered the midnight feasts of her own youthful schooldays and smiled indulgently, thinking we should be allowed some freedom — after all, this was not the Middle Ages. She decided it was better not to interfere.

The night watchman, John Mazaboko, the tall Zulu from Natal, who was later to die tragically in his room in a fire, said he heard a noise coming from Kitchener but considered it was not his role, a black night watchman in a white girls' school, to report on them.

He also heard footsteps in the very early hours of the morning, when the sky was a faint pink. He was wandering up and down the gravel path under the ancient oaks, the light of his torch punching holes through the dark of the hydrangeas. He looked up and saw a blond girl wrapped in a striped towel, drifting toward the pool in the dawn light.

He said that he called out, "*Sala khale*," the Zulu greeting, telling her to go carefully, but when she did not respond, he did not follow her, because he, too, had been drinking skokiaan to pass the interminable hours of the empty night, and he thought he might have seen a ghost.

What Miss G did at the feast

NONE OF US had ever seen Fiamma drink so much. She drank from the tin of condensed milk, the thick liquid trickling down her chin. She drank glass after glass of the spiked pineapple juice, which the Trevelyans passed her. She drank the white wine mixed with red that Miss G had provided. She broke a glass, and we had to try to scoop up the pieces with our bare hands in the half-light so that no one would cut her bare feet.

The Trevelyans said afterward that they'd heard what no one else had, a first soft knock on the door, and they said that when they heard it, they had a feeling of anticipation and dread. They feared that it would all end badly.

Then there was a louder knock, which everyone heard. We all kept very still, and some of us, who were naked, crouched down behind the basins, which Fiamma had filled with food and which were now almost empty. The door opened slowly, and Miss G appeared. She loomed, barefooted in her jumpsuit, a long, dark shadow in the light from the corridor. She shut the door behind her quickly and stood there, legs apart, hands on her hips, staring at the disorderly scene in the moonlight. We were all standing around drunkenly, half naked, linked in pairs, flowers in our loose hair, or false mustaches running into our mouths.

She called for Fiamma. She called again, and Fiamma emerged slowly from the shadows. She tottered forward, or perhaps Bobby Joe pushed her, though Bobby Joe denied it later. Bobby Jean, who became a social worker, said she saw her twin pull Fiamma from beside the bed where she was hiding when Miss G called for her. Then Fiamma floated forward. Everyone else was too drunk to speak.

We did recall that Fiamma had remained half naked since early in the evening. Her sheet had slipped down to her waist, baring her full, white bosoms. Her hair was loose. Her crown of daisies tilted across her brow into one eye. Her gold eye shadow was smudged, her lipstick, spread wide like a clown's. Like all of us she smelled of alcohol and sweat.

We moved away from her, as Miss G strode toward her and grabbed her by the arm and held her close as though she were smelling her. She placed her hands on Fiamma's shoulders and looked into her eyes. Then she picked up a scarf that had fallen to the floor and slung it around Fiamma's neck like a halter. "Now you come with me," she said and led her away like a horse. Fiamma stumbled forward blindly. We watched in amazement as the door opened, and they disappeared into the garish neon light.

It was after Fiamma had gone that the batteries in Ann's torch went dead, and only moonlight remained. We clasped one another deliriously in it; we stroked one another's skin, our soft new breasts; we rolled around in one another's beds and pretended to be Fiamma and Miss G and made the sorts of noises we hoped they were making at last.

PART FIVE

DISAPPEARANCE

→>-<←

What happened on the day of
Fiamma's disappearance

O N THE DAY Fiamma was to disappear, she rose at dawn to swim. Ann saw her sit up in her bed in the silence of the sleeping dormitory. In the faint light she already looked like a specter in her soft, long-sleeved nightdress that she had washed, despite regulations, so that the school soap would not aggravate her sensitive skin. Her heavy hair was plaited down her back in a long, limp rope. She told Ann, speaking softly so as not to awaken the others, she had dreamed that she was swimming through the still, trapped water of her lake at home, the mist rising from its gray surface. She felt her body buoyed up by the water and slowly spinning free, escaping into the cool air. She rose, she soared. But when she awoke under her white sheet, she was soaked with sweat.

Ann had acquired a reputation as a remarkable interpreter of dreams, because she had read Freud's dream book, but she did not attempt to interpret that one.

Fiamma said that she had hardly slept, but she was going swimming. Ann reminded her it was Sunday, and she was not supposed to practice but to dress for chapel. Miss G would not be up this early, anyway. "I need to cool off," Fiamma said.

Ann watched her remove her nightdress and wander around the disarrayed dormitory, already hot, though not as hot as it was to become that day. Adorned only with the camphor bag, which trailed on the end of a string, bouncing against her back, she skated her hand across the identical iron bed ends, lined up side-by-side, looking for her racing costume. Her once-proud step, arched and smooth, as if she had never worn shoes, seemed to Ann to have lost its spring. She picked her way with the blank gaze of the sleepwalker, lips slightly parted.

Ann couldn't help staring at her firm white bosoms, the smooth swell of her stomach. She felt the affliction of her own bony body, thick neck, protruding collarbones, shortsightedness. She imagined Fiamma on her hands and knees, begging for mercy.

Fiamma stepped unsteadily into her thin, black racing costume. She tied a striped towel about her waist and picked up her green plastic cap by the buckle from a heap of dead flowers.

Fiamma said nothing about the events of the night before as she walked slowly barefooted past Ann, along the length of the dormitory called Kitchener, now looking like a trash heap, and out the door into the gold light of the early December morning.

In chapel that day

TWELVE OF THE thirteen girls on Miss G's team trooped in late for Sunday chapel. Fiamma was not among us. Ann had promised Fiamma that she would wait for her at the door, but when she did not arrive, Ann came in with the rest of us. We stumbled in one behind another, our hatted heads bent. We were all still dazed; we floated up the blue velvet carpet that lines the center aisle, sweating, light-headed, dry-mouthed, and nauseated.

The twins, who had been up later than anyone, had come in through the side door and were still clumsily arranging the carnations, lilies, and baby's breath in two identical silver flutes on the altar. As scholarship girls, they were made to perform certain functions in the school, despite their lack of artistic ability.

Fuzzie was playing "All Things Bright and Beautiful" on the upright piano, using the damper pedal for dramatic effect, and thumping loudly. Usually, we would make the sign for the organ grinder behind her back, but today we were not doing so; from the corners of our eyes we were watching Miss G's entrance.

She strode down the aisle, her long arms swinging martially at her sides. Her sable eyes blazed, and she held her head high, tipped by her aquiline nose. Like the prow of a ship she dipped and rose proudly over the waves. Her tanned skin glowed. She stirred us with the rustle of her impeccably starched jumpsuit and the triumphant creak of her highly polished boots. She was no longer scratching with the tips of her blunt fingers, and we stopped scratching, too. She had regained her exciting air of recklessness.

The rest of the staff filed in at a distance from her, as usual. They came in pairs, hands folded and heads bowed demurely, in belted cotton dresses of pale pastel colors: mauve, light blue, and beige; Mrs. Willis wore gray, as if to match her skin, discolored from smoking too many cigarettes.

The teachers slipped silently into their places in the chapel pews and sank with a sigh of soft dresses onto their knees, burying their pale faces in their arms or hiding them in their hands. Miss G sat on the other side of the aisle from them, head back, one leg crossed over the other, one arm dangling irreverently over the back of the pew.

What happened to Fiamma in chapel

W E HEARD a great clatter at the back of the church, and the whole school turned around with a rustle of starched white Sunday dresses, sounding like a wave breaking on the shore. "I heard her swear under her breath, saying something in Italian that sounded like a curse," Fuzzie told us afterward. Fiamma was at the back door of the chapel, looking very pale, pumping her inhaler for breath and, when she had regained it, crossing herself, as she deep-curtsied in the aisle.

We had just sat down after singing to Fuzzie's accompaniment when Fiamma came in and knocked a heavy hymnbook onto the floor from the table that stood between the two back doors.

She slid into the last pew and sat beside Di, who rose to her full height and moved further along so that Fiamma would be sitting at the end of the pew, beside Ann. We turned around to catch a glimpse of Fiamma as she sat down, an expression of defiance on her face.

She said nothing to Ann, who moved slightly away from her as well, sliding onto the blue kneeler for the prayer.

While we sang "Ride On! Ride On in Majesty," Fiamma grew increasingly pale, and even Ann's sallow skin looked rosy beside hers. Then we heard a dull thud, as Fiamma slumped forward in the pew and her head struck the wood. She had never fainted before — never made herself faint for Miss G the way we all had done — but she fainted that Sunday morning. Perhaps she did not make herself faint at all; perhaps she just fainted.

Miss Nieven, who was at that moment climbing the steps to

take up her high position in the granite pulpit for her sermon, glanced back on hearing the thud, clasping her ivory-backed prayerbook to her flat spinster breast, as if she would rush down from the stone steps to assist the Princess. But we heard the squelch of Miss G's crepe soled boots as she strode fast along the blue-carpeted aisle to rescue Fiamma. Miss G stood over Fiamma possessively and glared about with a look which was both menacing and aghast.

It was Fiamma whom Miss G rescued on the Sunday Fiamma disappeared.

Our hearts fluttered, as we watched Miss G making Fiamma put her head down between her knees and then leading her down the aisle, her head drooping limply onto Miss G's shoulder, feeling Miss G's breath on her cheek, the soft swell of her boosie, we could see. We saw the light streaming in aslant through the narrow stained-glass windows: red and blue and yellow, like a rainbow.

Miss G led Fiamma out into the cool of the garden, and Fiamma sat on the whitewashed wall under the loquat tree in her white Sunday dress and undid the mother-of-pearl button at her neck, we all imagined, as we stood to say the Nicene Creed. *I believe in God the Father, and God the son,* we intoned, thinking of Miss G sitting on the wall beside Fiamma and smoking a cigarette, holding it under her hand, so Miss Nieven would not notice if she came upon her suddenly. When Miss G told Fiamma to, she must have taken off her panama hat and set it down on the wall. Fiamma must have leaned her head against Miss G's shoulder. It was Fiamma who got to sit there under the cool dark leaves of the loquat tree and feel the breeze lift the hem of her tunic very gently and watch Miss G blow smoke rings, until she asked if Fiamma felt all right now, in her deep hoarse man's voice.

On the front steps

ON THE AFTERNOON Fiamma disappeared we were told to gather on the front steps of the Dutch-gabled school building. We milled around on the red, polished front steps where the two friable sandstone lions stood, and still stand, like sentinels.

Our heads throbbed, and we were nauseated. The twins threw up in the hydrangeas, then sprawled on the steps, their knees apart, wiping the spittle from their wide mouths and holding their flat foreheads in their hands. The sickly scent hung in the heavy air.

The sun disappeared behind clouds, but it was still hot. The oak trees dipped down, dark and heavy. There was a whine of mosquitoes, and from time to time a hand slapped against an arm or a leg, catching a slow one. We waited to line up, grumbling about having to go off on a walk in the early afternoon, rather than being allowed to plunge into the cool of the pool, just because of reports of a thundershower and the other teachers' fears of lightning. Usually, Miss G would shield us from their fears, but not today. Perhaps it was Miss G herself who had suggested this walk.

No one knew why we were kept waiting so long in the heat before starting on the walk. Perhaps, had we left sooner, nothing more would have occurred.

Preparations for a walk

EVEN WITH THE CLOUD cover it was getting hotter by the minute. We sweated in our earth-colored tunics, our heavy lace-up shoes. We were trying to shake off the aftereffects of the midnight feast: the sardines floating in oil, the peaches swimming in syrup, the spiked pineapple juice. We were thinking of Fiamma fainting in chapel.

Meg said her mother had often fainted when she was preggie. One time Meg saw her mother fall down from the table where she was turning around, having a hem pinned up. Perhaps that was Fiamma's problem, Meg lisped. Ann told her not to be so dumb: Fiamma had not even got the curse, so how could she possibly be preggie?

Fuzzie said, "Maybe, if you do it with another woman in the dark, you can get preggie." Ann told her not to be so absurd, that you needed a man, obviously.

"Well, she could have been more of a sport and waited a couple of weeks before taking her turn to faint; she was just showing off, again," Di said, scornfully.

"And did you see how she upset Miss G?" Mary added.

Fiamma at last sauntered up and sprawled alone in silence in the shadows of the lions on the last step of the Dutch-gabled building. She sat, tracing letters in the dust with the end of a stick and then erasing them with her lace-up shoe. No one sat near her. Ann remained perched on the step above Sheila and began reading *The Life of Charlotte Brontë* by Gaskell in a small, blue, leather-backed volume Sheila had lent her.

We grew silent when Miss G approached.

Miss G and Fiamma

WE TURNED QUIET as Miss G came striding through a side door in her usual uniform of crepe-soled boots and khaki jumpsuit. She stood before us; she looked up the stairs. Her clothes were as neat as ever, her boots as highly lacquered, but, for the first time, Miss G's eyes were shaded from the glare and from us by small, round, wire-rimmed sunglasses. The glasses glinted at us ominously in the glare. She asked us what we were waiting for, kingdom come? Why had we not lined up by now? She told us to hurry up and get lined up two by two. We could see she was in an anxious mood.

Miss G strode over to Fiamma and bent toward her and asked her something, probably if she was feeling better. Fiamma slumped sulkily in the shadows. She traced letters in the sand, her head slightly to one side, her skin so white and her hair so pale she looked almost as though she did not exist. She did not bother to look up. We heard her say quite clearly in her bored, truculent tone that she was suffering from pains. Miss G bent her head down further and whispered something softly. She must have told her to hush.

There was a pause, a moment of silence. We all looked at one another, raised our eyebrows, goggled our eyes. Miss G crouched down beside Fiamma; she put her arm around her shoulder, and whispered in her ear. We could see there was more than longing in Miss G's eyes now; there was fear. Cajoling, we could see, Miss G was cajoling; she was making promises. She was placating. She was making jokes. She was trying to make Fiamma smile.

But Fiamma did not smile. She did not even pay attention to Miss G. Fiamma was enjoying her moment of power, we were sure. Instead the same distant look came over her face as it had the first time we had seen her in the dormitory. She seemed to look through Miss G, as though she did not recognize her, or as though she were not there, as though Fiamma were staring at the hydrangea bushes behind her where the Trevelyan twins had vomited.

Fiamma flicked her pale plait back from her shoulder and looked around distractedly. She rose and walked away from Miss G slowly in her careless way and went toward Ann, but Ann already had a partner. Ann was standing next to Mary Skeen, so Fiamma was obliged to follow along at the end of the line, alone.

The walk itself

> There was nothing but heat
> And above, the white sky.
> We did not know whom we would meet
> Or where Fiamma was to lie.

WE FOLLOWED Miss G down the driveway in silence. The sun had softened the recently tarred surface, and our heavy lace-up shoes pressed into it. We smelled the tar, as we walked, two-by-two, through the iron gates and across the veld. We stumbled on in our dark brown tunics. We were lost out there. There was nothing to see except dull fields and a sky, scattered with an occasional cloud, black-bellied and bulbous, and in the distance a shimmer of heat.

The light, the odors, the fatigue, the nausea, the memories of the night before — flashes of white flesh in the moonlight, Miss G standing with the scarf like a halter around Fiamma's neck, made it hard for us to think straight. Occasionally, one of us dropped down into the long grass and wriggled forward in the dust on our stomach and elbows, playing Red Indians, as we had done as small children. The twins and Mary started to play horsie, but Miss G soon put a stop to childish games. Fiamma dragged her feet at the end of the line. She looked sullen, with her pouting mouth.

Miss G suddenly burst into song. She had a sweet Welsh voice that her strong appearance belied. As she sang, she swung her arms. She recovered more and more of the bounce in her step as we went along, going farther and farther from the school into the wilderness. She strode on beside us, hatless, slim, and strong. She looked brave and beautiful. Behind her dark head the sky seemed whiter. We took it all in: the vast sky, the gray branches of a dead tree, the silver wattle leaves scintillant in the valley, the low, blue hills crouched menacingly in the distance.

We, too, swung our arms, as we attempted to march as straight as she, picking up our step. We sang lustily, tears in our eyes, moved by the sound of her alto voice and by the words of the hymn, which was her, and therefore our, favorite hymn. She lifted her head, and her voice rang out to the horizon:

> Bring me my Bow of burning gold:
> Bring me my Arrows of desire:
> Bring me my Spear: O Clouds unfold!
> Bring me my Chariot of fire.

Even Meg Donovan sang our Protestant hymn, as we strode across the dry veld. The only one not singing was Fiamma. She was dragging her feet in silence, flicking her long plait back from her face. She looked sulky and disconsolate. She pumped her inhaler, breathing loudly and coughing her shallow cough. She was not sweating like the rest of us, and her face was pale.

Miss G glanced back at her from time to time, and when she did so, we could see the dark turmoil in her face. She interrupted her singing to encourage Fiamma onward.

"Why do you want to go so far in this beastly heat?" Fiamma asked in a loud voice. But Miss G pressed forward, as though there were some urgent purpose to our march.

When we looked back we could see Fiamma receding slowly, dissolving in the haze of heat and dust. She was farther and farther behind. We realized she must have stopped dead in her tracks. Miss G halted the march.

Her face was as somber as the clouds above us. We watched her stride back to Fiamma, a frail, flickering figure in the heat, standing in the dusty tracks, her head hanging on her chest. We could see from the way Fiamma waved her slender arms and hands about that she was objecting to going further. Miss G was exhorting Fiamma onward. We stood in a silent crescent, watching the drama unfold, waiting. We saw Miss G put her hand to her wire-rimmed glasses to slide them down her nose, we presumed, to make Fiamma look her in the eye. They returned to us together.

When we approached the shade trees along the banks of the river, we broke ranks before being told to do so. We rushed impulsively toward the water, pulling off our shoes, tucking up our tunics, and scrambling down the bank. We waded in; we splashed one another's hot faces; we skipped over the burning stones. Fuzzie slipped and fell in the gray mud and had to be helped to her feet.

We watched Fiamma stroll off downstream. No one followed. From a distance we saw her bend over, staring at her reflection in the water. It appeared that she was trying to splash some of the cool water up between her legs.

What we remember most clearly about that afternoon

THE HEAT and the mosquitoes and the flies. The flies were black and iridescent green and numberless. They alighted on our sweating flesh; they tickled; they gorged; they bit.

The stench of the latrines.

The disk of the sun, a dull silver. The stifling air in the valley. The hot air seemed white.

The afternoon wore on, hazy and dreadful with damp heat. The air was as heavy as steam on our faces. It was too hot to climb up the bank again. We all stayed down at the edge of the water, our heads pounding with the sun, the aftereffects of the alcohol, the lack of sleep. Our mouths were dry; our temples pulsed. Mosquitoes buzzed around our ankles and our calves. We kept moving slowly, driven onward by the heat, the mosquitoes, the flies, the dullness of the long Sunday afternoon. We all sauntered along the bank chewing on pieces of grass, arms thrown loosely around one another's waists or shoulders, smacking at mosquitoes, wiping the sweat from our brows, our shadows mingling.

There was nothing to do.

Di, with her arm slung lazily around Meg's shoulder, walked in front; the Trevelyan twins, arms around one another's waists, followed. Then came Ann, walking beside Mary and Sheila and Pamela, with Ann sucking on the end of a piece of grass and holding forth about the dangers of polio and the risks of contagion in our school. Lizzie, pale and alone, her hair tied back neatly in a ponytail, walked behind; and, coming last, picking her way with her soft-soled feet and her odd, catlike walk and complaining, Fuzzie, saying she had a terrible headache and was particularly hot because of the vest her dead mother had told her to wear at all times and because the mosquitoes were attacking her.

From time to time thunder struck in the distance. Fuzzie limped and called out, "I wish it would rain."

"It will never rain again," Sheila predicted, turning her head and speaking over her shoulder.

None of us could think clearly because of the heat and our hangovers and the muffled boom of thunder. Our minds were blank in the glare.

We inched forward slowly, sweating in the silence and the heat, drawn by a strange sort of curiosity toward the rock where Fiamma lay in the shade of the wattles and the willows that leaned down over the water. From that distance she was a blur of white and pink. "Do you think she might tell on Miss G?" Meg asked Ann.

"If she is given a chance, in all probability she will," Ann said.

What we were thinking on the bank of the river

M EG WAS STILL feeling sick from all the sweet peaches swimming in syrup and the sardines floating in oil. As she walked in the shadows of the wattles along the bank of the river toward Fiamma, she remembered the afternoon when she had told Miss G about her father beating her and her sisters, when Miss G had responded by touching her knee, making everything swing around her.

Di walked by the bank of the river and remembered a game she and her sister had played when they were very young. They rolled down the bank with their hands over their heads and their eyes shut, rolling over and over down the bank, helplessly.

Sheila wanted something exciting to happen, at that moment. She imagined someone might drown accidentally, or be struck by lightning, just to relieve the boredom of the afternoon.

Fuzzie walked along the bank and remembered the voices she had heard as a lonely child. She was afraid she might hear them again. She felt as though her heart had escaped her; she could feel it beating steadily, but it felt like someone else's heart, not hers.

Fiamma among the wattles

WE ALL ADVANCED toward Fiamma in silence, a compact group, our shadows mingling. We saw things obscurely through the tremble of the heat and the steamy air. There was little sign of the approaching storm now, apart from the continuous growl of thunder. The riverbanks were swept clean, like scoured blades; the trees cast somber shadows. Reflected in the surface of the water were the heavy sky, the clouds, the occasional swallows, dipping down around us.

Fiamma was still stretched out on the gray rock in the shade of the wattles. We were moving toward her slowly. Wild white irises grew nearby, and bright butterflies danced around one another over her head. One hand trailed in the water, the other, behind her head. Her legs looked very pale and slim. She seemed asleep or, at least, content and calm. The only thing moving was the hem of her dress, fluttered by a faint breeze.

When she felt us draw near, she sat up and looked at us. She put her hand to her eyes to shield them from the sun.

We all stood there in the silence by the river.

She said, "What are you all staring at, anyway?"

It was then that we got the idea: "Let's play the game of truth!"

Di Radfield and Miss G

MISS G STRODE through the wattles, snapping the twigs beneath the soles of her boots. Her impeccably ironed jumpsuit rustled, and her round glasses glinted once again. "Come with me, Radfield," she called out imperiously.

Miss G offered her a cigarette. They went off for a smoke all on their own. We watched them go together, whispering. Miss G had never allowed anyone to smoke with her before. She had always forbidden it. For years afterward Di could remember the taste of that cigarette.

They sat under the wattles, smoking and watching the dragonflies skim over the water. Di did not really like it; it made her feel sick, particularly because she was already feeling so, but after that day she took it up: she kept reaching for another.

They dipped their hands into the water. Miss G had often told her, before Fiamma's arrival, that she was the best swimmer on the team, the strongest, the most enduring, but that day, while they were smoking, Miss G told her that she should know the truth. Di already knew what she was going to say, which was that Fiamma was a much better swimmer than Di would ever be, that Fiamma would always beat her in the end, that what Di had was simply endurance, but that Fiamma had it all.

"She's the real thing," Miss G told Di, while the sun beat

down on the gray water, and Di learned to pull hard on a cigarette and then stub it out beneath the heel of her shoe.

Rain

O N THE DECEMBER DAY Fiamma disappeared, it rained
for the first time in months. We could hardly remember
the last time. It suddenly started raining hard while we were
down by the river, and we had to take shelter in the picnic hut.
It was because of the rain that we came to play the game of
truth with Fiamma.

We heard it in the leaves before we felt it, a rustling, like the
wind. Then everything came on very fast. The clouds opened,
and a waterfall descended on us. The wind picked up so hard, it
blew the water sideways. The big drops became hailstones that
came down brutally, like grapeshot. Lightning forked across the
sky, scattering us. Some ran, screaming, to shelter under the
nearest trees; some rushed into the thatched picnic hut, which
was set up below the graves by the side of the river with a few
rickety wooden tables and benches and a beaten-earth floor.

The two privies, deep holes in the earth infested with flies,
were at the back. Their stench was barely mitigated by the smell
of lime, and when it rained, it became overpowering.

The hail continued to pound down steadily on the thatched
roof, while we huddled at the tables. We listened and watched
the red earth spatter, forming deep pools, and played the game
of truth. We wanted Fiamma to tell us what had happened with
Miss G the night before.

Where was Miss G?

N O ONE WAS SURE exactly where Miss G had gone after Di came back to us. She seemed to have vanished with the coming of rain. When Fuzzie asked after her, Meg said she had seen her go to the privy, that she must have been in there all the while, but we could not imagine how anyone could have shut herself up there for so long. Pamela said she thought she had fallen asleep at the back of the picnic hut, where she had heard heavy breathing. Fuzzie said she was certain that she had smelled smoke while we were playing. Afterward we thought she might very well have been sitting at the back, listening and watching, able to overhear the rude things Fiamma was saying.

Fiamma resisted playing the game with us, but not for the reason we had expected: she was not interested in keeping her secret; she wanted us to know what she had done for us, but she no longer thought of it as a game. Nothing obliged her to say what she did. Afterward we wondered what Miss G must have thought, if she had overheard us.

Fuzzie said, "Perhaps Fiamma had always wanted to play with us, and she was just doing her Princess act and waiting to be asked."

The game of truth

I T WAS ANN'S TURN on the sidelines. It was she who caught Fiamma with her hand at the bottom of the pile. We held Fiamma's hand down, so she would have to answer the question.

Ann looked at Fiamma, and her small red eyes shimmered behind her glasses in the shadows of the picnic hut. We could hear the hail beating down on the thatched roof as Ann asked Fiamma, "What happened with Miss G last night? Why do you have pains? Are you bleeding?"

Fuzzie said, "You are only supposed to ask her one question."

Fiamma said nothing. There was a long silence as we all stared at Fiamma and waited. We could hear her shallow, ragged breathing and saw her hand going to her pocket for her inhaler. Meg clutched the little camphor bag around her neck and asked, "Did you play St. Agnes's Eve with Miss G?"

Bobby Joe put up her hands in prayer and made little kissing movements with her lips.

We all laughed.

Fiamma took out her inhaler and pumped.

The hail was coming down hard as stones, tearing at the wild irises that grew along the bank of the river, the low scrub, and the thatched roof of the picnic hut. We all gathered around Fiamma, listening to the hail and smelling the latrines and the wet earth and the faint odor of smoke. The red mud was running down the bank to the river, while we were laughing and making kissing noises and waiting for Fiamma's reply. After a while Di said, "You have to answer," and we all took it up, clapping and chanting, "Answer, answer, answer. Give us the truth, Princess Fiamma! Princess Fiamma!" Fiamma sat in silence, looking stiff and bored and watching the hail fall.

Sheila asked, "Why did you faint in chapel this morning?"

Fiamma said, "I told you. I have pains," and she got up and tried to walk out of the circle, but we were barring her way. We pulled at her tunic; we grabbed at her legs; Di got up and pushed on her shoulders; we made her sit down. Besides, there was nowhere to go in the rain. "Not so fast, Princess Fiamma.

Sit down, sit down," Di said. Fiamma sat. She crossed her arms. She scowled.

Di said, "You have to tell us what happened last night. It's the rule of the game."

Fiamma sat cross-legged, her head held high. She said, "What do you think happened?"

Ann said, "Did you *do* it with Miss G? Did you do it for *real*? Is that why you're in pain?"

Di asked, "You're not a *virgin* anymore?"

Meg said, "You actually did it with *Miss G?*" and pulled her mouth down in a grimace of disgust.

Fiamma looked at us with her blank stare. She looked very bored and tired, and she pulled at the end of her plait. There were dark circles under her eyes, and her breathing was fast and shallow. She said, "I did what you asked me to do."

Meg said, "But we just asked you to be *nice.*"

Di, who had confessed to letting a boy put his finger up her winkie, said, "You were a *lezzie* with Miss G? Yuck. *Disgusting,*" and sounded as if she were going to be sick.

Fuzzie said, "You played Madeline and Porphyro *for real* with Miss G?"

Fiamma shrugged her shoulders and said in her low, slow voice, "Oh, grow up, all of you, can't you?" She put her hand to her pocket again, searching for her inhaler, and said in a loud, firm voice, "Someone should report your Miss G to the authorities. Someone should close this prison down. I'm going to make sure my father hears about all of this."

Di said, "But Miss G thinks you are the best."

Fiamma looked around at us with her clear gaze. She pumped and said, "And I am the best."

We were all gathered around by now, smelling blood. Everyone drew closer, elbowing Fuzzie out of the way. The hail stopped suddenly, or perhaps it had stopped earlier, and we had not noticed. The breeze had died, too. There was the strong scent of wet earth and wet grass and the rising stench from the latrines, the smell of smoke. It was very quiet again; all we could hear was Fiamma's ragged breathing and the screaming of the cicadas. Fiamma looked down, and her face seemed to reflect the color of the beaten red earth. Then she looked up at us. She said, "Don't you understand? Miss G doesn't tell you the truth. She tells you what you want to hear, what is convenient for her. She's not all that powerful. No one learned to swim or do anything else by *desiring* it. You either know how to, or you don't. I happen to know how, and you don't."

Miss G's reaction

EVERYTHING SHIMMERED in the steamy air. The flies attacked us in droves as we ran up the bank to the graves. Miss G appeared again and told us to line up. It was getting late. It was time to go back.

She asked for Fiamma. When no one answered, she called her loudly, again and again, in her deep, mellow, man's voice. Then she sent us all off to search along the bank of the river, where she had last seen her. Fiamma was not on the edge of the bank in the high, wet grass, under the trees, in the picnic area, or on the dark, shiny rocks.

We called her name and received in reply the buzz of the flies and the scream of the cicadas, the cry of the sparrow hawk. We slapped at our legs, cheeks, and arms. We wiped the sweat from our brows. Miss G removed and wiped her steel-rimmed sunglasses with trembling hands and told us to search farther down the riverbed. The cuffs of her khaki jumpsuit were stained green, and there was red mud on her boots and her hands. She was smoking one cigarette after the other and stamping out the butts. She was striding up and down along the edge of the river. She was scratching again. She looked wild; her face and dark hair were streaked with red earth.

We ran down into the river, the damp sand seeping between our toes. The brown water looked so still we felt we could walk on it. We waded in up to our waists, looking behind rocks and rotted tree trunks and ferns, calling for her. Finally, exhausted, our clothes wet and our faces smudged and burned and bitten, we straggled back to Miss G.

The sun was sinking as she blew her whistle and told us to line up. She marched the twelve of us in silence, double-file, back across the muddy veld.

The search

IT STARTED RAINING hard again after we got back. Following months of drought, the constant rain turned the veld to mud, washed away the thin topsoil, eroded the land, and swelled the rivers. It rained on and off for days, making the search for Fiamma increasingly difficult.

Search parties were sent out with bloodhounds, as Miss Nieven had informed us they would be; they combed the long, wet grass all along the banks. The next day the river was dragged. The police searched the area for miles around. An advertisement was placed in the local papers with a photo of Fiamma in her school uniform, her swimming team badge, and her panama hat with the brim turned down so that the shadow fell on her face. It mentioned something we had never noticed, a strawberry-shaped birthmark on her shoulder. Someone reported hearing screams coming from the graves.

The detective questioned us again, this time as a group. We repeated what Di had already told him, that the last we saw of Fiamma was her lying very calmly in the shade of the frangipanis.

John Mazaboko, too, was questioned by the detective, because he knew the area where Fiamma had last been seen. It was he who tended the graves. We presumed he had not noticed anything unusual, or at any rate had not seen fit to say anything about it to the detective. But whether he had reported anything further to Miss Nieven, which she had felt it wiser not to pass on, we were never to find out.

No one mentioned Miss G.

Miss G's departure

MISS G DROVE OFF in her old, square, maroon Buick as we watched from the same dormitory window from which we had watched Fiamma arrive. Only Di went to say good-bye. We saw them sitting on the red polished steps between the sandstone lions for a moment, before Miss G rose, squared her shoulders bravely, soldierlike, and strode off to her car in her lacquered boots.

Afterward we asked Di what Miss G had said to her. Did she mention where she was while we played the game of truth? Had she heard what Fiamma had said?

Di told us that Miss G had said that she could understand very well why she had been fired. "They needed a scapegoat, and, of course, it had to be me. With their inhibited imaginations, they could not simply accept that she had disappeared. Why, she might have gone off anywhere. Anywhere there is a scandal, someone's head must roll."

Di went on to say that she had objected strenuously. "The injustice of it! After all those years of hard work. This school has never had such a successful swimming team. All those trophies we won for them! And all because of your coaching. You would have left anyway, I know, after what happened. You always sacrificed yourself for us."

Our parents' reaction

MISS NIEVEN EXPERIENCED a brief period of difficulties after Fiamma's disappearance. When the name of the school was linked to the disappearance in several articles that appeared in the local papers, there were long telephone calls; telegrams arrived in stacks. There were descriptions of Fiamma's prominent family, the area where she disappeared, the isolation and lack of supervision in our school.

The *Johannesburg Star* wrote indignantly: "What was a band of innocent young girls doing, marching for miles across bare veld in the burning heat? Why were they left to their own devices by the banks of a bilharzia-infested river? Where were the teachers? And all of this during the polio scare, which has already wrecked so many of our precious children's lives."

Initially, many of the girls' parents threatened to take them out of the school. Meg's father arrived and wanted to take all five girls home. A teacher himself, he had driven up all the way from Barberton. We watched him jump out of his battered old car in the driving rain, slamming the door, holding his worn tweed jacket with the patches on the elbows to cover his and his wife's heads, though covering more of his than hers, so that her hair clung to her damp forehead. He charged ahead, driven by righteous indignation — how could the school have been so negligent? — ascending the stairs two at a time, dragging his frumpy and faded wife between the sandstone lions, dispatching her to pack up the girls' belongings in their cardboard suitcases and to wrap up their books in brown paper parcels.

He closeted himself with Miss Nieven in her study. She had just placed a frantic call to the hospital where Fiamma's father was confined with his recurrent fevers, trying to communicate to him what she knew, and to gather his responses.

She persuaded Meg's father to leave the girls by hinting that Meg would most likely become head girl, and she did; most of the other parents eventually followed suit. It was said that if a father of five had confidence in our school, the other parents could too. None of our parents came to take us home.

Our reactions to Fiamma's disappearance

D I SAID she could not feel anything, anymore; nothing made her sad or happy. Meg acquired that blank look in her sloe eyes. She told everyone she was going to marry a rich husband, and of course, she did. Sheila stopped telling stories of doom and destruction at night in the dormitory. It was only many years later that she dared to take up her pen again, and then only to write thrillers. Mary gave all her horse books to the twins and said she was never going to ride again. Lizzie said she would become a librarian and found work in a bookstore. Fuzzie sat and stared in silence. But it was Ann, our Logical Lindt, who was the one who could not get over the loss. Sobs shook her thin body through day and night. Mrs. Looney sent her to the san, but the respite did not help. After some weeks Miss Nieven wired her parents, and she was sent alone on the endless train ride back to Salisbury. She went back to the mother who had drooping bosoms and hair on her upper lip and a maths degree from Oxford.

Ann was told not to take her books along, because she had overreached herself. Her weeping was put down to excessive reading and ambition. She was given a piece of cross-stitch and told to do it on the train and to lie down in her room on her arrival with the curtains drawn. She told us she stuffed the cross-stitch down the back of her train seat.

None of us wanted to stay on the team, now that Miss G was gone. We dropped out, one by one. We became studious, diligent. We took to listening in class and copying down exactly what the teachers said. We repeated their words verbatim in our examination papers. We toned down our natural rebelliousness. We wore pale powder to cover our blemishes. We walked in silence down the long corridors, our heads lowered slightly, our gaze on the ground, our books clutched to our chests. Even Di spoke softly, and blushed, and began stooping to hide her height. We spent our time bent over our books, trying to absorb all the facts we had avoided until then, too busy swimming for Miss G and God.

We spent our free time preparing for the school dance. Some of our parents ordered our dresses from overseas. Di's white, strapless dress, which showed off her smooth, broad shoulders, came from Harrods, Sheila's, from Liberty's. Meg made her own dress out of pink taffeta and sewed seed pearls around the high neck, and she looked lovelier than anyone else.

We decorated the hall with an Oriental theme: we put fans on the walls and Chinese lanterns around the lights. We invited boys this time, and we rehearsed the presentation of our choices to Miss Nieven over and over. Sheila kept muttering, "Miss Nieven, this is Mark Bell. Miss Nieven this is Mark Bell," as she walked up and down the pergola, but when the time came, she said, "Mark Bell, this is Miss Nieven."

Miss Nieven wore a long Black Watch tartan skirt and a black velvet top. To our surprise and amusement, she joined in when we did the hokeypokey. She put her left foot in, took her left foot out, then shook it all about, lifting her scrawny arms and turning herself. We all joined in.

Our bodies had grown soft, curvaceous, by then. We lolloped around in the water and tittered for effect. No one swam the crawl, that powerful oceangoing stroke; we swam sidestroke or breaststroke, or we did not swim at all. We all feared muscles in our arms and legs. We decided that what Miss G had had to teach us was not very useful for the business of living, after all. We were too old for cracks now. We were worried about our future. Some of us wanted to go on to the universities, where we hoped to meet a mate.

We no longer ran across the veld out-of-bounds to the river and the graves. We avoided the graves. We never climbed up on the grave and played dead again; we never played the game of truth; we kept our secrets to ourselves. We had no secrets; we no longer dreamed, or if we dreamed, it was of boys, real boys with crew cuts and thick white socks and thick-soled boots.

PART SIX

REMEMBRANCE

→>·<←

Sunday morning

IT IS ALREADY HOT, and the palms beyond the window rustle. We sit in the dining room and sip our tea from tin mugs that scald our lips. There is the familiar odor of oranges and dust.

Ann's gray hair is still wet from her shower and falls over her high, shiny forehead. She cracks open an egg, and her small eyes squint in the bright light. Fuzzie has forgotten to brush her hair. She dusts bread crumbs from her chest. Di stares in gloomy silence, writing with a thick silver pen. She coughs her smoker's cough. Meg and Mary, still late sleepers, have not yet come down from the dormitory.

Miss Nieven wanders in for a moment, wearing the same mauve dress with the amber beads, as though she has not slept all night. She hovers, a dark figure, with the sun at her back. She looks so frail we feel death could come at any moment and whisk her away from the thin anchorage of her cane. She whistles as she wishes us a good day. We start to rise from our seats, scraping back our chairs as we did so many years ago, but she gestures to us to sit down. We expect her to say grace as she always did: "For what we are about to receive, may the Lord make us truly thankful," but instead, she suggests we take a picnic to the riverbank. She says, "You will find the place quite unchanged," and she looks at us blindly, until Di rises and goes over to her and gives her our check. She clutches the folded paper in her knotted hands. She puts on thick glasses and opens it and holds it up close to read the sum and then slips it into her pocket. She leans toward Di and whispers something in her ear and kisses her cheek. She smiles at us, nods, and then wanders out the door into the bright light, tapping with her cane on the stone floor.

Fuzzie says she dreamed her old dream of the child drowning, but this time she knew it was Fiamma she was trying to rescue from the water. She was trying to hold on to her, but she was slipping from her arms. Her body was naked and slippery as though she were covered with grease, and she was falling down into the darkness at the bottom of the sea.

Di tells us how she met up with Miss G years later, when Di was out here to visit. She found Miss G sitting in a faded raincoat on the steps of a department store. Miss G rose and accosted her and insisted she have tea. They took the double-decker bus to her small but spotless studio in Hillbrow. Di had had no desire to have tea with her, but she had insisted. She told Di she had not been able to find work teaching after they fired her. She said she had been obliged to take a housekeeper's job. She kept feeding Di one slice of cake after another and bringing out more sandwiches and little packets of sugar she must have stolen from some tearoom.

She brought up Fiamma. She said that Fiamma, to her surprise, had thrown herself at her wildly. "The truth is, she seduced me. At fourteen she was no virgin. She knew how to go about it, I assure you. She was such an exasperating brat, after all, and yet . . ."

At the graves

THE MIXTURE of flies, mosquitoes, and heat is the same as it was years ago, as it is, everywhere, in places of this sort. We can hear the buzzing of the fat flies from the latrines — the kind with glossy, green wings — and the hum of the mosquitoes. "Enough to drive you mad," Ann says, as we all walk up from the riverbank toward the graves.

We are here together again, going through the long, wet grass and the low scrub, up the bank to the graves of Sir George Harrow and his dog, Jock. The gray-branched frangipanis still spread their pale blossoms. Nothing seems changed except the dog's gravestone, which has been spray-painted yellow.

First we talk, then we fall silent. It is the dead quiet we noticed when Fiamma first walked into the dormitory and stood there, blinking her dark eyelashes, and it all began.

We are crowded together around the cracked marble tombstone with its worn inscription. We can hear the soft gurgle of the slowly flowing water and the call of the dove. There is the dreamlike intensity of things.

Di stands at one end of Sir George's tomb and says, "Meg, perhaps you should say a proper prayer." Meg kneels down and recites the Twenty-third Psalm.

We all remember how Meg spread Fiamma's loose hair around her shoulders and crossed her hands on her still chest. We covered her slender body with the white irises that still grow here, and the honeysuckle that climbs around the tomb. We had never seen Fiamma look as lovely: her delicate features, her flaxen ringlets, her oval face — as exquisite a countenance as we had ever beheld, with her chin tilted slightly upward, as though there were something she still wanted to offer us.

Together we manage now to move the slab of heavy marble that covers the airtight tomb. We make an opening wide enough to slip through, as she did years ago. Dust rises in the air and drops onto the gray branches and leaves of the frangipani. We look down into the darkness, and see Sir George's bones, which have been lying there for so long, so peacefully. They are as white and dry as shells, and beside them lies another set, along with the scraps of brown tunic and the shriveled brown lace-up shoes.

We remember

WHILE FIAMMA was talking about Miss G during the game of truth, Di says she passed out. For a momemt Di saw black as Fiamma spoke about Miss G. When Fiamma said Miss G did not tell the truth, Di lost consciousness for a moment. When she came back to herself, she told Fiamma that if she could be Miss G's Madeline, she could be ours, too. "You have to be our Madeline now," Di said firmly and put her hand over Fiamma's mouth.

Fiamma started up and struggled with Di. They wrestled, holding on to each other, pulling and scratching and biting, but Fiamma was no match for Di. Di had her by the arm; she was twisting it. All Fiamma could do was escape from her grip. She broke loose and smacked Di hard across the face, panting. For a moment Di, stunned, stood motionless.

No one moved.

Fiamma ran from us. She bolted through the circle and ran

out of the picnic hut up the bank toward the graves. She ran as fast as she could in her brown tunic, her little camphor bag bouncing on her back, her heavy lace-up shoes sinking and slipping in the red mud, the long grass, wetting her legs but racing on in the steamy air.

Fiamma, who was so fast in the water, was not fast on land.

"After her," Di yelled. We shouted and rushed forward as a group, running through long grass and scrub, excited by the chase. "Madeline, Madeline, you are going to be our Madeline," we shouted wildly.

The shouting made us feel brave and reckless. Our faces were shouting masks. In the hot, steamy sunlight we were running and slipping and jumping over everything in sight: deep dongas, rocks. Our sweating bodies were close, but we were running separately, in our distinctive ways. Meg ran gracefully, her well-turned ankles and her wasp waist revolving swiftly; Di ran aggressively, long-legged, knobby-kneed, arms swinging; the twins, side-by-side, indistinguishable, snub-nosed, white-haired, their sinewy calves shining; Ann, spindly and thin, coming behind; Sheila, like an ostrich, as if on stilts; and finally Fuzzie, her peg legs visible in the glare. We were a pack, giving off high-pitched screams.

The sound of our voices came back to us, bouncing off the wattle trees. We were hot, feverish, nauseated. Our minds were blank. Our nerves were jangled from lack of sleep, the long walk, the singing, Fiamma's words. For a moment, we lost her under the trees. It was cooler and darker there. We all stopped and looked about, our eyes glinting. "Where did she go?" Di cried and wiped her forehead and blinked. We could see the red imprint of Fiamma's fingers on Di's cheek. The faint smell of Miss G's smoke hung in the air like a pall.

Then we heard a shallow cough.

Fiamma had flung herself down under a bush to steady her breathing. She was halfway up the bank.

"Leave me alone," Fiamma cried, as she staggered out into the bright light and up the bank toward the graves and the open air. We hesitated. Perhaps we would have given up. But then she tripped and fell over something.

We were onto her.

Meg, who was the fastest runner, caught up with her at the graves and gave her a playful tap on her behind. "Lie down and be our Madeline," she said, giggling, accustomed to watching her father beat her younger sisters.

Fiamma panted, clutching her throat, "Leave me alone. I can't breathe. Ann, make them go away," she begged and clambered up onto Sir George's tomb to escape. We were sure she was only pretending not to be able to breathe, just playing at being the victim, the martyr, once again.

Ann, who had followed along with the rest of us, still clutching her blue book in her hands, shook her head and said, "Too late, Princess Fiamma."

"Get her! Get her!" Sheila said, pulling a piece of long, wet grass from the ground and pretending to whip Fiamma's white legs. Fiamma jumped up and down on the gray marble as though she were trampling on grapes, kicking out at us as we slapped at her. She did not seem to understand that we were only playing.

"Smack her! Smack her!" Pamela shouted, grabbing a stick from the ground and waving it in the air. "Down, down, down on your bed, Madeline!" she commanded.

We were all gathered around now in the shade of the frangipani tree. Sweat blinded us. Our heads throbbed, and our mouths were dry. The mosquitoes swarmed in droves, biting our arms and calves. We smacked at them. We echoed Pamela, "Madeline, Madeline, you have to be our Madeline."

Fiamma's jiggling white legs made us giggle. She looked like a puppet on a string, her arms and legs jerking. Our eyes glinted with merriment. There was Princess Fiamma, her face streaked with mud and sweat, jumping up and down on the gray marble slab that covered the illustrious bones of Sir George. She had lost her velvet hair ribbon in the chase, and her pale hair tumbled crazily across her forehead and into her eyes. Her chest rose and fell. She was panting and wheezing.

Sheila was putting it all down in her head.

Fiamma's face was puce, and a thin trickle of blood seeped down her calf where someone had scratched her with a stick. The blood frightened her, and she whispered hoarsely, "Stop it, please. You are behaving like a bunch of barbarians." She was slowing down, as though treading water. She was jumping back and forth, from one side to the other of the tomb, driven by our hands, our sticks, and pieces of wet grass. She was breathing loudly.

Di was growing impatient. "Keep still! Do what you did for Miss G," she shouted and threw her stick hard at Fiamma. It caught her in the right eye. Fiamma lifted her hand to it and plumped down blindly on the marble. She lunged out at us and scratched and bit and pulled at hair; she kicked at us angrily, catching Di in the bosom.

"You idjut, you got my boosie!" she shouted, suddenly furious. "Get her! Get her!" she urged, and the twins jumped up onto the tomb. One on each side, they held Fiamma down.

"Go for the bum! Go for the bum!" Pamela shouted. Then we all took up the chant: "Go for the bum!"

When Fiamma tried to get up, the twins pushed her down hard, one on either side. They flipped her over onto her stomach and pulled up her tunic and smacked her behind with a stick. We all smacked her behind with sticks. Meg smacked harder and harder, yelling loudly, her dark hair falling into her eyes.

Fiamma was scratching and biting desperately, more and more frightened, and the more she fought, the tighter the twins were obliged to hold her down. If she had let us play with her, perhaps, nothing much would have happened. She tried to cry out, but only her ragged breathing escaped. Anyway, the only ones who could have heard her were the swimmers and God and, perhaps, Miss G.

"Give me a snot rag. Shut her up," Di shouted, while we all watched, fascinated. Di grabbed Ann's dirty handkerchief and shoved it into Fiamma's mouth. Her face was purple now, her eyes bloodshot. She was trying to say something or reach her inhaler with her waving hands, but Ann grabbed them and tied them with her tunic belt. Mary tied her feet together. Then all we could hear was Fiamma's ragged heaving and panting.

"Hey, quit hurting her, she can't breathe properly," Fuzzie said softly, but no one heeded. We did not let her through the circle we had formed around the tomb. We pushed Fiamma's gag further into her mouth, and someone pulled down her knickers, exposing her bare behind. She lay sprawled before us, a white doll, helpless, our plaything.

"I'm Porphyro, and she's my Madeline," Meg cried.

"Do her, do her," everyone chanted.

"Up the bum, up the bum," Di called out.

No one was paying attention to Fiamma's face.

In the blinding white light she lay on the marble tomb, our victim, bound hands and feet, as on an altar, with the priestess, Ann, brandishing her book, watching what was happening, the slaves gathered around the victim, leaning over her, the rest of us, inserting whatever came to hand — it was mainly sticks, though Lizzie, who was always more elegant than the rest, had found the stem of a wild rose — into Fiamma's behind. One by one we thrust something hard and sharp into her tight, child's orifices, while she gagged and tried to scream.

Swimming

W E STARE into one another's eyes from both sides of the grave, as though gathered around a table for an evening meal. Our faces are brought nearer by the light of the southern sunset. Our makeup has washed away. We wear no jewelry, no fancy clothes, no camouflage. We see the lines, the sag and fall, the indistinct, watery gazes. We see ourselves in one another's sad eyes, relieved that this reunion has ended. No one speaks.

A change goes through us: Meg slings an arm around Di's shoulder; Fuzzie hands Ann a handkerchief; Bobby Joe removes a burr from Bobby Jean's sleeve. For a moment we huddle together, as though the presence of one another can shut out the outside world, the watery wastes, the fast-encroaching dark.

We stand together and watch the sunset char the sky, as if for the first time. We look across the marble grave as the red light kindles the river's memory, sparks down the hills, flames the frangipanis, ignites the vast sky. Lit up, our small world widens.

Fuzzie suggests we swim the river. We mention bilharzia and the possibility of quicksand. She does not listen but runs through the lion-colored grass down the bank to the water. Her modesty vanishes in the blinding glare. Piece by garish piece, she strips. We notice she still wears her vest, as her mother told her to do, so many years ago. Fuzzie's milky, freckled flesh is still firm and fresh. Without her clothes she looks almost like the girl we remember from long before, the tender, plump body, tight in its pink skin, and the tight auburn curls. We watch her wade into the brown water and pat the surface with her palms. "It's warm. Come on in," she says and floats on her back, staring up at the blazing sky. Then she swims out to the middle of the river and dives down and comes up somewhere else. She keeps plunging.

The twins are the next to discard their identical long gray skirts and worn tennis shoes. Then everyone undresses. Ann removes her glasses, unbuttons her shirt, and says, "Oh, hell, why not?" You can still see her ribs, and her skin looks greenish in the glare. Even Di pulls off her dark dress and lace corsets, and rolls down the dark stockings she still wears. She lumbers into the water. Meg's bare body dazzles, her breasts still firm, her nipples pink, her stomach smooth. We splash one another and shout like the wild girls we once were.

We imagine Miss G striding up and down the bank, her yellow whistle between her lips, watching us swim, exhorting us to slice through the water, to knock them flat.

Meg swims sidestroke swiftly, going through the clinging reeds and the glistening rocks. She bobs up and down. Di does a fast crawl, avoiding rocks and rotted tree trunks and ferns. Sheila turns on her back and strikes out, stretching her arms straight, brushing her ears with her arms, kicking with the regular rhythm that Miss G taught her.

We all swim down the river. There is a distant call as of a dreamer's voice, clear and shrill. We go onward in silence, expectant.

Then, look, there she is, out there, kicking up a rainbow spray. We feel her presence drawing us on, as we swim fast, striking out bravely through the dark water.

We see Fiamma, our dead sister, our wild girlhood, our lost dreams. We watch her, so slow and languorous on land, cutting

RAW LAND

G·K
Hall
&Cº

**Also by Luke Short
in Large Print:**

Savage Range
Barren Land Showdown
High Vermilion
A Man Could Get Killed
Station West

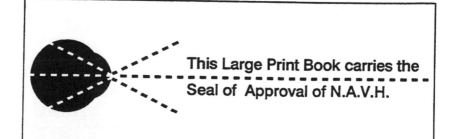

This Large Print Book carries the
Seal of Approval of N.A.V.H.

RAW LAND

Luke Short

G.K. Hall & Co.
Thorndike, Maine

Published in 1996 by arrangement with
Kate Hirson and Daniel Glidden.

G.K. Hall Large Print Western Collection.

The text of this Large Print edition is unabridged.
Other aspects of the book may vary from the original edition.

Set in 16 pt. News Plantin by Minnie B. Raven.

Printed in the United States on permanent paper.

Library of Congress Cataloging in Publication Data

Short, Luke, 1908–1975.
    Raw land / Luke Short.
       p.   cm.
    ISBN 0-7838-1463-1 (lg. print : hc)
    1. Large type books. I. Title.
  [PS3513.L68158R39   1996]
  813'.54—dc20   95-24421

RAW LAND

Chapter One

A Bleak Welcome

As the long freight train rolled to a groaning halt, Will Danning stepped out of the caboose door onto the rear platform and sniffed the desert night. A brakeman was framed in the door by the light of the lantern behind him.

Will said in the deep silence, "This is the Long Grade tank, isn't it?"

"That's right."

"And how long have we got?"

"Ten — fifteen minutes."

Will grunted and swung down onto the roadbed. Beside the red lantern glow, he paused to touch a match to the cigarette he had already rolled. The confusion of lights, with the match flaring suddenly, pointed up his lean, bored face for the brakeman to see. It was the face of just another big puncher, maybe twenty-five, with town clothes and a new shave and haircut, the brakeman thought. He'd got on at Hortense and he'd get off at Yellow Jacket, and now he was sick of the long ride and he'd take a stroll down the long line of cars for the night air, like they all did. The brakeman wasn't surprised to see Will

7

Danning stretch his thick shoulders and long legs, and then, whistling thinly, stroll out of sight forward. The brakeman spat over the rail and forgot him.

Which was what Will Danning hoped he would do. Once out of sight, Will tossed away his cigarette and increased his pace. Far ahead, he could see the high water tank and its skeleton legs against the star-spangled sky, and this side of it there was a tool shed, he remembered.

He was hurrying toward it when he heard a low whistle off in the brush beyond the right of way. He headed for it, his high heels digging into the steep slope of the bank and checking his speed. At the bottom of the slope he paused, and then he heard a low laugh in the night.

"Milt?" he called softly.

The laugh came again, and close to him. A voice said, "You even remembered the name, Will?"

"Just so you do," Will said gently, and they met and shook hands briefly, in silence.

Will said, "What about it? Have any trouble?"

"You wouldn't call it trouble," the other voice said. "They spotted us coming in, and they stopped us and asked questions."

"Who's they?"

"Their ponies were branded Nine X."

Will grunted. "That's Case, all right. What did they want?"

"To count the herd. That seemed important to the surly blond devil bossing them. He named

8

our boundaries and asked for you and then warned us to stay close to home until he'd talked with you."

"But he didn't warn you off?"

"No." There was a pause, and the voice said with quiet humor, "You picked a lonesome spot, Will. The world ends right there, just forty feet north of the shack."

"That's what you wanted, wasn't it?"

"Exactly. But will they let us stay?"

"I'll tell you that tomorrow," Will said. The locomotive ahead began to thrash, and then the long line of cars jerked noisily. Will raised a careless hand in parting and climbed up the bank, swinging on the caboose as it trundled by.

Three hours later and some two thousand feet higher, Will Danning saw the sparse lights of Yellow Jacket blotted out by the stock pens. He threw his sacked saddle off against the pens, shouldered his war bag, and stepped off the moving train, waving to the brakeman when he came to a full stop. The train picked up speed and vanished. Will went back along the right of way, found his saddle, carried it as far as the depot platform where he left it and his war bag, and then surveyed the town. Its principal street held a few lights and a half-dozen hipshot horses at the tie rail of Hal Mohr's saloon.

The depot was at the head of the street. Will cut across the cinder apron and hit the boardwalk by Settlemeir's feed stable on the corner. Nothing had changed in ten years, not even the smell of rotting wood from the horse trough in front of the stable. He tramped on down the street, his footsteps ringing hollowly along the deserted street. As he neared the saloon the ponies lined out there turned their heads and lifted their ears as they watched him.

He didn't pause but shouldered through the swing doors of the saloon and squinted against the bright lamplight. At that moment he wore the face of a truculent man, but that might have been because of the scowl. The two men at the bar, wearing guns, who didn't turn around but observed him in the back mirror, felt a small stir of excitement at sight of him. And then his eyes became accustomed to the light, the truculence disappeared, and he tramped past them. He was a tall man, they saw, big mostly at the shoulders and in his fists, which were scarred and tufted with black hair. His face was faintly hollow-cheeked, burned brown, and his gray eyes were hooded under thick black eyebrows as dark as his hair that was covered by a very worn Stetson. The black suit with the trousers tucked into half boots they recognized as the town-going outfit of any prosperous cattleman.

He tramped past them, heading for a table in the rear that held two men. Behind them, against the back wall, there was another puncher playing solitaire.

Will came up to the table where the two men were and said to the older, "You never take a chance, do you, Case?"

The man addressed thoughtfully played a card, then raised his glance to Will. He might have been sixty, for his hair was plentifully sprinkled with gray. It capped a squarish, stubborn face, seamed and weathered and made alive only by a pair of troubled and suspicious blue eyes. He wore a mussed and careless dark suit, and carried a gun in his outside coat pocket.

He said, "Not very often. Sit down, Danning."

Will looked around the room, at the two punchers at the bar, at the single man studiously playing solitaire, and finally at the other man at the table. Then he said, "Chase these bums out of here first."

The man at the table with Case started to rise in anger, when Case shook his head. This man was thick-bodied, blond, and ugly, and the pale skin of his face was burned a deep red instead of tan. The air of iron authority in his pale eyes and the loose set of his lips told Will he was Case's foreman, the man who had questioned Milt.

Case said, "You stay, Pres. Send the boys out."

Will watched in silence while Pres whistled. The solitaire player looked up, got his boss's nod, rose, and took the other two at the bar out with him. Then Will sat down and rammed his hands deep in his pockets, after thumb-prodding his Stetson to the back of his head. He regarded the two men with taciturn hostility and waited for them to speak.

11

Case said, "You keep your engagements, any-way."

Will said dryly, "Don't bother to be polite, because I won't. This isn't any engagement. It's an order from you. The only reason I'm following it is because I figure I'll have to talk to you sooner or later, anyway. We might as well get this settled now."

Case nodded. "Chap Hale sent you word?"

"He wrote me you wanted to see me the minute I got here."

"That's right. I wanted to ask you some ques-tions."

"I'm ready."

"You've bought the old Harkins place out by the brakes, the Pitchfork brand, Chap said. That right?" When Will nodded, Case said, "I'm won-dering why."

Will smiled faintly. "Maybe I like it."

"The grass is no good. Water's scarce over there. It's a bad buy, I'd say."

"Nobody asked you," Will murmured inso-lently.

Pres Milo looked at his boss, but Case was not to be prodded. He looked baffled and un-certain, but not angry. He leaned forward now and said earnestly, "Just so we understand each other, let me tell you what we both know. The Pitchfork is against the Sevier Brakes. Nobody knows all those trails through there, but lots of people know that they lead to Sevier Valley on the other side, where a lot of vented beef is shipped. You agree?"

Will nodded.

"Now," Case said slowly, "I had a little experience with that place until I wiped Harkins and his rustlers out."

"Harkins wasn't a rustler," Will murmured. "Go on."

"And you worked for Harkins," Case finished. "You were fifteen then."

Again Will nodded. "I even took a couple of pot shots at your Nine X men before they got Harkins," he said gently. "Go on."

"That's all there is," Case said flatly. "You worked for a rustler once. And now you've bought his God-forgotten, dreary place."

"Yes."

"And I'm wondering why."

"To ranch."

Pres Milo broke in bluntly. "With five hundred head of beef?"

Will regarded him lazily. "You counted 'em?"

"I took your ramrod's word. He said you were bringin' in five hundred. It looked more like two hundred to me, but you can fill out the count with beef you steal."

Will said gently, "Fella, you're a damn liar. Milt told you two hundred."

Pres flushed. "That's enough to screen a rustlin' business."

Will raised a foot under the table and shoved Pres's knee. Pres lost his balance and went over backward in his chair. Slowly, almost indolently,

13

Will came out of his chair and around the table just as Pres crashed onto the floor on his back. Pres clawed for his gun, and Will placed a boot firmly on the wrist of Pres's gun hand and looked up at Case. Will's hands were still rammed in his pockets, and he said mildly to Case, "He's got a pretty big mouth, ain't he?"

Case was looking at his foreman, surprise in his eyes. And then a subtle shift in expression crossed his face, a look of alarm, and Will looked down. Pres had crossed his free arm over his body and drawn his gun. It was just clearing leather as Will looked down. Swiftly, savagely, Will kicked the gun out of Pres's hand, and then leaned down and hauled Pres to his feet. Pres swung wildly, and Will blocked the blow and then drove his fist into Pres's face. The heavy man fell into the next table, its legs gave way, and he crashed to the floor.

Rubbing his knuckles gently, Will looked again at Case. "If I'm goin' to get shot in the back," he drawled, "I'd better stop this, hadn't I?"

Case came out of his chair and said sharply, "Pres! Drop it, now!"

Will looked over just in time to see a chair leave Pres's hands. Will dodged it, and then Pres came at him. Will shot a fleeting glance at Case, saw that his gun wasn't drawn, and then turned his attention to Pres. He didn't wait for him; he went toward him, a low growl in his throat, knowing this would have to be short and final. The two of them met with such force that the

14

tables danced. Will brought up a knee in Pres's groin as they grappled, and when Pres knifed over in pain, he lifted an upper-cut into Pres's face that straightened the man up. Then he sent two savage hooks, a left and right, into Pres's face, following them with an elbow into his jaw. Will caught him, then, as Pres sagged unconscious into his arms. Without pausing, Will started lugging him to the door. He shifted his grip to the seat of Pres's trousers and to his collar and then, almost running, literally threw him through the door just as two of the Nine X men swung in. Pres bowled them over, and the three of them fell into a moiling tangle on the boardwalk.

Will turned his back and walked over to the table where Case, goggle-eyed and mouth agape, stood and stared at him.

"I think I'd better hide behind you," Will drawled. "They'll likely come up shootin'."

Case started for the door, and a second later two of his crew, guns in hand, rushed through the door.

Case bawled, "Put those guns away, you fools!"

They stopped and looked at Will. Sheepishly they obeyed Case's orders.

As they were going Case said to them, "Put Pres on a horse and take him home with you. Now get out!"

At that moment the bartender, who had been absent, came through the doors. Case snarled at him, "Send me a bill for this stuff, Hal," and to Will he said, "Come on!"

Will fell in beside him. They swung under the tie rail, passed the silent trio of Nine X men loading Pres on his horse, and crossed to the hotel directly opposite.

There was a dim light in the lobby, and Case stepped just inside the door. He turned and surveyed Will and said, "We'll finish this right here, Danning. I admit I tried to bluff you and scare you tonight. It kicked back on me. But I can say everything I was going to say." He paused, isolating what came next. "I've looked you up. You rodded Murray Broome's spread until he got in this shootin' scrape and disappeared. Nobody I talked to connected you with Broome at all. Everybody had a good word for you, even Chap Hale." His voice lowered to a half snarl. "All right. I'll take a man at face value! I'm a neighbor of yours until I miss cattle! Then, by God, I'll run you out of the country or kill you!"

He turned and bumped into a girl that neither of them had noticed approaching.

"Becky!" he said sharply. "What are you doing down here?"

Will couldn't see very well in that half-light. He heard a cool voice say, "Waiting for you, until I got run into, Dad. Now I'm trying to keep from yelling over a mashed foot."

Will could make out only a girl of medium height whose light hair was golden even in that half-light. He couldn't even see the color of her dress.

Case said impatiently, "Becky, meet Will Dan-

16

ning. He's our neighbor over on Harkins's old Pitchfork. Now come to bed. Good night, sir."

Becky Case didn't even have time to speak. Angus Case took a firm grip on his daughter's hand and headed resolutely for the stairs.

Will said sharply, "Wait a minute, Case!"

Case and his daughter paused, and Will tramped over to them. He still couldn't make out the girl's face, but he wouldn't be talking to her anyway. He said flatly to the older man, "You spoke your piece, and I'll speak mine. I don't aim to rustle your beef. All I want out there is to be let alone. If I'm not, you'll have more trouble on your hands than seven swarms of hornets. That's a promise. And this time, you won't be fightin' an old man that can't fight back, like Harkins."

Case watched him in the half-darkness for five full seconds, then he swung around and tramped upstairs, propelling his daughter beside him.

Will, legs spraddled, hat on the back of his head, watched them go, and his anger died. He turned his head, and through the lobby window he saw four men, one leaning far over in his saddle, line out down the street, heading north.

This, he thought bleakly, was his welcome. Anyway, he'd called Angus Case's bluff, and he would keep the Pitchfork, and that was enough. A man couldn't ask for a whole lot in this world.

A tired voice said, from the depths of one of the lobby chairs, "Still the same fire-eater, aren't you, Will?"

Will's head swiveled, and he walked toward

17

the sound of the voice. Out of the gloom an old man rose. While he couldn't see Chap Hale's face, Will remembered it — old, shrunken, paper-white, and delicately veined. He shook Chap's hand and was saddened to feel its frail bones and leathery skin.

"What are you up to, old-timer?" Will asked.

"Waiting for you."

"Let's go where I can see you," Will said. "Let's get a drink."

"If you don't mind, let's not," Chap said wearily. "I'm an old man, Will, and liquor's lost its kick. I'm tired and I'm sleepy and I'm going home. I just wanted to see you didn't come to any harm, son."

"But I want to talk to you."

"And I want to talk to you, Will, but not now. You're not in any shape to talk."

Will scowled in the dark, and Chap went on. "You're mad now, son. You'll keep me up till daylight asking me about Case and Preston Milo and how to beat them. I don't know, Will. Case is a good man, a friend of mine, one of my oldest friends. But he's scared of you. I bought your place for you. From now on, it's your fight." He paused, and then said mildly, "I'd like to ask a question, Will."

"Go ahead."

"I'm not going to be so foolish as Case and consider that you might want the Pitchfork for a cattle-stealing gang. I'm only wondering why you want it at all."

18

Will said gently, "You, too, Chap?"

"Yes, me, too. It's an ugly place, Will. It's set in the deep jaws of a canyon where the sun never rightly reaches it. Those bare hills crowd it. It's worn out, dead, evil. You're a young man and you've earned your stake. You want a place in the sun, Will, not a rathole. Why did you buy it?"

"I'm going to ranch, Chap."

Chap sighed. "I didn't think you'd tell me. Come see me in a couple of days, Will, when all this fighting is out of your blood. Good night."

Will watched him go. He was an old man now, crowding eighty, and his steps were uncertain and feeble as he pushed his way out the lobby door. Will watched him turn upstreet and lost him in the dark.

Chap, too, wanted to know why he'd bought it. And he could no more tell Chap than he could tell Case, or anyone else.

He suddenly felt lonely, and knew the burden of keeping a secret. It was only fleeting, and then he soberly took a key off the board behind the desk and went upstairs.

Hal Mohr was sweeping up the last of the chair splinters in his saloon when a man came in.

"Too late for a drink?" the man asked pleasantly.

"Be with you in a minute," Hal said.

He dumped the splinters in the cold stove in the corner, rearranged the chairs, shoved the bro-

19

ken table against the wall, and came behind the bar. He was breathing hard when he finished, for his body was sheathed in a thick layer of fat that made every movement an exertion. He had a heavy, cunning face, and his tight lips and opaque eyes told the stranger that here was a man who kept his own counsel.

The stranger said, "Whisky. Pour one for yourself."

"Thanks," Hal said. He regarded the stranger briefly, cataloging him in the custom of his profession. He saw only a man of medium size and middle age, stocky, dressed in Levis and jumper. He had ruddy cheeks burned a deep red. Probably a top hand or foreman from one of the spreads over north in the Sevier here on business.

The stranger scrubbed his face with a thick and calloused hand and looked at the wreckage of the table while Hal poured two drinks. They nodded to each other and drank, and Hal poured out two more drinks.

"Ruckus, tonight?" the stranger asked idly.

Hal leaned against the back bar and nodded. "A good one, looks like. I didn't see it."

"Anybody hurt?"

"Nine X foreman lost a tooth and got beat up."

"Pres Milo?" The stranger's eyebrows lifted. "That'd take a pretty good man."

"He looked like one. Will Danning. New here."

The stranger scowled. "Will Danning," he murmured. "Seems like I've read that name in the newspapers."

Hal nodded. "You have. You remember that shootin' a couple months ago over in the capital? Newspaper editor name of Murray Broome gunned Senator Mason, and then jumped the country."

"I remember."

"This here Will Danning was at the inquest to testify, what I read. They was tryin' to find out where Broome had gone to, and this Danning, he ups and tells them they're persecutin' a good man. There was a fight there at the inquest. Danning hit the sheriff after he'd called Broome a murderer and announced a reward on his head."

"That's it," the stranger said. "I remember. And this was Will Danning that hit Milo?"

"Same fella. He's a hardcase, all right." He paused, and when the stranger seemed incurious, Hal went on. "He's bought a place out here by the Sevier Brakes, the Pitchfork. That's what the row was over."

The stranger said, "How's that?"

"It's an old rustlers' hangout. Case, he's the Big Augur around here, figured Danning was goin' to set himself up as a rustler. He didn't know whether to leave him take the place or not."

The stranger asked idly, "What did he decide?"

Hal laughed noiselessly. "I reckon Danning will stay there. He beat up Case's foreman, but him

21

and Case went out of here friends. I seen it my-self."

The stranger said nothing. He finished his drink, bade Hal good night, and went out. Afterward Hal reflected that the stranger seemed to wait just long enough to learn that Will Danning was going to be allowed to keep his new place, and then he went out. Hal didn't think anything more about it.

Chapter Two

A Bluff That Failed

Next morning Will was up early, breakfasted, and was riding out of Yellow Jacket on a livery-stable horse before the breakfast fires were lifting their smoke above the town.

The country he slowly rode through during those early hours jogged something in his memory. He had forgotten what good graze it was, thick, sun-cured grama grass with the new green thrusting up to crowd out the old. It was a rolling country, well watered, the hills sloping down to copses of cottonwood and willows in the valleys, and piñon and cedar capping the crests. It was better than the country he was used to farther south, and a piece of it could have been his if he hadn't chosen Harkins's Pitchfork instead.

In midmorning, he judged he was onto Nine X range. Scattered groups of whiteface cattle watched him pass, and long-legged calves high-tailed it away from the rutted wagon road.

He topped a rise sometime in early morning and saw ahead of him, where the road forded a stream, a buckboard and team. Only — one horse of the team was grazing off the road; the other, still hitched to the buckboard, was haltered to a tree.

As Will rode up to it, a girl came off the grass from under some willows and regarded him quizzically. Will touched his Stetson and looked at her in silence. She was a tall slim girl, leggy in tight Levis and blue shirt. Her wide friendly mouth was faintly smiling, and when she spoke her voice was low, a little mocking.

"It was too dark to see in that lobby last night, but you must be Will Danning."

Will grinned.

"Your hair looks familiar. That's all I saw."

She appraised him silently for a moment as he swung down, and then said, "I've lamed one of my horses, and that other one is too salty for me to tackle bareback." She laughed a little. "I thought I wanted to get home in a hurry, but I guess it doesn't matter."

Will said, "If you're in a hurry, we could swap."

Becky Case flushed a little. "No, I'm not really in a hurry. I — just don't like town." She looked almost shyly at Will and continued. "I woke up before daylight and decided to hit out for home. I've been in town two days, and that's too long for me."

Will said mockingly, "I thought all women wanted to stay in town."

"Here's one that doesn't," Becky said, and she laughed.

Will considered her a long moment, wondering if her father had told her of last night's quarrel.

24

If he had, she didn't seem concerned about it. And this was his chance to prove to Angus Case that he would be a good neighbor.

He said, "If you really aren't in a hurry, Miss Case —"

"Becky, please. We're neighbors, aren't we?"

Will nodded and went on. "If you aren't in a hurry, I'll hitch up my horse, and we'll drive on to my place. There used to be a short cut through the brakes that came out close to the Nine X."

"You're anxious to see your place, aren't you?" Becky asked.

Will nodded.

"I'm in no hurry," she went on. "I'd like to see the old place myself."

Will offsaddled and hitched his livery horse to the buckboard. The lame horse was turned loose; Becky climbed up on the buckboard seat beside Will, and they were off.

The girl was silent a long while, and Will was aware that she was covertly studying him. When he had given her a good look at him, he said, "I reckon you heard about the ruckus I had with your foreman last night, Miss Becky."

"I'm glad you had it," Becky Case said quietly. Will looked at her in surprise, and she laughed shortly. "What's the use of pretending? I don't like Pres Milo and I never did." She hesitated and then said in a low voice, "Sometimes I think he knows something about Dad that makes Dad afraid to fire him. He obeys orders when he wants

25

to, and when he doesn't, Dad won't do anything."

Will remembered Angus Case trying to stop the fight last night. Certainly Pres Milo had disregarded orders then. Will said, "Do you really reckon he has somethin' on your dad?"

"Dad wouldn't have let him try to kill you last night if he didn't, would he?"

Will saw the truth in that, yet something else was puzzling him.

"Why do you reckon Pres got so redheaded about my buyin' the Pitchfork if he don't pay any attention to your father, Miss Becky? If your dad won't fire him, then why should he care if Nine X beef is stole or not?"

Becky looked thoughtfully at him, as if she wasn't sure if she should talk further. "That's easy to see. Pres wants the Pitchfork. He always has."

Will looked puzzled.

"He's tried to buy it?" he asked.

"Many a time. You know Harkins only leased it, and it went back to some land company when he was killed. For the last six years Pres has been trying to get money enough to buy it. Several times he's almost had enough, and then he gambles to make up the rest and he loses his whole stake."

"What does he want it for?"

"I don't know. He's tried to get Dad to loan him the money, and Dad won't do it. He's afraid Pres will start rustling Nine X beef if he does."

"Then whatever Pres has got on your dad, it

can't be very bad, or else your dad would loan him the money."

"That's the only thing that comforts me," Becky said in a low voice. "Still, it's all queer." She looked curiously at Will. "Did you know that some men lived on the Pitchfork for a while three years ago?"

"Rustlers?"

"I don't think so. At least we didn't miss any beef. But Pres was friendly with two of them. He saw them all the time and talked with them. But he hated the third man. He beat him up so badly the man almost died. Dad's friendship with Sheriff Phipps was the only thing that saved Pres. Then the three of them went away."

Will scowled.

"What's that supposed to mean?"

"I wish I knew," Becky said. "I'm only telling you. And warning you, too. Because Dad can't stop Pres. And Pres hates you."

"Thanks," Will said.

The conversation was switched to other things, and Will listened carefully for further light on what had been said. But Becky Case wouldn't talk about it any more. It was as if she had only wanted to tell him everything she knew, so he might be warned.

It was almost noon when the shape of the country began to change. Clay dunes and long ugly limestone outcrops began to appear along the road, and the trees were stunted and discouraged-looking. This was the first hint of the Sevier

Brakes, that wide, bleak wasteland of myriad canyons, of fantastic wind erosions, of sparse grass, and of mysterious trails that few men knew. It was hot here, shut off from the breezes of the bench, and the faint wagon road twisted and turned into rougher country. Will recalled Chap's description of it last night. "It's worn out, dead, evil," and thought how right he was.

And then, almost at high noon, the team climbed a steep grade that put them on a short and bare mesa, and from its farther edge they could see Will's place, the Pitchfork brand.

It lay on the bare floor of a bleak valley backed up against a red-clay ridge, a black cut of a canyon to the west. The house itself was stone, with slab wings and a slab roof that had taken on the color of the red clay of the canyon floor. It was ugly, with no vegetation except an occasional mesquite bush around it. It lay there raw and naked under the high sun — the house, a root cellar dug into the slope of the ridge, a wagon shed, a windmill, and the rickety barns and corrals bleached a bone-white and tinted also with the dust of the red clay.

Becky Case studied it in silence and looked obliquely at Will.

"I can't see what Pres would want with that. I can't see what you'd want with it, either."

Will only shrugged, keeping his attention on the narrow and worn wagon road that snaked down to the valley floor. They crossed a dry wash that came out of the dark canyon; they pulled up beside the corral in the shade of the barn.

Three punchers and one fat little Mexican came out of the house. Will advanced to meet them, Becky following a little way behind, and sight of the man approaching first brought a wide and friendly smile to Will's face.

"Howdy, Milt," Will said, and gripped the man's hand.

Milt was a little shorter than Will, lean, and his flashing smile was affectionate. His blue eyes were bold, almost arrogant. His lean face was burned a deep brown, and he was clean-shaven. He wore his worn Levis and faded checked shirt with a certain elegance, and he gripped Will's hand with both hands. Then his eyes shifted to Becky, appraised her briefly, and then he said, "Will, you didn't tell me you were bringing a bride with you."

Becky Case flushed, and Will, too, was embarrassed. "Becky, this is Milt Barron, my foreman. This is Miss Case, our neighbor and not my wife."

Becky shook hands with Milt, and Will turned to greet the other three men. Pinky Sharp, little and bowlegged and ugly, got his name from his bright-red hair. Ollie Gargan was a sour-faced, rawhide-lean man with a ruff of stiff gray hair. The third man, in a singlet, was Pablo, a grinning Mexican, fat and merry-looking and dark as an Indian. Becky met them all, and then Will led the way to the house. Milt was beside Becky. The others drifted off toward the corrals.

29

The main room of the house in the stone part of it looked as if it had never known a woman's touch. There were no rugs, no curtains, and solid, heavy tables and stump chairs. Bridles, guns, odd pieces of leather, and old magazines littered the big room, and in one corner four saddles were stacked.

Milt cleared a chair for Becky, and then Will looked around. One wing of the house was the mess shack and cookshack. The other wing was the bunkhouse. Will looked through the dark and ugly rooms, remembering it all from ten years back. Only then it had been new and exciting — his first job. He'd been fifteen then, and old man Harkins had been a good boss. Now — well, it was different.

He turned back down the passage between the big room and bunkhouse wing, and paused in the doorway, looking at Milt and Becky. They were laughing over something, and Will frowned a little. Milt's dark hair was too neat, his smile too quick, and his speech too facile. Will knew a little fear then, but quickly dismissed it as he tramped into the room.

At that moment Pablo appeared in the doorway.

"Somebody, she's come, Will."

Will looked out the door. There, cutting across the wash were four riders. Milt rose and came over beside him, his dark inquiring eyes on Will.

"Go see, Milt," Will said quietly.

He had already recognized the man in the lead

as Pres Milo. His squat and burly body, erect in the saddle, looked as if it were carved out of stone.

Becky, from beside him, suddenly whispered, "That's Pres, Will."

Will put out his hand. "Stay here, Becky. I want to see what he does."

Two riders dropped off by the barn, on the sunny side of it, so the buckboard and team were hidden from them. Pres and the other rider came toward the porch.

Milt paused just beyond the porch and said civilly, "Howdy."

Pres reined up and looked around him, his hard blue eyes calculating and cold. Then his gaze rested on Milt, and he folded his thick arms and leaned on the saddle horn. Cuffing his Stetson back off his forehead, he said, "Got anything in that house you want?"

Milt regarded him carefully. The two riders he had dropped at the barn were talking with Pinky and Ollie Gargan.

Milt said cautiously, "A lot of things. Why?"

Pres turned his beet-red face aside and spat, then turned clear around and called, "All right, boys."

Milt saw the two men by the barn whip up six-guns and cover Ollie and Pinky. At the same time he heard footsteps behind him and looked. Around the side of the house two more riders, guns in hand, appeared. Pablo came to the cookshack door then. One of the riders hauled

31

Pablo out into the open and rammed a gun in his back.

"Because," Pres Milo said curtly, "I'm goin' to fire the place. Make a nice present for your boss when he comes."

Milt had no gun. He looked quietly at Pres, and then said, "There's nothin' much I can do, is there? I'd like a saddle out of that big room."

"I'll watch you get it," Pres said. He swung down from his horse.

Will drew Becky into the corridor then, picked up a rifle that leaned against the table, and faded against the front wall of the room. He looked at Becky and raised a finger to his lips. She nodded and disappeared.

Milt walked in the door and, without looking around him, tramped toward the far corner where the saddles were stacked. Pres Milo followed him in, six-gun hanging at his side.

Inside the room, Pres looked around him. His eyes traveled the side wall, and then something attracted his attention to the front wall.

Will stood there, his rifle pointing at Pres's belly.

For three long seconds, nobody spoke. Pres, swollen lips parted a little in surprise, stared. There was a welt on his right cheek that remained from last night, and it gave his face a lop-sided look.

Will said quietly, "Drop that iron, and drop it now!"

The gun clattered to the floor. Pres licked his

lips, and a kind of cold fear crept into his pale eyes. Milt was grinning behind him.

Will said, "Step up to the door and call your crew of gunnies to the porch."

Pres, eyeing Will's rifle, moved toward the door. Will stayed away from it. Pres stopped in the door and called out, "Bring 'em up here!"

Will waited two long minutes until he heard the sound of scuffling boots. He came up behind Pres, looked over his shoulder, saw the others assembled outside. Then he placed his foot in the middle of Pres's back and shoved.

Pres flew out the door, off balance, tripped, and sprawled on his face in the dirt beyond the porch.

At the same time Will, rifle to shoulder, appeared in the door and said, "I've got nine shots in here. Anybody want to take a chance?"

At that moment Milt stepped out of the kitchen door behind them, six-gun in hand, and drawled, "Go ahead and try it!"

The Nine X crew was caught. They dropped their guns, and at that moment Becky brushed past Will. Pres had struggled to his feet, and now he saw Becky. Some of the color flushed out of his face as he saw her.

Becky looked at him, her lip curled in contempt, and then shifted her gaze to the rest of the crew.

"Tip, maybe you can tell me what this means. Or you, Wallie. Or you, Fred!"

"It was orders," one of the punchers growled.

Becky turned on Pres, her eyes blazing with

wrath. "From you, I suppose, Pres?"

Pres sneered at her. "That's right. You think I'm goin' to let that coyote get away with clubbin' me with a chair when my back was turned like he did last night?" He looked balefully at Will and then back at Becky.

Will saw that Becky was so furious she couldn't speak. He drawled mildly, "That means you think you could take me in a fair fight, don't it, Pres?"

"Any time," Pres sneered. "After I burned your place, I was goin' to wait for you and prove it."

Will stepped past Becky and nodded to Pinky and held out his rifle to him. "You keep the customers in hand, Pinky." Then he peeled off his coat, dropped it on the porch, and laid his hat carefully alongside.

"I never disappoint anybody," Will drawled gently as he stepped off the porch. "Least of all would I disappoint you, Pres."

Pres regarded him coldly. "You think I'd fight you with your men holdin' a gun on my back?"

"I think you're goin' to," Will murmured. He walked slowly toward the Nine X foreman.

"Wait," Pres said. "I admit you got me, Danning. It ain't a fair fight, and I won't have any of it."

For answer, Will lashed out with a blow that thudded loud in that noon stillness, and Pres sprawled on his back in the red dust. Slowly he pulled himself up on one elbow, shook his head, and made no effort to rise.

Will turned to the Nine X crew and looked

them over. They were a sheepish-looking lot, but they didn't look like saddle bums.

He said dryly, "You sure got a tough ramrod. He talks as mean a fight as any man I know."

Behind him, Will heard a soft scuffle in the dust, and he knew what was happening. To cover up his knowledge, to make it look as if he didn't know, he went on rapidly. "What kind of an outfit are you, anyway? Did Case tell you to ride over here? I doubt it, because he's in —"

"Look out, Will!" Becky cried.

Will looked at her, puzzled, but he braced himself. A second later Pres Milo's hulking weight hit him in the back, and he went sprawling on his face in the dust. He landed lightly and rolled out of the way just as Pres kicked out at him. Will came to his feet, his gray eyes sultry, his mouth twisted in a crooked smile.

"I thought I'd toll you into it if I turned my back, Pres. Now I aim to show your crew what a joker Case has got for a foreman. You remember seein' a buckboard on the other side of the barn, Pres?"

Pres stood there, breathing hard, unwilling to crowd the fight now that Will was on his feet. He didn't answer.

"I'll show you," Will murmured. "I'm goin' to fight you clean over to that buckboard, Pres. And when we get over there, I'll lift you into that buckboard and cover you up, and Miss Case will drive you back to the spread. She'll have to, because you won't be able to ride."

He started for Pres then, and Pres, knowing what was in store for him, decided to fight. They stood toe to toe, slugging, for about ten seconds, and then Pres backed up. Will crowded him and knocked him down. Pres scrambled to his feet, and before he was fully erect, Will knocked him down again. They were forty of the two hundred feet to the buckboard.

The fight had settled now into a grim, wordless, grunting battle. Pres knew he was licked; all he wanted was to save his face and not let Will crowd him to the buckboard.

And Will was implacable. He hoped that now, for once and all, Pres Milo could be taught to leave him alone. He wanted to beat the man's spirit, to humiliate him in front of his crew so that Becky could go back to Case with the story.

He fought with a cruel relish. What Pres had over him in weight, Will gained back in height and reach. And slowly, stubbornly, with both crews silently watching, Will took advantage of every inch of this reach and height. When Pres tried to circle him, Will cut him off. When Pres tried to grapple with him, Will kept him at arm's length, rocking him back on his heels. In the hot blaze of afternoon sun, shirts ribboned down around their trousers, the two of them slugged it out. Gagging for breath, stubborn as winter, Will looped long, slogging blows at Pres's face, driving him back foot by foot.

And Pres gave ground. Twice he was knocked down, and twice Will waited for him to rise.

The third time, when Pres fell against the barn, he came up slowly. His face was bruised beyond recognition, his nose mashed, and both eyes were slowly closing. He came to his feet, weaving, holding up his guard blindly, and Will knocked him down again. He fell around the corner of the barn and lay senseless at the feet of the buckboard team.

The Nine X crew watched in bleak silence while Will, staggering with weariness, made one last supreme effort. He hauled Pres to his feet, stooped, jackknifed the Nine X foreman over his shoulder, and loaded him like a sack of flour into the buckboard.

Afterward, Will put both hands on the buckboard frame and hung his head, sucking in great gagging breaths of air. Presently he lifted his head to regard the onlookers. His chest and belly held big red bruises, and it hurt him to breathe.

He said meagerly, "Next time, I'll shoot him." To Pinky, he added, "Go offsaddle those Nine X ponies and load the saddles in here. Put their guns in here, too."

One of the Nine X men stirred uneasily. "What do you aim to do, Danning?"

"You're goin' to walk home," Will said quietly. "It's only ten miles. You can start off now. Miss Case will bring your saddles and your tough foreman with her. Your ponies will follow her."

The Nine X crew looked at each other. One man said bitterly, "I told you we was damn fools to string along with him."

Then they broke and slowly filed out toward the wash.

Only then did Will see Becky Case. She stood a little way off, Milt at her side. On her face was a look of distaste and distress and a faint anger.

When Will paused in front of her, she said, "Is it necessary to make those men pay for what Pres did?"

Will nodded. "I seem to have a hard time getting across to your crew that I want to be let alone," he drawled. "Maybe they'll believe me now."

Becky didn't say anything. She only went over to the buckboard and looked at the still figure Pinky had covered with a tarp.

"I think they'll let you alone," she said quietly, and added, "I'm sorry this had to happen. I wanted to be neighbors with you."

"You're always welcome here," Will said levelly. "So's your father. But if any of these men or Pres set foot on this spread again, there'll be a coroner's inquest in Yellow Jacket. That's a promise."

Milt helped Becky up to the seat. She smiled her thanks and drove off.

Will tramped wearily over to the horse trough and plunged his head into it. When he looked up, Milt was standing beside him, watching him, a look of curiosity and respect in eyes that were usually mocking.

"Now I know," he drawled, "why you made

such a good foreman for these last two years, Will."

Will wheeled and looked around him.

"It's all right," Milt went on. "They've gone up to eat."

Will and Milt went up to the big room, and while Will pulled a clean shirt out of his war bag, Milt leaned against the table regarding him curiously.

"You haven't told me what this is all about," Milt said.

Will told him about last night's brush with Pres Milo. He also told Milt what Becky had told him of Pres's desire for this place.

"But why does he want it?" Milt said curiously.

Will shrugged and buttoned his shirt. "I don't know. Let's forget it. What about you?"

"Your crew figures me for a remittance man from the East," Milt said. "They're good men."

"While I think of it," Will said, "you've got to rough yourself up, Murray."

"Milt," Murray Broome corrected him.

"Your hair's too neat, your talk's too good. You're too friendly."

"With that girl?" Milt suggested mockingly. "I won't steal her from you, Will."

Will felt his face getting hot, and he didn't know why. He said brusquely, "I didn't mean that. But you've taken off close to ninety pounds, fella. You've —"

"I've been hungry for two months," Milt said bitterly.

"You've shaved your mustache, you've dyed your hair. You've lost your white office skin. Nobody in the world would spot you for a white-faced, blond-mustached, overweight newspaper editor. But if you keep talkin' like a newspaper reads, if you keep dressin' like a dude —"

Milt cut in. "But I've got to keep shaved, Will. If I don't my beard grows out blond."

"All right, keep shaved," Will said. "Only act like a puncher, Milt. Shy or surly or dirty — anything, just so you can drift in with the rest of the boys and nobody will pick you out."

Milt nodded wearily. "All right." He straightened up. "Did anybody ask you questions about me in town?"

"No," Will said grimly. "They all want to know why I'm here. I tell 'em because I want to be let alone. And I reckon they'll believe me, after today."

Milt put out his hand and squeezed Will's arm. "You'll do to ride the river with, Will," he said quietly. "If I get impatient or tough with you, keep me in line. Because if you don't hide me, I'll hang."

Will looked at him briefly and then smiled. "Let's eat."

Chapter Three

VALUABLE KNOWLEDGE

The Nine X outfit was so different from the hardscrabble spread Will Danning had bought that it was hard to concede they existed for the same purpose. The Nine X buildings nestled against one of the rolling hills to the west and north of the Sevier Brakes. Its house was a big frame affair built of lumber that was shipped in the second month after the railroad was completed to Yellow Jacket. It was painted white and looked like a big house in a town. Coming on it, a casual rider was first surprised and then admiring and then, if he reflected awhile, amused. For Angus Case had built a pleasant house, a banker's house, out in a lonesome country where only an occasional cattle buyer or a rider on the grub line could admire it. The out-buildings off to the north against the shoulder of the hill were more in character with the country. They did not have big cottonwoods screening them, and they were of logs. The barn was big, and the corrals were spacious, and the bunkhouse and cookshack, midway between house and barn, were built of stone.

Becky drove into the place after dark, left the

buckboard by the bunkhouse with orders for a couple of the riders to see to Pres, and then went on into the house.

Pres had come to soon after he left Danning's place. With a bleak realization that Will Danning had made good his brag, he lay there under the tarp, too sore and beaten to care about it. Later, his shame would not allow him to rise and sit beside Becky, so he endured the jolting trip home under the sweltering tarp.

When he heard Becky give the orders to carry him into his bunk he lay there until he heard her go. One of the crew pulled the tarp off, and Pres sat up.

"You want some help, Pres?" one of the men asked.

"Get the hell away from me!" Pres snarled.

The two men disappeared in the bunkhouse, and Pres staggered over to the wash bucket on the cookshack bench. He stripped off his tattered shirt and washed the dried blood off his face and body. His face felt soft, mashed, beaten, and he could barely see. Afterward, he went into the office at the end of the bunkhouse. It held a big roll-top desk, a small iron safe, and two chairs. In the rear was his cot, above it a row of nails on which hung his clothes.

He fumbled the lamp alight, then dried himself off and looked at his image in the mirror. It was hard for him to recognize himself. He looked as if he'd run full tilt into the butt end of a big blue spruce. He swore savagely and turned away from the mirror, searching for a shirt. If he'd only read those tracks right today, he'd never have been tolled into Danning's place. But how did he know that it was Becky's buckboard or that she'd already made friends with Danning? But he'd gone, and he'd got beat up for his pains. He wasn't afraid of what the Nine X crew thought of him. He could handle them. If they spoke to him about it, he'd beat them up and fire them, and they knew it.

He was buttoning his shirt over his hairy barrel chest when he heard somebody approaching. That would be Angus, and Pres tried to smile. His face was redder than ever, the lips of his loose mouth swollen so that they hurt when his mouth curved into an unaccustomed grin.

There was a knock on the door, and then Angus Case stepped inside. Pres didn't even speak as the older man closed the door and came over to the desk.

Angus Case looked at him and said dryly, "Well, you're a beauty."

Pres said nothing. He tucked his shirttail in and ran puffed and sore hands over his sandy hair to comb it.

"Becky told me all about it," Angus said.

"And how do you like it?" Pres asked.

"I'm waiting for you to explain why you went over there in the first place."

"To burn him out," Pres said bluntly. "Didn't she tell you that?"

Case's square, stubborn jaw clamped shut, and

his eyes had tiny pin points of anger in them. "She told me, yes."

Pres laughed. "You're scared of Will Danning. You're scared he'll steal you blind, but you ain't got the guts to do anything about it."

"I did everything I could do legally," Case said angrily.

"Like hell you did," Pres sneered. "Chap Hale's your best friend. Why'd you let him get the place for Danning?"

"I couldn't stop him."

"Well, I aim to stop Danning," Pres went on. "How do you like that?"

Case didn't answer for a long moment, and then he said, "Pres, you're about washed up here."

Pres stared at him, and then laughed again. He picked up a sack of tobacco and began to roll a cigarette. "Sure," he said mildly. "I'll leave tomorrow."

"I wish to God you would!" Case said bitterly.

"I'll pack up and ride into town," Pres drawled. "I'll have to say good-by to Sheriff Phipps, though." He looked up at Case. "We'll get to talkin' about things, rememberin' things, and then I'll tell him about why you killed Harkins." He paused. "I was pretty young then, a squirt of a Nine X horse wrangler, but I remember about it."

He was looking at Case now, and suddenly the older man's gaze faltered.

"I'll tell him how this was a company ranch

44

then and you was just a manager trying to get money to buy it by rustlin' company stock. I'll tell him the truth because I saw you steal the cattle and change the upside-down T brand to your own damn Nine X. I'll tell him how the company crowded you into the corner and you had to get a goat for your stealin' and you accused Harkins. I'll tell him how you was afraid for Harkins to be tried for rustlin' because he was innocent so you had him killed. I'll tell him how you bought out the company with money you got from stealin' their cattle. I'll tell him — or do you reckon that's enough?"

Angus Case's eyes looked haunted. He settled into a chair and rolled a cigarette with trembling fingers.

"You still want to fire me?" Pres jeered.

"I want to kill you, Pres," Case said quietly. "And some day I will."

Pres laughed. "You ain't got the guts, Case," he jeered. "You ain't got guts enough to kill a man. You had Harkins killed, and it's been hauntin' you for ten years. You'd shoot yourself before you'd shoot another man, and I know it!"

Case only glared at him. In his eyes was a bitterness and a hatred and a fear that was not pleasant to see.

Pres lounged on the desk and looked down at Case. "Go on with your speech."

Case straightened up and said crisply, "All right, I'll go at it this way. I can't stop you from doin' a damn thing you want around here, Pres. But

Will Danning is going to kill you if you don't leave him alone."

"If I don't kill him first," Pres said easily.

"But why do you aim to bother him? Why do you hate him?" Pres said nothing. Case nodded. "It's the old reason, isn't it, Pres? You want to buy the Pitchfork."

Pres nodded. "If you'd given me the money a long time ago, I'd have it."

"And have you steal me blind, and me not able to fight you? Oh, no. I can be pushed so far, Pres. But when a man steals my cattle, even you, I'll fight. And damn Harkins's killin'!"

"You'd be rid of me if you'd bought it."

"I'll never be rid of you," Case said bitterly.

Pres yawned. "That all you want to tell me?"

Case nodded bleakly and came to his feet. His shoulders under his black suit coat seemed bowed and shrunken. "That's all," he said quietly. "I can't stop you from rawhidin' Danning. But I can tell you, if you don't stop, he'll kill you."

"Maybe."

Case said curiously, "In the last three years, Pres, I've asked you a hundred times what you want of that damned hardscrabble spread. You won't tell me. Will you tell me now?"

"You," Pres said gently, "go to hell, Angus."

Case went out without another word. Pres, grinning, slacked into the chair and rammed his hands deep in his pockets. He stared musingly at the stuffed pigeonholes of the desk, and his forehead was puckered in a frown.

46

Presently, he rose and went outside and tramped over to the barn. At the door in one corner of it, he paused, listened, knocked, and then went in.

"Tomás!"

"*Sí*, Señor Pres," a soft voice answered.

"Where the hell is your lamp here?"

"She's not there, señor," Tomás answered. "Because I sleep in the barn, I have no lamp, so you say."

Pres remembered. He'd forbidden this Mexican stable hand to smoke or have a lamp in his quarters here in the barn. Consequently, the poor devil retired at sunset each night rather than sit up in the dark.

Pres stumbled across the room toward the cot in the corner. "You awake?"

"*Sí*. For two hours, maybe."

"Listen. Have we still got that Star 88 pony the boys picked up a couple of days ago?"

"*Sí.*"

"Then listen. Tomorrow morning saddle up that pony, and you and me are goin' to ride over to the Pitchfork. This Danning and his crew will be out, I reckon. He's got a Mexican cook over there. I want you to toll that cook out of the shack, understand?"

"But how?"

"All you spicks like horses," Pres said sneeringly. "Take him out and show him this Star 88 pony. He won't know you're from Nine X. Try and sell him the pony."

47

"Why do I do that, señor?"

"So I can search the place, you damned dumb greaser!" Pres said.

"*Sí,* señor," Tomás said. There was nothing in the man's tone to indicate his hatred of this man who detested Mexicans so much that he made them sleep in the barn. But Pres knew the hatred was there. He went out, kicking over a chair and cursing on his way out.

By midmorning next day Pres and Tomás had worked their way carefully to the top of one of the red hills hard to the east of Will Danning's Pitchfork, and from there Pres looked the place over. He regarded the small horse pasture, which held only one horse, and the corral, which was empty, and then the house, where smoke was rising from the cookshack wing. His hunch was right. Will Danning, on his second day home, would have ridden out to locate his cattle and boundaries and get a look at the place he had left ten years ago. Pres cursed when he thought of it. This was a sorry excuse for a ranch, yet he wanted it more than anything he knew.

He said to Tomás without turning, *"Vamos!"* and heard the Mexican scramble down to his horse ground-haltered in the wash.

Presently Tomás rode in from the east and pulled up in the yard and yelled, puncher-fashion, "Hello — the house!"

The cookshack door opened, and Pablo, Will's cook, stepped out. Tomás pulled his horse over. As compatriots will do in a strange country,

48

Tomás and Pablo shook hands, and Tomás dismounted. Pres watched impatiently. If he remembered rightly, there was a ceremony for them to go through — cigarettes to be lighted, some courteous, leisurely talk, and then the hunting of shade in which to squat and resume their palaver.

It all worked out that way. In a few minutes, Tomás gestured to the horse trough. Pablo followed, and they wound up in the shade of the barn.

Pres grunted with satisfaction and started his circle of the house behind the shelter of the clay hills. When he was on the north side of the house, he tied the horse he had been leading, climbed the hill, then cautiously descended the other slope. It levelled off directly in back of the house. Pres approached the west corner, listened, heard nothing; he made sure the barn hid the two Mexicans, then stepped around the corner and into the open door of the bunkhouse wing.

Once inside he paused, looking around at the double tier of bunks and the heavy table in the middle of the room. Now that he was here he felt a little foolish. In his mind last night there had been room for only anger and a single idea — he had to get Will Danning off this place by any means he could. The most obvious way, by violence, had failed, and the next most obvious way was legal eviction. For that, of course, he'd been prepared. Ever since he'd heard Chap Hale had bought the place, he'd been watching the county records in town for the recording of the deed. It had not been recorded, which meant that either Will or Chap had the deed. And last night he wondered if a search of the house would turn up the deed. If he could steal it, then it would give him the time it took Will to get another deed in which to plan some way of getting the place. But this bunkhouse didn't look as if it held any deed.

Nevertheless, he was going to look. Half the bunks were unoccupied; the rest held blankets and clothes. Hanging from the post of each occupied bunk was the war bag of its occupant. Since Pres didn't know which was which, he set about looking through all. He would dump the contents of the war bags on the floor, look through them for any papers, and then put the stuff back.

He had gone through two of them and found only old letters and pictures from magazines and catalogs, besides a change of clothes. On the third bunk, he found a newer war bag, shook it out, and knelt over its contents.

This war bag reflected a different type of owner, and he thought he had Will Danning's. For instance, there was a good pair of gloves; there was a magazine he'd never heard the name of before, and there was also a can of a good and different tobacco. Besides what was in a deerskin sack.

Pres opened the sack. There was a thick silver watch, a cameo pin and a small painted miniature of a woman, framed in glass. There were no papers.

In disgust, Pres threw the stuff to the floor. The miniature hit the boards, and its glass shattered with a small tinkle. It came open, also, and Pres picked it up angrily. Maybe the absence of the glass wouldn't be noticed if he cleaned up the shards of it. He tried to shut the back of it, and it stuck; he turned it over to get a better grip. Curiosity prompted him, then, to look inside. There was another miniature there, of a man with mutton-chop whiskers. Engraved on the inside of the back was this message: *To Murray, from Mother and Dad, on his fifteenth birthday.*

Pres read it, scowled, and closed the lid, but the message set his mind ticking. Murray. There was no Murray in this outfit, unless Milt Barron had lied to him that first day. Maybe Pinky was really named Murray.

And then it came to Pres in a flash. Murray — Murray Broome! That was the man Will Danning worked for, and who had a reward of five thousand on his head for the murder of a senator!

Pres stared at the miniature, his mind working swiftly. Then his glance traveled to a shirt lying on the floor. This was the shirt Milt Barron had been wearing yesterday. This wasn't Will Danning's war bag; it was Milt Barron's!

Pres stared again at the miniature, a thousand things running through his mind. Yellow Jacket, to a man, was wondering why Will Danning wanted the Pitchfork. Here was the answer — to hide Murray Broome!

But which man of them was Murray Broome?

51

Pres didn't have to wonder more than a few seconds, and then his mind settled unerringly on Milt Barron. Something about him, his look, his speech, his clothes, told a man he wasn't an ordinary puncher. Yes, it was Milt Barron.

For one long minute Pres stared at the object in his hand, his swollen face creasing into a smile. He wasn't thinking of the five thousand dollars reward; it was too late to use that money for the only thing he wanted. But better than money, better than anything he could have invented, was the knowledge he held.

It was the pry he needed. At long last he saw a way to get Will Danning's place.

Chapter Four

BLACKMAIL

It was late morning when Will and Milt rode into Yellow Jacket. It looked like any cow town drowsing in the hot summer sun — one main street, dusty and wide, a cross street bisecting it. The buildings were all frame, with their false fronts scaling paint under the blistering sun and winds of the bench. On one of the four corners, Will noticed, was a new bank, across from it Dunn's General Store. Hal Mohr's big saloon was in the middle of the block where Dunn's used to be, and down-street a few doors and across the way was the sheriff's office and jail, converted from Mohr's old saloon. Across from the new saloon and in the middle of the block the hotel still stood at its same dark location. The only trees in town grew on the back streets where the homes were. The whole town seemed to point to the station at the head of the street, and it was dominated by the long tangle of dirty stock pens next to it. Yellow Jacket was a cow town, living for cattle and dominated by cattle.

Cow ponies were tied in clusters at the rails, and an occasional team and buckboard or spring wagon added variety.

Will and Milt pulled in at the tie rail a couple of doors down from the hotel.

Will said, "Want to meet Chap?"

Milt shook his head. "I met him once, a long time ago. And he looked like he had a memory. No, I'll look around."

Will said briefly, "You got to face it some time. Go ahead."

He watched Milt tramp across the dusty street, whistling carelessly, and he was troubled. This furtive hiding, the bleak spread, the barren red-clay badlands, and the long hours of riding were galling Milt, he knew — Will even made himself think of Murray as Milt now.

The night of the shooting, months ago, when Will had taken a horse out to him where he was waiting in the old stage station east of Mesilla, they had settled this. Milt had told him briefly about the fight, how he was crowded into going for his gun, and how he had killed old Senator Mason. Milt had been bitter and discouraged that night, and had seen himself as the victim of a cheap political frame-up. It was then he had asked Will to hide him for a year until the next elections. Then, Milt was confident, a reform party would be elected, his reward would be lifted, and he could come out of hiding. It was all politics, he had insisted, and he was being savagely persecuted for his crusades to clean up the Territory. And Will, who was a loyal friend, knowing nothing of politics and caring less, had remembered old

Harkins's place, lonely and remote and unfriendly. He had made his decision that night,
and he had never questioned the rightness of it.
Milt was his friend.

Five years before, when Milt's father had given
him the ranch and the newspaper, Milt had hired
him, a lonely, broke puncher riding the grub line.
During those five years and countless weekends,
they had come to know each other on pack and
hunting and fishing trips. And Milt, because he
knew a man with cow savvy when he saw him,
had promoted Will to foreman of his Double Bar
O. It had been a strange and deep friendship
of a volatile, brilliant, and educated young man
with a taciturn, hard-to-know young puncher. It
was a friendship that few suspected, for they were
both careful to guard it as something private.

But a friendship it was. Will had proven
that when he had taken his savings to buy this
place where Milt was to hide. Will had accepted
Milt completely as his friend, and he saw nothing strange in running a constant risk, of spending
all his money and a year of his life in helping
Milt. Milt was his friend; it was as simple as
that.

He turned away, his face sober. Before it was
over, Milt would be a lot sicker of hiding, a lot
more impatient, and inclined to carelessness. Then
the real trouble would begin. This was only the
beginning.

Three doors down from the hotel, Will swung
into the entrance of a covered stairway that lifted

to Chap Hale's office.

He found Chap in a musty room lined on three sides with law books and smelling of good cigars and dust. Will was shocked to see Chap in daylight. Ten years had done a lot to him. He was frail as old china, and his skin was almost transparent. His white hair was thin, and his eyes had lost some of their sparkle.

He shook hands with Will without getting up, and waved Will to a chair.

"How does it look?" he asked, leaning back in his chair.

"Just like I thought it would," Will murmured.

"Worth a life's savings?"

Will nodded. He smiled a little, the skin around his eyes wrinkling with some inner amusement.

Chap said, "Funny, your liking that place, after Broome's Double Bar O."

"That was a big ranch. It cost a hundred thousand and grazed eight thousand head of beef. This is — well, it's a poor man's start, Chap."

Chap said, "I read about this Broome business in the papers." He looked out the window. "Young Murray Broome must have been a thorough-going scoundrel."

Will said nothing, and presently Chap looked at him. "You don't say anything."

"He was a good boss," Will said quietly. "Outside of that I don't know or care what he was, I reckon."

"He libeled Senator Mason, and when Mason

56

won the suit he killed him. What do you think of that?"

Will shifted impatiently in his seat. "I don't think about it, Chap. I don't care about it." He had himself under control and he knew it. But he was sorry and a little angry to hear Chap say what he was saying.

"Well, no matter," Chap said, sighing. He looked keenly at Will. "You're finished with him, I hope."

"I'm a rancher," Will said flatly.

Chap grinned then. "You'll need to be, out there. You're determined to stick it out?"

Will nodded.

"With Case a poor neighbor to you and suspicious?"

Will nodded and said slowly, "What about Case, Chap? You're his friend, you say."

Chap nodded. "Angus is a good man. But he's suspicious. He remembers Harkins and the rustling. And he's crazy on one subject, like all of us."

"And what's that?"

"He'll kill a man who steals a steer of his. He'd kill his mother if she stole one. He'll put up with anything from his crew but stealing. And sooner or later, Will, he's apt to think you're a thief. And then you'll have trouble, real trouble." Will only nodded, and Chap said in a tired voice, "You're willing to risk that? You still want to go through with it?"

"I do."

"All right," Chap said. "I'll sign it over to you, then."

"Sign it over to me?" Will echoed.

Chap nodded. "I bought the Pitchfork in my name, with my own money. I thought — I hoped — you'd change your mind. If you had, it didn't matter that I'd bought it and was stuck with it. I'm old, Will, and money's nothing. I just don't want you to get a wrong start."

"I want the place," Will said. "Sign it over, Chap, because I'm here to stay."

Chap murmured, "I can remember a fifteen-year-old kid I singled out of a bunch of so-called rustlers brought into the sheriff's office. I can remember thinking he looked pretty stubborn. When I pleaded his case privately with the judge, and the judge asked to see him, he still looked stubborn. The judge said so, when he dismissed charges." Chap shook his head. "You haven't changed much, Will."

"No," Will said.

Chap turned to his desk. "Well, I'll sign it over to you."

Will rose, ready to go. Chap said, "Oh, I almost forgot, Will. There's a young woman in town staying at the hotel. Her name is Norman. She asked me about you. She wants to talk to you."

Will scowled. "Norman? I don't know any Norman. What's she like?"

"Young. Pretty in a hard way. She wouldn't state her business. I told her you'd see her."

Will nodded. They chatted a few minutes

longer, and then Will left.

His lean face was grave as he hit the boardwalk and turned down it. He was touched by old Chap's effort to get him to reconsider buying the place, and he was disturbed by what Chap had said of the Murray Broome-Senator Mason fight. Chap was wrong, of course.

Milt was tying a package across the cantle of his saddle when Will came up to the tie rail.

"I'll be with you in a minute," Will said.

Milt looked at him, saw his scowl, and asked, "Bad news?"

Will laughed. "No. Only damn these people who don't give a man credit for knowin' his own mind."

"Meanin' what?"

Will said grimly, "Chap Hale was so sure I wouldn't want to buy the place after I looked at it that he bought it in his own name. Now I buy it from him."

Milt laughed with quiet irony. "Chap's right, Will. It's a damned sand pile. If you can do better, don't buy it."

"Damned if I won't," Will growled. "I don't care what kind of graze it is. We're buyin' it because it's lonesome."

Milt said quietly, "On my account, isn't it, Will?"

Will said briefly, "That's what we're here for, isn't it?" Milt nodded bleakly, and Will said, quick to change the subject, "Go get a drink. I'll pick you up at Mohr's," and went on toward the hotel.

At the hotel desk he inquired for a Miss Norman and was told to go up to room ten.

Upstairs, at the door of the room next to the last he knocked, and a woman's voice said, "Come in."

Will stepped inside, yanking off his Stetson. A girl was standing by the bed, a girl he had never seen before. Will caught the faint scent of cigarette smoke in the room, but he couldn't be sure. He immediately thought of Chap's description of her, "Pretty in a hard way," and he thought that described her. She was dark-haired, and her dress was of a dull-red silk that closely molded her figure. Her brown eyes were watchful and smiling.

"Mr. Danning? I'm Mary Norman." She smiled and extended her hand, and Will shook hands with her. She offered him a chair by a connecting door into the next room and then sat on the bed facing him. He was more curious than ever about her as he sat down and waited for her to begin.

"I understand you've bought a spread around here."

"That's right."

"It's a lovely country," Mary Norman said, and smiled a little. "A lot better cattle country than where you were, isn't it?"

"Why, yes," Will said. His gray eyes were searching, and the girl returned his level stare.

"I saw you around the Double Bar O," she said. "That's how I happened to know of you."

60

"I see," Will said. He didn't remember her.

Mary Norman seemed calm enough, but Will noticed that she was pleating the goods of her skirt with nervous fingers. Suddenly, she said, "Oh, I'm no good at hiding anything, Mr. Danning. I've come to ask you a question."

Will nodded, still puzzled.

"Have you ever heard Murray Broome speak of me?" she asked quietly.

Will felt a vague uneasiness as he shook his head. "No, ma'am."

"He and I were — well, good friends," Mary Norman said.

Will said nothing, and his silence seemed to embarrass the girl. She looked away from him, and her cheeks were slowly coloring, Will saw.

Suddenly, she blurted out, "You know, we were going to be married."

"I didn't know," Will said blankly.

The girl stood up and turned her back to him. "I don't know how to say this with you looking at me that way. But Murray and I were more than friends. He — he was going to marry me when all this trouble was over." She whirled now, and her skirts billowed as she turned. "I — you can guess now why I want to see him," she said defiantly.

Will didn't speak, only inclined his head. It was a nicely acted mixture of embarrassment and a declaration of love, intended to be a show of maidenly modesty. Only it didn't quite carry; it was too expert, Will thought.

"I can't guess, no," he said slowly.

"I want to see Murray," Mary Norman said.

Will said, frowning, "I understand that, yes. But I don't understand why you came to see me. You want me to find him for you?"

"Yes," the girl said swiftly.

"And where should I look?" There was a faint touch of irony in Will's voice.

"You must know where he is!" the girl cried. "Somebody does, and you were his closest friend!"

Will shook his head and came to his feet. "Sorry, ma'am. But I'm not workin' for Murray Broome any more. I've got a spread of my own. Murray's disappeared, so I've heard."

"You didn't answer my question," Mary Norman said stubbornly.

"What was it?"

"Do you know where Murray is?"

Will looked at her levelly, and the lie came easy. "No, I don't."

The girl didn't believe him; he could see it in her eyes. "Please," she said. "I won't tell. Do you think I'd sell out the man I'm going to marry? Do you think I ever believed anything they wrote about him?"

Will drawled, "You've got a bum steer somewhere, miss. Why do you think I know where he is?"

"Call it a hunch," the girl said swiftly. "I know you do. You must."

Will shook his head. "I wish I could help you. I can't."

"You won't tell me?"

"I can't," Will repeated.

There was a long silence. During it, Will heard a muffled movement in the next room. It sounded as if somebody had scuffed a chair in passing. Only a deep silence would have allowed him to hear it. The girl heard it, too, for she said swiftly, "Please, please tell me!"

And then she made the fatal mistake of looking toward the connecting door.

Will knew instantly there was someone in the next room, someone listening to this conversation.

He wheeled and lunged for the door, brushing his chair out of the way. The door opened easily, and he had only the briefest glimpse of a room like the one he had left before something crashed down on his head, and a curtain of blackness wrapped him in oblivion.

Mary Norman ran to the door and stood looking down at Will's broad back as he lay on the floor. Then she raised her eyes to regard the stocky, ruddy-cheeked man against the wall who was just holstering his gun.

"I had to do it. He knows me," the man said quietly, defensively.

"Well, are you satisfied now?" Mary Norman asked angrily.

"No. Not at all."

"He said he didn't know where he was!" Mary Norman said hotly.

"Why would he tell you?" the man asked. "He doesn't know you. But you stick around here for a while and give him a chance to see you. If Murray Broome's around, he'll find out you're here. You stick."

Mary Norman looked at the man and said passionately, "It's wrong! It's a sneaking, cruel thing to do, and you know it!"

The ruddy-cheeked man grunted. "Well, you can always go to jail, sister, if you don't like it."

"I don't hate it that much," Mary Norman said bleakly. "What's my next move?"

"I'll hide in your closet. Get some water and douse his face with it. He'll be proddy when he comes to. Tell him you don't know anything about who was in this room. He won't believe you, but tell him. Or," he suggested dryly, "you can cry. But he looks too tough to fall for that."

Mary Norman said in a low, passionate voice, "I hope you choke, Charlie Sommers! I hope you die in your sleep tonight!"

Charlie Sommers's plain face broke into a smile. "I won't," he drawled. "When you get to hatin' yourself too much for tryin' to trap your old sweetheart, just think how jail looks from inside — for a long time."

He went back into Mary's room, took a hand towel, soaked it in water from the pitcher, and gave it to her. Afterward, saying nothing more, he went back and opened the door to her closet and went inside.

Mary Norman knelt and laid the towel on Will's forehead. She worked over him a full minute be-

fore he stirred, opened his eyes, looked about him, and then pushed himself unsteadily to his feet.

"Are — are you all right?" Mary asked. "What happened?"

Will shook his head, and then his sultry gray glance settled on her. "Don't bother," he murmured.

"But what happened? I only saw —"

"Don't bother, I said," Will said curtly. "It was a cheap frame-up by a pair of cheap bounty-hunters. But it didn't work, did it?"

Mary Norman started to cry then. Will picked up his Stetson and left.

During his first look at the town Milt Barron made the pleasant discovery that nobody paid any attention to him. Among the scattering of punchers on the street and in the stores, he was inconspicuous. The only hostile glance he received was from a man he thought was one of the Nine X crew. Milt looked at him blankly and didn't speak.

After he met Will at the horses and talked with him, he headed idly for the big saloon across the street. Will's words were still in his mind, and he felt the anger that comes with helplessness. For it wasn't pleasant to see a friend break himself buying a squalid stone shack and a handful of stony acres so that he could hide a friend there. Milt felt a hot loyalty to Will. Some day, of course, he could and would repay Will tenfold for this

help, but that didn't comfort him now. He looked at the movement on the street with a kind of childlike hunger, thinking of the loneliness of the spread. He reflected, with a touch of irony, that Will had bought a place to hide him that was so much like prison that there was hardly any difference. An angry restlessness was on him as he shouldered through Hal Mohr's swing doors and tramped up to the bar and ordered a drink.

He gulped it down and poured another, feeling it warm his belly. He leaned both elbows on the bar and hunched his shoulders and stared in the bar mirror, seeing the image of a man he scarcely recognized. This was what hunger did to a man, he thought. Nature intended him to be a thick-bodied, burly man; and he had starved himself into this slim, work-worn-looking puncher in the mirror. His stomach protested at the liquor, and with a sudden recklessness he wondered how much it would protest at several more drinks. He took the bottle and his glass and tramped over to one of the tables where a dirty pack of cards was scattered. There was a desultory game of poker going on at one of the back tables.

He had another drink, shuffled the thick cards, and laid out a game of solitaire.

He was barely into it when he was aware of the bartender calling sharply to someone. He looked up, and standing in front of his table was a small Mexican boy.

"Get out of here, kid," the fat bartender called.

The boy extended a soiled envelope to Milt,

and Milt took it. On it, written in pencil, was the name: *Milt Barron*. Milt gave the boy a coin, and he ran out of the saloon.

Milt looked at the envelope. The drinks he had taken were working now, and he regarded the envelope with dispassionate curiosity. Only a handful of people here knew his name, and of them he couldn't think of one who didn't dislike him. Oh, yes, there was Becky Case. He looked at the writing, and it didn't seem like a woman's hand, but you never could tell. He propped the letter against the bottle and went on playing solitaire. He wanted to open it and read it, but his amusements were small enough these days. To prolong his curiosity was a form of enjoyment.

He played out his game of solitaire, poured himself another drink, and then reached for the letter. He opened it without haste, unfolded it, and read:

There's a drift fence a half mile up the wash from your place. You come there alone tonight, Murray Broome, or I may decide to collect your reward. Remember, I said alone. If you tell Danning about this I'll turn you up tomorrow morning. If you don't come I will too.

A sudden paralyzing nausea gripped Milt's belly, and when it passed he was dead sober. He folded the note, took a deep breath, and came to his feet, fighting down the urge to run. He went over to the bar, paid for the drinks, and

67

looked at the door. Walking through that door was the hardest thing he would ever have to do. He got a grip on himself then, reasoning that whoever sent the note wouldn't be waiting out there, and wouldn't have the law there. Whoever sent it wanted to talk to him first — for blackmail, probably.

He went out, and paused on the boardwalk in front of the saloon and looked up and down the street. Nobody was watching him, yet panic clawed inside him.

He made himself swing slowly under the tie rail and head for the horses. At that moment Will stepped out of the hotel and headed for the tie rail, too.

They met at the tie rail, and Will looked at him keenly. "What's the matter with you?" he asked. "You look sick."

Milt remembered the note said not to tell Will. He said in an unsteady voice, "I drank too much booze, Will. Lay off, will you, and let's get out of here."

He looked at Will and laughed shortly. "You don't look so good yourself."

"I'm all right," Will said. He wasn't going to tell Murray what happened in the hotel. If Mary Norman really was one of Milt's old sweethearts, he didn't want Milt to know she was in town. And he wanted to get Milt out of here right now.

"Let's ride," he agreed.

Chapter Five

Double Cross for a Pal

Supper that night was a dismal affair. Will was moody and silent, and Milt, for the first time in two months, left part of his food. Afterward, the crew drifted out, and Will and Milt went into the big room and lighted smokes. Will hauled up a stool by the big table and brought out his new tally book, while Milt watched from the door. There was something prophetic about Will's act; it told Milt that Will had decided irrevocably to buy this place and live here. Milt wanted to stride over, yank the book away from Will, and tell him why they couldn't stay, why they had to run. But time was slipping, and if he did that it meant that tonight he would have to run. To where? How could he hide? He remembered the long misery of riding the grub line, of hunger, of blistered hands, of long, lonely nights, of fear during the two months he had waited for Will to get this place. No, the place was bad enough, but it was better than being on the dodge.

Milt paced the floor in slow restlessness and finally stopped beside Will.

"I'm goin' out for air, Will. I shouldn't have

drunk that stuff today."

"Walk it off," Will murmured, not even glancing up from his tally book.

Milt went into the bunkhouse, which was empty now, took down his gun, rammed it in his waistband, and stepped out into the night.

He went down to the arroyo, cut up the canyon, and was soon lost in its gloom. Who had written the note he'd got today? Nobody knew him here, and he knew with utter certainty that any of his old friends couldn't recognize him. Had Will let it slip to someone? He rejected that, knowing wild horses couldn't drag his identity from Will.

Whoever it was, though, man or woman, would have to be killed. Milt faced that fact calmly. It didn't occur to him that whoever was waiting for him at the drift fence might have this same thought and might be prepared for him. In his mind, Milt knew that if he was to live, this person must die.

He came to the drift fence sooner than he expected. A dark tangle of brush on the other side of the fence sagged it, and he stopped and examined it in the deep gloom of the canyon. The walls sloped away here, so that the sides were not steep.

Nothing moved, and he could hear nothing. He rolled a smoke and lighted it. As the match flare died, a voice said from somewhere above him, "Throw that gun up here."

Milt started a little at the sound of the voice

70

and peered through the darkness. "It's Pres Milo, isn't it?"

"That's right. Throw that gun up here."

"I haven't got one."

"Throw it up here," Pres requested, "or I'll ride off and head for town."

For a moment, Milt didn't move. Milo hadn't seen the gun, he was sure. He simply knew he'd brought one. Why hadn't he brought two, so that he could have thrown one gun away and then, when Milo came down, used the other?

"Well?"

Silently, Milt took the gun out of his waistband and tossed it in the direction from which Milo's voice came. Milt heard a sound of cascading gravel, and then the dark bulk of Pres Milo stopped, some feet away from him.

"Stay right there," Milo said. "I can see pretty good, and I've got a gun in my hand."

Milt was silent a moment, gauging his chances. They weren't good. Pres might miss the first shot, he wouldn't the second or third.

Pres murmured, "Don't look so good, does it?"

"No."

"Sit down in the sand. You and me are goin' to parley."

Milt sat down. Pres, ten feet away, hunkered down on his heels, and the two of them peered through the darkness at each other.

"So I was right," Pres murmured.

"I'm here," Milt said dryly. "How did you find out my name?"

"I searched your shack yesterday. I found that pitcher of your mother and father."

"I thought I could hide that," Milt reflected. "How'd you get it open? I thought it was jammed shut."

"Dropped it and it come open," Pres said.

"Then let's get down to business," Milt said meagerly. "I suppose you're here to blackmail me. You're out of luck, my friend, I'm broke."

Pres Milo laughed shortly. "I don't give a damn about that. I don't give a damn about the five thousand on your head."

"A public servant," Milt sneered. "You just want to turn me up because you're a law-abiding citizen."

"Did I say I'd turn you up?" Pres murmured.

"Then get to it, man!" Milt said harshly.

"I need you," Pres said frankly, "to make some money."

Milt said nothing.

Pres shifted his position and said in a low voice, "Tell me some things first I need to know. You ain't got any money?"

"No. I was sued for libel, and the judgment went against me. It cleaned me out. You know that."

"Will Danning bought this place with his money?"

"That's right."

"He bought it so's he could hide you, didn't he?"

"Why else would he? It's no good for cattle."

72

There was a long pause, and Pres asked, "But has he bought it? The deed ain't recorded."

"As good as bought it," Milt said idly. "Chap Hale bought it for him. The title hasn't been transferred yet."

"Ah, hah!" Pres exclaimed delightedly, softly. "So it ain't his yet?"

"What are you gettin' at?" Milt said sharply.

Pres ignored him. "Do you think you could talk him into selling it?"

"No."

"Not even," Pres suggested slyly, "if I was to turn you up if you couldn't make him sell in a week?"

Milt remembered that Pres had already said he needed him. He realized suddenly that Pres Milo was a dull-witted man, that he had already tipped his hand. Milt seized on this shrewdly and he said immediately, "No."

"Why not?" Pres asked, surprised.

"Maybe I don't want to," Milt drawled. Pres was too surprised to answer, and Milt went on. "You want this place. I want to know why."

"You ain't goin' to," Pres said in a hard voice.

Milt came slowly to his feet. "Okay, you can go to hell."

Pres stood up, too. "Feelin' salty, eh? Maybe I'll just ride into town and see Phipps tonight and take you with me."

Milt laughed. It was a brash, arrogant laugh that Pres had never heard before, and didn't like. "You will like hell," Milt drawled. "I won't do you any good in jail. And I can do you some good outside of jail. You just said so."

Pres's slow understanding took that in, and he realized bitterly that he had tipped his hand too soon. He needed Barron's help, and Barron knew it. For a bleak three seconds, Pres contemplated shooting him, but plain, hard-headed sense cautioned him against it. Once already this lean-faced young man had led him into trouble with Will Danning. He should have been warned.

He considered Milt's spare dark figure standing there, hands on hips, and he felt a grudging admiration for him. It occurred to him with slow conviction that if this Milt Barron was that quick in his thinking, it would be better to have him on his side, instead of fighting him. Afterward, when it was done, he could turn him up and have him safely in prison. All this ribboned through Pres's mind, and then he lowered his gun.

"I'll make a bargain with you," he said.

"Let's hear it."

"You help me get Danning's place, and I'll forget what I know about you."

"The trouble with saddle tramps like you," Milt drawled, "is that you never forget. I still want to know why you want Danning's place."

Pres laughed. "I'll tell you. And you'll help me to get it. And like you said, I won't forget. I don't see no reason why you shouldn't know."

"That's what I'm telling you," Milt jeered.

"Sit down. This'll take some time."

Milt sat in the still-warm sand again, and again Pres hunkered down.

"This here Pitchfork spread, including a big chunk of the Sevier Brakes, used to be owned by the Gold Seal Land and Development Company. It was bought from the railroad. This here was an eastern company, and they had a crooked manager. He bought the land from the railroad for fifteen cents an acre, told the company he bought it for a dollar an acre, and then kept the difference and jumped the country. Soon's the company found out nobody'd buy the land, they sent a man out here and he seen it was just a gravel pile. They was stuck for a big piece of money. Harkins is the only man that ever leased an acre of it. Well, I know these brakes pretty good —"

"You've probably run enough stolen cattle through them, haven't you?" Milt said dryly.

"That's right," Pres said, unperturbed. "I know 'em pretty good, every trail, every canyon, every water hole. About six years back I come across somethin' in one of those deep cuts over toward Sevier Creek. That ground was green, kind of like."

Milt said sharply, "What does that mean?"

"This one meant a copper deposit," Pres said quietly. "I got a prospector in here from Butte to make sure. He disappeared."

He paused, and Milt shivered a little in the night. He knew what Pres meant, but he said nothing.

When Milt didn't comment, Pres went on. "As soon as I was sure, I tried to get the money to buy that piece. But the company wouldn't sell an acre unless I bought enough to cost ten thousand dollars. I tried to talk 'em out of it. That got them wonderin'. They hired a mining engineer and sent him to Yellow Jacket. He was lookin' for somebody to guide him around in them brakes. I sent a couple of men to him, and they guided him. But they steered clear of that canyon. The day this engineer was goin' to look over that canyon, I caught him the night before and beat him up."

"So I heard," Milt said. "He left, didn't he?"

"Where'd you hear?"

"Miss Case."

Pres said, "So she told you, huh? Well, she don't know why I beat him. That's why. Because he was gettin' close. And he never come back. So for the last five years I been tryin' to get hold of the money to buy the place from the company. I almost had it once, but I lost in a poker game. And then Will Danning comes along."

"And buys it out from under you."

"That's right. And he's goin' to sell it back to me. And you're goin' to talk him into it."

Milt said dryly, "I haven't heard you mention my cut."

"You'll git a cut, soon's I see if you can swing the deal."

Milt was quiet a long moment, considering what

76

Pres had told him. He felt a vague excitement stirring within him as a man will when his ability is challenged. Pres Milo was onto something big, just how big even he didn't realize. Yet Milt couldn't tell Will of it, or else Pres would turn him over to the law. But why would Will ever have to know? It wouldn't be hurting Will if the place was sold and Will got his money back. Once that was done, Pres could buy the place and go ahead with the mining end of it. And he would have to kick through with Milt's share of the cut, or else Milt could start a search for the prospector's body. Pres blackmailed him, he blackmailed Pres. Yes, he could do business with Pres if he was driven to it — but not before he'd tried something else.

Milt rose and said softly, "*Bueno.* You're sure there's a big deposit?"

"Dead sure. The prospector said there was hundreds of thousands of tons."

Milt came slowly toward Pres, holding out his hand. "It's a deal. We're partners, eh, Pres?"

"You mean you'll swing it?"

"That's what I mean."

Pres put out his big paw, and they shook hands.

Milt said, "Now put that gun away. You won't need it any more. Where's your horse?"

"Up over the ridge."

Milt took Pres's arm and gently turned him toward the bank and started to talk of his chances with Will. While he talked, he steered Pres, who was listening carefully, in the direction in which he had thrown his gun. When they came to the bank, he stepped behind and Pres clambered up the steep slope, Milt at his heels.

Milt felt in the loose gravel as he walked, searching frantically for the gun. Pres was talking now, ahead of him, but Milt paid no attention.

And then his fingers touched the cool metal of the six-gun which had been buried under an inch of earthslide.

His fingers wrapped around it, and at that moment Pres ceased talking and turned around, wondering at Milt's silence. He saw Milt straighten up, something in his hand, and Pres's intuition told him what it was.

He lunged frantically for the top of the ridge and heard the gun cock. He dived wildly over the crest as the gun hammered out behind him. He felt something nudge him in the shoulder, and then he was rolling down the other side. He drew his own gun and, softly swearing, started back up the slope.

And then he realized that he couldn't kill Milt. He needed Milt, and Milt didn't need him; in fact, Milt wanted him dead.

He saw Milt's head sky-lined, and then Pres ran. Another shot roared out in the night, and he felt the passing of the bullet over his head. He dived into the nearest brush, lost his hat, and started running again, bent over. Another and yet another shot hammered out, but they were farther away now. And then he achieved the next ridge, and he paused to listen.

He heard a high, wild cursing off in the direction from which he had run.

He raised his voice and yelled, "Remember what I said, Barron!"

For answer, he got more of Milt's vicious cursing. Afterward Milt rammed his gun in his waistband and slid down to the arroyo. A wicked and savage anger had its way with him for a while. He had almost done it, almost killed the only man beside Will who knew his real identity. One second longer there on the slope and his slug would have caught Pres in the back, silencing him forever.

As he tramped down the arroyo again, he became calm. He wasn't afraid of Pres turning him up; the man wouldn't lose his last chance of getting Will's place just for revenge. But it left Milt with the other alternative, that of persuading Will to get rid of the place. And deep down within him, Milt, knowing Will's bottomless stubbornness, figured it might not be so easy.

He heard the sound of horses approaching down the arroyo. That would be Will, who couldn't have helped but hear the shots.

Out of the darkness, a horseman suddenly appeared, and Will called harshly, "That you, Milt?"

"Will!" Milt called.

Will rode up, holstering his gun. "What were those shots?"

"I don't know," Milt said, his voice spuriously excited. "Somebody took a shot at me, Will!"

Just then Pinky and Ollie rode up, too. Will

told them everything was all right, and they headed down the arroyo again. Will dismounted and led his horse over to Milt.

"What happened, now?"

"I walked as far as the drift fence and had a smoke! All of a sudden, somebody shot at me from the arroyo bank! Who was it, Will?" His voice was tense with excitement.

Will said slowly, "I dunno. Likely somebody hangin' around watchin' our beef, and they thought you had 'em spotted."

There was a short silence, and then Milt burst out, "No! You're just sayin' that, Will. I tell you, somebody knows me here! They knew it was me! They were tryin' to kill me!"

Will said gently, "Easy, fella. Nobody knows you here."

Milt came closer to him, and his voice was low and strained. "Look, Will. Let's pull out of here! I tell you, somebody knows who I am. It isn't safe!"

"You're excited," Will said calmly. "Hell, it was some of Pres Milo's crew prowlin' around, and they figured to scare you off."

But Milt shook his head violently and grabbed Will's arm. "I tell you, Will, they know me here! I've felt it! Look." His voice was pleading now. "You don't own the place yet, Will! Don't buy it! Tell Chap Hale you've changed your mind, and let's pull out of here!"

"And leave Chap stuck with this place he can't use? I couldn't, Milt."

80

"Pres Milo wants it, Becky Case said! Let Chap sell it to him!"

"I couldn't," Will said gently, patiently. "Look, fella. You're spooky. Somewhere else looks better now. But they're all the same, Milt — not so good as this. They'll let us alone here. And if they crowd us, we can live back there in the Sevier Brakes for a year. We can't do better, Milt."

Milt said desperately, "But they'll kill me, Will. I tell you, they know! I've got to get out of here!"

It was one last desperate plea, and for a full minute Will regarded him in the silence. He was glad he couldn't see Milt's face, for Milt was afraid. He'd been scared, and scared badly. But Will wasn't going to let Milt's fear stampede him. He said gently, "You're spooked, Milt. Nobody knows you."

"You won't let Chap have it and pull out?"

"I can't."

Milt turned away, and tramped down the arroyo. His anger was more than half genuine, for he knew that Will was being stubborn, and that he'd failed in his first attempt. Now, he'd have to approach it some other way, and with Pres's help — if he could get it.

Chapter Six

DOWN A SINISTER TRAIL

Milt sulked the next morning. Will and Pinky tended to a long-overdue shoeing job on the *remuda*. It was hot in the wagon shed, which Will was using as the temporary blacksmith shop, and their equipment was none too good. Three of the horses were sore-footed, and between their temper and the heat, Will was in an edgy temper. He was remembering Milt's talk of last night, and he couldn't see much but trouble ahead for them. They had been here on the spread less than a week, and already Milt was moody. But what was worse, when he was in one of his sulking moods, he refused to work. Will didn't mind that, except that Pinky and Ollie, noting it, would think it queer and might start wondering. And all morning Milt, whose rightful job this was, piddled around with a hammer and a handful of nails, trying to patch up the rotten boards of the horse trough.

Finished with his job, he came over to the wagon shed and lounged in the doorway. It was his big bay gelding, still sore-footed from the long drive across the stony Capitan desert, that Will was shoeing. He was an ugly devil, shy of anyone but Milt, and he kept sidling away, ears back, waiting for the chance he wanted.

Pinky, sensing his mood, backed wide in a circle and cursed him in tuneless passion, adding, "If I get close enough to you, you walleyed jughead, I'll kick you in the belly so hard I'll curl your toes."

Milt said quietly from the door, "I don't reckon you will." Milt's eyes were sultry and wild, and on his face was a look of insufferable insolence that could be a red flag to a man in Pinky's harassed mood.

Will said quickly, "Pink, go get us a bucket of water and let me handle him."

Pinky looked belligerently at Milt and walked out. Will was stripped to the waist in the heat. He walked up to the big bay's head and started to stroke his nose. His long, lean muscles rippled as his arms moved, and he absently clucked at the horse, watching Milt. He said gently to Milt, "Maybe I ought to tell each man to shoe his own string."

Milt said quietly, "Maybe you had."

Will left the horse and walked slowly over to Milt, a smile on his face. "Look, fella. You want to be careful with Pinky and Ollie. They don't know you. If they don't like your talk, they'll tie into you."

Milt looked amused. "I can take care of that, too."

"You don't get it," Will said. "They think you're my foreman. They'll take orders from you as long as you work with 'em."

"Meanin' I'm not workin' this morning?"

"That's it."

Milt straightened up and went to his horse and untied his halter.

"Let it ride," he murmured.

Will was puzzled. He knew Milt in all his moodiness, and now he was a little afraid of it. He glanced up at the house, saw that Pinky was still in the kitchen, and came over to Milt.

"Look, fella," he said affectionately. "Forget last night, can't you? Nothin' will happen. We're safe here."

Milt said, "Sure," and didn't look at him. He led the bay out to the corral, turned him in, then took his rope off his saddle on the poles.

Scowling, Will drifted over to the corral. Milt was working out his little chestnut mare from the bunch in the corral that had already been shod. He separated her, spooked her back away from the others, shook out his rope, made his cast, and led her over to his saddle and bridle on the corral poles.

Will came up and leaned on the corral, the skin of his back and arms a dead white compared to his hands and face. He said idly, "Goin' to take a look around?"

Milt looked at him quickly, hotly.

"What if I am?" he asked.

Will shrugged and said nothing, only regarded Milt with puzzled affection.

Milt swung the saddle on, cinched it up, and

then said, "I'm goin' to town."

Immediately Will thought of Mary Norman. "Think you ought to?" he murmured.

Milt wheeled and stared at him. "Hell, Will, am I a prisoner here?"

Will shook his head. "If you ain't in town, then nobody can see you," he pointed out. "Besides, you'll hit town about dark. You aim to stay all night?"

"Do you care?" Milt asked hotly.

Will straightened up. "I don't care, Milt. I'm thinkin' of you. But if you want to head for town, go ahead. It's your risk."

"That's what I've been tryin' to tell you, Will," Milt said shortly.

He led the mare out the gate, closed it, swung into the saddle, and slowly lined out for town. His back was straight, cocky, somehow arrogant.

Will watched him go with a mingled exasperation and foreboding. He didn't want him to go to Yellow Jacket, and yet he couldn't tell Milt the reason. For if he did, Milt would laugh and then seek out Mary Norman the first time he was lonely for a woman. It was his way never to think of the risk, to always choose the reckless way, to damn the consequences. It was this in him that Will knew he would have to fight. It was Milt's neck, yet he was more careless of it than anybody else.

The appearance of Pinky, lugging a bucket of water from the cookshack, stirred Will to action. He went into the wagon shed, donned his shirt, and, when Pinky appeared, said, "Let's call it a mornin', Pinky. I've got to go to town."

Will's first impulse was to catch up with Milt and ride in with him. But when he was finished giving Pinky orders for the afternoon's work, Milt was already out of sight over the mesa's rimrock. It came to Will with a feeling of small hurt that Milt had foreseen his coming along, and that he'd ridden ahead on purpose.

Will didn't hurry. He never caught sight of Milt on the ride, and he drifted into Yellow Jacket at suppertime. He had supper alone, and afterward strolled down the long street in the dusk, a big, lonely man who nodded to everyone and yet really spoke to nobody.

At full dark, he drifted into Hal Mohr's saloon, collected the papers, and took a seat at one of the back tables where he could watch the door.

By ten o'clock, Will had dropped two dollars in a poker game that bored him, when Milt came in. Milt's face was sulky, faintly wicked-looking, and the way he came up to the bar, abruptly pushed his hat off his forehead, folded his arms, and let his shoulders sink with deep exhaustion, told Will that Milt's mood had not left him. Will concentrated on his cards.

Soon he looked up to see Milt standing over him watching him with smoky, sultry eyes. Milt suddenly grinned then, as if apologizing. Will cashed in his chips, and he and Milt drifted over to the bar.

They ordered drinks, and then Milt said, "I'm sorry for the raggin', Will. I'm just edgy." He rubbed his eyes with his thumb and third finger and then stared in the bar mirror, grinning at Will.

"Forget it," Will said. He straightened up. "Well, I'm ridin' out."

Milt fell in behind him as they left the saloon. Out on the boardwalk, Will stopped and took a deep breath of air, clearing the smoke of the saloon out of his lungs. Upstreet, a single puncher was tramping toward the four corners, whistling cheerfully, his boots ringing hollowly on the boardwalk.

And then, crashing into that silence, came the boom of a single gunshot.

Following it, there was a heavy thudding, as of something falling down a stairs.

Will looked across and upstreet in the direction from which the sound had come. He and Milt exchanged brief glances and headed upstreet. The puncher had stopped his whistling and was staring across the street.

Then there was the added sound of a man running downstairs, taking the steps four at a time. And suddenly, from out of the stairwell that led to Chap Hale's office, the shadowy figure of a man appeared, paused, then cut in back between the buildings

Will ran, then. He dodged under the tie rail and hauled up in front of Chap Hale's stairs.

There on the bottom landing, half sprawled

onto the boardwalk, was Chap Hale.

Will stopped, knelt, took one look at Chap's chest, saw the stain spreading there, and knew Chap was dead.

The puncher came up beside them then; and Will rose, pulling out his gun.

"He went this way," he said. "Come on."

Will knifed in between the two buildings, Milt and the puncher at his heels. It was Will who first burst out into the dark alley, looking up and down it. Toward the four-corners end of the alley, he saw a man running.

Will snapped a shot at him, and the running man turned and fired wildly at them. Then he cut to one side and disappeared into the tangle of sheds and barns to the left.

Will reached the spot first and saw a door of a barn on the left swinging shut and heard a sound inside the barn. He turned and shouted to Milt and the puncher, "He's in here! Surround it!"

He followed his own orders then, and cut around to the front of the barn. The puncher was next, and he paused at the long side of the barn.

Will couldn't see Milt, but he yelled, "You in the alley, Milt?"

"Back here," Milt called.

"He's in here," Will said. "I'm damn sure of it."

The puncher drawled, "Well, if he is, he ain't goin' to get out, then."

Will said, "Move up this way a little where you can see the door here. I'm goin' in after him."

"Better be careful," the puncher protested.

Will paid no attention. He yanked the door open and dodged inside. Then he stopped to listen. He heard the nervous stomping of animals in their stalls, and that was all. A cold anger hammered through his veins as he listened, knowing that unless he had a light here, he could pass within a foot of the man without knowing it. On the other hand, a light would attract the man's fire.

Will lifted his hand and felt along the wall just inside the door where a lantern usually hangs. He found it, took it down, then stepped outside, and closed the door. He lighted the lantern, opened the door, and set it on the floor inside.

Nothing happened. He stepped inside carefully, and still nothing happened. Three stalled horses regarded him with mild and uneasy curiosity. Will watched them, alert for any indication by their actions that someone was hiding in their stalls. He couldn't see anything strange.

Picking up the lantern, holding his gun in the other hand, he drifted back down the barn, knowing he made a good target and not caring. Beyond the stalls, there was a wagon, a buggy, a workbench, a tangle of harness, and some miscellaneous gear. A door opened from this room to the outside of the barn, and there was a pass-door in the big back door of the barn. *Both doors are covered,*

Will thought, *He's in here and he can't get out.*

But a slow examination of the room revealed nothing. That left the loft above the stalls.

Will put his lantern down, swung onto the loft ladder, and climbed it slowly. When he was at the top, he dived swiftly into the hay and waited. No sound. He came to his feet and slowly beat along the hay. He tramped every square foot of the small loft, knowing how easy it would be to hide in it. But there was nobody there.

He came down and stood in the middle of the barn, looking around him carefully. He had missed nothing, yet there was nobody there.

Taking the lantern, he stepped out into the alley. Milt was waiting there, gun drawn.

"Anybody come out, Milt?"

"No. I could have seen 'em," Milt said.

The puncher, hearing voices, drifted around the corner. Will looked at him bleakly, suspicion slowly forming. The puncher was a middle-aged responsible-looking man, and Will was puzzled.

"He didn't dodge out your side?" Will asked.

The puncher shook his head.

"He went in there," Will said grimly. "I saw the door swinging. I heard him."

The puncher looked at him sharply. "You must have been mistaken, mister, because he never come out."

Will kept looking at him and, still keeping his gaze on the man, he said to Milt, "You say you didn't see him come out, Milt?"

"He didn't," Milt said firmly. "I couldn't have

helped but see him, Will."

"And you didn't see anything?" he asked the puncher again.

The puncher said coldly, "No, I didn't see anything. You think I'm lyin'?"

"That's what I think," Will said softly.

The two of them stared at each other, each with a gun in his hand. Will said, "You drop that gun, fella, and come along with me. Whoever got Chap Hale was a friend of yours, because you let him get away."

"You go to hell," the puncher said angrily. "I ain't handing over my gun to you nor anybody else."

The lantern was midway between the two men. His gun still at his side, Will started toward the puncher. The man kicked out the lantern, plunging them into immediate darkness. Will shot blindly, and the puncher shot. Will's eyes were not yet washed clear of the lantern light, but he felt the bullet miss him by inches and heard it slam into the barn.

He heard the man running, and shot wildly again, moving after him.

Now he saw the man, and shot once more. The puncher dived behind a rain barrel set against the back of one of the buildings, and then he shot twice. His shots were close, and Will ducked in behind a shed on the other side of the alley.

He loaded his gun, calling, "Better give up, fella. I'm comin' after you."

The puncher yelled, "Go to hell!"

Will called, "Circle him, Milt."

And Milt, from back by the barn, answered, "Here comes a bunch of men, Will. Be careful."

Will took aim and sent three slugs slamming into the barrel. The sound of men running toward him made him turn his head. The man in the lead was carrying a lantern, and there must have been a dozen others behind him.

He came to a halt beside Will, flattened against the wall. Will could see the sheriff's star on the man's vest. "Over there behind the barrel," Will said, jerking his head. "There's the man you want."

Sheriff Phipps called toward the puncher, "Throw your gun away and come out of there." He was an old man, with a seamed face and a mustache the color of straw. His eyes were pale and tired-looking, but they were fearless. He handed the lantern to one of the other men and started for the barrel, gun in hand.

"That you, John?" the puncher called.

Sheriff Phipps stopped, and turned slowly to look at Will. "Hell, that's Harry Mygrave."

Will said, "I don't care who he is, sheriff. He let Chap Hale's killer escape."

Phipps turned and said, "Come out, Harry."

"You taken that damn maniac's gun away from him?"

"Drop your gun," Phipps said to Will.

Will drawled, "I reckon I'll keep it."

Phipps looked searchingly at him and then

turned and called, "Keep your gun, Harry. But come out of there."

Slowly the puncher rose from behind the barrel, gun in hand, and walked toward the sheriff.

Will walked slowly over to the pair of them, and the others trailed behind.

Phipps said to Will, "I've known Harry Mygrave for twenty years. There ain't a crooked thing about him."

"He let Chap's killer go," Will said stubbornly. "You aim to arrest him?"

Phipps turned to Mygrave. The puncher was really angry now. His eyes flashed wickedly, and he was so mad his lips trembled.

"What happened, Harry?" Sheriff Phipps asked.

Harry told him. The three of them were attracted by the shot. They saw the killer flee. Will took after him, the other two following. He went into a barn. They surrounded it, the barn was searched, but the man wasn't there.

"Who's the third man?" the sheriff rapped out.

Milt stepped up. His face was pale, his eyes wary and careful in that dim lantern light.

"He's my foreman," Will said. "He's new here. I don't have to wonder about him. He didn't know Hale and he doesn't know a man in town."

Sheriff Phipps regarded Milt briefly and then said to Will, "And you think Harry let him go?"

"He had to," Will said stubbornly, his voice hard in anger. "I didn't let him go. Milt didn't. And he was in the barn!"

Harry said hotly, "Damn you, Chap Hale was a friend of mine, too! If anyone let him go, that ramrod of yours was the man!"

"You're a liar!" Will said in cold wrath. "You were in with Chap's killer!"

Harry Mygrave lunged for Will. Phipps grabbed him, and Will dived for Mygrave. A dozen men grabbed him, and Will fought blindly, trying to get at Mygrave. There was a babel of voices, some bitter cursing, and then Will bucked loose. He lunged at Mygrave, grappled with him, and they fell in the dust of the alley. A red, murdering rage flamed through Will. He wrapped his big hands around Mygrave's throat and throttled him. He was aware of Mygrave bucking under him, and of a dozen men trying to tear his hands away. And then something smashed across his skull, and his muscles seemed turned to water.

When he came to, his arms were pinned by two men, and he could hear Sheriff Phipps's wrathful voice saying, "— and stay out of town until he's calmed down. You understand that, Harry?"

"I'll kill him!" Harry said bitterly. "The damn murderin' fool!"

Will was propelled down the alley, his steps dragging. He tried to shake his head but it wasn't clear. He was aware of entering a room, a lighted room, and then he was hauled through it, a door was opened, and he was set on a cot. A dipper of ice-cold water slashed into his face, taking his breath away.

When he opened his eyes, still shaking his head, he was alone with Sheriff Phipps in a jail cell. Will looked around him and then up at Phipps's face. The old man's expression was of bleak anger.

"You're goin' to cool off," Phipps said grimly. "I'm sorry I had to buffalo you, but you'd of killed Harry."

"What am I in here for?" Will asked slowly.

"It's an arrest, assault and battery. Maybe in the morning after you've cooled off a fine will make you see sense."

Will came weakly to his feet, his anger returning. "And you're lettin' this Mygrave go?"

"Listen," Phipps said in a hard voice. "I know Mygrave. I don't know you. Mygrave is the straightest, most honest and peaceful man I've known in twenty years! You're crazy-mad, that's all, Danning."

"But he let Chap's killer go!" Will shouted.

"You're wrong," Phipps said flatly. "Either your man let him go, he sneaked out unbeknownst to anybody, or else he was never in there."

"He was in there!"

Phipps came over and pushed Will gently to a seat on the cot. "Listen, son," he said, almost with gentleness. "I know how you feel. But you ain't thinkin' straight. Sleep on it, and then you'll see how it could have happened."

Will said nothing. He heard the cell door shut, and he put his face in his hands and closed his eyes. His head ached miserably, but he wasn't mad any more. He was only puzzled. He was positive, dead-sure, that whoever it was he chased had gone into that barn. He was also dead-sure that when he looked through the barn the man wasn't there. That left only Milt and this Harry Mygrave responsible for his escape. Milt was out; he couldn't have been blind enough to miss seeing the man, and he wouldn't let him go on purpose. No, it was Mygrave who did it. Yet he seemed a plain, decent sort of man, and the sheriff seemed honest enough, too. It didn't make sense.

He heard the corridor door open and footsteps in the cell corridor and he looked up.

"Charlie Sommers!" he said in a low, amazed voice.

"Howdy, Will." Charlie Sommers's ruddy cheeks were as shiny as new apples. He was dressed in a black suit, and he extended his hand in friendly fashion, leaning on the bars.

Will rose and shook hands with him. "What are you doin' here?"

"I had some business here. Come in tonight on the freight. I heard all the ruckus, and they told me it was Will Danning. Thought I'd look you up and see if I could help."

Will sat down because his knees threatened to give way. But he wasn't so exhausted he couldn't realize the threat in Sommers's presence. For Charlie Sommers was a deputy U. S. marshal, the man who had been delegated by the Commissioner and Marshal to work on the Murray Broome case. He wasn't a brilliant man, but a more dogged one never lived. He was friendly,

96

reasonable, implacable as an Indian, the best peace officer in the Territory. Will liked him — and feared him. His presence here now might be accident, or it might be a hunch. And Milt was in town.

All this flashed swiftly through Will's mind as he sat down.

Sommers said, "Phipps is a good man, Will. They don't come better. So is Mygrave, Phipps says, and I'll take his word. You must have been mistaken."

Will said, "What happened to Chap?"

"Nearest they can figure is that whoever killed him waited on the top landing. The old boy was coming upstairs, reached the landing, and was shot in the chest by someone on the landing. He fell downstairs, and his killer ducked out behind him."

Will said bleakly, "Well, he was ready to die. But not that way, Charlie, not that way."

Sommers nodded somberly. "I told Phipps about you. The judge will suspend the fine at the hearing tomorrow, and let you off with a scolding."

"Thanks," Will said.

Sommers grinned at him. "You know, Will, you got a real honin' for trouble. I figured after you'd slugged that sheriff in the courtroom a couple months ago, you'd kind of learn to hold your temper."

Will smiled faintly and shook his head.

Sommers said pleasantly, "Well, I'm still lookin'

for Murray Broome, Will. You ain't ready to tell me where he is, are you?"

Will looked slowly at Sommers, who was grinning cheerfully. Will said wearily, "That's an old joke, Charlie. I wish you'd forget it."

Charlie Sommers said meagerly, "I don't aim to forget it, Will. You see, you liked Chap Hale, and a dirty killer got him. Senator Mason was as nice an old fellow as Chap. And a dirty killer got him, too. Only difference is, we know Mason's killer. It was Broome, and all we got to do is catch him. Think it over."

"I've thought it over," Will said angrily. "I'm through with it, Charlie. Murray Broome was a good boss to me! That's all I know!"

Charlie Sommers straightened up. "It had better be all you know, Will. Because when we get Broome, anybody that stands in our way is goin' to get it, too." He waved carelessly. "See you tomorrow. Get some sleep."

He went out, and Will felt the old angry fear return. Where was Milt? He knew Charlie Sommers, too. Would he have heard about Charlie's presence and have sense enough to dodge out of town? He wished savagely that he could warn Milt before he walked into Sommers.

He heard the corridor door open again, and looked up.

Becky Case stood there, an expression of puzzled friendliness in her face.

Will rose and came over to the bars. Becky was dressed in blue, and Will was a little awed.

This wasn't the rather sober girl in Levis he remembered; this was a woman, a beautiful woman, too.

Becky said, "I heard about it, Will. I — don't blame you."

"This don't matter," Will said bleakly. "Chap's dead."

Becky nodded. It occurred swiftly to Will that here was his way to get a message out. He said, "Becky, you're the only friend I've got in this country. I — want to ask you a favor."

"Go ahead, Will."

"Will you find Milt and tell him to go back to the spread, tonight, right now, without comin' to see me, even?"

"Of course," Becky said slowly, and then added in a low tone, "Are you worried for fear they'll question him, Will?"

Will's face was smooth, impassive, but he felt a cold apprehension at Becky's words. He said slowly, "I'm afraid to leave the ranch without a boss in case there's trouble out there." He drawled, "What do you mean, question?"

Slow color crept into Becky's face, but she said stubbornly, "You won't get mad, Will, if I tell you about something that happened tonight?"

"No."

Becky said earnestly, "The other day when Pres and our men rode up to your place and were going to burn it, I told Dad. I was there so he knew it was the truth. I asked him to fire Pres." She hesitated and then went on in a dull voice.

99

"You remember, I told you I thought Pres was blackmailing Dad?"

"Yes."

"Well, he is. Dad admitted it to me. He said he couldn't fire Pres. I argued with him for five days. I never gave him a moment's peace. I wanted him to come to Chap Hale and tell him the story. Chap's his oldest friend. He didn't want to, but he finally agreed that if anyone could tell him what to do to get rid of Pres, it would be Chap. You understand?"

Will nodded, listening intently.

"This afternoon we drove in together, Dad and I. We got in after dark, and went straight to Chap's office. But there was somebody there ahead of us. I heard him, there in the office. He and Chap were arguing, and they didn't hear us. We went away, but I recognized the man's voice who was talking to Chap."

"Who was it?"

"That's what's queer, Will." Becky said slowly. "It was Milt Barron."

Milt watched Will, sagging between two men, hauled into the lighted sheriff's office. From his position between two dark stores across the street, he could see that Will was walking, and that he wasn't hurt. And then, for the first time since the fight in the alley, he turned his thoughts to what had happened there. Right now, it seemed as if it hadn't happened.

He'd been standing in the alley, gun drawn,

and had just shouted to Will reassuring him he had the alley covered, when he had heard a soft voice from inside the barn. "Milt?"

It was Pres. For a moment, he had stood there, stunned. Pres Milo was the man who killed Chap Hale!

Then Pres had opened the door and slipped out, gun in hand. Pres had whispered, "When this is over, come to the station."

And before Milt had had a chance to answer, Pres slipped off in the dark. Pres had assumed that Milt would have to help him, and he'd been right. Milt had let him escape.

Milt looked bleakly toward the dark hulk of the station upstreet. Pres was a cheap killer. Why in hell had he ever told Pres tonight before he met Will in the saloon that he had talked with Chap Hale? That was what did it, that was what caused Chap's death. He'd met Pres by the hotel, just after he'd left Chap. They'd walked to the edge of town and back in the darkness, and he'd told Pres that Will was determined to buy the ranch. He told him how he'd gone to Chap and pleaded with him not to sell the ranch to Will. His grounds for pleading had sounded sensible — as Will's friend and foreman, he didn't want to see him stuck with a piece of worthless property. Chap agreed, but said it was Will's business. Milt insisted, Chap refused, and there had been an argument. But Chap was adamant, and Milt left him.

Pres had listened to all this, grunted, said good-by; and Milt went over to the saloon where Will was. Pres had gone up Chap's stairs, waited for him, and killed him.

Across the street now in the sheriff's office men were talking. Milt stepped out on the walk and headed slowly, reluctantly for the station where Pres said he would be. He knew with dismal conviction that the time for him to act had passed. If he'd shot Pres there in the alley, he would be clear. But he couldn't shoot Pres now; it was too late, and he couldn't explain it.

Milt approached the dark station and walked around to the platform in front.

A man stirred in the shadows and said, "Here."

Milt walked up to him and said in a small wicked voice, "I don't know why I don't kill you now, Pres."

Pres laughed. "Yes you do, fella. I'm through worryin' about you. You cut down on me now and Will Danning will know you let me out of the barn, won't he? And what'll you tell him?"

Milt said hotly, "What did you kill Hale for? What sense does it make?"

"You don't see?"

"Hell, no!" Milt said savagely. "He had nothin' to do with it, nothin' at all."

"Listen," Pres sneered. "You told me Will Danning didn't own the place yet, didn't you?"

"Yes."

"And that Chap Hale had the deed?"

"Yes."

"Then Danning ain't goin' to own it. Chap

102

can't deed him the place if he's dead, can he?"

Milt was mute. It was the truth, a truth that hadn't dawned on him. He felt a loathing for Pres, but beyond that he had to admit Pres had done the only thing that would forestall Will's getting the place.

Milt said, "Now what'll happen to the place?"

"I dunno," Pres said. "It'll give us time, anyway."

Milt said tonelessly, "You're a hardcase, aren't you, Pres? You'd kill any man that stands in your way, wouldn't you?"

Pres was silent, uneasy.

"There's nothin' I can do about Hale," Milt went on. "He's dead, and I didn't know you'd kill him or I'd never have told you what I did. But I'm goin' to make you a promise, Pres."

"Yeah?" Pres asked slowly.

"You hurt Will Danning, and, by God, I'll kill you!" His voice was low, passionate, wild, and in it was more threat than was in his words.

Pres said uneasily, "Take it easy, Milt. Hell, I won't hurt Danning. We can get the place now."

Milt said nothing more. He turned on his heel and walked away. His thoughts were bleak and terrible as he tramped across the cinders to the boardwalk. He felt a guilt in Chap Hale's death. True, the old man was eighty; death didn't matter so much. But what did matter was that Pres was drawing him into something evil and sinister, and he was helpless to pull out. Slowly and irrevocably, he was being drawn into it.

He passed the sheriff's office, and immediately afterward the door opened. He heard it shut, heard a woman's footsteps on the boardwalk, and then a voice called, "Milt Barron!"

Milt waited. It was Becky Case, he saw, as she came closer. He touched his hat and smiled, feeling a lift at the sight of something as beautiful and clean as this girl.

She fell in beside him and said, "I just saw Will."

"He's all right, isn't he?"

"Yes. He had a message for you."

Milt looked at her curiously, and Becky went on. "He said he wanted you to go out to the ranch tonight, right now, without coming to see him, even."

Milt said uneasily, "Did he say why?"

"He said he was afraid to leave the ranch alone in case — well, in case it was raided again. By us, I suppose."

Milt laughed boyishly. "That's a funny message comin' from the people he's supposed to be afraid of."

Becky laughed. They were even with the hotel now, and Milt wanted to go in and talk with her. He was hungry for a woman's company, hungry for just a look at a pretty woman. There was a scattering of men in the lobby, Milt could see as he glanced through the lobby window.

And then, just as he was about to look away, he yanked his gaze back.

There, half turned to him, sitting under one

of the overhead lamps and talking to a couple of men, was Charlie Sommers.

Milt felt his stomach coil in fear. He stared at the man, fascinated, and then Becky's voice said, "You've been holding that door handle for a half minute, Milt. Aren't you going to let me in?"

"Sure. Yes, sure," Milt said hastily. He looked at Becky, a sick smile on his face, and touched his hat.

"Good night."

He was gone down street, head turned toward the opposite sidewalk, before Becky had time to answer him.

Chapter Seven

FRAME-UP

A little before noon next day Will was hauled before the justice of the peace, whose chambers were the Masonic Hall over Dunn's General Store, and fined twenty-five dollars. The fine was suspended, but not before the judge, true to Charlie Sommers's prediction, gave Will a scolding for accusing innocent people of serious crimes. Will took it without a word, and afterward was freed. Sheriff Phipps, with Chap Hale's murder on his hands, put in only a perfunctory appearance, warned Will to keep away from Harry Mygrave, and then went out to resume his investigation at Chap's office.

Will went to the barbershop to get cleaned up. Lying there in the chair, eyes closed, while the barber shaved him, he had several things to think about. First was Milt. Will had stayed awake far into the night trying to puzzle out why Milt would have wanted to see Chap. And did his talk with Chap have any connection with Chap's death? With a stern impartiality, Will made himself consider that, but he couldn't see any connection. Milt was with him when Chap was killed, and he'd joined in the hunt for the killer. No, Milt was clear — but why had he argued so violently with Chap?

The other thing that troubled Will was the disposition of the spread. Chap still owned it. There might be some tiresome court requirements to go through before Will could get it. However, Chap's letters and the fact that he had accepted Will's money would be proof enough to the court that the executors of Chap's estate would be morally bound to turn over the spread to him.

He didn't know what to think of Chap's death. Who could have killed him, and why? Will met a blank there. He knew nothing about Chap, about his enemies. Chap had lived a lifetime here, and all men have enemies. Will didn't have a clue to his death; only Phipps could unravel that killing.

The other thing that troubled him was the presence of Charlie Sommers. It could mean that he was on Milt's trail, or it could mean nothing except that he was passing through on business of his office.

Before he ate Will had a drink in Mohr's saloon and learned that Chap was to be buried early that afternoon from the small white church down one of the back streets. Will didn't go to the services, but he was the first one at the small bleak cemetery out on the flats where the fresh earth from Chap's grave was drying in the sun.

A lot of people were at Chap's funeral, among them Phipps, Case and Becky, and Pres Milo.

The words that were spoken there didn't mean much to Will; he thought of Chap only as an old man with a passionate interest in justice, a man who had befriended him and counseled him — and whose counsel he had not followed. And during that service he made a private vow that he would get Chap's killer if it turned out to be Milt himself. He would see Mygrave, too — sheriff or no sheriff.

After the services, Will hunted out Sheriff Phipps, who was dressed in a hot black suit. The old man looked sad, for Chap Hale was one of his friends. He greeted Will coolly when Will spoke to him, and led him out of the slow stream of people who were heading for their buggies and horses at the cemetery tie rail.

"I'd like to ask a couple of questions, sheriff," Will began.

Phipps nodded.

Will asked, "Do you know the man that waited on the landing for Chap?"

Phipps angrily shook his head. "If I did, would I be here now?"

"Who are Chap's heirs?"

"Relatives back East."

"Who's handlin' his property?"

Phipps looked at him curiously.

"His executor is Angus Case."

Will was inwardly dismayed at that, but his lean face was impassive. Only the gray eyes gave a hint of trouble as he thanked Phipps, and the sheriff went on.

Will saw Becky and Angus Case walking slowly toward their buggy, and he followed them, determined to learn everything now.

Case was just picking up the reins when he saw Will approach. Over his face came an expression of stolid dislike.

Will touched his hat to Becky and then said to Case, "I understand you're Chap's executor, Case."

"That's right."

"I want to explain what you'll find when you look over Chap's papers," Will said evenly. "He bought the Pitchfork place for me, you know."

"So I heard."

"But the title is still in his name," Will said.

Case stared at him, frowning.

"How's that?"

"Chap thought maybe after I'd seen the place that I'd change my mind about wantin' it. So he bought it in his own name. I didn't change my mind, and he was goin' to make over the title to me. I don't think he got around to it before he died."

Case said slowly, "Then the spread ain't yours legally?"

"It was bought with my money, but the title's in Chap's name."

Case looked at him a long moment, and then cleared his throat.

"You'll get your money back," he said.

Will flushed. "I don't want the money, Case. I want the spread."

Case said, smiling thinly, "I'm to be the judge of that, I reckon. As Chap's executor, I have the right to dispose of the property."

Will was getting mad, and he knew it and didn't care. "You'll sell it to me, Case, or I'll make you!" he said thickly.

"How?"

"I've got Chap's letters. I've got a receipt for the money spent. It'll stand up in any court in the Territory. I'll tell Chap's heirs of this swindle."

"It'll have to hold up in court," Case said grimly, "because that's where it'll wind up."

"You'll fight it then?"

"Till hell freezes over, and then I'll buy it to keep it from you," Case said curtly. "Good day."

Will watched them drive off. Becky looked at him, fear in her eyes, and she smiled nervously. Will didn't see her smile and wouldn't have cared, anyway. Slowly, surely, he was growing to hate Case with a hatred that scared him. The thought that checked his anger was the knowledge that the court would award him the Pitchfork.

He stepped into the saddle and headed back for the main street. Once there, he wondered why he hadn't ridden around the town to pick up the north road. He had no business here; he disliked the place, he wanted to get out.

Passing Dunn's big store, idly watching the street, he saw the legend: *Post Office* printed under the sign: *General Merchandise*. He remembered then that he hadn't called for his mail since he'd been here.

He swung down and tramped inside the big store. One front corner was walled off by racks of pigeonholes, and he stepped up to the wicket and asked for his mail.

One letter was waiting for him. He pocketed it absently in his jumper, turned to go, and found Mary Norman confronting him.

Mary said, "I'd like to talk to you, Mr. Danning."

"We've got nothin' to talk about," Will said coldly.

"Please," Mary said, and she smiled. She was wearing a pale yellow dress with a flower design spangled through it, and the men gathered around the cold stove in the center of the store were watching her. She was handsome, and the smile she turned on Will was melting. Will was uncomfortably aware that people were watching him, and he wanted to get away.

"Over here," Mary Norman said. They went over to the counter opposite the post-office wicket, and Mary came close to him.

"Do you still think I tried to trap you by our talk the other day?"

"I do," Will said coldly.

Mary Norman looked distressed. "But please, you've got to believe me, Mr. Danning. I wasn't. I only wanted to learn about Murray."

"Why ask me?" Will said wearily. "I told you what I knew."

Mary Norman's eyes were filling with tears. "If I could only make you believe me!" she cried passionately. "I don't want to live without him! I can't!"

And then she began to cry.

Will was not prepared for this. He was aware that the men were watching him, and he was embarrassed. Mary's sobbing, quiet as it was, could be heard halfway through the store.

Will made a clumsy, embarrassed, angry gesture, and said in a low, alarmed voice, "Quit it, now! Quit it!"

And then Mary Norman came into his arms and put her hands on his chest and wept bitterly. Will tried to back away, but she clung to him obstinately. A sudden anger made him put all pretense aside. He pushed her away, grabbed her shoulders, and shook her.

"Damn it, stop it!" Will said angrily. "I've told you what I know! I can't tell you any more!"

Mary was still sobbing. She looked beaten and helpless, and Will knew that it was an act. She was trying by every scheme known to woman to pry information out of him.

Will heard somebody approach and he turned to find big Joe Dunn, the storekeeper, looking at him angrily.

"What are you doing to the lady?" he demanded.

Will said sardonically, "I just kicked her in the shins. What are you goin' to do about it?"

"I'll call the sheriff, mister, that's what I'll do," Joe Dunn said.

Will shrugged and turned away from Mary.

"All right, call the sheriff. Call the governor. To hell with it!"

He tramped out of the store under the hard and threatening gaze of a dozen onlookers, his face a flaming red. He swung on his horse and headed out of town, swearing under his breath. Once outside of town he lifted the horse into a long lope. After five minutes running, the horse cooled off and slacked into a walk. Will's anger was gone now.

It was only then he remembered the letter in his jumper pocket. He felt for it, but it wasn't there. He pulled up and looked back down the road. He'd forgotten about the letter entirely, and in that long gallop it had slipped out of his pocket. He debated going back for it, and then decided against it. It was probably a saddle-company dodger, or something similar. He didn't know anybody who'd bother to write to him, anyway. He rode on.

Back in Dunn's store, Mary Norman stopped her crying as soon as it was decently possible. Joe Dunn, sad and clucking his sympathy, tried to comfort her. Mary wiped her eyes, straightened her back, and said sadly, "You're so kind. Thank you so much."

She went out under the sympathetic gaze of every man in the place. Once on the street, she hurried back to the hotel and went up to her room, locking the door behind her.

Only then did she look at the letter she had taken from Will's jumper pocket when she leaned against him to cry. She was trembling so that she could scarcely open the letter. She was certain that it was from Murray. Hadn't Charlie Sommers told her that he was sure Will either knew where Murray was or was in touch with him?

Mary ripped the letter open, and a paper fell out. She stooped to pick it up, and then her heart sank. It was a signed legal form, a deed made out to Will Danning. The other paper was a brief note. It said:

Friend Will:

I think you'd better have this now. Something queer is up, Will, but that's your problem.

— Chap.

Mary sank down on the bed, bitter disappointment welling up within her. She threw the papers on the dresser and looked bleakly out the window. And then she began to cry; it was real this time — a bitter, heartbroken weeping.

Will rode into the spread after dark, tired and hungry. He offsaddled, turned his horse into the corral, and tramped up to the house and let himself in the cookshack.

Milt heard him and came out just as Will was pouring cold coffee into a cup. In his other hand was a cold biscuit.

Milt closed the door behind him and grinned affectionately at Will. He came over and sat on the table and said softly, "Old jailbird. Did you get fined?"

"It was suspended." Will looked at him, trying to plumb behind the grinning, careless front of Milt's good nature. "Did Becky Case get to you?"

Milt's grin died, and his face was suddenly serious.

"I couldn't figure it out and then I saw Sommers. Did he ask about me?"

Will nodded.

"Does he suspect I'm hidin' here?"

"Said he was just passin' through," Will said. "You can have it for what it's worth."

Will drank his coffee and munched on the biscuit, and Milt regarded him somberly. "Still think it's a good idea to stick, Will?"

Will didn't look at him. "If we run away now, Sommers will think it's on account of him."

Milt didn't say anything right away. He rolled a cigarette, and Will went on eating. He wondered if Milt was going to tell him of his call on Chap last night, and he soon saw that he wasn't.

Will finished his coffee, rolled a smoke, and then touched a match to it. He said then, "Milt, you and me have got somethin' to settle. Right now."

Milt frowned.

"What's that?" he asked.

"Just who's boss around here?"

Milt studied him carefully, and then said, "That's settled already, Will. You are."

"Then you better keep your nose out of my business," Will said bluntly.

The two friends looked at each other, and Milt's

eyes lighted up with a slow anger. His voice was calm, though, when he said, "You mean about keepin' the place?"

"That, and other things."

A long pause. "Like what?" Milt drawled.

"Goin' to Chap behind my back."

Milt's eyes were steady on him, but Will could see the flush creep up under his tanned skin. He could see the anger in Milt's eyes, too.

"So you know that, eh?"

Will nodded.

"I didn't want to tell you," Milt said slowly. "I didn't figure it was any of your business."

Will said levelly, "You could have gone to Chap for only one thing I reckon. About buyin' the place."

"That was it," Milt said curtly. "I told him not to sell it to you."

"What did he say?"

"He said it was your business," Milt said. "But I wanted to try."

Will took a long drag on his cigarette and studied the coal, then looked up at Milt's wild dark face. "You're scared," he said.

"Sure I'm scared!" Milt said swiftly, angrily. "I've told you that!"

"You can't run away from fear," Will drawled gently. "It follows you."

"Careful, fella," Milt murmured.

"I'm not sayin' you're yellow," Will explained grimly. "I'm just tellin' you this because it's the last time I aim to. You'll have to fight this wher-

116

ever you go, Milt. I haven't got the money to move every time you get spooked. I won't do it. I won't let you do it. I offered to hide you, and I spent every dime I ever earned or could beg or borrow doin' it. And I'm goin' to keep hidin' you, you understand? You let me do it. Keep out of my way."

Milt's face was wicked-looking with anger and humiliation, and Will's hard gaze didn't give him any mercy. They regarded each other a long time in that dim lamplight, and then Milt said softly, "You're a hard man, Will — even to your friends."

"Just so you remember it," Will said. He lounged away from the wall and went into the house, and Milt watched him go, in bitter and angry silence.

Chapter Eight

THE MISSING DEED

Pres said good-by to the poker game at nine o'clock. Yellow Jacket's main street was deserted except for a handful of ponies at the tie rails. Pres mounted his horse, wishing there were someone to watch him ride out, and then headed out the north road. On the outskirts of town he turned and came back down the alleys. Behind Chap's office he tied his horse, picked up the small bundle and the burlap sack he had cached in a trash can there, then knifed his big hulk between the two buildings and reached the sidewalk. The street was still deserted.

He climbed the stairs where Chap had fallen only last night, and paused on the landing from which he had shot the old man. There was a door at the landing. Pres tried it; it was locked. He backed off and kicked it. The lock snapped, and Pres waited, watching the street. Nobody came. He went into a small corridor, turned right, and came to the locked door of Chap's office. Again he kicked the door open, but this time he didn't bother to wait and see if he'd been heard. He knew he hadn't.

Once in the office, he went directly to the windows, pulled the shades, then went into the closet and struck a match. He lighted the stump of candle, set it on a low closet shelf, and came out into the office. Systematically, then, he carried all the drawers in Chap's desk to the closet and dumped their contents on the floor.

Afterward he sat on the closet floor and patiently went through the papers he had found. He was looking for one thing only — the deed to the Pitchfork from the Gold Seal Land and Development Company to Chap Hale. Milt said Chap hadn't given it to Will, so it must be here.

It took him a long time to run through the papers; it was not here. The candle burned down, and he lighted another. It was hot in here, and this was dull work, but it was important. Case was the executor of Chap Hale's estate. If Case got the deed to the Pitchfork, he, as executor, could do anything he wanted with it. And two things he certainly would not do with it — he would not sell the place to Will Danning, and he would not sell it to his foreman, Pres Milo. The only thing to do, then, was get the deed before Case got it.

Pres didn't find the deed, after an hour's search. He rolled a smoke and lighted it and considered what to do next. He knew, without looking, that Chap Hale's small safe over there behind the desk held the rest of the papers. He'd hoped he wouldn't have to open it, but now it was necessary.

Finished with his smoke, he went over to look at the safe. It was small, of iron, and if he didn't care how much noise he made he could open it with a sledge. But the pounding would bring somebody, that was certain.

Next best thing, of course, was to blow it. He felt around the edges of the door and saw they weren't tight. Then he took a drill from his sack and began work.

In half an hour he had a hole big enough for the powder to sift through. He poured in a quantity of black powder, put a length of fuse in, and then stood up. He did not light the fuse right away.

He went out into the corridor and walked the length of it to another door, which led into another office. Again Pres kicked the door, and the flimsy lock broke. He went straight through to the rear window, opened it, and peered out. Below the window, perhaps five feet, was the sloping roof of a shed. Twenty feet from it his horse was tied in the alley.

Pres went back to Chap's office, collected his tools and candle and even his cigarette butts, and put them in the sack in the hall. Then he came back to the safe, saw that everything was ready, and lighted the short fuse.

He dodged out into the hall, flattened himself against the wall and waited.

There came a muffled explosion, soft and thunderous, dragging a rush of air past him. At the same time there was a jarring thud against the wall, and Pres picked up his sack and went in. The safe door lay against the foot of the opposite wall. A half-dozen books had tumbled down from their places, and Pres tripped over them in his haste.

He knew Chap Hale's safe. Anybody did who had seen it standing open behind Chap for the last thirty years. There was a double rack of drawers in the safe. Pres ripped them out and dumped their contents into the sack.

He was on the last drawer when he heard someone hit the stairs below. Swiftly, Pres dropped the drawer into the sack and headed down the corridor. Whoever was coming up took the stairs three at a time.

Pres hurried on through the back office, slammed into a chair, overturned it, cursing softly, and put a leg out the window. The footsteps were in the corridor now, and turning toward him. The overturned chair had given him away.

He slipped out the window, dropped, hit the roof, rolled, and then fell off, landing on his feet in the alley. The sack was still in his hand. He raced for his horse, swung onto him, and then a shot slapped out into the night.

Pres lay over his horse's neck and roweled him, and another shot cracked out. But it was dark as pitch down here, and whoever shot was aiming for the sound.

He raced down the continuous alley until he reached the stock pens, turned west, rode to the edge of town, then doubled back north at a slow walk. A block away toward town he heard men shouting and the sound of running horses.

Leisurely, the sack across his saddle horn, he rode north out of town. A twenty-minute ride brought him to an arroyo, and he turned up to it. A half mile farther he dismounted, built a small fire of dead chamiso stalks, and then settled down to look at his loot.

The deed to Chap Hale from the company was not there.

Pres rolled a smoke and considered his next move, wishing he knew where the deed was. A deep disgust rose within him as he realized that Will Danning might have it by now in spite of what Milt had told him. He didn't think so, though. But his next move was certain. He sacked the papers, kicked sand over the fire, and rode back to town. There was nobody near Chap's office, but all the horses were gone from in front of the saloon. He threw the sack of papers in the doorway without dismounting, rode on to the livery stable, turned his horse into the corral, and went back to the hotel.

He took a key down from the board, noted on the register which room Angus Case had, then went upstairs. The room he had picked out for himself had pen and paper on the desk. Tearing the hotel letterhead off the paper, he sat down and was a long hour composing a note.

At the finish of it, he rose, turned down his light, and went down the corridor to Angus Case's room. He knocked loudly, and presently the door

122

opened. Angus Case stood there, his pants drawn on over his underwear.

Pres brushed past him into the room, and Case shut the door behind him.

"What do you want?" Case asked without enthusiasm.

Pres didn't answer immediately. He sat down in the only chair, and Case came over and sat nervously on the bed. Pres's face was still swollen, but his features were slowly settling into their brutal thick-lipped naturalness. He shoved his hat back on his sandy hair, yawned, and said, "Hear anything tonight?"

"Like what?"

"An explosion?"

"No." Case peered at him. "What was it?"

"I blew Hale's safe. I figured the whole town would be awake."

"You — did what?"

Pres smiled faintly. "Blew his safe. I was lookin' for that deed from the land company so you wouldn't get it."

Case only stared at him. Pres yawned again and said, "It ain't there. I looked through all the stuff."

"Then Danning's got it?"

"I don't reckon." Pres gestured with a thick thumb toward the paper he'd laid on the desk. "Read that."

He made no move to hand it to Case, and Case rose and came over to the table. He fumbled around in his coat for his iron-rimmed glasses, put them on, and then read what Pres had just written.

Dear Mr. Hale:
I might have took your body gard job if you hadent tolt me who you was afrade of. Im a marryed man now mr. Hale and I now you done me favirs but I dont hone to go agenst will Daning or his gunnies, you beter get some yung man who aint got a fambly and who aint scaired to go agenst danning like me. If he sed hed kill you he will, you beter go away.

— *Tod Rinker*

Case looked at Pres, and there was puzzlement in his face. "Where'd you get this?"

"I wrote it."

"But what for?"

Pres stifled another yawn and said carelessly, "You got to go over Hale's papers, ain't you? You're his executor."

"Yes, what's this got to do with that?"

"Slip that in your pocket," Pres said. "When you and Phipps start picking up Chap's stuff tomorrow just slip that in with the other stuff."

Case straightened up slowly and took off his glasses. "I see," he mused. "You want it to look like Danning quarreled with Chap, or maybe murdered him?"

"Maybe he did," Pres suggested.

On Case's face was a look of loathing. "You mean you'd frame a man with a murder?"

"Not me," Pres said gently. "You will."

"I won't!"

Pres rose and yawned again. "You'll do it," he said carelessly. "You'll get to thinkin' after I go. You'll find you'd like to have Danning off the Pitchfork, too. Then" — here he smiled faintly and looked at Case — "you'll do it because I say so."

"But —"

"Save it," Pres said. He went out, shutting the door gently behind him.

Chapter Nine

ONE AGAINST THE LAW

Land, like houses or dogs, can grow old and wear out. And the Sevier Brakes, Will thought that morning, were worn out. He had started out early with sour-faced old Ollie Gargan to locate the east boundary and take a look at what few of their cattle they could see.

The brakes were really the lands draining the headwaters of the Sevier river, far to the east and south. They were clay dunes, mostly, capped by a rotting schist that gave them a scabby appearance. Wind and rains had fantastically eroded them, but their labyrinthine canyons had some order if you understood them. All the arroyos, in spite of endless twisting and turning, drained down from a height of land that was obscured by the fantastic spires and spines of the ridges. A wiry bunch grass and the stubborn grama were scattered on the lesser slopes and the rare flats, and the only water was in scattered springs. It was a sorry range, Will thought; even old man Harkins, who located the springs, never conceded cattle would thrive on it. The beef they saw during that morning's ride was gaunt-ribbed from foraging, and Will was glad that nobody but the crew ever saw his beef. If they did, they would be certain that Will Danning was raising cattle as a screen for something else, since he couldn't possibly make money ranching.

Ollie regarded the land and the cattle in glum silence all morning. Will thought the desolate wasteland was depressing him, but when they had spotted their east boundary corner and turned back toward the spread, Ollie shook his head and spat.

"How long you aim to keep me working here, Danning?" he asked.

"As long as you do your work. Why?"

"What work?" Ollie made a hopeless gesture indicating the country. "You won't have no beef left after a rain. They'll shelter up in them deep arroyos, and when the head of water comes down they'll drown. Or break their legs."

"It's not that bad, Ollie."

"It's worse," Ollie said. "You stick here and you'll raise a runty breed of culls you can't give away. It ain't in a cow to scrounge for grass the way they'll have to. And what about roundup?"

"What about it?"

Ollie spat again in disgust. "You can't drive 'em. Hell, you'll have to build traps at every water hole."

Will smiled, but Ollie regarded him accusingly. Ollie was trying to gauge just how far he could go with his new boss, and he was encouraged by Will's easy way with him. He was determined to get everything off his chest.

He said grimly, "Another thing. Am I 'sposed to take orders from you or Barron?"

"Barron's my foreman," Will said flatly. "He'll give you orders when I don't."

"And who'm I 'sposed to tell things I see?"

Will glanced at him curiously. The old man's jaw was clamped shut, and he was looking straight ahead. "I don't get it," Will murmured.

"What you do ain't any of my business," Ollie went on. "But what I do is your business, and what your foreman does is your business, ain't it?"

"It depends," Will said slowly.

"Well, I'm goin' to tell you what I saw and then shut up," Ollie went on. "The other night when we heard them shots and rode up to the drift fence, I heard Milt tell you he was smokin' by the fence and somebody cut down on him. Is that right?"

Will nodded.

"He was talkin' to somebody," Ollie said. "He was sittin' down in the arroyo, and the other man was standin' off a ways. They started off together up the bank. Milt did all the shootin', too."

"How do you know?" Will said, after a moment's pause.

"I was ridin' that fence next day, like you told me. I seen the tracks. I don't snoop, but I seen it and I figured to tell you, that's all."

Will was silent. Presently, he said, "Thanks,

Ollie," and lapsed into silence again. He didn't understand the implications of what Ollie told him. Whom had Milt talked to, and then shot at? Milt didn't know anybody here that he could sit down in the sand and talk to — except Becky Case. And he wouldn't shoot at her. Then it must have been somebody from outside, somebody Milt had known before. But why was it necessary to lie to everyone? Will didn't know, but he felt a vague uneasiness about Milt. There was something about Milt's actions that wasn't right, and yet he couldn't put his finger on it. One thing that angered him was that Milt, by his actions, was making the crew suspicious. He'd have to have another talk with Milt and, even if hard words were passed, make him understand the suicidal risk he was running.

It was late afternoon when they rode into the place. Will rode past the house, noticed nobody seemed to be around, and went on down to the corral where he turned his horse in. Afterward, he came into the cookshack for a drink of water and listened. Pablo wasn't even here. There was absolute silence. He heard Ollie walk into the big room and, apparently, sit down.

Wearily, Will tramped through the passageway into the big room, his eyes on the floor. When he stepped into the big room, he looked up to see where Ollie was.

He was looking into Sheriff Phipps's two guns. The whole crew, including Milt, was sitting against the far wall. There were four other men besides Sheriff Phipps there, and they all held guns on the crew.

Will looked at them and then at Phipps, an immediate anger mounting into his smoky eyes. He said, "So that's why the place looked dead."

"We've been waitin' an hour," Phipps said. "I'm takin' no chances on you, Danning."

Will said nothing.

"I'm arresting you," Phipps said slowly, "for the murder of Chap Hale."

Will's jaw sagged in amazement and then he said with savage scorn, "You damned old fool, I heard Mygrave tell you that both me and Milt were standin' in front of the saloon when Chap was shot. You think I can shoot around corners?"

Phipps said harshly, "Let me finish, Danning. I don't claim you murdered him yourself; I claim you had him murdered by one of your men. The only man in your crew besides yourself that couldn't have done it is Barron, here. As for the rest, one of them done it!"

"And *why* would they kill him?" Will demanded angrily. "Chap was the only friend I had here. Why would I hire him killed?"

"Because he wouldn't sell you this place."

"But he would!"

"You got the deed?" Phipps asked.

Will shook his head. "You know damn well I haven't! He didn't have time to make it out to me before he was killed!"

"I know he *wouldn't* make it out to you," Phipps

said grimly. "Where were you last night?"

"Right here."

"With your crew?"

"Every man jack of 'em."

"And I suppose you played poker for a couple of hours and then went to bed," Phipps said angrily.

"That's right, except it was rummy."

Phipps said thinly, "Chap Hale's office was robbed last night. The safe was blown. You aim to tell me now that it wasn't you that done it, lookin' for that deed?"

Will was speechless; he stared at Phipps with bleak, murderous eyes, not knowing what to say.

And then he said in a flat, toneless voice, "You ain't got proof anyone killed him, you ain't got proof of any motive, you ain't got proof I was even in town last night, and still you aim to arrest me and my crew for Chap's murder?"

"A couple of other things figure in it," Phipps said. "One of them is that Case heard a man arguing in Hale's office the night Chap was killed. He figures it was you."

Will didn't even look at Milt, and Milt didn't deny it. Behind his anger, Will wondered at that and was unreasonably hurt. But Phipps was taking something out of his pocket, a piece of paper, and he extended it to Will.

It was Pres's note. Will read it and read it again, and then looked up at Phipps, eyes questioning.

"That was found in Chap's papers," Phipps said.

"And where were the papers?" Will asked softly.

"Scattered to hell and gone."

Will smiled wickedly. "Whoever wrote this could've left it lyin' with the rest of the papers when he blew the safe, couldn't he?"

Phipps shook his head. "That was in a drawer in the desk you missed, Danning. Case, Chap's executor, and me searched the office this mornin'. Case found that in a locked drawer."

"Case found it," Will sneered. "Well, well. Of course he couldn't put it there, and pretend he'd just come on it."

Phipps said calmly, "I figured you'd say that. You claim Harry Mygrave let Chap's killer go, too, and Mygrave is the straightest man I know. Angus Case is about the next straightest, and now you claim he's a crook." Phipps shook his head. "Trouble with you is, you figure everybody's as crooked as you, Danning. You'll have time to think about that in jail, though."

"And you're goin' to take my whole crew to jail?" Will drawled.

"All except Barron. He couldn't have shot Chap, because he was with you."

Then it was safe to act, Will thought. Milt wouldn't be arrested if he kept his mouth shut and didn't lose his temper.

Will frowned, pushed his hat back, put his hands on his hips, and said, "All right, Phipps.

I'll go with you. But the law don't give you the right to ruin a man when you arrest him on suspicion of murder, does it?"

"What do you mean?"

"I got a busted shaft on that windmill out there." He pointed out the door. "My stock can't get water unless you leave Milt a man to help with that."

Phipps, who had never taken his eyes off Will, glanced out the door. In that moment, Will dived for him.

One of Phipps's men yelled, "Watch out!"

Phipps was a quick thinker. He heard the man yell and he pulled the trigger of his six-gun immediately. Will, foreseeing that, had stepped to one side when he moved. The slug plucked at his shirt, and then he slammed up against Phipps, his iron grip on the wrist of Phipps's gun hand, Phipps's body between him and the deputies.

Will whirled the frail old man around, and said swiftly, "Stay there, boys. Don't move. Drop your gun, sheriff!"

Phipps's gun slipped to the floor, and Will backed toward the door with the sheriff in front of him. At the door, he realized that while he was going to make a break for it, he didn't have a horse. Then he could take one of the sheriff's.

"Where are your horses, Phipps?"

"Behind the house," Phipps said.

Before anyone could say anything, Will gave Phipps a savage shove into the room, slamming him into his deputies, turned, and ran toward the cookshack end of the house. He heard Milt's voice yell at him as he ran, but he couldn't make out the words.

Just as he reached the corner of the cookshack, the first shot slammed out behind him, kicking a geyser of dust up at his feet.

He turned the corner, out of sight of his pursuers now, and made a quick decision as to what he would do. He could take a horse, ride back the other way behind the house, cut for the wash, and ride up it and then into the brakes, where they would never find him.

He turned the rear corner of the house at a dead run, then hauled up.

There were no horses here! Phipps had trapped him.

Will whirled, knowing he was cut off from the corral now, and even if he wasn't he couldn't saddle a horse under the fire of three deputies.

And then he saw the stone-sided root cellar, buried in the side of the hill.

He ran for that, some twenty yards off, and dived down its steps, just as a pair of shots from the corner of the house chipped the stone face.

He slammed into the door, and it gave, and he was in the gloom of the cellar. He turned, crawled up the steps again, raised his head, and sent two shots at the feet of Sheriff Phipps. Phipps stopped, turned, and ran for the shelter of the house. Two more shots hurried his passage.

And now he heard Phipps bawling, "Surround the cellar! He's forted up inside."

In less than five minutes, one of the deputies was on the hill above him, a second was in the wagon shed to the left, and Phipps was posted at the corner of the house. He was trapped, neatly as any sheriff could want. The fourth deputy, of course, was guarding Milt and the rest of the crew.

Will squatted in the doorway out of the line of fire and considered his position. He had a belt of shells, his own gun, and Phipps's. He could fight off capture as long as his shells held out. On the other hand, it would be the purest luck if he could break through Phipps and his crew. The thought that right behind him, not fifty yards away, lay the Sevier Brakes with all their canyons, was maddening. The idea of giving himself up had not occurred to him. A kind of hot and wicked stubbornness was in him now; someone had framed him, and he would not submit to it. Milt wasn't in trouble, so he could put his mind at rest on that score. He knew, with cynical certainty, that if they got him, they would hang him. People hate what they are not used to, and they hated him because he was a stranger, because they thought he killed Chap, and because he didn't mind their hatred. They would hang him as certainly as they would be deaf to his defense. Phipps's voice roused him. "You're surrounded, Danning. Better give up, or we'll come in smokin'!"

"Come ahead!" Will called.

He gauged his chances carefully. The three of

them couldn't take him. And by the time they had sent to town for reinforcements it would be dark. And under cover of darkness his chances for escaping would be a hundredfold. He decided instantly and definitely to fight them off till dark and then try to escape.

Phipps again demanded his surrender, and all he got for his pains was a brief, "Go to hell!" After that, the three deputies poured a steady stream of fire at the steps which Will did not even bother to return. Toward dusk, some gravel from the hill up above him rolled onto the steps, and he knew the man up above was inching down the slope with the intention of shooting over the roof edge.

Will only retired a foot inside the door where, by raising himself up, he could see the house and the shed, and send a slug toward each.

He waited tensely until dusk fell. Occasionally when he rose, he could see Pinky and Ollie carrying wood up and stacking it by the corner of the house. Phipps, apparently, wasn't going to take any chances of escape under cover of darkness.

When night came, Phipps tried again to get him to surrender, and again Will refused. Afterward, the fire was lighted. It cast a bright light over the area in front of the root cellar, and Will considered it with dark foreboding. It was brighter than daylight. And then the deputy at the wagon shed opened up again, and so did Phipps.

Will squatted on his haunches, facing the door,

and tried to think. This looked like the payoff, unless something broke. And nothing would. He was here till help came and then they'd dynamite him. He considered that, and still there was no thought of surrender in his mind.

Sporadic shooting at him livened the night. He hunkered in a constant cloud of dust, raised by the slugs slamming into the roof over the far wall.

The shooting slacked off now, and he wondered if they were content to rest for a few minutes.

And then in the following silence he heard, "Will! Will Danning!"

It was Becky Case's voice. Or was it? Was this a trick to draw him to the stairs where a man above could put a slug in his back?

"I'm coming over, Will. Don't shoot!"

Will raised himself up and looked. Becky Case was on this side of the fire, walking slowly toward him. There was nobody behind her.

Will waited, and when she reached the steps she called, "Are you all right, Will?"

"I'm all right," Will drawled. "Watch those steps."

Becky came down then into the gloom of the root cellar. She paused in the doorway and peered in.

Will said, "What are you doin' here, Becky?"

"I — heard in town they were going to arrest you, and I came out, Will. I — well, Sheriff Phipps was a friend of Chap's, and I wasn't sure if he wouldn't lose his head."

137

"He kept it," Will said wearily. "He's got me nailed down now."

Becky came over to him and knelt on the floor facing him. "Will," she said quietly, "I don't know much about this, only I know you didn't kill Chap Hale. You never killed anybody!"

"Tell Phipps that," Will said bitterly.

"But what are they doing to you, Will? Why do they think you did it?"

"A note your dad says he found in Chap's papers — a note from a gunnie claimin' he wouldn't go against Will Danning for pay. It makes out I was threatenin' Chap and he was scared of me. They figure one of my crew killed Chap, from that note."

Becky was silent. "And Dad found it?"

"That's what Phipps said."

"Will," Becky said. "Something's wrong with Dad. He's afraid. He doesn't sleep, he's worried, and he's ashamed of himself. I — I think he put that note in Chap's papers."

"But why?"

"Because Pres made him."

"But why would Pres do it?" Will demanded.

"Oh, Will, it all goes back to something I don't understand. Pres wants this place. He's crazy wild to get it, and he'd do anything to drive you off, don't you see?"

"He robbed Chap's office for the deed?"

"He could have."

"And now he's made your dad plant that note." Will was silent, thinking, and then he swore softly.

"Becky, if I could get out of here I'd find out what's behind this. I'd do it if I had to take your dad and wring his neck!"

Becky said nothing. Will stood up and looked out at the fire. It was burning brightly as ever, and Phipps was watching the place. Will turned and paced down the narrow cellar, beating his fist against his palm in time with his slow steps. He had to get out of here, he *had* to!

"Will."

Will came up to her.

Becky said, "You can't do it. I met one of Phipps's deputies riding to town. He's after help. They'll get you."

"I know," Will said grimly.

"If you'll go to jail, Will, they'll leave you alone," Becky said.

Will scowled. "How's that?"

"Now they're waiting for you with guns. But once they have you locked up, they'll forget you. And wouldn't it be easier to escape from jail than here?"

Will smiled in the dark. "I've got a gun here, Becky."

"But what if you had one in jail?"

"In jail?" Will echoed.

"Oh, don't you see what I'm trying to tell you?" Becky burst out. "I don't think you killed Chap, Will. I want to know about Dad. I don't want you killed! And some way I'll help you break jail if you'll give yourself up! I promise it."

"And go to jail yourself?"

"I don't care. They won't touch me. Oh, Will, you can't wait down here like a stubborn rat in a hole and let them cave this place down on top of you! They hate you in town! They'd like to kill you! Have you thought of that?"

"Yeah," Will said.

"Then let me go out and tell Phipps you'll surrender. And once you're in jail, we can figure out some way to break you out. I'll even hire gunmen to rescue you."

"Becky," Will said slowly, "you could almost make me do it."

"Do it, Will! I'm your friend. We'll find a way."

Will stood there undecided a moment, and then he said, "All right, Becky. Here are my guns."

He held out both guns. Becky didn't take them immediately. She kissed him swiftly and lightly, then took the guns and fled up the steps.

When Phipps came down the steps, Will was still staring at the door after Becky.

Phipps prodded him outside, and the other two deputies, both holding guns on him, came up, too.

Will said, "I'd like to talk to Barron for a few minutes, alone."

"Go ahead," Phipps said. "Only make it quick."

Milt was brought out from the big room. Phipps left him and Will by the fire, and backed out of earshot, although not out of gunshot.

Milt's face was dark with anger. They had been kept sitting on the floor, just where Will had left them, for fear they would try for a break.

Milt said swiftly, "You all right?" Will nodded, and Milt said bitterly, "Those damn murderin' lawdogs! You won't stay in jail long, Will, if I have to blow it up!"

"Listen careful, fella," Will said. "Get this straight and remember it. You don't make a move to help me, understand?"

"Why not?" Milt demanded angrily.

"Because they'll pick you up then, and once they get you, the jig's up. Can't you see that?"

Milt nodded reluctantly, and Will went on. "Don't even come in to see me. Sommers may still be in town. Stay on the place, talk soft, and say nothin'."

"But damn it!" Milt protested. "I can't let you stay there, Will! You're in there on my account!"

Will smiled faintly. "I won't be in long," he murmured, wondering if it was true.

Chapter Ten

JAILBREAK

After breakfast, Charlie Sommers went upstairs, as if he were going to his own room. Instead, he looked up and down the hall, saw nobody was in the corridor, and knocked softly on Mary Norman's door.

A sleepy voice bade him enter, and he went in. Mary Norman was still in bed. Her black hair was braided in a long rope on her pillow, and when Charlie stepped inside she pulled the covers up to her chin. Charlie wondered idly, for about the four-thousandth time, how an ex-honkytonk girl, gambler's shill, and petty crook, could keep her looks the way this girl had.

She said curtly, "You might give me time to dress."

Charlie, a married man, wasn't impressed by the feminine clothes scattered on the lone chair. He shoved them on the floor, sat down, and regarded the girl.

"Try gettin' up at a decent hour and I wouldn't catch you in bed."

"There's nothing to do in this town but sleep," Mary Norman said bitterly.

"There will be now," Charlie said.

Mary Norman looked interested, but she said nothing. Charlie glanced around the room, at the paper, the clothes, the letters littering the dresser top, and then he pulled out a sack of tobacco and rolled a cigarette.

"Will Danning was brought in last night. They're holdin' him for murderin' Chap Hale."

"Did he do it?"

"He did not," Charlie said flatly. "He's bein' framed, near as I can make out. I dunno who's framin' him, either. But that ain't the point. What I come to tell you is I'm likely to be away for a while."

"Where?"

"Jail."

Mary Norman laughed briefly. "That's a laugh. A deputy U. S. marshal in jail."

"It won't be funny," Charlie said stolidly. "I mean it."

"But why?"

"Never mind why. All I want to tell you is that when I go away or I'm locked up, that's no chance for you to hit the grit. Don't try and run out on me, you understand?"

Mary Norman said nothing, and Charlie went on in a matter-of-fact voice. "I'm still goin' to find Murray Broome. This is part of it. And you're still goin' to help me, unless you'd rather go to jail. So when I get in trouble, don't figure you can dodge out and me not know it."

Still Mary Norman said nothing.

"I sent a letter off last night to Hortense, and another up the line to Seven Troughs. They'll watch for you. This jerk-line stage that dumps you over in Sevier is no good either, because I've tipped the Sevier marshal off."

"What do you want me to do?" Mary Norman asked.

"Stay put. Keep your eyes open for Broome. Stay clear of me and keep your mouth shut and wait till I'm out. If you get any news of Broome, send me a message by someone you can trust. That's all."

Mary Norman watched him get up and walk over to the door. She said then, "What if you never get Murray?"

"You keep tryin' to help us for a year, and the judge'll likely let you off."

"And the rest of my life I try to live down being a squealer, is that it?"

Charlie nodded. "That's what you get for pickin' up with crooks like Broome. They buy you clothes and jewels and show you a good time — but, sister, they're poison. You're findin' it out."

Charlie went out. He didn't go near the sheriff's office on his way down to the livery stable. There, he hired a horse and rode north out of town. He'd never have a better opportunity than now to do what he'd been wanting to do for weeks.

He rode into Will's place around noon and hailed the house. Nobody answered. Will's foreman, who Charlie had heard was the only one of the crew to escape arrest, was not around. Charlie dismounted and went up to the door, which was open. The room looked as if someone had just walked out of it, but when Charlie looked about for proof of this he couldn't find any. It was just an impression, that was all. He went through the rooms, calling out for anybody, and there was no answer. He had to be satisfied with this, so he turned to the bunkhouse wing. Swiftly, expertly, he searched all the war bags, at least glanced at the contents of every letter he could find. To Will's stuff he paid special attention, but found nothing. Will's worldly goods were less than his Mexican cook's, his letters nonexistent. This puzzled Charlie. Surely somewhere among Will's possessions must be something to indicate he had worked for Murray Broome, knew where he was, or had heard from him. If this wasn't so, then Charlie's hunch, on which he'd staked his reputation with the Commissioner, was wrong — and he knew it wasn't. But there was nothing in this whole house to indicate that Will Danning had ever heard of Murray Broome.

Twice Charlie went to the bunkhouse door and looked over the place. He still had the uneasy feeling that there was somebody here — somebody watching him. When he was finished with his job, however, and nobody had disturbed him, he rolled a cigarette and stood in the doorway of the big room, his ruddy face set in a scowl, his sharp eyes musing. He had found exactly noth-

145

ing, and yet, contrariwise, he was more firmly convinced than ever that Will was in touch with Murray Broome. It was intuition, a hunch, call it whatever you would, it was still there. And he determined to go through with his original plan.

He rode back to Yellow Jacket, arriving after dark, ate his supper, and then strolled over to the sheriff's office.

Phipps greeted him cordially, and they talked for a while, mostly about Will Danning. Charlie listened and didn't talk, and from what he gathered Phipps was ready to rush through Will's arraignment and trial. In that stubborn way some courageous men have, Phipps had blinded himself to any doubts. Will Danning was guilty of Hale's murder and would hang.

Afterward Charlie asked if he might talk with the prisoner, and he was let into the cellblock. It consisted of four cells. Pinky and Ollie were in the far cell, Pablo next to them. There was an empty cell between him and Will, who was next to the office. An overhead kerosene lamp in the corridor supplied the light.

Will rose on his elbow when Charlie Sommers came in, and he said, "Hello," not very enthusiastically. Charlie was an expert at reading on an imprisoned man's face just how much confinement galled him. What he saw on Will's face pleased him; Will was not resigned. Charlie pulled a stool across the corridor, parked it by Will's cell, and sat down.

"Luck seems to be runnin' against you, Will," Charlie observed.

Will sat up and stretched, his face drawn with boredom. "You don't call a frame-up luck, do you?"

"I call it a crime," Charlie said briefly.

Will glanced at him and grunted. "You can't call it, though, Charlie. This here is Phipps's party."

"What can I do for you?" Charlie asked.

Will shrugged and didn't look at him. "Nothin'. Hell, I could hire a crew of lawyers and it still wouldn't change the jury I'll draw."

"Break out," Charlie said.

Will looked at him and said, "Hah," humorlessly and looked away.

Charlie said, "Will."

Will's glance shuttled to him. In Charlie's hands, thrust halfway between the bars, was his gun. Will saw it and then raised his glance to Charlie, questioning. Then he said wryly, "Ain't you rode me enough, Charlie? Now you want me to take a busted gun, so Phipps'll have a chance to cut down on me."

"Look at the gun, then," Charlie said.

Will took it. He saw the hammer wasn't filed. He looked at the cartridges, supposing the powder had been pulled. Charlie knew what he was thinking. He said, "Pull out a slug and look for yourself."

Will did. It was good black powder in the shells. He hefted the gun, glanced sharply at Charlie, and handed it back. "No, thanks, not from a lawman."

"You figure there's a catch, don't you?" Charlie asked softly. He knew the others were watching this scene, but if they were as loyal to Will as his crew at the Double Bar O had been, Phipps would never find out.

"What do you think?" Will said derisively. His smoky eyes were angry, like a man's who has been goaded beyond toleration.

"I don't think so," Charlie said. "I'll tell you why. I watched you for quite a spell when you were workin' for Broome, Will. I saw you come up from a kid horse wrangler to roddin' that outfit. I watched you grade up that Double Bar O beef, I talked to your neighbors, I kept my eyes open. I've never heard a man say anything against you yet — except that you're stubborn."

Will listened in silence. Charlie nodded toward the outer office. "I just come from talkin' with Phipps. He thinks you had Chap killed. And he aims to hang you."

"I know that," Will growled.

Charlie smiled faintly. "You and me was on opposite sides of the fence durin' that Broome business, Will. We still are, I reckon. Only I don't think you'd kill a man. I don't think you're a crook."

"Try tellin' Phipps that."

"No, I'm goin' to play it another way," Charlie said slowly. "I'm goin' to risk a job I like and

148

a badge I got a lot of respect for."

"How?"

Charlie held out the gun. "Take it. Shove it in Phipps's face and walk out of here."

For a long moment Will stared at him, and then he said softly, "What's the catch, Charlie? You want somethin', and I know what it is, too."

Charlie nodded. "I want somethin', and you think you know what it is, do you? You figure I'll give you the gun if you'll tell me where Murray Broome is?"

"That's it."

Charlie shook his head. "I ain't even goin' to ask you where he is, Will, I think you know, but I'm not goin' to ask you, because you wouldn't tell me."

"No."

"Here's all I ask," Charlie said quietly, looking Will straight in the eye. "Take that gun and get out of here. You'll be on the dodge with a reward on your head. I don't know where you'll go, and I don't give a damn. You'll meet Murray Broome. You and him are friends, and I know it, Will. I know how much he used to depend on you." He paused now, driving his point home. "Here's what I ask — when you find out that Murray Broome is the cheap, flashy crook I know him to be, I want you to come to me and help me bring him to justice."

Anger stirred in Will's eyes, but before he could answer Charlie held up his hand. "There's no promise you got to make, Will. Understand, I

149

said *if* and *when* you find out Broome's just plumb narrow-gauge, you come help me."

"And if I don't find this out about him?"

"You will," Charlie said bluntly. "You ain't a crook, Will. You're decent and honest. Murray Broome ain't. Some day he'll prove it to you. If he don't —" Charlie spread his hands and shrugged — "I just made a bum guess, that's all. You'll be free, and I'll lose my job and likely go to jail. I'm riskin' it."

"You're pretty sure of yourself, aren't you, Charlie?" Will drawled slowly, still puzzled. "You're pretty sure of Murray, too."

Charlie nodded. Will was mute, impressed by Charlie's quiet conviction. For a moment, he wondered if Charlie was right about Milt, and then he knew he wasn't. Charlie Sommers thought that any man who kills another is automatically a killer, never seeing through to the motive or the justification. Will didn't pretend to understand all the politics behind Murray Broome's killing of Senator Mason, but he felt deep within him that it was justified. A queer thought fled through his mind then; he remembered Chap Hale saying this same thing about Murray Broome.

But Milt was straight. You can't know a man's innermost thoughts for five years and not know that about him. He had to cling to that, remember it. As for Charlie's proposition, it was fair, straightforward, and Will knew he must accept it. The reason had become plain to him during these hours in jail; he couldn't let Becky help him break out. Phipps was a man who wouldn't spare a woman, and if the break was successful and Becky was implicated, Phipps wouldn't spare her. Last night, faced with hopeless odds and persuaded by Becky, he had thought it might work. Now he knew he couldn't accept her help. And he could accept Charlie's.

Charlie's voice roused him, saying, "Better take the gun, Will."

"What about you?" Will said softly. "Hell, they'll get you, Charlie. And there's nobody folks hate like a renegade lawman. They'll nail up your hide, sure."

Charlie nodded, smiling a little. "It'll be pretty rough. But once they find out you're innocent and that you turn up Murray Broome, I'll be all right."

"But I won't turn up Murray!" Will said swiftly. "Forget that. You can't count on that, Charlie."

"I am countin' on it."

"And you're willin' to risk roostin' in jail for twenty years on it?"

"Hell, I'd risk hangin'."

"You're a sucker. Give me the gun," Will said meagerly.

"You promise that when you find Broome's a crook, you'll help me get him?"

"If I find he's a crook, I'll come to you and help you get him," Will promised.

Charlie handed him the gun and rose. "I don't have to tell you that Phipps is an honest lawman.

Don't hurt him." He shook hands with Will and went out, a ruddy-faced, stocky man who saw nothing strange in what he had just done. At the door he paused to button his coat so that his empty holster would not show to the men in the office.

When he was gone, Will hid the gun under the blanket on his cot. The others watched him, speechless with surprise. Then Ollie Gargan growled, "Will, you're goin' to walk into a trap. That-there marshal will have a dozen men with rifles planted across the street."

"You boys want to try it with me?" Will countered.

Ollie considered, and then said, "I reckon."

"How about you, Pinky?"

"I'll take a chance."

"Pablo?"

"Me, too."

Will sat back to consider. Unless he played this cagey, none of them would get out. You couldn't stick a gun in Phipps's face and tell him to open up. What if he didn't have the keys with him? But he carried them, Will remembered. What if he refused, knowing you wouldn't shoot? You'd have to get him in the cell, and that meant waiting till meal time. And that meant making an escape in daylight, which would be more dangerous.

No, he'd have to try it at night — tonight.

Every night at ten or so either Phipps or one of his deputies would come in and blow out the lamp. This was the time to act. The other three were looking at him, and Will said, "Let me play this my way. Just watch."

He smoked two cigarettes in quick succession and then waited impatiently. The others were lying on their cots, watching him.

Presently, one of the deputies, a big young puncher, came in to blow out the lamp.

"Roll in, you bums," he said cheerfully.

Will was sitting on his cot. He yawned and said idly, "Phipps still here?"

"Yeah, but he won't talk to you," the deputy said.

Will stood up and took out his gun and stepped to the bars. The deputy reached up for the lamp and Will said quietly, "Leave that alone."

The deputy glanced at him, then his gaze traveled down to the gun. His mouth sagged open, and slowly he raised his eyes to Will's face.

"One yelp out of you and I'll blow out your short ribs," Will drawled tonelessly. "You got it?"

The deputy nodded in speechless assent.

Will saw he didn't have a gun. He said, "Come over here by the door. Make it quick!"

The deputy did as he was bidden. Will knew he was too scared to bluff it out and too dumb to gauge a prisoner's desperation, as Phipps would do.

Will rammed the gun in his midriff and said swiftly, "Does Phipps carry the cell keys with him?"

The man shook his head in negation, and for

153

a moment Will knew despair. He thought quickly, wracking his brain for some way to get Phipps in here with the keys. He didn't dare let the deputy go. Then he said, "Listen careful, now. Tiptoe over to that corridor door and open it, soft. Then come back here, stand in front of that Mexican's cell, and yell for Phipps to bring the keys. Wait a second."

Still keeping his eyes on the deputy, Will said, "Pablo, lie down on the floor away from your cot. When Phipps comes in, don't move, don't say anything. You *sabe?*"

"*Sí*, I'm seeck," Pablo said.

"That's right." To the deputy Will said, "Phipps don't smoke, does he?"

"No."

"Give me your tobacco."

The deputy was too scared to be mystified at the request. He handed over his sack of dust, and Will pocketed it. Then Will said, "If that door squeaks when you open it, I'll shoot you in the back. Hurry it!"

The deputy went over to the corridor door and silently pulled it ajar under Will's gun. Getting Will's nod, he came back to Pablo's cell, where the Mexican was lying on the floor, and then called, "Hey, sheriff! Bring in them cell keys, will you?"

It was good. There was just enough urgency and excitement in his voice to arouse curiosity. Will sank on the cot, put the gun behind him, and waited.

Phipps stalked in, hand on gun. When he got into the cell block the deputy pointed. "He's sick or somethin'. You want to look at him?"

Phipps was an old hand at all the dodges. He came up to the cell, looked at Pablo, who was jerking his legs in a strange manner.

"Go out and get a doc," Phipps said meagerly.

The deputy looked at Will, and Will realized he'd have to stop him.

Will came to his feet, gun in his waistband in the small of his back and drawled, "No need for that, sheriff. You got the keys?"

"I got 'em."

"Then roll him over and blow tobacco in his nose. It makes him sneeze and he comes out of them fits."

Phipps looked as if he didn't believe it, but he said to the deputy, "Got some tobacco?" The deputy, deprived of his tobacco, shook his head.

"Here," Will said, and held out the sack through the bars. The deputy made a start for it but hauled up at Will's warning glance. Phipps didn't notice it. He came over, reached absently for the sack, and then Will grabbed his wrist. He swung him round, yanked him to the bars, and wrapped his arms around Phipps's neck, choking him. Phipps kicked like a horse and tried to grab his gun, but Will had his hand on it. Will said swiftly to the deputy, "Unlock this door, fella."

"Don't!" Phipps gasped.

And then the deputy caught his meaning. He

155

stopped, undecided, and Will saw he was wavering. He clamped down on Phipps's throat and yanked out the gun and pointed it at the deputy.

"Open up or I'll gut-shoot you!"

"No!" Phipps gasped.

Will knew he would have to act, regardless of the danger. He shot once. The slug plucked at the deputy's sleeve and slammed into the stone wall. The report bellowed in the cell block.

"Next time it's dead center!" Will snarled. "Get them keys!"

The deputy was really scared now. He lunged for the keys in Phipps's pocket and the game sheriff tried to fight him off. But Will was choking him savagely.

The deputy got the keys and fumbled them into the lock; the door swung open. Will dived through it, brushing the deputy aside. Phipps was just coming to his feet then, and Will swung a left into his jaw that knocked him flat. Will didn't even wait to watch him. He swung the gun on the deputy and said, "Open the rest!"

"Go on, Will!" Ollie yelled. "You ain't got time for us!"

Already they could hear shouting in the street.

But Will stubbornly prodded the deputy over to the end cell. He let Pinky and Ollie out. Just as they came through the door they heard footsteps pound through the office.

Will raced for the corridor door, and he was halfway to it when it slammed open and a puncher tumbled through shooting wildly. Will shot low and the puncher went down, and then Will yelled, "Come on!" and jumped over the downed man and through the door. Two more men from the saloon across the street boiled into the office and slammed into Will. Immediately they were at such close quarters they couldn't shoot, and Will slashed out with his gun. He caught one man on the side of the head, and he went down, and then Will kicked out at the other, who was bringing up his gun. The shot boomed hollowly in the room, and the slug slammed into the roof, and then the gun went kiting after it. Will picked up a chair and smashed it down on the man's head, then turned to look back. The downed puncher had Ollie and Pinky covered, and they were backed against the wall, hands overhead. Ollie saw him and yelled, "Go on, Will!" and the puncher turned and snapped a shot at him. At the same moment someone from across the street let go with a rifle, and the slug bored into the doorjamb beside Will's head. It was too late to help his crew now, Will knew. He lunged out into the night, and was immediately caught in a cross fire along the boardwalk. He vaulted the tie rail and then saw the stream of men pouring out of the saloon toward the sheriff's office. It was so dark out here that nobody was recognizable, and Will knew they couldn't spot him unless they heard the shouting of their companions. He ran out into the street, shouting:

"Surround the place! Get around in back!" Exhorting each man as he passed him, he ran for the horses at the tie rail in front of the saloon.

But now he was in the dim lamplight cast through the saloon windows, and he heard men yelling behind him. He was recognized now.

He piled into the protection of the horses and swiftly untied the reins of one. Before he mounted, he looked across the street. Men were running up the boardwalk now, flanking him, cutting him off. As soon as he pulled out from the tangle of horses he would run a gantlet of fire. And yet he had to have a horse to escape.

He made up his mind after one bitter moment of indecision. He swung into the saddle of a big chestnut, crouching low on his neck. He roweled him through the narrow passage between two tie rails onto the boardwalk. Then he reined him straight into the door of Hal Mohr's saloon. A tattoo of gunfire beat on the sign above the door.

Will savagely roweled the horse which brushed open the door with his shoulder and ran across the sawdust floor of the saloon. Will lifted him over one long table and snaked him in between two others. Hal Mohr's shotgun blasted across the room, and Will heard the buckshot slap on the opposite wall. Will reined him through the back door, the horse slipping and almost going down and catching himself, and then lunging forward through the open door into the alley. A parting blast from the shotgun stung Will's back and the horse's rump, but the distance was ineffective for shooting.

Will turned the horse up the alley and let him

stretch out into a lope, heading north. He knew that darkness would hide him until he was swallowed up hours later in the Sevier Brakes.

Chapter Eleven

FUGITIVE

Case had left the house for the barn some time ago, and Becky was cleaning up in the kitchen. There was a worried frown on her face, and a kind of dread excitement within her. Case was going to town this afternoon, and she was going with him. Sometime during the evening she would call on Will in jail, and when she left he would have the gun she smuggled to him. She had given much thought to how she could help, and had settled on the gun. All other ways were closed to a lone woman, and she was exasperated by her helplessness. What if they caught Will with the gun, using that as an excuse to shoot him?

She put that out of her mind and ran through the things she must finish before she left. There was Tomás to see. Last night in the darkness he had walked into his quarters in the barn where Pres Milo had forbidden him to have any light. Some one of the hands, during the day, had thrown a harness into Tomás's room for him to patch. When Tomás came in, he tripped on the harness, fell into the table, and peeled two square inches of hide off his shins.

160

Becky found her salves and stepped out the back door. The slow wind rustled her skirts, and she smelled the warm summer scent of wind on grass and the faint smoky odor of cedar.

She had passed the bunkhouse, humming softly to herself, when she saw Pres Milo ride through the gate and out directly toward the big corral where a couple of hands had the wheels off a spring wagon and were greasing it. Becky wondered why he was in such a hurry, but she made her way to the barn.

She saw Pres start for the barn and one of the hands called, "He's in the loft, Pres."

Pres dismounted at the door of the barn, ground-haltering his horse, and strode inside, not even seeing Becky. She made her way to Tomás's door, knocked, heard no answer, and went in. Tomás was asleep on his cot, snoring softly. On his legs were two bloody bandages. Becky came across the room, intending to wake him, when she heard Pres's voice say gruffly from behind the partition, "Well, Angus, he's done it! Damn his eyes, he busted out!"

"Danning?"

"Shot his way out last night. Fought through the whole gang from Mohr's and rode his horse through the saloon and made it."

Case said wearily, "So your little frame-up was wasted?"

Pres swore savagely, but Becky didn't even notice. A wild elation was in her. She heard Pres say, "What nobody can figure out is how he got

161

the gun. Phipps claims nobody but that U. S. marshal could have give it to him."

"Nonsense."

Pres said grimly, "Well, he's out, and he'll be harder to catch than a muley steer."

Her father said nothing, and Becky heard Pres sit down on a bale of hay.

"Tomás inside?" Pres asked.

"He's sleepin'."

"All right. I want to talk to you, Angus. I want to know some things. What are you goin' to do about that deed that's missin'?"

"Just what I told you," Case said flatly. "The Gold Seal outfit has a record of who they deeded that land to. It'll be Hale. I'll get another deed. That's all there is to it."

"And you won't sell it to me?"

"Not ever," Case said flatly. "That's out. If a buyer comes to me and wants it and takes it to court, I'll buy it myself before I'll let it get out of my hands."

Pres laughed nastily. "Would you buy it, say, if you found it was worth a lot of money?"

"Of course I would," Case snapped. "It isn't worth money, though, except to a crook. And I'll tell Chap's heirs that, too."

"It is, though," Pres murmured.

Case was silent for a long moment, and Becky tried to picture him. She couldn't, nor could she understand what Pres was driving at.

"Why is it?" Case demanded.

Pres chuckled. "You don't think I'd be sucker

enough to tell you, unless I had a signed and sealed paper givin' me half of it, do you?"

"And you don't think I'd give it to you, do you?" Case countered.

"I think you will," Pres drawled. "You just make out a deed sayin' *if* I can prove that Danning's place is worth more than a hundred thousand dollars to a buyer, then I'm to share half the profits with you in further development."

Case said softly, "Did you say worth more than a hundred thousand dollars?"

"That's it. If I can't prove to you that it's worth more than that to anybody, then I don't get a cent. But if it is, then I get a fifty-fifty cut."

"On what?"

"On the money we'll make."

Becky's heart hammered riotously and she held her breath.

Her father said, "What is it over there, Pres?"

Pres laughed. "Hell, for three years I've known it. I've tried to get the money to buy the place, so I'd have it all to myself. But I couldn't swing it. Then Danning came in. I tried to drive him off, but all I done was make him mad. There's only one way left now, and that's to split it with the only gent that can buy it. That's you, Angus."

"But split what?" Case demanded. "Gold. Is that it?"

"You'll know when you sign the paper. Will you sign it — a ten-thousand-dollar risk on more than a hundred thousand?"

"I'll have to see what you're talkin' about first."

"You will like hell!" Pres snapped. "You'll buy the place blind and take my word for it. Even if I'm lyin' to you, and I ain't, you'll still have the place, won't you?"

"Yes."

"Then you're goin' in town with me this afternoon and buy it for yourself. Make out a deed to yourself, get the deed from the Gold Seal, deposit the ten thousand, and you've got the place."

"If you're lyin' to me, Pres, I'll —"

"Lie to you!" Pres shouted angrily. "I'm comin' to you because I can't swing it any other way! You think I like you good enough to make you rich, you damned old fool?"

Becky heard her father answer wearily, "No, I don't. If you ever came to me for help, it's because you couldn't help it."

"Then saddle up," Pres said. Becky heard him get up, and she fled out the door, leaving Tomás still sleeping.

She was in the kitchen again when she saw the two men come out of the barn. Becky thought swiftly. Will Danning was being cheated out of his rightful property. She'd told her father that, but her father was stubborn in his intention of resorting to legal trickery to keep Will off the place. And now he was going to cheat Will out of a fortune by the same method. She was sick at the thought, angry at her father, and bewildered. What did Pres have on her father that he could make him do these evil things?

Case came into the kitchen and said, "Ready, Becky?"

"I've got a headache, Dad. I think I'll stay home."

Case looked at her and frowned. "I'll be away a week."

Becky laughed and came over and kissed him lightly. "Since when have I been afraid to stay here alone?"

Her father grumbled a bit more and went out. Soon he and Pres rode off toward Yellow Jacket together. Becky, now that they were gone, sank into a chair and considered what she had heard. She felt a weak excitement and a kind of pride when she thought of Will's escape. If she could only get to him now with the news she had heard. But what could he do if she did reach him? Nothing. He was a fugitive. Besides, she couldn't reach him. He'd be smart enough to stay away from the Pitchfork, because they'd watch that. All she could do was sit by, helpless, and watch this steal.

The afternoon and evening were torment, and she wished she'd gone with her father. Anything, so that she wouldn't think of what was happening.

After supper she was sitting by the lamp in the kitchen reading week-old newspapers when she heard a faint tap on the window. She looked up, listening, and the tap came again. She went to the door and stood in it, and then she heard a whisper, "Becky."

It was Will. Without answering him, she stepped back into the room, blew the lamp, and

165

then came outside. Will was flattened against the side of the house, big and shadowy.

"Nobody's home, Will. Come in," she said.

"I just came for some grub," Will said. "Can you let me have some?"

"But Will, I've got to talk to you. Come in."

"No thanks," Will said bitterly. "I'll have a bounty on my head by now that any Nine X puncher hones to collect. Besides, I don't want you in on this."

"Will, are you hurt?"

"Not even scratched." Will smiled wryly in the dark. "Still, they won. I'm holed up back in the Sevier Brakes and I'm runnin' to you for grub. I reckon they got me off the place, all right."

"Do you know why, Will?"

"I don't, and that's a fact."

Becky told him swiftly of the conversation she had overheard between Pres and her father. Will listened in silence, and when she was finished he still didn't speak.

"What is it they're after, Will?"

"Gold, silver, I dunno. Whatever it is, they've got it, all right. Your dad can sell the place to himself. Likely he's done it. And Pres will get his split."

"And you're outlawed! Will, are you going to take it?"

"No," Will said quietly, stubbornly.

"What are you going to do?"

"You won't like this, Becky. Maybe I'd better not tell you."

"But I'm in it, Will. You've got to tell me."

"I been crowded into my last corner," Will said bleakly. "I come here wantin' to be let alone, and I got swindled out of every dollar I ever saved. I aim to fight."

"How?"

"I don't know, but I'm goin' to fight your old man. I'm goin' to make him sorry for the day he ever saw me. So help me, I'll run him out of this country, Becky. I'm goin' to break him, and then I'm goin' to kill that crooked partner of his!"

Becky was silent, awed, and afraid of the passion in his voice. Will said then, "You asked me what I was goin' to do. That's it. Now, I don't reckon you'll want to feed the man that's goin' to ruin your dad."

"Do you have to do it, Will?"

"Either that or quit. And I won't quit." He paused. "Thanks for what you've done for me."

"Will, are you going without grub?"

"I'll get it, steal it."

"Not while there's some here!" Becky said angrily. "You wait here."

She disappeared into the house and was gone a long time. When she came back, she had a sack full of groceries. Under her arm was a carbine, and over her shoulder two shell belts. "Tell me where your hideout is, Will. I'll bring more grub when this is gone."

"But your dad, Becky!"

"He raised me to be honest and decent, and

I believed him!" Becky said passionately. "If he's a crook, then he'll pay for it!"

"He's your dad, Becky. You don't mean that."

Becky hesitated. It was true what he said. She couldn't betray her father, help his enemies, the man who had sworn to ruin him. But neither could she help him; it was wrong.

"Becky," Will said softly. "If this wasn't me, would you feel like helpin' me?"

"I — I'd feel like it," Becky said softly. "But I wouldn't, Will."

Will put his hands on her shoulders, and spoke in a low voice. "I did a lot of thinkin' there in jail, Becky. I thought how a lot of things might have been — if this hadn't happened. I thought of a woman with me, and a little place of our own, afterwhile — not that dark hole where I was. I thought of a lot of things like that — and then I knew it couldn't happen till I was clear of this. And tonight I reckon I found out it can't happen at all. Because I won't ask any girl to fight her family, her blood, like I'm goin' to fight them."

Becky nodded mutely, and Will's hands dropped to his side. "It's goin' to be wicked, Becky. I'm going to fight like hell, and I'm goin' to hurt you. Only I wanted you to know what I thought of you before you start hatin' me."

"I'll never hate you, Will — never."

"You will. Good night, Becky. And thanks."

Before Becky could say good night, Will had vanished into the night.

168

Chapter Twelve

A Renegade Lawman

It was past noon when Charlie Sommers heard the knock on his door. He opened it to find one of Phipps's deputies, standing in the hall.

"Sheriff'd like to see you, marshal," the deputy said.

"Sure," Charlie said. He went back to get his hat, knowing it had come. Phipps was too good a man, too honest a man to ignore his duty.

Sommers and the deputy went downstairs, marched through the lobby and downstreet to the sheriff's office. Phipps was there; so were three other deputies, among them Ed Brown, the big puncher whom Will had cornered the night before.

Phipps's face was grave as he got out of the chair. "Sit down, Sommers. We got some questions to ask."

Charlie sat down, his ruddy face impassive. Should he lie to them, or should he admit it? If he admitted it, they would want to know why he'd done it, and he couldn't tell them. Even if they believed him, which they wouldn't, he couldn't have this story getting out. It would only serve to warn Murray Broome to watch his step, and his plan would be defeated. No, he'd lie, and pay the price if he had to.

Phipps sat on the desk and said, "There's one thing worryin' us, Sommers. We thought you might clear it up."

"What's that?"

"We can't figure out where Will Danning got the gun he used to crowd Ed into that play last night."

Sommers looked at Ed. "Sure he had a gun?"

"Hell, he shot at me, didn't he?" Ed asked indignantly.

Sommers shrugged. "Maybe he had it hid on him."

"We searched him, searched him good, even his boots. No, he never brought it in with him."

"Then somebody snuck it in."

"Through a window? No. There's a wire screen on the cell-block window. He couldn't have got it in his food neither. And the only folks that was in that cell block yesterday was the boys here and Angus Case and you."

Charlie smiled broadly. "Don't tell me you think Case brought it in?"

"He couldn't," Phipps said quietly. "I was with him."

"Well, that leaves me," Charlie said cheerfully.

"That's right."

They were all silent, watching him. Charlie crossed his legs and said dryly, "I always figured it was a marshal's job to land a man in jail, not let him out."

"So did we!" Ed blurted out.

"Easy," Phipps said to his deputy. He turned to Charlie and asked bluntly, "Did you give him a gun, Charlie?"

"No," Charlie lied.

"Where is your gun?"

Charlie handed a gun over. Phipps looked at it briefly and said, "Then you got two. You had your initials cut in the cedar handle of one gun."

"You're mistaken," Charlie said.

Phipps looked at him sharply. "I ain't mistaken, and you damn well know it. Where's your other gun?"

"I only carry one."

Phipps put the gun down on the desk and looked long at him. The faces of the other deputies were hard and tough with suspicion.

Phipps said then in a barren voice, "Why'd you give him the gun, Charlie?"

"I don't know what you're talking about."

"I'll give you a chance to tell me," Phipps said stubbornly. "Is Will Danning an undercover marshal? If he is, all you got to do is say so, and I'll telegraph the Commissioner for confirmation."

"Not that I know of, he isn't," Charlie said.

"Then why'd you do it?"

Charlie shook his head. "There must be a mistake, John. You're going off half-cocked."

"Then you explain to me how he got the gun."

171

"I don't know."

"I do," Phipps said quietly. "It looks like you give it to him, Charlie. This thing busted right after you left. His crew in there won't say a word, so we ain't got proof. But you had two guns and now you say you only had one. You're lyin', and if you're lyin' over that it must mean that Danning has your other gun."

"But I'm a deputy U. S. marshal," Charlie said gently. "Marshals don't do that, John."

"You're a renegade, then, because you done it!" Phipps said flatly.

Charlie said, "You're the sheriff. You've got my story. Do whatever you want."

Phipps didn't speak for a moment, but his eyes were bleak with contempt. "All my life," he said wryly, "I've hated crooked lawmen. And all my life I believed that the man wearin' Uncle Sam's badge couldn't be bought. No matter how bad other lawmen were, there was always a U. S. marshal to do the job that needed doin'. Now I dunno."

"I know," one of the deputies said hotly. "He swore on his oath that he'd be straight. But he ain't! He's as crooked as any damn bank robber or killer!"

Charlie's ruddy face flushed. That hurt, and he came to his feet slowly. "You're a liar," he said quietly.

The deputy hit him first, and Charlie slugged back. And then the four deputies swarmed on him. Charlie was a better than average saloon brawler, and for a few seconds he held his own. But he couldn't win. These men were fighting for something they believed — the honor of a government lawman. And to them he was a renegade, worse than a killer, for he had let a killer escape.

He kicked out and caught Ed in the groin, and another deputy smashed him flush in the jaw. His head slammed back against the wall, and then someone drove a fist into his belly. Charlie doubled up, and a blow caught him alongside the ear. Another slammed him in the face and he fought weakly, blindly, hearing Phipps's shrill cursing. Charlie's whole body was aching, bruised; his breath was gone, and his face felt mashed, but he fought on. Time and again, they cornered him, raining blows into his chest and face.

And then his knees gave way and buckled, and he sat down, and slowly a curtain of oblivion slipped over him. He didn't bear these men any ill will; they were doing what he would have done in their place. That was the last thought in his mind before everything faded away into blessed blackness.

Chapter Thirteen

Rustling Without Risk

There was a light in the big room. Will had been watching it for an hour, edging down yard by yard, off the red- clay banks toward the house. He would move, then listen, then move some more, certain that the house would be watched. Or maybe they were inside, waiting to decoy him in.

Slowly, patiently he worked around until he could see through the door into the big room. Milt was sitting there reading at the big table. Will watched him for half an hour, noting every move to see if Milt would give away the presence of another man in there. But there was nothing strange in Milt's actions, and he decided to chance it.

He whistled thinly, and he saw Milt's head jerk around, peering out into the night. He whistled again, and Milt rose and came to the door.

At the next whistle Milt came outside walking toward the corral. There was nobody following him. Then Will called his name, and Milt ran over to him. They shook hands, and Milt laughed with relief.

174

"Will, damn you, I thought you'd never show up! You all right?"

"Fine. Nobody's here?"

"No. They gave up and rode back this afternoon. And I made sure they went, too."

They hunkered down against the corral, content with silence and companionship. They rolled cigarettes and lighted them, and then Milt said, "What are you doin' for grub, Will? I had some cached down by the drift fence, but they took it."

"Becky," Will said. Presently, he added, "I know why Case and Pres want us off here now, Milt."

Milt jerked his head around and then said in a strained voice, "You do?"

Will told him what Becky had overheard. "It's gold or silver or somethin', she didn't know. But Case is goin' to buy the place for himself."

"You say Pres and Case are in on it?"

"That's right. Pres finally give up tryin' to get it by himself and took in Case."

"Nobody else with them?" Milt asked idly.

"No. Why?"

"I dunno. I can't imagine either of them killin' Hale. But maybe they did."

His voice had an odd timbre that puzzled Will for a moment. And Will was reminded of something. He said, "Milt, there's somethin' I've been wantin' to ask you."

"What's that?"

"Remember that night you was at the drift

175

fence and somebody took a shot at you?"

"Yeah," Milt said cautiously.

"Ollie says he looked at the tracks. He said you were talkin' to somebody. He said you were sittin' down when you did it."

Milt said instantly, "He's a liar!"

"You weren't talkin' to anybody?"

"Hell, no!" Milt said angrily. "Sure I sat down. I smoked a lot of cigarettes. I tramped around. But damned if I saw anybody, or talked to anybody."

"Okay," Will said gently. "I just wanted to ask you."

Milt grunted angrily, and they were silent. Presently, Milt said, "What do you want me to do now, Will? Light a shuck?"

"Sit tight," Will said. "They won't evict you until they've had confirmation from the company that the deed was made out to Chap. That'll take a while."

"And you'll do what?"

Will flipped his cigarette away. "I'm goin' in for rustlin', to begin with, Milt."

"Rustlin'?"

"Nine X beef," Will said grimly. "Case and Pres, as far as I can make out, hate each other. Case doesn't trust him, but now they're partners. Supposin', all of a sudden, that Case starts missin' beef. He'll blame it on me at first, maybe. But then I'll leave enough sign to show him there are three or four of us in on it. All my crew's in jail, so he can't figure out where I'd get the men. Then he'll trace the beef, and I'll leave plenty of hints that it's Pres. He'll accuse Pres of it, and unless I miss my guess they'll fight. That's the first move." He looked at Milt in the dark. "How does it sound?"

"Huh?" Milt yanked himself up, and then laughed uneasily. "I must be gettin' old, Will. I wasn't payin' attention."

Will told him again, and Milt agreed it was a good idea. Will added, "I want you to ride to Yellow Jacket tomorrow and write the railroad orderin' enough cars for a hundred and fifty head of cattle to be on the Sevier Creek siding the night of the nineteenth."

"All right."

"That's done. Now, has Phipps got a bounty on me yet?"

"A thousand," Milt said. "And say. There's the damnedest story goin' around Yellow Jacket. They claim that Phipps has arrested Sommers for givin' you the gun to escape with." Milt laughed and went on. "Imagine that? Charlie Sommers handin' you a gun, so you could bust loose. Phipps must be crazy."

"He's not crazy," Will said. "He's right."

Milt turned his head slowly, peering at Will. "He's — what?"

"Sommers gave me the gun."

"But — he's a deputy U. S. marshal."

"But he gave it to me."

"Why?"

Will said quietly, "He thinks I know where

you are, Milt. He don't know, but he's playin' a hunch. He put me a proposition. He said he knew you were crooked, Milt. He said I'd find out some day that you were forked. When I did, he said, he wanted me to come to him and help him get you. If I'd promise, he'd give me a gun to bust loose with."

There was a long silence and Milt said stiffly, "And what did you say?"

"I told him I would. I took the gun."

There was a long, long silence, and then Milt said in a voice in which there was an underlying wildness, "That's comin' pretty close to promisin' to sell me out, Will."

Will was dumb with amazement. When he could speak, he said simply, "You aren't a crook, are you, Milt?"

"No."

"Then why am I sellin' you out? What have you got to fear?"

Milt said passionately, "But, Will, dammit, you hear stories! You can't help but hear stories about me! And when you hear 'em enough, you might begin to believe 'em."

"I've heard stories," Will countered angrily. "Hell, if I believed them, I wouldn't have given you help!"

Milt sighed. "Oh, hell, Will. I didn't mean that. I'm edgy. Hell, no, you don't believe 'em, and you never will. You know me. Let the others talk." He squeezed Will's arm, and the old careless, brash way was with him again. "Will, I'm

178

edgy, I tell you. And I don't like it when you take that kind of help from a man tryin' to hang me. It — scares me."

"But —"

"I know. You did right," Milt said, and added with bitter humor: "Take his help. Sure. You did right. Let him roost in jail, where he belongs, and remember how he tried to bribe my friends."

"That wasn't a bribe," Will said quietly. "That was a promise, and I'll keep it, Milt."

Milt looked at him in the night and then laughed his old reckless laugh. "Good. That'll keep me in line better than advice from my mother."

Will laughed then and rose to go. He told Milt where he was hiding out, a cave close to one of the springs in the brakes. When Milt wanted him, he was to come to this spring where Will would pick him up.

They shook hands; Will rode off, and Milt watched him go, his face sober and narrow-eyed and touched with a pinching fear. Then he laughed to himself and walked slowly toward the house. He had never realized how implacable a man's honesty could be, as Will's was.

Will broke camp before daylight and had a hard time starting his fire. Everything was wet from the rain of yesterday, including his blankets, and he felt cold and miserable. It had cleared during the night, and he yearned for the warm sunlight that would thaw and dry him out. He had ridden all day yesterday and late into the night in a driving rain that turned the brakes into a greasy mud and set its arroyos churning with a brown weight of water. His horse was red-clay color to his withers, and the legs of Will's Levis were the same color. Beard stubble shadowed his face, and his gray eyes were dismal with discomfort.

Clean sunup, however, changed things. He came to the north edge of the brakes at sunrise, and could look over the rain-clean Sevier Basin for sixty miles to the distant Cecils. This slope before him was like the range immediately around his place — hard-scrabble, as poor as a man might find outside of a desert.

And Will was counting on just this poverty of the range to help him in his plans. He took the first trail he came to; it wound out of the clay dunes and soon joined another. Barely an hour later he rode into the yard of a stone-and-adobe shack set among the cheerless dunes.

A man stepped to the door, and Will greeted him, observing him carefully. A child peeked out from behind the man's legs, and the face of the man was work-worn and fearless and friendly. A rose bush struggled out of the clay beside the door, testifying to a woman's presence.

"Light and have some breakfast," the man invited.

"Thanks, but I'm ridin' through," Will said. "I'm lookin' for some Circle 5 strays. Haven't seen 'em, have you?"

180

The man eyed him steadily. "Can't say I have."

Will knew this wasn't the kind of man he was looking for, and he rode on. But the very look of the man, his quiet defiance, told Will that the kind of men he did want was close here.

Three miles beyond the place a road forked off east and soon started to climb again. Two hours later, Will saw a mean stone shack at the head of a bunch-grass meadow, a single tall cottonwood an eye-hurting emerald-green against the red hills.

Two men watched him ride in, one from the doorway of the place, the other from the corner of one of the shabby outbuildings.

Will reined up in the yard and looked around him, finally eyeing the silent man in the doorway. This was more like it, Will thought; there were no children, no rosebushes here. Cans littered the yard, and the man in the doorway hadn't worn clean clothes in months. He was thirty-odd, dirty, and his eyes bored into Will with the hard suspicion of men who do not welcome callers.

Will said, "Fine day."

"Yeah."

"I'm lookin' for a couple of hands to work for me," Will said.

The man delicately shifted a cud of tobacco to his other cheek and said, "Why come here?"

"I pick my men," Will said. "I'm lookin' around."

The other man had come up now, and was leaning against a corner of the house. Will didn't look at him, but he talked loud enough so the man could hear.

The one in the doorway looked long at Will and shook his head. "We got jobs."

Will nodded agreeably and picked up his reins. "Maybe," he said slowly, "you could steer me on to a couple of men who know these brakes."

"Mebbe I could," the man said, "but mebbe I won't."

The man at the corner spoke. "You ain't ranchin' out there, mister."

"Did I say I was?" Will murmured. He pulled his horse around and started walking it out of the yard.

"Wait a minute," the man in the door called.

Will pulled up and waited patiently as the two men converged on him. The one he'd spoken to first was older, more seasoned-looking than his hungry looking companion.

"We know them brakes some," the first speaker said.

"But you got jobs, you said," Will answered mildly.

"What you aim to pay, and for what kind of work?"

Will didn't answer immediately and then he smiled faintly.

"What you make depends on how good you work. The job? Well, there'll be some cattle drivin'."

"Where you from?" the second man said. "You ain't from the Sevier."

"No, I'm from the other side of the brakes," Will drawled. He saw them look at each other and knew both were thinking of the same thing — that here might be a chance to pick up some money.

The first man said obliquely, "What kind of cattle drivin'?"

"Mostly night drivin'," Will murmured.

"How much?"

"Depends on what you want to draw in a month," Will murmured.

"Where you aim to drive 'em to?"

"Sevier Creek pens," Will said.

A pause. "Who you aim to sell 'em to?"

"Stockyards."

The men looked puzzled. "Why the hell don't you ship out of Yellow Jacket, then?"

"Because I'm goin' to start with about three hundred and wind up shippin' a hundred and fifty."

"Where are the others goin'?"

"To whoever helps me drive 'em."

"Wait a minute," the older man said. "I don't get this. If they're wet cattle, they'll check at the yards, hold 'em, wire the owner, and credit him."

"They're not wet. The bill of lading is signed by the owner's foreman."

"You're his foreman?"

"Pres Milo from the Nine X."

The two men considered this, eyeing him carefully and respectfully. "What's the catch?" the younger man answered.

Will folded his arms and leaned on the horn and said, "There's no catch. I've got my boss by the short hairs. Once it's done, he can't move. But gettin' it done is what's hard. If I drive to Yellow Jacket he can stop me, but if I drive through these brakes, he won't know it. The railroad won't check back with him, because the stuff is shipped to the yards and is his brand, signed for by his foreman. By the time he gets his check from the yards, tallies, and misses three hundred head instead of a hundred and fifty, you can have them vent-branded and out of the way. I admit it, and he can't move."

"Sure he can't?"

"That's my risk. And where's yours? There ain't any."

"What's your cut?"

"A third."

The older man pondered. "We may need another man or two."

"Pay 'em fifty dollars, if you know any."

The older man nodded. "What about cars?"

"I wrote for 'em. They'll be on the Sevier Creek siding on the nineteenth — five nights from tonight."

The younger man looked at his companion. "What's wrong with that?"

"Nothin', except the time. We'd have to start now," the other said.

"What's stoppin' you?" Will murmured.

The older man grinned. "Nothin'. Light and give us fifteen minutes."

184

Chapter Fourteen

Fight for Life

Milt came awake to hear the rain drumming on the roof. He stood in the doorway, watching the gray morning light seep up from the ground like a dreary fog. Last night's talk with Will and the discovery that Pres was double-crossing him had put a wicked edge on his temper.

He ate a cold meal swiftly, then donned his slicker, and splashed out to the corral. He saddled his big chestnut, turned the other horses out to pasture, and headed for town to mail the car order.

All morning the drizzle kept up, slow and implacable. Within an hour it had channeled down inside the collar of his slicker and inside his boots. It was all fuel for his anger, which was cold and wicked now. Pres's double cross was like a sore in his mind. He knew what had happened — Pres, knowing there was no other way but to share the loot with someone who could get the Pitchfork, had thrown in his lot with Case. Pres had brushed him aside without even bothering to tell him so, now that he didn't need him any more. In Pres's mind, Milt had failed to persuade

185

Will, so now he was no longer of any use. And Milt could do nothing about it.

Out on the Nine X range, a cold raw wind drove the rain before it, and Milt hunched over in dismal discomfort. Pres would be in town; if he wasn't, Milt would wait for him. If he didn't come, Milt would go after him. The arroyos were running now, and Milt had to force his horse into the swiftly running water.

In midmorning he came to the arroyo where Will had met Becky. But instead of finding a creek, he was looking at a raging torrent of brown boiling water some thirty yards from bank to bank. And there, barely visible through the pelting rain, was someone in a slicker, back to Milt, huddled under the cottonwood over a smoldering fire. The thunder of the flood drowned out all the noise of his approach.

Milt rode down and looked at the water, a sinking feeling in the pit of his stomach. He couldn't cross this; it was too swift and treacherous. He moved down the bank, closer to the cottonwood, and peered incuriously at the figure over the fire, barely visible in the rain. Something about that back, its squat barrel-shape, was familiar. Milt pulled his horse around and headed upstream again, so that he could see the man's horse now hidden by a plum thicket. And then he saw the horse, a big black gelding — Pres Milo's horse.

Without a moment's pause, Milt roweled his horse into the flood. The force of the water immediately swept the horse off its feet. It didn't even try to breast the torrent, but fought to keep its head up above the churning waves. A log slammed into the horse's rump, turning it sideways and sending it under. Frantically, Milt kicked the log off, yanking his horse's head above water. They were like corks, bobbing downstream, now afloat, now hidden by the boiling waves. The banks raced by with a breath-taking speed, and they were soon out of sight or possible earshot of Pres. Once, when the arroyo bent abruptly, Milt thought they were lost. The savage current piled them against the bend, pounding and dragging the tired horse against the clay bank with a violence that caved dirt on them. And then, as unreasonably as it had swept them into the bank, the current swept them out again. And this time, out of pure panic, the gelding spent his last effort in getting to the other shore.

It floundered up the bank and stood there shaking, head hung. Milt gave him a bare minute for a breather, and then put him upstream.

Pres heard the approach of the horse when Milt was almost to the cottonwood, and by the time he rose Milt had slipped out of the saddle and tramped over to him. Both men were drenched, both burly in their heavy slickers, and Milt's lips were blue with cold.

Pres started to greet him with a friendly smile, but when he saw Milt's eyes he checked himself. His great loose face, still scarred from Will's beating, was a flushed and angry red.

"I been lookin' for you," Milt said ominously. "I got somethin' to talk over with you."

"Well, you found me," Pres said. They both had to talk loud above the roar of the water twenty feet away.

"I hear you got a new partner," Milt said angrily.

Pres regarded him shrewdly and said, "That's right. Case. How'd you know?"

Milt ignored the question. "A three-way cut now," he sneered. "Maybe you'd like to ask some more of your friends in on it."

"It's still a two-way cut," Pres answered bluntly. "Me and Case."

"And I'm out?"

"That's right," Pres said bluntly. "You're out. I gave you a chance, and you threw it. You couldn't swing Will Danning, so I got hold of the man who can."

Milt said thickly, "Damn you, Pres! You can't do that to me! I've got enough on you to hang you, and I'll tell it!"

Pres laughed then, his thick lips curling up over yellow teeth. "You ain't goin' to tell anybody anything, Murray Broome. Now git on your horse and go home and sulk."

A red rage came over Milt; he clawed wildly at the buttons of his slicker to get inside for his gun. Pres saw him, and went for his own, and it was buttoned tight inside his slicker, and then he acted quickly. He dived at Milt, pinning his arms. Milt twisted loose and looped a blow in

188

his face, and then clinched with him. A kind of maniac fury had seized Milt; Pres was taller and heavier than he, but as they wrestled there, clumsy in their cold, stiff slickers, Milt's wild slugging backed Pres toward the arroyo.

Pres grappled with him and tried to speak. "Take it easy — I can still — turn you up."

But Milt fought with a maniac fury, and Pres was scared. Time and again he tried to fumble under his slicker for his gun, and each time Milt slammed into him with a viciousness that took his breath away. The footing was slippery now, and they were standing toe to toe, slugging at each other. Milt missed a looping left that curled his arm around Pres's neck and he slammed the whole weight of his body into him. Pres skidded backward, and when he finally checked the slide, the water was lapping around his ankles.

He fought to circle Milt, putting his back to the arroyo, but Milt fought with the stubborn wildness of a jungle animal. He tried to bring an elbow into Pres's face, and when he missed he stamped savagely on Pres's feet. Pres hauled his foot away, cursing wildly, and then Milt dove into him, shoulder in his belly. Pres went over backward into the shallow water, but before he could move Milt was clawing up onto him, fighting for a hold on his throat. Pres rolled over onto his hands and knees, and again Milt slammed into him, fighting for his throat. Pres put up his arms in front of him; Milt rose and kicked him savagely in the belly.

189

And now all Pres thought of was escaping from this wild man. He fought to his knees and tried to cut off downstream toward the point. Milt lunged on his back, winding both arms around his shoulders; then Pres tripped and fell into the knee-deep water, Milt on his back. Panic seized him then. He reared up in a great mooselike heave, then he lost his footing and went over backward into the deep water, Milt's arm wrapped around his throat, choking him.

Now Pres fought with all his wild strength, fought against drowning as the flood swept him out into the torrent. The cold water took the breath out of him and seemed to make him more certain he was drowning. Milt's arm was like a vice around his neck, immovable. He came to the surface once, and was tumbled under again, Milt clinging to him like a burr. A wild desperation was on Pres. He opened his mouth, and the muddy water boiled in. With both hands he forced Milt's arm up to his mouth and sank his teeth in it.

Milt let go, and the torrent rolled Pres to the surface again. He saw Milt's rage-contorted face close to him. Milt struck out again, and hit him in the face; then Pres felt his shoulder seized again. Blind panic was on him, the terror of a drowning man added to the jungle fear of a more savage animal that is sure to kill.

The sodden slicker was like a coat of lead, holding him under water. His lungs were bursting, and he already had breathed water. Now he felt

Milt's boots tromping him down, down to the very bottom of this thick flood. Pres knew death then. With every instinct he fought to reach the surface. His hand touched something solid, and he grabbed for it. It was a root of some kind, and he pulled himself to the surface. He was under the overhang of a bank; it was the root of a cedar tree he was holding.

The flood tore at him, and he saw it tumbling Milt out in midstream. Milt, with a maniacal stubbornness, was trying to swim against the stream to the spot where he last saw Pres. And then, in a few seconds, he was swept out of sight.

Pres clung to the branch and gagged for air. The stream was tugging at him like a thousand hands trying to pull him loose. When the worst of the coughing and choking had passed, Pres felt around with his feet, trying for bottom. There wasn't any. He looked about him for some hold to cling to so he could work his way out from under this bank, which might cave at any moment. There was no other branch. The thought of drifting out into that flood again made him tighten his hold on the branch until his fingers ached.

He tried to fight down his fear and to reason. If he could stay here till this flash flood subsided, he would be safe. He was too weak, too exhausted to hunt for a place downstream where the bank wasn't so high. But it was still raining, and it would be hours after the rain ceased before the flood decreased. A bleak despair settled on him; it was his own bull strength against the flood.

He could help by shedding his slicker. He started, then stopped.

On the opposite bank he saw Milt.

Like an animal frightened into immobility, Pres didn't move. Milt was slowly pacing up the bank, looking at the flood. His slicker was gone now, and he held a gun in his hand. He looked as wild and implacable as a jungle animal and he slowly walked along the shore, wet and filthy and muddy.

When he was out of sight, Pres moved. His first thought was his gun, which he had forgotten. It was gone. Sometime, in that turmoil, it had slipped out of its holster. He contemplated this with a kind of fatalistic indifference. He was completely at Milt's mercy now, and unless he stayed where he was, hidden from Milt by the tangle of roots in front of him, he was gone. His teeth chattered with the cold and with naked fear.

Fifteen minutes had passed before he saw Milt again. This time Milt had a pole, and was prodding under each overhang of the bank. He worked with an implacable patience, his head bare in the rain, the gun rammed in his waistband. Pres watched him with a dismal fascination. If Milt was so thorough with that bank, surely he would cross over to this one. Hysteria seized Pres then; he knew he'd have to get out of here, and he knew he couldn't. No, he'd wait like an animal in a trap until the trapper came along and disposed of him.

An hour passed, an hour of the purest misery

Pres had ever known. In spite of the great strength in his arms and shoulders, his grip on the root was lessening. He had to change hands more often. And the cold of this water was eating into his very bones; he couldn't stop his teeth chattering, and his body seemed to be only a chunk of heavy wood, refusing to respond to the orders from his brain.

Soon he knew he could stand it no longer. He decided to risk everything on holding his breath and letting the stream whirl him down to a less steep shore. He didn't even care if he drowned.

It took some minutes to work up to the decision, but he did it. He relaxed his hold on the branch and pushed the small sucker roots out of the way ahead of him.

And then he saw a pole lowered from the bank above. He knew instantly, with cold terror, that it was Milt prodding. He dodged back under the bank and shrank into its farthest corner. Slowly, the pole came toward him. Milt felt the sucker roots and brushed them aside and then the pole started to explore the cave. It started at the far end and worked toward him, and in voiceless terror Pres shrank his great hulking body into the mud. The pole was almost on him now, and then it stopped moving. It had met a stubborn sucker root. It gave a couple of tentative lunges that did not seem to dislodge the root, and then it was withdrawn.

Pres almost fainted with relief. He abandoned

all thought of leaving his cave now. Gathering every ounce of strength, he clung to the root and was utterly motionless, except for the chattering of his teeth.

The rain kept on, the gray sky slowly darkening as evening approached, and still Pres did not move. Toward dusk, the pole came again. And again, Pres clung to his old position, watching it with the fatalism of a man who is prepared to die. And again it missed him, stopped by the tough sucker root.

Afterward he concentrated all his strength on holding out until darkness. The water was falling a little, but it was still tumbling past in a brown turgid boiling that was a constant roar in his ears.

When darkness came, Pres knew that he was safe from Milt. Yet the dark moil of the flood in front of him was even more terrifying. He made up his mind to stay here until he drowned. It was later, much later, that he felt a log nudging into his cave. He felt it, saw that it was thick, and with fumbling and numb hands, grasped it to see if it would support him. It did.

He gave himself up to the flood, pushing out from his cave into the torrent. It had ceased its boiling now and flowed in a swift and steady stream, draining the grasslands of the bench and the barren clay hills of the brakes. It seized him like some strong hand, and Pres clung blindly to his log, holding his head out of water.

Time and again he felt for bottom, and sometimes found it, but he did not have strength enough to buck the current. Miles below his cave, the stream seemed to broaden, the current to relax a little. Gently, wearily, he guided the log toward shore. And he found the slope was not steep.

He abandoned his log then, and summoned all the strength left to pull himself out of the flood. Inch by inch, he clawed his way up the bank in the cold drizzle. When his feet were clear he stopped to rest. And when he tried to start again, he was too tired, too sleepy. This cold rain seemed warm beside the stream. He relaxed and let it warm him, and then went to sleep that way, the muddy earth for a pillow.

He wakened at dawn, with the rain still pelting down on him. It was agony to move, and he was so cold that his hands were numb claws. Pulling himself to his feet, he looked around him. He knew where he was. A Nine X line camp lay a couple of miles down the arroyo. If he could make that, he was safe, for it was miles back to his horse. His matches were wet, he was exhausted, hungry, and in fever.

Pres didn't remember much of that walk. He remembered falling time and again; he remembered cattle watching him with dull and kindly curiosity. He remembered seeing the shack where it lay between a couple of big piñons against the hill, and he remembered how it took him longer to make it after he'd seen it than it took him to walk from the arroyo.

But he made it, and he fell into the bunk and pulled the straw over him and slept.

For how long he didn't know. When he woke it was night, and he was weak with hunger. He staggered out of the bunk and over to the table and lighted a candle. He built a fire in the rickety stove and wolfed down some moldy pan bread that had been cached in a sack hung by a wire from the ridgepole.

The shack was just warming up when he heard the horses outside. He forgot his bread, forgot his hunger, forgot his weakness, and staggered to the door and threw it open.

"Tip? Barney? That you?" he yelled hoarsely.

Out in the darkness he heard a quiet chuckle, and then a man walked into the light of the doorway.

"Pres Milo," the voice drawled. "Sittin' up to meet us, eh?"

Pres almost cried. It was Will Danning, tall and unshaven, his eyes a smoky, sultry gray, who came into the room and pushed him back onto the bunk.

Chapter Fifteen

A FOOLPROOF SCHEME

Will looked at Pres's beefy face, drawn and harried-looking and unshaven, and then regarded his clothes, torn and muddy and holding a fine sand in each crease. The Rainey brothers, Jack and Phil, stepped into the room behind him.

"Who's this?" Jack Rainey growled.

Will's eyes glinted with a secret amusement. "This? Why, he's the man that signs the bill of sale, boys."

Jack looked at him. "Then you ain't Milo?"

Will shook his head. "I was goin' to forge his name. Now I don't reckon we'll have to."

Pres was bewildered by all this talk. Will had to repeat his question. "What happened to you, Pres?"

Pres flagged his weary brain into action. He knew that if he told Will Danning the true story of how Milt Barron had almost killed him, Will would want to know why. And in learning why, Will would learn that he knew Milt's name. Will would kill him then. If he didn't, Milt would. The memory of Milt pacing that bank yesterday

— or was it the day before — would never leave his mind. He didn't want another man like Milt after him, too.

He said weakly, "I got caught in the storm and set afoot in a floodin' arroyo. I damn near died."

Will's long face was touched with sardonic enjoyment of this.

Pres said, "I don't care what you do with me, Danning. Only I got to eat! I'm starved!"

Will's glance traveled to the cans up on the shelf. "Rig up some grub, Phil," he said to the younger man. To Pres he said dryly, "Do you think you can stagger to the door while I show you somethin'?"

He stepped out into the night and struck a match. There, among their horses was Pres's own black gelding still saddled, its fetlocks muddy, its hair dried curly.

"He was standin' at the ford when we passed it this mornin'," Will drawled. "We figured to use him, but now we got you, and we won't need him. I'll give him to you."

Pres said shakily, "What you aimin' to do, Danning?"

Will laughed softly. "Now that," he drawled, "is a surprise. I wouldn't aim to spoil your grub."

"You ain't —"

Will's face changed, and the match died, but his voice was thoughtful. "No, we don't aim to kill you, Pres. Maybe you'll wish we had when we're through with you, though."

Pres didn't pay attention to anything but the food. But once he was finished eating, he looked at the two men with Will. They were hardcases, all right, tight-lipped, silent, suspicious-looking men. They didn't talk and looked to Will for a cue to their behavior. Will was silent, smiling now and then in secret amusement.

When they were finished, Will rose. "Well, we better get to work, boys."

"Where you goin'?" Pres asked suspiciously.

"We're goin' to take your horse with us," Will drawled. "You just go to bed, and we'll call you around daylight."

Pres watched them file out into the night, and his curiosity was whetted. Something was up, but he was too tired to figure it out. He had a feeling that if he was smart he'd light out afoot tonight, but he knew he couldn't make more than a couple of miles in his condition.

Outside, when they had ridden out of earshot, Jack Rainey pulled up. "Better tell us about this," he said to Will.

"I lied to you," Will said calmly. "I figured I couldn't get you to throw in with me any other way. There was no risk for you. I ain't Pres Milo. That's Pres Milo back there. He'll ride with us, and I reckon he'll do anything I say."

"But if he ain't in on this, he'll squeal."

"Nobody'll believe him," Will said. "He's forked himself, and his boss knows it. By the time I let him go, you'll have your stuff clear, and nobody will look for you. Case will settle with him."

"And not us?"

"It's his name will be on the bill of lading," Will pointed out. "That's all Case needs, that's all he wants."

Jack Rainey said dubiously, "How do we know?"

"You don't," Will said. "But will you take a chance on it for my third of the cattle?"

Both the Raineys were silent. Finally Phil blurted out, "Then what in hell are you doin' this for?"

"Not money," Will said calmly. "I'm doin' it to get him in a jam. You got it all right there. And I won't get him in any jam if I let you two get caught with the beef, will I?"

"No," Rainey said reluctantly.

"Then you'll be clear. I got to have you get away with the beef to nail him. I can't double-cross you, any way you look at it." He paused. "I'm not crowdin' you into it. If you don't want a hundred and fifty head of beef, pull out. If you do, stick."

"I'll take a chance on it," Rainey said. "I don't understand it, but I'll take the chance."

"Wait a minute," Will said. "You'll have those two men you hired waitin' for you in the brakes, won't you? You figured to have them drive the shippin' beef down, and you aimed to drive the stolen beef off, didn't you?"

"That's what we said."

"Then you come along with me, Jack, and let Phil go with them. That way, you'll see I won't cross you."

"Okay."

There was a moon at ten, and with the aid of its light they rounded up the small clusters of beef that dotted this rolling Nine X range. It was open country, and the bedded cattle were not hard to spot.

It was like a leisurely, fumbling roundup. Jack held the herd while Will and Phil rode the ridges pushing down the stuff. At their approach, even the cattle hidden in the brush came to their feet with an alarmed snort. By daylight, Jack was easing the growing herd north and east toward the brakes, while the other two pushed the other cattle down to join the big herd. By midmorning, they had an easy three hundred head moving north, and Will dropped out and rode back to the line shack, on his way picking up Pres's horse, which they had staked out.

Pres, looking haggard but rested, was waiting for him at the shack. Will ordered him to mount, and they set out after the herd. Pres kept watching Will with an uneasy expression that made Will smile. Then, topping a ridge, they caught sight of the herd trailing north.

Pres hauled up, looked at it, and turned to Will, eyes goggling.

"You're runnin' off Nine X beef!"

"And you'll help us," Will said gently. "This time we got the guns, Pres, and you haven't.

So line out there and ride drag with the boys."

"Case'll get you for this!" Pres said savagely. "You can't get away with it."

"Will he?" Will grinned. "Light a shuck, now."

Pres sullenly joined Phil at drag, and Jack moved up to swing. Will rode point, heading toward the nearest jut of the brakes.

That afternoon the herd was swallowed up in the canyons. It was better driving here, for the cattle couldn't scatter, and the Raineys hazed them unmercifully.

Late that night, cutting in from a western canyon, they came to the Quartz Wells, which were on Will's land. Quartz Wells lay at the head of a broad canyon barren of graze but big enough so that the herd could be accommodated and easily held.

Two men of the same type as the Rainey boys were camped there, and after a quick meal, Will told them off as night herders, and the rest rolled into blankets. Will gave Pres his own blankets and kept watch himself. This was too perfect to be spoiled by Pres's seizing a gun and escaping.

At daylight next morning, the herd was split. Phil Rainey and the two hired hands took half the herd up an arroyo that led off to the north. Will and Jack and Pres headed east with the rest toward the Sevier Creek pens on the east edge of the brakes where the railroad skirted it.

They made a dry camp that night in a blind canyon, and Jack Rainey spelled Will. Pres had not spoken all day; the splitting of the herd had given him some clue to what was happening. Nor did he speak the next day.

The cattle were tired and hungry that last day, but they were hazed unmercifully all through it underneath an overcast sky.

In late afternoon, the arroyos began to slope steeply, and they could see beyond the ramparts of the brakes the faint green of Sevier. The Sevier Creek pens were halfway down the long valley, placed there so that the shippers in the south end of the valley would not have to make the long drive to Sevier.

The cattle finally pushed out into grass, and Rainey and Pres and Will hauled up.

Will dismounted and rolled a smoke; the others did, too. Two miles distant were the Sevier Creek pens, a weathered tangle of boards rising out of the prairie beside a sun-scoured way station. On the siding stood a locomotive ahead of a string of cattle cars, its smoke pluming lazily into the overcast sky, then mushrooming above the train. This was their string of cars.

Will lighted his smoke and regarded Pres. "Guessed what's up, Pres?"

"Nothin' except you're stealin' Nine X beef that you'll hang for."

"We're not stealin' beef, Pres — you are," Will corrected gently.

Pres stared at him with blank eyes, not understanding. Will went on. "See those cars? They're ordered in your name. And you're goin' to sign the bill of lading, too."

"Who said I was?"

Will shrugged. "Nobody'll make you. But if you don't I'm ridin' down to the office and telegraphin' to Case. I'll ask confirmation for this shipment. He'll know somethin's up, catch the eastbound tomorrow, and come over here. You'll be waitin' with a hundred and fifty head of gaunted beef, and so will the cars. What are you goin' to say to him?"

"That you stole 'em and took me along."

"How you aim to prove it?"

Pres started to speak, and then his voice died. He looked at Rainey, who was grinning, and back to Will. "Oh," he said. "Well, I'll show him the camps."

"Sure you will," Will drawled. "He'd never think you could've drove a hundred and fifty head over here alone. He'll think you refused your hired rustlers their cut and they give you away with that telegram, and then dodged out."

"I'll prove you done it!" Pres shouted.

"How?" Will drawled. "Case knows my crew is locked up. You don't even know the names of the rannies you rode with. And as for the other hundred and fifty head, they'll be scattered fifty ways to Sunday by the time you trail 'em."

Press face was black with anger. Will Danning had played this with a cunning that was perfect. Somehow Will knew that Case hated cattle stealing worse than anything in the world; he knew, too, that Case didn't trust his foreman. Only one thing remained for Pres, and that was to bluff it out.

204

He laughed gruffly. "You sucker, Danning. You think I could have worked for Case for fifteen years, and him not trust me?"

"Nobody trusts a man that keeps his job by blackmail," Will drawled. Pres blinked, and Will went on. "Now that you and Case are partners, he'll figure that you think you can get away with anything, even rustlin'."

Pres's face flushed. "What are you talkin' about?"

"You know what I'm talkin' about," Will murmured. He threw away his cigarette. "Well, make up your mind, Pres. You goin' to sign that bill of lading and load the cattle, or do you refuse and aim to wait until Case catches you with the goods?"

Pres was caught and he knew it. Will Danning knew about the deal with Case. How? Milt wouldn't dare tell him, lest his own guilt come out. Then how did he know? Pres thought a moment, and knew that Will couldn't do anything about it. But the fact that he knew worried Pres. And now Will's work had put him in a spot that would take some careful squirming. He throttled his anger and considered this from both angles. He decided immediately that an honest foreman's duty would be to salvage what he could out of the mess and ship the cattle, making the best of a bad deal, then explain. Tell the truth.

"I'll ship," he said curtly.

Will grinned faintly and murmured, "I figured you would."

They loaded by lantern light in the hot and muggy night that presaged a storm. Pres, lest he grab a gun from the agent's quarters, was set by the loading chutes to tally, while Will and Jack prodded the cattle into the cars. Finished, the bill of lading was signed by Pres, and the train clanged out into the darkness, showering a rain of cinders on them.

Will watched the agent bid them good night, then he strolled over toward Pres, who was following the agent inside.

"Where you goin', Pres?"

"To send Case a telegram," Pres snarled. "You think I'm goin' to take this without fightin'?"

Will palmed his gun up and said quietly, "Get on your horse. I'm not through with you yet."

"But —"

"Get over there."

Rainey watched, grinning, while Pres went over to his horse. Then, Pres in the middle, the three of them headed back up the arroyo into the brakes. They rode all that night, and at dawn next morning it started to drizzle. They camped, ate, and rode deeper into the brakes.

At noon, Will pulled up and said to Jack Rainey, "How much time do you need, Jack, to get the beef clear?"

"Three more days would do it with this rain. Less, even."

Pres looked at them, puzzled. Will said to him, "Get off that horse, Pres."

Pres dismounted, his little pig eyes wary and angry.

Will reached back, tossed his saddlebag with

the remainder of the grub to Pres, then reached down for the reins of Pres's horse.

"What are you doin'?" Pres demanded.

"Leavin' you here," Will said.

"But I'm lost!" Pres howled. "Why don't you shoot a man and be done with it?"

Will said quietly, "We're over the height of land. All you got to do is follow one of these arroyos out and you'll reach Nine X range."

"And you're goin' to take my horse?"

Will nodded. "It'll take you three days, I figure. This rain will give you water. If you save your grub it'll last you."

Pres stood there, rain dripping off his head, his red face covered with a sandy beard stubble. In his eyes was pure murder. Rainey, observing him, drawled, "Don't cry."

A fury seized Pres at these words. He rushed at Rainey, and Rainey put a foot on his chest and pushed him over. In his raging helplessness, Pres started to hunt for rocks to throw. There were none, just sand and mud.

Will left him that way, helpless and furious and afoot, and Rainey headed north. Will, dog-tired, headed for his hide-out to the south and east. He was too tired to wonder if his scheme would work. All he could do now was wait.

Chapter Sixteen

FALSE AS HELL

Case was in Yellow Jacket for a week after the morning Pres left him for the ranch. During that time, Charlie Sommers had a preliminary hearing and was held on charges of aiding a prisoner to escape. The preliminary hearing for Will Danning's crew was postponed; without Will, there was no case. And during that week, Case had telegraphed all four of Chap's heirs stating the sale of Chap's property and asking if there was any dissent. He got permission from three on the fifth day, and on the morning of the seventh the last telegram came. Will Danning's property was his.

On the evening of the eighth day he rode into his spread, and Becky came to meet him out by the corral. She kissed him and then said, "Where's Pres, Dad? Tip has some news for him."

"Isn't he here?" Becky shook her head, and Case said, "But he left town a week ago."

"He's not been here."

Case scowled and turned his horse into the corral. The sun was just setting, and Case, walking toward the bunkhouse with Becky, felt at peace

208

with the world. Riding through his range today he had seen the new green after the rains. The prospect of good grass, on top of the knowledge that all the grass in the Territory could die and it wouldn't affect his bank balance in another year, gave him a feeling of solid prosperity.

He saw Tip, Pres's *segundo,* step out of the bunkhouse and come toward him. Tip was a grave-faced young man, a far better man than Pres. Right now he looked saddle-worn and hungry.

"What is it, Tip? Where's Pres?"

"I figured he was with you," Tip said. "There's plenty up, too. You're havin' your beef rustled, Mr. Case."

Case's good humor shriveled instantly. These were the words he had feared more than anything else for the last ten years. He recognized his feeling for what it was — a thief's hatred of being robbed — but it didn't help. He knew instant, savage anger.

"How do you know?"

Tip told him how he and Barney had come across the sign of cattle being moved into the brakes. They followed the sign until the herd split, one half going east, one half north, and then it started to rain. An hour's drizzle in that sandy stuff blotted out the tracks, then the arroyos began to run, wiping out the last signs. He recited it in a tired, excited voice.

When he finished, Case said, "How many head?"

"A pretty big herd, looked like," Tip said.

"And Pres hasn't been here?"

Tip shook his head. Becky knew what her father was thinking and she saw his squarish face settle into a stubborn cast. He had never made a secret of his hatred for cattle thieves, and she remembered dimly that long-distant fight with Harkins. It was something he never talked about, but it had left its scar on him, she knew. And now Pres was absent. Intuitively, she knew her father's suspicions.

He said to Tip in a kindly voice, "Thanks, Tip. Tomorrow you better start shovin' the stuff away from the brakes and put a line rider over there."

"I'll take a couple of men and comb them brakes if you say so," Tip offered.

Case made a wry face. "It'd take a year," he said and turned toward the house.

Becky laid out a cold meal for him in the kitchen; he ate in silence. Becky watched him with troubled eyes, wanting to help him and not daring to let on she knew why Pres thought he could get away with this.

Presently she said, "Dad, do you think Pres is behind this?"

Her father looked startled. "What makes you think he is?"

"Because he knows you're afraid of him. He'd dare to do anything, knowing that."

Case's gaze wavered, then fell. He pushed his plate away and went upstairs to his room. Becky heard him pacing the floor far into the night.

Next morning, Case was wearing a gun. The last time he'd worn one, Becky remembered, was the day he'd ridden in to greet Will Danning. Before that, he hadn't worn one for years.

That morning Tip sent out a line rider; and afterward, Becky saw them break out the roundup wagon and start repairing it. Case worked with them, just like one of his hands.

At noon, Becky couldn't hold her curiosity. "What are you doing with the wagon, Dad?"

"Roundup," Case said briefly. "I'm goin' to find out how much beef I'm missin'."

"But can't you wait until fall?"

Case looked bleakly at her, his eyes fanatic. "No," he said bluntly.

It was after supper when Tomás knocked at the back door, and when Becky opened it, he said, "Pres, she's come back."

Case, in the other room, heard him. He put on his coat and went outside.

Pres was dismounted, standing in the doorway of the bunkhouse talking to the crew when Case came up.

Pres said, "I got a story to tell you, Case, that's goin' to hurt."

Case said nothing. Pres went into the office, lighted the lamp, and sat down wearily. He looked as if he'd lost ten pounds; his clothes were filthy, his beard stubble ragged, his eyes wicked and red from sleeplessness.

"You've had some beef stole," Pres announced.

"I know that," Case said narrowly. "Where have you been?"

"I was kidnaped!" Pres said viciously. "That damn Danning picked me up at the piñon line camp, took my gun away from me, and made me help rustle a herd of Nine X stuff!"

Case said nothing. Pres, watching him, had the uneasy feeling that he had never seen Case like this before.

"Where'd the beef go?" Case asked.

"It's shipped. They made me sign the bill of lading for the stuff. Half the stuff was shipped, the other half run off north into the brakes."

"Why was half of it shipped?" Case asked in a meager voice.

"Because Danning wanted my name on the bill of lading to frame me with you!" Pres said hotly.

Case looked as if he didn't believe it, and Pres made the mistake of insisting. "Damn it, don't you see he knows about our setup?"

"How would he?" Case said thinly.

"I don't know, but he does! I tell you, he's tryin' to queer our deal, Case! He figures you'll think that now we're partners, I can steal you blind and you can't yell."

"How does he know I can't yell?" Case asked softly. "How does he know you're blackmailin' me?"

Pres settled into sullen silence. Case went on, his voice implacable. "Tell me what happened — all of it."

Pres started by telling him of being picked up

212

at the piñon line camp.

"What were you doin' there?" Case interrupted immediately.

Pres squirmed, and then lied. He'd lost his horse in the rain and made for the camp. Then he told of Will and two of his crew finding him, of gathering the beef, of pushing it into the brakes and of meeting two more men.

Again Case interrupted. "Where'd he get the men? His crew is in jail."

"How do I know?" Pres shouted angrily. "He had 'em."

"Go on."

Pres took up the story, but now he had the conviction that it sounded false as hell, and he was angry. And the more angry he got, the more he tried to insist that it was the truth he was telling. He got to the loading, and Case cut in again.

"How'd the cars get there?"

"Danning ordered 'em!" Pres shouted. "I tell you, it was a frame-up from the beginning."

Case said nothing, and Pres went on, explaining how he was taken back to the brakes and set afoot, and how it took him two days to reach here.

"But that's your own horse you're ridin'," Case pointed out.

"I picked him up at the edge of the brakes," Pres said desperately. "Danning left him there."

Case didn't speak. He stared at Pres, his gray glance boring into him. Then he said softly,

"You're lyin', Pres. You're lying in your throat. Your story stinks to heaven. You knew I'd be in town for a week. You figured now that our partnership was signed, you could do any damn thing you pleased to me, and I wouldn't kick, couldn't kick. You'd cut in on the big money anyway, and I couldn't shake you. So you rounded up a bunch of saloon bums and rustled my stock. To alibi yourself with this cock-and-bull story about Danning, you shipped half the stuff and drove the other half off for your crew to sell."

"I swear, I never —"

"You didn't even bother to go over your story," Case went on implacably, his voice getting harsher. "Where would Danning get the men? He's hidin' alone. And you forgot to mention Milt Barron, his foreman. Wouldn't Milt have been with him? And you say you were afoot, and yet you ride in on your own horse. And best of all, you say Danning knew about our partnership. That's a damn crude lie, Pres — it's the one I gag on."

This was a new Case, one who wasn't afraid to stand up and fight. Pres, seeing it, fell back on the old sneering bluff.

"Take it easy, Case. You can get just so tough with me, and then I remember Harkins."

"Harkins be damned!" Case said savagely. "Where you're goin' there won't be any sheriffs to tell it to!"

Pres saw Case's hand streak for his gun, and he acted automatically. He dived for the lamp on the desk, slamming into Case as he lunged. The lamp went out, and a gun boomed savagely in the small room. Pres picked up the chair and swung it wildly and heard it crash into Case, and Case shot again. The shot was so close it scorched the sleeve of Pres's shirt.

In a wild panic, Pres clawed for the door, yanked it open, and boiled out into the night. He ran for his horse, leaped in the saddle, and roweled the tired gelding savagely.

Three more shots came from the door in rapid succession, all misses. Pres rode out beyond the gun range and then pulled up, the lights of the ranch behind him.

His rage almost strangled him. He'd kill Angus Case the moment he could get his hands on a gun. He'd go back and kill him tonight with an ax, a singletree, anything! And then it dawned on him that he couldn't. If any harm came to Angus Case, then everything he'd worked for these five years past, everything he'd dreamed of, would be gone. For Angus Case held the deed to the Pitchfork, and unless Case worked the deposit back there in the brakes, Pres would never get a dime.

He turned thoughtfully toward town then. He'd taken a beating from Milt, a licking from Danning, and was shot at by Case. Yet he was alive, bound to make a fortune if Case made one. The only thing wrong with that was that he'd have to get Danning before Danning spoiled everything again. He thought he knew a way.

Chapter Seventeen

Just About Licked

Milt was still in his blankets in the bunkhouse when he heard the horse come into the yard. He rolled out of the bunk, pulled his boots on, and grabbed a gun. He was still a bit shaky from last night's drinking, but not so shaky that he wanted to take a chance on somebody trapping him.

He went swiftly into the big room and put his head around the doorjamb.

Becky Case, standing on the porch, watched him with curiosity.

A sheepish look came over Milt's face; he ran his fingers through his hair to comb it and put his gun down.

"Mornin'," he said thickly and stepped aside.

"Good morning," Becky answered. She was wearing Levis, a checked shirt, and a flat-brimmed Stetson. Walking into the room, she paused just beyond the doorway and looked at the litter. Food, clothes, bottles, everything that Milt had used for a week, seemed to be scattered about the room.

Becky said nothing, and Milt felt a sullen resentment at her silence. He cleared a seat for her, mumbling, "I'm not a very good house-keeper, looks like."

Becky only smiled, looking at him with covert curiosity. Was this the cheerful chap she'd known as Will's foreman? Something was changed about him. In the first place, the beard stubble that blurred his face was blond. It looked queer in contrast to his dark hair. And then he seemed to be heavier; his cheeks had filled out, and his tan was lighter, and his Levis seemed tight at the waist, as if he were putting on weight. His eyes were bloodshot and bleary, as if he'd been drinking too much. His sultry temper was evident in the sullen set of his mouth.

Becky said swiftly, "I came over to see if you'd take me to Will."

"Anything wrong?" Milt asked.

"Pres and Dad have quarreled at last."

Milt stared at her, openmouthed. Becky said quickly, "Is there anything wrong?"

"No. No," Milt said hurriedly. He hadn't been sure that day, but he'd thought he'd killed Pres. And he hadn't.

"Will you take me to him?"

Milt grinned faintly, and it was the kind of a grin that Becky didn't like. What it intimated was that he knew she was in love with Will and had to see him. The fact that it was partly true made Becky resent it all the more.

"Sure I will," Milt drawled. "I'm due with grub up there tonight."

Becky sat back with relief.

Milt said, "I'll clean up a little, and then we'll start."

He built a fire in the kitchen, and Becky heard the rattle of dishes. He came back into the room, his face lathered, and went straight to a bottle of whisky on the table and poured himself a drink.

"That's breakfast," he said. "Won't join me, will you?"

"No, thanks," Becky said. She had acquired a sudden and definite distaste for his company, but it had to be tolerated if she were to see Will.

A long time later, Milt reappeared. He was shaved, his face washed, his hair combed, his clothes changed. He looked more like the man she remembered, but not wholly. He was in a surly mood, too.

Milt collected some groceries in a sack and went out to the corral and saddled up. Becky was waiting when he rode up and started off in the direction of the arroyo.

"Hadn't you better make sure we're not being watched and followed?" Becky asked.

"How?"

"Make a circle of the place and see if there are any new tracks."

Milt laughed. "They haven't watched me for a week. No, we're safe."

Becky wasn't certain, but then Milt should know what he was doing. He settled into a surly silence after that, and all afternoon they rode without speaking. Once he lost his way in the maze

218

of canyons, and they had to backtrack a mile.

Darkness came, and Becky was getting tired and hungry, but Milt made no suggestion that they stop and eat. Idly, Becky wondered how much Will had confided in Milt, and hoped it wasn't much. Somehow, she didn't like him.

They were in the deep canyons now, and the gloom was so profound that Becky could not see her way. But Milt evidently knew every twist and turn. They rounded a sharp bend, and a faint light seemed to relieve the gloom. Then they cut left again, and a campfire lay ahead of them a hundred yards away. Under the overhang of a high cliff and raised some six feet above the arroyo bed was a cave, its entrance black and deserted-looking in the firelight.

Milt rode up and dismounted and said, "Come over here by the fire."

Becky went over, and immediately, from up-river, she heard the sound of someone walking.

Will Danning stepped into the circle of firelight, a slow smile breaking his wolf-hungry face.

He greeted Becky quietly and looked at Milt. "Good thing you came, fella, or I'd be eatin' my boots." He looked sharply at Milt. "You're changed, Milt."

"Solitude," Milt said, scowling.

A fleeting frown crossed Will's face as he saw how a week of soft living, of drinking, of eating had changed Milt. There was the faint suggestion about him now of the way he used to be — stocky, well-fed, with pallor in his face. And then

219

Will looked at Becky.

She was hungry for a sight of him, but these days had made a difference in him, too. He looked like the men who had come off roundup — saddle-worn and weary and gaunted with sleepless nights and fourteen hours of riding. His shirt and Levis were faded-looking and worn, and a black stubble of beard seemed to further lean his cheeks.

They regarded each other with troubled understanding, both of them remembering the night Will had taken leave.

"Anything wrong, Becky?" Will asked. Becky nodded mutely toward Milt, and Will said immediately, "He knows what I know, Becky. There are no secrets."

Becky sat by the fire, and Will hunkered down on the other side of it. Milt, a faintly sardonic expression on his face, watched Becky.

"Dad has kicked Pres off the place," Becky began.

She didn't expect to see Will smile, but he did. "I thought he would," Will remarked.

"Why? Did you know about Pres's rustling?"

"I did the rustlin'," Will said.

"Then Pres told the truth!"

Will nodded. Milt, his gaze intent, watched Becky as she told the story of her father's quarrel with Pres. She finished by saying, "And I'm afraid now, Will, terribly afraid."

"That Pres will do somethin' to your dad?"

Becky nodded.

Will shook his head. "He's got to keep your

dad safe, Becky. If the deed to my spread is in your dad's name, then Pres wouldn't dare to make trouble right away. He won't get any money out of it if he does."

"But I know Dad won't do anything with the Pitchfork now, Will. He's stubborn. If he thinks it'll help Pres, he'll let the house rot and pay taxes for the next twenty years and not touch it. And Pres will get tired of waiting."

Will looked at her levelly and said, "Sure he will. He'll make trouble, too."

"But —" Becky stopped talking, sudden knowledge flooding into her eyes. She nodded slowly and said, "That's what you want, isn't it?"

Will nodded. "I told you."

"And you won't do anything to change it, will you?"

Will shook his head. They looked at each other in troubled silence, Milt watching them.

And then it happened.

Crack!

The sharp, flat slap of a rifle broke the night. Will spun around and fell sprawling by the fire. Becky screamed. Milt lunged to his feet, kicked out the fire, and whipped out his six-gun. He emptied it at nothing, and then they listened. The sound of a galloping horse faded, and then there was silence.

"Will!" Becky said. She ran toward him and knelt by him.

"I— it's nothin'," Will whispered. "In the leg."

"Milt, build up a fire!" Becky ordered swiftly.

221

"But they'll see us!"

"If you'd made sure they weren't following us, this wouldn't have happened!" Becky flared. "We've got to see if he's hurt. Hurry, now!"

Milt gathered the coals, and Becky was silent, still. She listened to Will's breathing, and knew he was in pain now, after the numbing shock.

When they had light again, Becky looked at Will's leg. His Levis were soaked with blood, and Becky glanced at his face. He was smiling wryly, his lip tight over his teeth. Becky borrowed Milt's knife and cut away the Levis leg. The wound was high in his thigh, and the bullet had gone clear through, just missing the bone. A small purple-mouthed depression in those muscles was welling a small stream of blood. The exit of the bullet was larger, the flesh jagged and torn, and this was the wound that was bleeding freely.

Becky bandaged it tightly with the clean shirt Milt had brought in the sack of grub. When she was finished, the blood was already seeping through the bandage.

"Help me up," Will said.

"You've got to lie still, Will," Becky protested.

"And let them come back and finish the job? No, I've got to get out of here if I can ride. Help me up, Milt."

Milt helped him to his feet. Becky watched Will's face and saw it slowly drained of color. Tentatively, he tried to flex his leg, and a spasm of pain crossed his face. He leaned on Milt's shoulder.

"Put me down and gather my stuff, Milt, and saddle up for me."

"But you can't!" Becky protested.

"I've got to," Will said stubbornly, his gray eyes bright with pain. "I don't aim to lie here and let them shoot me!"

"Where will you go?"

Will didn't answer. He didn't know. The Pitchfork was out; whoever shot him would look there first for him. There were other caves in the brakes but none close to water.

Milt said, "We could go back farther in the brakes, Will."

Will said flatly, meaningly, "You're goin' back to the place and stay there, Milt."

"But you can't stay alone," Becky said.

The three of them were silent, baffled. A wounded man was hard to hide, and beyond that, Will had to have attention, and Becky knew it.

"Why can't Milt take care of you?" she asked.

"I'm all right!" Will said angrily. "A couple of days and I'll be all right. Besides, he has to stay at the place!"

Becky didn't understand, but she knew Will was too stubborn to give in. And then she thought of something.

"Will, I know a place!" And then the excitement faded out of her eyes as she added, "Only it's too far."

"Where?" Milt asked.

"Our line camp, the piñon line camp. Dad ordered roundup yesterday. Today they've pushed all the stuff past the piñon line camp down into Sinking Valley. From there, they'll move west. Oh, if we could only reach it! Nobody would bother you there."

"I can reach it," Will said.

"But you can't! Your leg is —"

"I can make it," Will said angrily. "I've got to make it. Put me down and saddle up, Milt."

Milt put him down. The wound was slowly bleeding now, soaking the bandage. Becky knelt by him and said softly, "Will, it'll kill you! You can't do it!"

"I'll make it there. Leave me water and grub and I'll be all right."

"You need a doctor."

Will shook his head and said bleakly, "Docs are people, Becky. He'll take care of my leg, but there's nothin' to keep his mouth shut. No. No doctor."

Becky learned the will of the man then. She knew he would get on his horse and try to make the line camp, and that it would probably kill him. She also knew she couldn't stop him.

Milt came up with Will's horse and his own and Becky's. Becky held Will's horse, and Milt helped him over to it. Will was sweating; the muscles along his jaw were corded with the effort. He grabbed the horse's mane with one hand, the horn with the other, and then paused. It was his hit leg which he would have to swing over. He gathered himself up; putting his foot in the stirrup, he hoisted, swinging his leg. It hit the cantle and then slid over, and when he settled into the saddle a small groan escaped him. Head hung, fists grasping the horn until the knuckles were white, he sat there, breathing deeply, slowly. When he looked up, his face was wet with perspiration. He said in an altered voice, "We'd better hurry."

It almost broke Becky's heart to watch him, and she turned away. Milt gathered up Will's blankets and guns, strapped the grub on his saddle, and they rode off in the dark.

"How is it, Will?" Becky asked softly.

"Fine." It was spoken in a small, breath-held voice, as if he were afraid anything, even the sound of his voice, would start the blood flowing in a torrent.

These were the most dismal hours Becky was ever to know. As the long night wore on, Becky was almost frantic with worry. She cursed Milt Barron in her heart. She hated him and she hated herself, for if either of them had not been so careless they would have discovered they were being watched back at the spread. And who had shot Will? Anyone could have, any of Phipps's deputies, any bounty hunter, Pres, or even her father. There was no use puzzling over that, for it was done.

Will didn't talk. When Becky looked at him the few times he was sky-lined on one of the ridges in the brakes, he was holding onto the saddle horn with both hands, his head low on his chest. Once, when Milt lighted a cigarette, she glanced down at Will's leg. It was brown with dried blood, with a crimson film over it of fresh bleeding. His boot was soaked dark; even the stirrup was dripping. He was slowly bleeding to death, and she was helpless to stop it.

They picked up the short cut through the brakes to the Nine X, and came out long after midnight onto the bench. This was easier riding, but Will could not bear a faster pace than a walk.

Nobody spoke now. It was a slow, implacable race with time. Every last ounce of Will's strength was concentrated in a hard core of fighting against the grinding pain that was slowly taking over his whole body.

Once he fell out of the saddle, and Becky and Milt were in a panic as they knelt by him.

"Help me up," he whispered. "I went to sleep."

"Oh, Milt, we can't do this to him! We can't!"

"Help me up," Will whispered doggedly.

They put him back in the saddle again, and Becky couldn't look at him.

The next time he fell off he didn't bother to lie about sleeping. He only kept demanding that they put him back in the saddle. This time his muscles were so loose that he could scarcely help them. Milt tied the stirrups under the horse's belly, thinking it might help to keep Will in the saddle.

It was just breaking dawn when they rode up to the line shack. Becky dismounted and ran over to Will. He was slumped in the saddle, his head almost touching his horse's neck, his body loose as a sack. Only some dim effort of will had kept him from entirely collapsing. His wounded leg was stuck to the saddle. Milt had to pry his hands off the saddle horn and pull him to the ground.

Milt and Becky carried him into the shack and put him on the bunk. While Becky built a fire Milt rustled water, and Becky bathed Will's leg and cleaned it. The wound looked ugly from constant irritation. Will roused to regard them with feverish eyes. His cheeks were shrunken, and there were two bright spots of color on his cheekbones. He smiled faintly and dozed off, muttering short snatches of sentences that made no sense.

Becky and Milt regarded him worriedly, and Becky said, "It's the fever. We shouldn't have brought him. Can't we get the doctor, Milt?"

"He's right," Milt said bitterly. "He can't take a chance. They're huntin' him in town, and even if the doc don't turn him up, somebody's liable to follow."

"He'll have to fight it out alone?"

"I'll stay with him."

"I didn't mean that. I'm going to stay with him, and you get back to the spread." She looked curiously at Milt. "Why was he so anxious for you to go back?"

Milt said evasively, "Worried about bein' burned out, I guess."

Becky wasn't satisfied, and her anger against Milt was still high. But there were other things to worry about. Unless her father received word from her, the whole country would be turned

227

out to search. And sooner or later they would look here. She found a stub of pencil and used a rumpled paper sack, the only thing she could find, to write her note. It told her father she was staying with Martha Forster, who had a ranch south of the Yellow Jacket, and that she might be gone a week and not to worry. It had been a surprise meeting, and she'd decided to go on the spur of the moment. She offered no excuse for the paper, knowing he would be uneasy but that the writing in her own hand would satisfy him.

She gave the note to Milt, told him to deliver it at the Nine X, and if he was asked where he got it to say that Becky had met him on the road and had asked him to deliver it.

Milt left, and she was alone with Will. She set about cleaning up the place, and when that was done, there was nothing left but to watch Will. He was in fever now. His big, bony hands plucked the blankets, and he tossed and muttered. She bathed his forehead, but it didn't seem to help. Nothing seemed to help. He was fighting that lonely fight with fever and pain in a country far beyond her reaching.

Late that night he opened his eyes and stared at her, and the look in his face frightened her. He didn't recognize her, only looked strangely around the room, then closed his eyes again.

Next morning, he was awake again. She tried to feed him, but he turned his face away. As the day wore on, he again settled into fever, and this time it was worse. He muttered of ranching and Murray Broome and Milt Barron and Chap Hale, and he was angry, but none of his talk made sense. His leg was angry-looking and swollen; and Becky was afraid. There was nothing she could do but watch him, and twice she went to sleep on the stump stool by his bunk. Later, in midafternoon, he dozed off, and Becky slept beside him, under his blanket. She listened to his troubled breathing and cried, and once she prayed.

The night after that day was torment. Will was deep in delirium, talking a weird nonsense with a strange passion that was frightening. Becky knew that this was the night when he would win or lose. She gazed upon that gaunt and beard-stubbled face, and it was a comfort to see the rugged strength there. His great gnarled and scarred hands were shrunken a little, as if shriveled by the fever. There was a wild strength in his eyes that were open but didn't see her.

She sat by the bunk, listening to his cursing and never flinching, her mind drugged with weariness. All she knew was that somehow, some way, he must pull through, and she would witness it.

After midnight, she was certain he was dying. The wild color in his face and the expression in his eyes were terrible to see. But toward morning, the color went away. His face was bathed with sweat, and he ceased talking. Then his breathing slowed, and she knew he was asleep.

He had won, conquered the fever.

She lay down beside him then, her head on his shoulder, and slept, too exhausted to be very happy.

She wakened in the afternoon and opened her eyes. Will was watching her, and now he smiled.

Becky was suddenly aware of where she was and she rose, blushing a little.

"I'm hungry," Will said, and grinned.

"You're going to get well, Will," Becky said happily. She threw back the blanket and looked at his leg. The swelling was receding, the angry color disappearing.

Will watched her cook some food, and when it was finished he wolfed it down and asked for more.

Afterward she rolled him a smoke and lighted it for him, and she was sitting on the bunk watching him when she heard a horseman approaching outside.

Will put out his cigarette, and Becky went to the door. It was Milt, and she told Will.

Milt tramped in, and when Will saw him he knew something was wrong. The old rash wildness was back in Milt's eyes. He grinned at Will, said, "How do you feel, boy?"

"Weak," Will said.

"Too weak to take some bad news?" Milt asked. Will scowled.

"Case and Phipps were out this morning, along with a pair of his deputies. We're kicked off. They helped me move. I'm camped under a spring wagon way off east over our boundary line."

Becky was watching Will, and she saw the bitterness mount in his eyes. He turned his head and looked out the small window. Surely he had known it was coming, she thought; but she was not prepared for this. There was no fight left in him, it seemed. Sickness and bad luck had burdened him too heavily. He was whipped. She remembered that rash brag he made to her that night at the Nine X. He had said he would ruin her father. Only now her father was in the saddle, and Will was licked. A man could fight only so much.

Will looked up at Milt, and Milt said, "The rest of it ain't so important. They've run Ollie and Pink and Pablo out of the county. Loaded 'em on the freight last night and kicked 'em out."

"No spread, no crew, and flat on my back with a price on my head," Will murmured. "Well, it looks like we're licked, Milt."

Milt nodded and sat on the bunk, his sullen face reflecting his discouragement. He and Will looked at each other in silence, as if understanding something that was not spoken. It made Becky sad to see Will this way, beaten and helpless. She didn't blame him, only it made her angry.

"We'll pull out when I can travel," Will said. "And the sooner the better."

Becky said, "Did — they say anything about Will getting shot — ask about him or anything?"

Milt shook his head. "I listened for that, tried to pump 'em. I don't think they did it, and I

231

don't think they know about it."

"Then who did?"

Milt shrugged.

Will said meagerly, "Well, we got our money to get out of this, Milt." He looked at Becky. "You figure your dad will pay back the money I gave to Chap?"

Becky nodded. "It wasn't the money he wanted; it was the place. He'll return it."

"To Milt?"

"If Milt has some kind of authorization, I know he will."

"Power of attorney, you mean?" Milt asked.

Becky nodded. They didn't speak for a few moments, and then Will sighed.

"All right, bring some paper with you when you come next time, Milt. I'll give you power of attorney. We'll get the money and light a shuck."

Becky listened to Will, her heart filled with bitterness, and said nothing.

Chapter Eighteen

STRANGE PARTNERSHIP

Milt and Becky both left the line camp at the same time, after Will's stubborn insistence. Becky was to go home for a change of clothes, a long sleep, and some food. Milt was to ride into Yellow Jacket, arrange with Phipps to have Case return the money, collect it, and return with it. In another day they would ride, if Will could stand it. They would drift slowly out of the country through the brakes, to look for another place where Will could hide Milt.

To Milt, as he rode away from the line camp that morning, the whole thing seemed like a reprieve. In another week he would not be living in constant fear that Pres, drunk some night, would tell a whole saloon full of punchers that he knew where Murray Broome was. True, Pres wouldn't tell when he was sober; he would be too afraid of Milt telling of Chap Hale's murder. But the risk was there. And then, too, Milt was bored. This last lonely week of hugging the ranch, lonesome, never seeing a woman, never having any companionship, was driving him crazy. He'd lost his chance for a fortune, too. And no money to spend, living like a damned homesteader. Anything, even prison, was preferable to this life — or almost, anyway.

He rode into Yellow Jacket at noon. The drowsy sun of midday made the town look half asleep. The usual saddle horses and teams were at the tie rails, and the town people went on their placid way.

Milt pulled up in front of the sheriff's office and dismounted. He remembered Charlie Sommers was back there in the cell block. Only a single wall barred Milt from possible recognition, but the risk had to be run, if it could really be called a risk.

He stepped into the sheriff's office and found Phipps seated at his desk, alone.

Phipps nodded coolly and said with a dry humor, "We seem to be doing considerable business together, Barron."

Milt nodded and sat down. The door to the cell block was closed so there was little risk of being overheard by Sommers. He crossed his legs and rolled a smoke.

"Phipps," he said when he had lighted it, "I'm pullin' out."

"That's smart," Phipps said, and added shrewdly, "I 'spose that means Will Danning is pullin' out, too."

Milt shrugged.

"It won't do him no good to run, of course," Phipps said. "He's got a price on his head. Somebody'll collect."

234

"Maybe," Milt said. "That ain't why I'm here, though. You claim to be honest. Are you honest to a man you think is a crook?"

Phipps's leathery face flushed deep. "I don't know what you mean by that."

"Case claims the Harkins place now. He's took over. Yet Will Danning paid ten thousand dollars to Chap Hale for it. You got a record of it in Chap's papers. Does Case aim to steal that money, too?"

"Have you asked him?" Phipps said.

"No. I figured he wouldn't let go of it unless the law made him."

"That money's in the bank, and has been for a week," Phipps said tartly. "Will Danning, or any authorized party, can ask Case for it and he'll get it. Does that satisfy you?"

Milt nodded and slipped a piece of paper on Phipps's desk. "There's my authority to collect," he said.

Phipps glanced at the paper and then at Milt. "So you saw him after we left?"

"That's dated the night he broke jail," Milt said smoothly. "That's all I know."

Phipps grunted and handed it back. "Find Case. He's in town and he'll pay you. And damned good riddance to the county, if you ask me."

Milt went out and looked in Hal Mohr's place. Case wasn't there. He went over to the hotel and inquired, and was told that Case left word he would be back at noon. It was almost noon now.

235

Milt bought a cigar, took a chair in the lobby, and relaxed. He had a view of both the street and the lobby, so that Case could not escape him.

He was smoking idly, when he heard the soft step of a woman on the stairs. He glanced over and saw Mary Norman descending the stairs.

Milt's first feeling was one of absolute panic. But he knew if he moved she would look at him and might recognize him. His second thought, as he watched her go to the desk and talk with the clerk, was one of admiration. She was as beautiful as ever, and the sight of her brought up memories that excited him. And then his old recklessness came over him. Mary Norman. Hell, she was in love with him once. He'd spent a fortune on her. She wouldn't give him away if they hanged her for it.

His eyes were amused now as he watched her, wondering if she would recognize him. She turned away from the desk, starting for the door. Milt cleared his throat; she looked up, saw him, and looked away. Immediately her gaze returned, and her pace slowed. There was a tiny frown of puzzlement on her handsome brow, and Milt couldn't refrain from smiling.

And it was that brash smile that shocked Mary Norman to a full stop. Milt came out of his chair and walked over to her, saying swiftly, "Not a word!"

Mary formed the name Murray with her lips, and then glanced swiftly over to the desk. The clerk had disappeared into the office.

"Follow me!" Mary whispered excitedly.

She started for the stairs and went up. Milt waited a moment, then went upstairs. She was standing down the hall in a doorway, beckoning him.

When Milt closed the door, she was in his arms. He kissed her, and Mary whispered, "Murray! You darling!"

Milt held her out at arm's length and looked at her and then kissed her again, and Mary returned his kisses.

"But you've changed," Mary said. "What have you done to your hair? And your mustache? And you're thinner, and you're tanned, Murray. Where have you been?"

Milt stemmed the flow of questions and pulled her onto his lap in the chair. If he had ever doubted Mary Norman's love, he didn't now. The joy in her face was obvious to anyone who wasn't blind.

Mary said, "Where have you been hiding? Tell me."

"Tell me first why you're here."

Mary's face sobered, and some of the joy went out of it. "To find you. They made me, Murray —"

"Milt's the name. Don't ever forget that."

"Milt. They've arrested me — for stealing."

"Stealing what?"

"Some papers from the Land Commissioner's rooms in the Capital hotel. I was hired by — you know — your old gang. Anyway, I was caught. But instead of jailing me the U. S. Commissioner promised me they'd drop the charges if I helped trap you."

Milt was amused. "And you took 'em up?"

Mary nodded and kissed him swiftly. "I did. Charlie Sommers brought me here. He was sure Will Danning would know where you were. I was bait."

"Well, it worked." Milt laughed.

"It did not!" Mary Norman said firmly. "Before Charlie Sommers went to jail, he told me I'd have to look for you for a year. After that, they'd let me go."

"Think you can hold out?" Milt teased.

Mary Norman said passionately, "I'd die before I'd tell them anything about you! Where have you been hiding?"

"With Will Danning, out at the Pitchfork."

"That reminds me," Mary said. She came off his knees and went over to the dresser and pawed through a heap of papers. She found what she wanted and handed it to Milt, saying, "I stole that from Will one day in the post office. I thought it was a letter from you."

"Will knew you were here!"

"I talked to him. Didn't you know?"

Milt said angrily, "Damn him, no." And he read the paper. A strange excitement came into his face as he read it.

"What's the matter?" Mary asked.

"Matter?" Milt said softly. "Mary, do you know what this is? It's the deed from Chap Hale! It's the deed to a fortune, a whole damned million-aire's fortune!"

"But — I don't understand."

"You don't have to understand," Milt said excitedly. Then he told her about Will's being outlawed, and his eviction from the place yesterday. This deed voided Case's claim. Will's money was paid down, deposited, and now he had the deed to the Pitchfork. Milt looked at it, his eyes strange with a bright greed. Then he looked up at Mary and said, "Mary, how would you like to go to South America, Europe, anywhere you want?"

"Alone?"

"No, you little fool! With me! Don't you see, this'll make me rich!"

Mary Norman was mute with surprise and pleasure. Milt slowly folded the deed, staring out the window. "Wait, Mary. I'll have to go now, but I'll be back later. This is the biggest thing that ever happened to me."

Mary kissed him again, and he slipped out into the hall. He stood there a moment, bemused by his good fortune. He had Will's power of attorney right here in his pocket, which meant he could steal the whole thing. But he wouldn't do that. He had another scheme, not so crude, safer, and Will would never know. Good old Will — dumb, loyal, and stupid. He'd served his usefulness and served it well, and it would be too cruel to let him down so abruptly.

Going down the stairs, Milt knew what he was going to do. He must find Case first. As he went through the lobby, the clerk said, "Mr. Barron, Mr. Case just went into the dining-room."

Milt thanked him and stepped into the dining-room. Only a couple of tables were occupied, and Case was at one of these.

Milt went over and sat down beside him. "Seen Phipps, Case?" he asked swiftly.

"I have."

"Going to pay over the money?"

"Naturally," Case said coldly. "I have the receipt here. It was signed by Chap and was among his papers, so there's no argument."

Milt couldn't stifle a feeling of elation. He said, "Let's see it."

Care took out his wallet and drew out a check and a folded paper. Milt took the paper and opened it. It merely acknowledged that ten thousand had been deposited by Will with him for the purchase of a ranch. The writing on it was the same as the writing on the deed, so there could be no mistake.

Milt folded the receipt, put it in his pocket and then picked up the check. He tore it in half, in fourths, in eighths, and then dropped the pieces on the floor, watching Case.

The older man's face was first surprised and then angry. He looked at the pieces, then up at Milt, and said, "In God's name, man! That's a check for ten thousand dollars!"

Milt took out the deed, unfolded it, laid it flat on the table, and held the edges down with his two hands.

"Don't touch it, Case," he drawled. "Just read it."

Case leaned over and read the deed. His face turned an ashy-white, and all the color drained out of his lips.

Milt grinned, pocketed the deed, and rose. "Try and bust that in any court in the Territory," Milt drawled. "I'll give you just two days to get the hell off that land, Case. Just two days."

He waved mockingly and walked out, and Case was dumb.

Milt had to find Pres now, find him before Case got the word to him and before Pres, swindled out of his share of the cut, told Phipps of Milt's real identity. Milt was smart enough to see that before anything could be done, he'd have to buy Pres off.

He went to Hal Mohr's, but Pres wasn't there. Nobody knew where he was. Milt tried a couple of the Mexican cantinas, with the same results. Pres wasn't at any of the restaurants or stores.

Time was passing, and he had to see Pres soon. Milt was undecided, after searching everywhere Pres might be. If he couldn't find him, then he could do the next best thing.

He went back to the hotel, chose a corner table in the lobby, pulled out a sheet of paper, and wrote:

Pres:
The deed to the Pitchfork made out to Will Danning and signed by Chap Hale has turned up and

is in my hands. This voids Case's deed and gives Danning the land, which is where we started. But with this difference. I think I can get Will to move now and release his claim on the place, leaving you and me with our original partnership. Let's forget our quarrel and work together again.

But you'll have to keep away from Will and stay hidden. Let me pretend you've learned my real name and will keep silence in return for the deed. But let me do it! Stay away from Danning.

You're sure of my co-operation in this, as this letter shows. And I'm sure you won't double-cross me again. You wouldn't want to have a fortune in sight and then have me tell Phipps how you shot Chap, would you? Get in touch with me as soon as you get this.

Milt Barron.

Milt read the letter over, made certain it would satisfy Pres, and then put it in an envelope. He addressed it to Pres Milo, General Delivery, and took it down to Dunn's store.

Dunn received the letter at the wicket, and Milt went out. Dunn looked at the address, saw the name, and tucked the letter in the pigeonhole marked: *Nine X Ranch.* He hadn't heard that Pres had left his job.

Milt went back to the hotel and ate with Mary Norman in public in the dining-room. He wasn't afraid of being seen with Mary now, for she told him that only Charlie Sommers and herself knew why she was here, and Charlie Sommers was discredited and in jail.

But all during the meal Milt's excitement would not let him eat, he was too anxious to see Pres. He sent Mary up to her room afterward, then started making the rounds again in search of Pres.

He found him bellied up to the bar in Hal Mohr's, the lone man in the saloon beside the fat owner. Pres saw Milt's entrance in the back bar mirror, and he backed away from his drink, his hand falling to his gun.

Milt, grinning, kept his hands at his side and walked up to Pres.

"A bottle and two glasses," he told Hal. Pres's thick face was wary, suspicious, ugly.

Milt took his gun out and laid it on the bar and then said to Pres, "Come over and have a drink with me."

Pres looked puzzled. He looked at the gun, then at Milt, and seemed undecided. Milt went over to one of the far tables and waited for him.

Pres came reluctantly and stopped beside the table. "You must want somethin'."

"Get your mail today, Pres?"

"No. Why?"

"There's a letter there that'll tell you everything. Sit down, and I'll explain."

Pres sat down warily. Milt drew the deed out of his pocket and handed it to Pres. Pres read it, read it again, and then looked up at Milt.

"It's no forgery," Milt said. "I just got it today. It voids Case's claim to the place, and gives it back to Will."

Pres was stupefied for a moment. And then he began to curse in a low and passionate voice, his face redder than usual. Milt grinned at him, and Pres stopped, stared.

"So you think it's funny," he said. "Well, Mr. Murray Broome, we'll see how funny it is."

He started to get up, and Milt drawled quietly, "Sit down, you damn fool. You ain't goin' to Phipps."

"Why not?"

"Because we're partners. And this time I can swing it."

Pres settled slowly into his chair, attentive, and Milt went on, "Will Danning's ready to pull out. He's whipped. Somebody shot at him and —" He paused, seeing Pres's faint grin. "You shot him," he cried.

"I don't know what you're talkin' about," Pres said.

Milt's eyes narrowed, and for a second there was a wicked light in his eyes. "Damn you, Pres!" he said softly. "If you and I weren't partners, I'd kill you."

Pres only shrugged, his thick lips pouting. Milt settled back and resumed his talk. "Danning's ready to leave. He sent me into town to get his money back. And then I turned up this deed. Don't you see what it means?"

"It means you and me, if we're partners, are right back where we started," Pres growled. "You couldn't get him off the place before, and you won't now."

"You're wrong," Milt said softly. "I'll get him off."

"How?"

"By tellin' him you're blackmailin' me. I'll tell him you found the deed, and you discovered my real name in that locket. I'll tell him you've decided to keep your mouth shut about me if you get the deed. If you don't, you'll turn me up."

"He'll laugh and tell you it's tough, but he ain't losin' a fortune just to protect you."

Milt shook his head. "You don't know Will Danning. In some ways he's the dumbest ranny that ever walked."

Pres said slowly, "You mean he'll lose the place rather than let me turn you up?"

Milt nodded.

"Why?"

Milt shrugged. "It's the way he's made. That's the reason I asked him to hide me. I knew damn well he'd die before he'd turn me up, and he will. Money doesn't mean anything to Will Danning where a friend's concerned."

Pres looked at him curiously, and then laughed a little. "Barron, you're a real hardcase, ain't you? You'd let a man cut his throat for you, and then laugh at him."

Milt's face flushed deeply, and there was an ugly glint to his eyes. "Careful, Pres," he murmured. "I'm just lookin' out for myself. If Will is dumb enough to do it, I'm not goin' to stop him. It ain't as if he didn't know what he was doin'. He knows that land is valuable. He'll know

245

what he's losin'. The only thing he won't know is that I'm makin' money off it. Even if I do, it won't hurt him — and I got to have money. I've got to have money to clear out of here where nobody'll care what my name is."

Pres shrugged. "You're sure he'll do it?"

"Positive."

Pres sat back in his chair, his little pig eyes dreamy, ignoring the drink Milt poured for him. Milt lifted his glass and said, "Here's to the new partnership."

Pres drank with him, and then smacked his glass on the table.

"Case know this?"

"I told him."

Pres grinned and put his hands on the table, ready to shove himself up. "Here's where I get even with that old coyote. For five years, he's kept me broke and wouldn't loan me money. And then he tried to kill me. We'll see, now." He stood up. "When you goin' to spring this on Danning?"

"Tomorrow."

Pres grinned, his eyes musing. "Keep your eyes open this afternoon. You'll see somethin'." And he went out.

Chapter Nineteen

Too Old for Prison

Angus Case sat in one of the lobby chairs, his thoughts bleak and somber. He realized that he should hunt up Pres Milo and beg him to come back again, but his pride kept him in his chair. He had known several days of the greatest peace he'd experienced in ten years, and now it was gone. The newly discovered deed had done that. The only thing that had kept Pres's mouth shut after he tried to kill Pres was the knowledge that Case could make money for him. And now Case couldn't, and Pres, disgruntled and out of a job, might make trouble for him. But he hated it. He hated it with all the passion of a proud man who has to grovel before a crook and a blackmailer.

Case lighted another cigar and thought of the ways in which he could avoid doing this. Pres would be furious that his secret, which he had guarded for five years, was useless now. Case might approach him in a friendly and businesslike way and say, "Look, Pres. I haven't got the land now, but Danning's got it. Why don't you go to him and make the same kind of a deal with him you made with me? You'll tell him how this money is to be made in return for a cut of it. And you can work back at your old job until the money starts coming in."

Yes, that would be the thing to do. It would save face for both of them. He decided to finish his cigar and then go hunt Pres.

He saw Sheriff Phipps come into the lobby. Phipps looked around, saw him, and then came over to him.

"Howdy, John."

"How are you, Angus?" Phipps said. He pulled up a chair beside Case and sat there in silence, his lean face grave and troubled.

Case said, "You look like hell. What's the matter?"

Phipps said glumly, "Sometimes I wish I'd never seen a law badge, and this is one of them times."

"What's the trouble now, John?"

Phipps was silent, looking at his old friend. He cleared his throat, was about to speak, and then didn't. His fingers drummed on the arm of his chair, and there was purest misery in his face.

Finally he said, "Angus, what would you do if you knew a friend of yours had committed a crime? If you was a sheriff, would you arrest him?"

Case frowned. "That's hard to answer, John. Do what your conscience tells you."

"Even if you hate it worse'n anything in the world?"

"A naggin' conscience is the worst thing in the world," Case said, suddenly grave. He might have added, "I ought to know," but he didn't.

Phipps said then, after a long pause, "I reckon you're right. I might's well do the job."

"What is it?" Case asked, interested now.

Phipps said quietly, "Angus, I know how Harkins died, and why."

Case didn't move. It was as if somebody had struck him. A raw, cold, despairing fear caught at his stomach, and then he slowly relaxed. Here it was, the thing he had been dreading for ten years. It had finally caught up with him. He thought with a bitter humor of his counsel to John Phipps to follow his conscience. Phipps had been talking of him, and Case hadn't even suspected it.

Case asked, "Was it Pres?"

Phipps nodded. "You don't have to tell me if you don't want to, Angus, but is it true? He told it all, your stealin' from your bosses and then coverin' up by blamin' Harkins and havin' him murdered. He named dates and times and the names of men and where I could reach 'em now. It all sounds true, Angus — but is it? Would you tell me?"

Case didn't speak for a long moment. His voice was almost a whisper as he said, "Yes. It's true."

Phipps didn't look at him. They both stared out the lobby window at the passers-by, each lost in his own dismal thoughts.

"He's known it for years," Case said quietly.

249

"He's been holdin' it over me all this time. Day and night, year in and year out, it was never out of my mind. He never let me forget it. He's crowded me into things I've been ashamed of, and I could never fire him for fear he'd go to you. Last week he stole some cattle from me. I won't take that, not from any man. I fired him then, John. I tried to kill him. And now he's got even with me."

Phipps said nothing. From the window they could see Hal Mohr's saloon. As they watched, they saw Pres's swaggering barrel-figure shoulder the doors aside and enter.

Case said quietly, "I won't go to prison, John. I'm too old."

Phipps didn't look at him, didn't say anything.

Case sighed and came slowly to his feet. His back was stooped, and he seemed older. He looked down at his old friend and said, "I didn't bring a gun with me, John. Can I borrow yours?"

Phipps looked at him then. Their glances locked, and then Phipps's gaze fell, and he slipped the gun out of its holster and gave it to Case.

"I won't be long," Case said.

He slipped the gun in his coat pocket and went out, not even saying good-by. Phipps didn't move, only sat there and watched him cross the street toward Hal Mohr's saloon and shoulder through the doors.

When Case entered the saloon, he saw Pres at the end of the bar talking with Milt Barron. Three other men were bellied up to the bar, and they turned to see who had entered.

Case stopped and motioned with his head for them to leave the bar. They backed away, and the men at the tables fell silent. Milt looked around at the silence, and saw Case.

"Get away from him," Case said thinly.

Milt backed away, too, and Hal Mohr ducked under the bar. Pres straightened up and let his hand fall to his side. He watched Case carefully, a kind of wry amusement in his eyes.

Case said, "It took you a long time, didn't it, Pres? Well, it won't take me long."

He reached in his pocket for his gun. Pres's hand streaked to his holster. Case yanked at his gun — and the sight caught on the edge of his pocket. He tugged savagely, and it came loose. But in that half second that the sight was tangled, Pres's gun swung up. He took careful sight and shot once.

The shot caught Case in the chest, slamming him backward. He caught himself, braced his feet, and raised his gun. He got it only chest-high when it boomed loudly in the room, and the slug slapped into the bar at Pres's feet.

Case looked at him with glassy eyes, tried to speak, and then his knees buckled. He fell on his side and rolled over on his back and lay still.

Men were bending over him when Phipps stepped in. Pres came up to him and offered his gun and said, "It was self-defense, Phipps. Ask anybody here."

Phipps listened to them absently. Man after

man told of how Case had come in, how he had threatened Pres. Phipps knew what the story would be. He pushed Pres's gun back and looked down at Case, at peace at last.

"Give a hand with him, will you?" he asked sadly.

He did not speak, did not look at Pres. He only followed the men who carried Case out, and did not once look back.

Afterward Milt went over to the hotel and wrote another note. It said: *Miss Becky: You'd better come to town at once. Your Father is ill. — Milt Barron.*

He signed it and took it down to the livery stable and paid a boy two dollars to ride out with it to the Nine X.

It was a wise move, and he was rather proud of it. It meant that Becky would not be on hand tomorrow when he talked with Will. She didn't like him, and he didn't want her influencing Will at this crucial moment.

Chapter Twenty

A Man's Promise

It was a gray morning, and Will was sleeping after breakfast. It had tired him even to cook a meal, and he was ashamed of it. All he wanted to do was sleep and eat. A Nine X rider could have walked in on him any time, and he wouldn't have known it.

He felt a hand on his shoulder and, coming awake, he realized it might be a stray rider. He opened his eyes and started to sit up, then saw it was Milt.

He had never seen Milt look this way before, never seen him so beaten and dispirited.

"What's the matter with you, fella?" Will drawled. And he asked instantly, "Wouldn't Case give you the money?"

Milt sat down on the edge of the bunk. "I dunno, Will. Before I had a chance to ask, somebody made me a proposition."

"What?"

"A lot's happened since yesterday," Milt went on. "First thing is Case is dead. He chose Pres, and Pres killed him."

"Poor Becky," Will said slowly. "She knew it

was comin', I reckon."

"Second thing is," Milt said bleakly, "somebody knows me here, Will."

Will sat upright, eyes wide. "Who?"

"Pres Milo."

For a long moment Will only stared at him, and then he murmured, "How'd he find out?"

"You remember that painted locket I've got of my mother? Well, I never told you, but it opens up. On the inside is a picture of my dad. On the inside of the back is some engraving, somethin' like: 'To Murray from Mother and Dad.' Well, yesterday Pres searched my camp at the wagon. He found the locket. I'd smashed it shut, and I didn't think it would open, but he opened it. He saw it and guessed it was me."

Will said nothing, and Milt went on doggedly, "Third thing is, Chap Hale made out a deed to you, Will, before he died." He handed the deed to Will, who opened it. "Pres stole it from the safe that night he robbed Chap's office."

Will looked from the deed to Milt.

"But why?"

"He didn't want you to get the land. He knew Case would be executor, and that if you couldn't show a deed, the land would go to Case. That's why he made the deal with Case."

"But why did he give it to you now?"

Milt laughed bitterly. "He figures he can make you deed the land to him now. If you don't, he says he'll turn me up and you, too, for hidin' me."

Will looked again at the deed. "Is that why Case tried to kill him?"

Milt nodded mutely, and Will let the deed fall to his lap. Milt got up and said, "Well, I'm goin' to drift, Will."

"Drift where?"

"I dunno, but I'm goin' to clear out of here today, now. Pres said he'd give you a day to decide. That'll give me time enough to get into the brakes. Then you can tell him to go to hell. You can ride into town and show the deed to Phipps. It'll show Phipps that you and Chap never quarreled about the deed, so you couldn't have killed him. Pres will try to hang the deadwood on you. He'll claim you been hidin' me. Deny it. When he brings out the locket, you can tell him I give it to you when we split up months ago. They can't find me to prove it, so you'll be in the clear."

"Wait a minute," Will said slowly. "You mean you're goin', clearin' out?"

Milt nodded.

"But why?"

Milt laughed shortly. "Don't be a damn fool, Will. If I stay here, it'll mean you got to deed your land to Pres. And that land's worth a fortune, so Pres says. It's worth enough that Case tried to kill him over losin' it."

Will threw the deed on the table. "Take it back to him and tell him to keep it. Tell him I'll deed him the damn land and welcome!"

"But you're losin' a fortune!" Milt said slowly.

"To hell with a fortune," Will said curtly. "I'm goin' to hide you, Milt. This deed will keep his mouth shut for a couple of weeks until I can ride out of here with you."

"But dammit, man —"

"It's settled," Will said flatly. "Money don't amount to a damn. The important thing is to keep him off our necks until I can drift with you, Milt."

Milt came over and stood looking down at Will. "Look, fella," he said quietly. "I been around your neck long enough. You've lost a place, you've got shot, and you're outlawed, all on account of me. I better drift alone. You've done all you could and more, Will. If you figure you owe it to me to keep your promise, forget it. You've done all a man could, and it's up to me, now."

"Where'll you go?"

Milt shrugged.

Will brought his hand down violently on the table. "No. Milt, you're cagey enough when it comes to business, but stickin' with me is your only chance! Sure as hell you'll give yourself away. You're too reckless! You don't care! And if you think I'm goin' to see you hanged, just because I dropped you to make some money, you're loco as hell! You're stickin' with me!"

"I can't let you do it!" Milt said doggedly.

"I've done it," Will said flatly. "You're goin' to ride into town tonight, tell Milo that I agree, pick up a deed form and bring it out here. You and Becky will be my witnesses to the deed. I'll sign it and show it to Pres. Tell him it's his if he gives me another week to get on my feet. After that, we'll mail it to him and ride out, and be damned to the land!"

"You can't do it, Will!"

"I can do anything for a friend," Will said simply.

Milt's gaze dropped, and he sat down on the bunk, staring at the floor. He felt a cold and dismal feeling of shame, and he couldn't look at Will. Will misinterpreted that. He said softly, "Look, Milt. Remember when I rode up to the Double Bar O, flat broke, ridin' the grub line? Remember when old Harley told me he'd feed me one meal and then for me to get out? Remember, you watched me eat, and then asked me if I could wrangle horses? Remember how you argued with Harley, and finally ordered him to hire me? In five years, you'd made me ramrod of your spread. I don't forget that, Milt. You gave me a hand when I was down. What kind of man would I be if I —"

"Quit it, Will!" Milt cried.

Milt looked at him. For an instant, an almost ungovernable impulse welled up in him to tell Will the whole rotten thing and ask his forgiveness. But he was afraid, afraid of Pres, afraid of Charlie Sommers, and afraid mostly of Will. For some day, surely as the sun rose, Will would find out the whole slimy story behind Senator Mason's killing. It was the story of how a young newspaperman, for more money than he'd ever seen, had boldly published lies and slander about a good man. He'd been brought to justice in the courts, but he couldn't tolerate a beating. He'd killed Senator Mason for it, and then fled. His innocence was fiction, although the men who first bribed him used it as a political rallying-cry. No, when Will found out the truth, he would hate him. It was too late to turn back now. It was too late for everything except to grab what money he could and flee to another country where he could start over. The time to tell Will was past, and Milt knew with dismal conviction that he could never look back, never have mercy, never ask it.

Will said gently, "All right, fella. But that's the way it stands."

Milt had to thank him now. He wondered if he'd choke as he spoke — if, as he had believed when he was a child, his tongue would turn black at mouthing such lies.

Will said gruffly, "If you try to thank me for this I'll break your neck. Get out of here."

Milt rose, not looking at him, put a hand on his shoulder, squeezed it, and went out.

Becky listened to Phipps's quiet story in the office that morning. She saw it as the tragic story of her father, aging and too ambitious, blinding his conscience to take a short cut to the ease which most men worked a lifetime for. He'd paid for it. Every hour of these last ten years had been payment. Death was welcome to him, she knew, and she couldn't feel much sorrow. Right now she couldn't even hate the man who'd killed him.

Phipps agreed with her when she said she wanted the burial that morning. Two of the three people Angus Case cared for most — his daughter and his friend, John Phipps — were there. Chap Hale was already dead. To get the crew in for the funeral would mean leaving roundup, and it would take days. And Becky couldn't, wouldn't wait that long.

It was a quiet service, only a handful of people attending. Angus Case had been an unfriendly and proud man during his lifetime, a person the town and the ranchers didn't understand and didn't like. And few would really mourn him, Becky knew.

Afterward she rode back to town in Phipps's buggy. There was only one person in the world she wanted to see now, and that was Will. But Will was leaving. Or was he? Wouldn't she inherit the land now, and couldn't she give it back to him? She was almost ashamed of her lightness of heart when she thought of that.

First, though, she remembered she was mistress of the Nine X. There was buying to do, for the ranch must run as it had always run under her father. She stopped in at Dunn's, ordered supplies, had a special sack of grub put up for Will, and then called for the Nine X mail.

She wanted to ride to see Will first, but she

knew she wouldn't. She must first ride out to the ranch, tell the men of her father's death, give orders to Tip. Afterward, her duty done, she could see Will.

The Nine X was deserted, except for Tomás and one of the punchers Becky had sent for last night when she'd got news of her father's illness. Now that her father was dead, she wondered if she should go on with this roundup, which was the whim of a man who feared his cattle had been stolen. But if the crew returned Will might be discovered. She told the puncher of her father's death and sent word to Tip to keep on with the roundup.

Afterward she went into the house. Will's grub she put on the table, and then she remembered the mail. She stepped to the door, called to the puncher, who was just riding out, to wait a moment, and then she returned to the mail. She began to sort it, and when she came to Pres's letter, put it aside. Then she put the crew's mail in a sack and gave it to the puncher, who rode off.

Coming back to the kitchen table, Becky looked again at Pres's letter, which Mr. Dunn had put with the Nine X mail by mistake. It came to her with a shock that she'd seen that bold writing before. She went over to a cabinet, took down a note, brought it over, and compared the writing. They were the same. The note was one she had received last night from Milt Barron!

What was Milt Barron doing writing to Pres?

They didn't know each other, hadn't seen each other except at Will's place before the fight. Or had they? Becky kept thinking of Milt, his sulky manner, his veiled insolence, and the fact that through his carelessness Will had been shot. And she thought of Pres, the man who had killed her father. For a moment, a suspicion arose within her and crystallized, the suspicion that Milt knew Pres well and was writing to him. She knew then that she would always think this, holding to it with a woman's stubbornness until it was proven otherwise.

Well, why not find out for herself? Why not open it? Some deep honesty in her told her that was shabby, dishonorable. But was it? If Pres was sent to the penitentiary, where he belonged, wouldn't people open his mail to make sure he wouldn't harm them further? Of course they would. Then why shouldn't she?

It was a devious argument, and she despised herself for resorting to it, yet the fact wasn't changed. Why was Milt writing Pres?

With sudden decision, she took Pres's letter, opened it, and read the note. Finished, she sank into a chair, her gaze still on the note. Milt was double-crossing Will, some way! And Pres was the one who had killed Chap Hale! Pres and Milt were partners — partners in looting Will of the Pitchfork!

Some of it she didn't understand, but Will might. Becky changed swiftly to Levis and blue shirt, put the letter in her pocket, and ran out

261

to the corral. She was in such a hurry that she completely forgot Will's grub. Tomás saddled her horse, and she set out for the line camp at a dead gallop, leaving the Mexican stable hand puzzled.

Becky arrived at the line camp just at dusk, her horse almost foundered. Will had seen her approach, and he was standing in the doorway, leaning on the jamb to favor his wounded leg.

Becky slipped out of the saddle and strode across to him. Now that she saw Will, her courage faltered. How could she tell him about Milt?

He hobbled out to meet her, his face grave. He had shaved while she was gone, and the hollowness in his cheeks, his sunken eyes made her sad.

He took her hands in his own rough ones. "Milt told me about your dad, Becky."

"He was lucky," Becky said bitterly, and then she shook her head. "I didn't mean that, Will. Come inside."

Will, puzzled at her brusque manner, followed her in. Becky struck a match, lighted the candle, and came over to Will and put her hands on his shoulders and forced him onto the stool.

She stood in front of him, her eyes grave and troubled. "I know you think I'm queer, Will. But don't judge me now. Just answer my questions, will you?"

Will nodded slowly.

"Do you know Milt's writing?" she asked.

Will nodded. Becky gave him the note Milt

had sent her, and Will glanced at it. "Yes, that's his." He looked up, as if waiting for the rest.

Becky bit her lip. Her resolution was failing her. This was going to hurt — hurt him terribly. She said softly, "You think a lot of Milt, don't you, Will?"

"You know I do," Will said.

"It — it would hurt you if he got in trouble?"

Will started to rise, and Becky put a restraining hand on his shoulder.

"Is Milt in trouble?"

Becky couldn't say any more. She took out Milt's letter to Pres and handed it to Will. "That came for Pres, Will. I opened it."

Will took out the letter and read it. Becky walked to the door; she didn't want to watch him. She listened, though. She could hear Will's breathing soften and then die away. There was a long, long silence that ran on until Becky couldn't bear it any longer. She glanced over her shoulder. The paper had fallen from Will's hand, and he was staring at the floor. Then he raised his hands and buried his face in them. Becky came slowly across to him and put her hand on his shoulder.

When Will looked up, minutes later, Becky could have cried with pity for him. His eyes were the eyes of a hurt animal, bright with pain, unbelieving, tortured.

Becky murmured, "Does it matter so much, Will?"

Will shuddered, and then he began to speak.

"Matter? I dunno, Becky. You see, Milt is Murray Broome."

"Murray Broome — the murderer?"

Becky could have bitten her tongue out after she said it, but Will only nodded. "I reckon he's a murderer. I don't know. I came here to hide him, Becky. That's why I bought the Pitchfork — to hide him. I thought he was my friend."

Becky knelt by him. "Will, what does it all mean? The note?"

Will said dully, "Just what it says. I dunno. He writes about the original partnership. I think way back when I first came, Becky, that Pres and Milt threw in together. That's why Milt wanted me to pull out and sell the place. That's why he was so mad when I wouldn't. Then I reckon Pres turned to your dad for help. I busted that up. And then this deed, Chap's deed to me, showed up. Milt said Pres had it all the time. He couldn't have." He looked at Becky now. "Today Milt came here and told me that Pres was blackmailin' him. Said Pres knew he was Murray Broome. Said Pres would keep quiet if I turned the place over to him."

"And you said you would?"

Will nodded.

"Oh, Will," Becky said softly. "How could he do it? He knew you were so loyal, so kind, that you'd give the place to Pres rather than betray a friend. He counted on it — that — that Judas! He and Pres were in partnership to swindle you out of whatever it is that's on your spread!"

264

Will nodded, staring at the floor.

"Will," Becky said. "Didn't you know Murray Broome was crooked? Hadn't you read about it?"

"He was good to me," Will said dully. "He gave me work when I was nothin' but a saddle bum. He was good to me. I figured they lied about him. He said they did, and I took his word." He glanced at her with a deep, dismal hurt in his eyes. "Chap told me he was crooked. Charlie Sommers did. Everybody did — only he was my friend, Becky."

Becky nodded. Will rose and hobbled to the door and stood there, looking out into the night. Becky knew she couldn't help him, that this was some deep hurt to his pride that would never heal. She sat quietly on the bed, watching him, silent.

Presently, Will turned to look at her. His stare was so intent that it almost hurt. Then he looked away again. Afterward, he came over to the table. His gun and shell belt lay there, and he picked up the belt and strapped it on. His eyes were distant, cold.

Alarm was in Becky's eyes as she watched him. She wanted to cry out — to stop him. She knew where he was going. She'd known it, in the back of her mind, when she read the letter, but now that it was here she couldn't bear it.

Will palmed the six-gun out, opened the loading-gate, spun the chamber, and holstered the gun. He picked up Milt's note to Pres and pocketed it.

"Wait, Will," Becky pleaded softly. "You can't make the ride."

"No."

"Then I'm going with you! I know where Milt hid your saddle and staked out your horse."

"You stay here," Will said mildly, absently.

Becky despaired then. She couldn't reach him, couldn't touch that part of him that was driving him to this. He couldn't make town! His wound would break open again, and he'd bleed to death. And even if he did make it, he wouldn't be a match for Milt. Becky was afraid. She came to her feet and went over to him.

"Will, have you got to?" she asked softly.

Will nodded. "I promised a man," he murmured. Becky didn't know what he meant, but she watched him hobble out to her horse. He swung up into the saddle and rode off, not looking back.

Becky watched him until he was out of sight, then she came back and blew out the candle. She ran out into the night now, heading down the slope. At the edge of the arroyo, she plunged into a thicket of willows and came out lugging Will's saddle and bridle from where Milt had cached it.

Taking the bridle, she headed down along the arroyo, running until she was out of breath, and then walking. Down here a half mile or so, in a cottonwood motte, Will's horse was staked out. She wasn't going to stay here and wait for somebody to tell her that he was dead.

The wound on his leg did break. The pain was so constant that the only way Will could tell was by the warm, wet feel of blood. He bound it with his handkerchief, not bothering to stop.

His thoughts during that ride into Yellow Jacket he could never recall later. They were not thoughts of shame at being taken in by a friend, nor at the thought of confronting Charlie Sommers. They were strange, unimportant thoughts, like Milt's laugh, or his way with women. Or of that time over in the Tetons when Milt shot that buck deer, wounding him. He came up to him, ready to put the last bullet into him, and the buck looked at him, proud, alert, sick, still fighting. Milt had walked away from him, and Will had to kill him. It was little things like this that filled Will's mind, as if he were recalling things about a person already dead.

His wound never stopped its slow seep. Will rode into the deserted street of Yellow Jacket, and it was late. He heard the wailing *whoosh* of the night freight piling into the west, not stopping. It was just the way it was that first night — the train wailing off to the upper reaches of the bench, the street silent, obscurely lighted, the cluster of ponies at the tie rail in front of Hal Mohr's saloon. There was a difference tonight, though; the window of the sheriff's office was lighted.

Will put his horse in there and sat in the saddle a moment, gathering his strength. Then he swung off — and fell flat on his face in the bitter dust as his leg gave way.

He pulled himself up by grasping the tie rail, and clung to it until the pain in his leg had subsided a little and the dizziness was gone. Then he hobbled toward the door of the sheriff's office, swinging up his gun as he went.

He opened the door and stepped inside. Phipps, reading at his desk, slowly turned his head. He was looking into the muzzle of Will's gun.

Swiftly, Phipps's gaze rose to Will's face. Will said, "You yell, and I'll shoot you this time."

There was something in his soft, tight voice, in his pale, fanatic face that told Phipps this was true. He was looking at the gaunt face of a man in whose cold gray eyes was naked murder. His reopened wound was pooling blood on the floor.

Phipps said softly, "What do you want?"

"Charlie Sommers. Get your keys and go let him out."

Phipps wanted to argue. Caution, his instinct of self-preservation told him not to. With one hand he picked up the lamp, with the other reached for his keys, and rose. Will followed him into the cell block.

Charlie Sommers came off his cot, blinking at the light. He saw Will, and then Will's leg, as he came to his feet. His cheeks were not so ruddy now; he was unshaven and pallid, his face still scarred from his beating, but his eyes were steady and curious. Phipps stood aside, watching them.

"I come back to keep my promise, Charlie," Will said.

"You found out he's a crook?"

Will nodded.

"Where is he?"

"Here. In town. I've been hidin' him, Charlie. He was my foreman all the time."

Charlie rapped out, "Phipps, let me out of here!" as if he were giving Phipps orders.

The sheriff opened the cell. Charlie took the lamp from him, put it on the floor, then ordered Phipps into the cell. He ripped up a blanket, said, "I'm takin' no chances, John. Afterward I'll explain," and proceeded to gag and bind the sheriff. Will leaned against the cell, taking the weight off his leg, closing his eyes.

Charlie's voice roused him. "You all right? You're bleedin', Will."

"I'm all right," Will said softly.

They passed through the sheriff's office. On the way, Charlie Sommers picked up Sheriff Phipps's gun and belt and strapped them on.

"Where is he?" Charlie asked.

Will eyed the saloon, and said softly, "Charlie, I kept my promise to you. But he's mine, you understand? He's mine."

"But —"

"I know what you'll say," Will said tonelessly. "You're a marshal, sworn to bring him to justice. But if you try to stop me, I'll kill you."

Charlie eyed him obliquely and said meagerly, "All right, Will."

They headed toward the saloon, crossing the empty street in the deep dust. Far upstreet there was a new horse at the tie rail, and someone was standing by it. Will noticed it but paid no attention.

On the boardwalk in front of the saloon, Will said, "There'll be someone with him, Charlie. Pres Milo. They'll fight."

He didn't wait for Charlie's answer, only shouldered through the doors. A couple of punchers were talking to Hal Mohr at the bar. There was a five-handed poker game going on at a table against the wall. Pres and Milt were sitting in on it.

Will started for the table, and Pres saw him first. Pres's face froze, and he kicked Milt under the table. Milt looked up and saw Will, and Charlie Sommers beyond him.

Will stopped there, some four feet from the table, facing Milt. Milt's face went loose and blank, and his eyes narrowed faintly, and the cards fell out of his hand. The other players slipped out of their chairs, leaving Milt and Pres side by side.

A slow, strained look of fear crept into Milt's eyes, and his upper lip was beaded with perspiration.

He didn't move, didn't take his eyes off Will. "Hello, Will," he said in a soft, dismal voice.

Will had Milt's note to Pres in his hand. He tossed it on the table. Milt reached for it, gaze still on Will, and unfolded it. His glance dropped to it for a brief second, then rose to Will's face.

"That does it," he said quietly.

"I reckon it does," Will drawled.

"I won't draw a gun on you, Will," Milt said quietly. "Go ahead."

It was this that almost changed Will's mind. The bleak look in his eyes altered for a moment, letting pity edge in. And then it came back, and his face was hard as iron.

"It won't do any good, Milt," he said in a far-off, distant voice. "You've worked that for the last time."

His hand fell to his gun. Milt exploded into action. He turned the table over in one sweeping heave. It caught Will on his game leg, and he went down. Pres dodged for the back of the room, and Charlie's gun lashed out at him. Charlie hit him, knocking him into the tables. Milt stepped out from behind the table. He wasn't going to run. His face was twisted with the hatred a man holds for another man whom he has sold out.

Back against the wall, Milt's gun swung up, and he shot. The slug whistled past Will's head, and it brought the bar glasses down in a metallic jangle.

Will's gun arced out and he fought to his feet. Again Milt shot wildly, savagely, hastily, stabbing his gun as if it were a knife. Will's gun swung up, and when Milt's shirt pocket lay between the sights he fired.

The slug knocked Milt back against the wall. His chin came up, a wild grimace contorted his face. He stayed that way, every muscle straining, and then he sagged. His filmed eyes looked bitterly at Will, and he reached out for the table that wasn't there. He fell then, on his face, sprawling across an overturned chair, one hand dangling in the rungs.

Will dropped his gun. Charlie was kneeling by Pres. His one shot had caught Pres under the armpit, ranging through his ribs to his heart. Will wiped his palm across his eyes, as if to get this sight forever out of his mind, and then tramped through the door.

Waiting outside the door was Becky. She came into his arms, a low moaning cry escaping her. She hugged him tightly, her head against his chest.

"Oh, Will! Are you all right?"

Will didn't answer, stroking her hair, holding her to him. Charlie Sommers passed him on the run, heading for the sheriff's office.

Afterward Becky led Will over to the hotel lobby, and the doctor came. While he was bandaging the leg, Charlie Sommers, Sheriff Phipps, and Mary Norman came into the lobby.

Mary, her face stony and bleak, came up to Will and stood before him.

"I don't blame you," she said softly, bitterly. "But damn you, Will Danning! Damn you, damn you!"

She turned and fled across the lobby and up the stairs, sobbing into the sleeve of her coat.

Phipps came up with the note, after the doctor had stepped away. "If this is his writin', Danning,

272

then I got nothin' on you for Hale's murder."
He turned to Charlie. "And if it's like he says
it is, that he let you out to get Broome, then
I got nothin' on him."

Will looked at Charlie Sommers. There was a
great pity in the marshal's eyes as he looked at
Will, and Will was grateful.

"He let me out to get him, Phipps," he said
in a toneless voice. "I got him."

Sommers motioned Phipps aside. The doctor
picked up his kit, said, "Get to bed as soon as
you can, young fellow," and left.

Becky slipped down beside him and looked up
at him.

"Will, I'll make up for all this. The world isn't
like this. You can't believe it is!"

Will stroked her hair and said, "No, I know
that, Becky. Remember what I told you that night
out at the Nine X? All the fightin' and the killin'
that stood between us is gone now. And I mean
it more than ever."

"I know you do, Will. I'll make up for it all."

Later, Becky lifted her head from Will's shoulder and said, "Will."

"What?"

"Do you know what Murray and Pres and Dad
were after, there on your place?"

"No. Do you?"

"No. Let's don't ever try to find out! Let's
leave it! We have everything we want now,
haven't we?"

Will smiled into the darkness and nodded.

The employees of G.K. HALL hope you have enjoyed this Large Print book. All our Large Print titles are designed for easy reading, and all our books are made to last. Other G.K. Hall Large Print books are available at your library, through selected bookstores, or directly from us. For more information about current and up-coming titles, please call or mail your name and address to:

G.K. HALL
PO Box 159
Thorndike, Maine 04986
800/223-6121
207/948-2962